Fleur McDonald lives on a large farm east of Esperance in Western Australia, where she and her husband Anthony produce prime lambs and cattle, run an Angus cattle and White Suffolk stud and produce a small amount of crops. They have two children, Rochelle and Hayden. Fleur snatches time for her writing in between helping on the farm. *Silver Clouds* is her fourth novel.

www.fleurmcdonald.com

Also by Fleur McDonald

Red Dust
Blue Skies
Purple Roads

Silver Clouds

FLEUR McDONALD

ARENA
ALLEN&UNWIN

First published in 2013
This edition published in 2014

Arena Books, an imprint of
Allen & Unwin

83 Alexander Street
Crows Nest NSW 2065
Australia
Phone: (61 2) 8425 0100
Email: info@allenandunwin.com
Web: www.allenandunwin.com

Cataloguing-in-Publication details are available
from the National Library of Australia
www.trove.nla.gov.au

ISBN 978 1 74331 881 2

Set in 13/17.5 pt ITC Garamond by Midland Typesetters, Australia
Printed and bound in Australia by Griffin Press

10 9 8 7 6 5 4 3 2 1

To my brother, Nicholas Parnell and sister, Susan Woolford: you are my strength, my rock, my core, as family is.

And, as always, to Anthony, Rochelle and Hayden, with much love.

Author's note

The Nullarbor is a very special place steeped in history. Although it is vast, and the distance between stations and people is great, the sense of community is strong.

None of the stations or people in this book are real or based on any one person or place. You may, however, recognise a mixture of family histories and stations all rolled into one to create Danjar Plains.

I have also taken liberties with the amount of plane action out there. Mostly people drive the distances.

Chapter 1

London, January 2010

Tessa's first realisation was that her head hurt. Not just hurt, but felt like it was going to explode.

She opened one eye, but shut it again quickly – the light was blinding. A familiar feeling of nausea rose in her throat. Swallowing hard, she tried to work out where she was. Her mouth was dry and she craved water. What on earth had happened last night?

She slowly turned over but froze in the tangled sheets when her hand made contact with a warm body. Her eyes flew open. *Not again. Please Lord, not again!*

But there was no avoiding it. Or the man lying beside her, for that matter. His face was half-hidden by the bedclothes, but she could see a gold earring in his left ear and a thick gold pinkie ring on his hand, which was thrown carelessly across the pillow.

'Oh no!' The words burst from her, but before she could say anything more she shot out of bed and ran from the room in search of the bathroom.

Frantically opening doors, she at last found the toilet.

Later, her head resting on the cool porcelain tiles, Tessa berated herself for getting so drunk she couldn't remember the previous evening.

After a while, she heard a deep, masculine cough through the paper-thin walls and wondered if it was her mysterious companion.

From the unfamiliar bed.

In the unfamiliar flat.

She dragged herself up off the floor. Catching sight of her reflection in the mirror, she gasped. She'd forgotten that only yesterday she'd had her thick dark hair cut so short the waves now hugged her skull, and on a dare from Jaz, had dyed her new locks blonde. There was more fun to be had, Jaz had assured her if you were blonde. She had apparently lived up to that expectation.

To top it off her olive skin was pasty, her eyes bloodshot and pink-rimmed. It wasn't Tessa Mathison staring back at her. It was a stranger. She groaned and shut her eyes, letting her head fall forward.

Now she had to go out and interact with someone she didn't even know, despite having already shared the most intimate of moments with him.

As she turned on the tap she heard another voice, female this time, and recognised her friend Jasmine's throaty giggle. 'Charlie, don't do that, you naughty boy!' said Jaz, though she didn't sound like she meant a word of it. Still, Tessa was pleased to know Jaz was in the flat, too.

She wasn't alone.

There was a gentle tap on the door. 'Tessa, are you finished? I'm a bit keen to use the loo.'

'Ah, I'll be right out,' she called and doused her face with cold water. Straightening, she ignored her pounding head and grabbed the nearby towel to wrap around her slight frame. She plastered on a smile. If only she could remember the man's name . . .

'Sorry,' she said as she opened the door.

She tried to pass him without being touched, but the man placed a hand on her bare shoulder and smiled. 'Good morning. How is my little Australian jillaroo today?'

Australian jillaroo? Hell. She must have been beyond pissed. Tessa hoped she hadn't done her kangaroo act with Jasmine in tow.

'Um, morning,' she muttered, blushing. 'Fine. Bit of a headache, that's all.'

'I've got something to help fix that problem. Top drawer, next to my bed.' He winked.

Tessa went to thank him but he'd already shut the door. Feeling like her head was about to fall off she found her way back to the bedroom.

Pulling open the drawer, she rummaged around in search of Panadol or something stronger. She found something much stronger: a small plastic bag of white powder. Tessa, being no stranger to the London party scene, guessed it was cocaine.

'Damn,' she whispered and slammed the drawer shut. Maybe she should just pretend she'd never seen it. Yes, that's what she'd do.

Clothes, she needed her clothes. Seeing them next to the bed, she dropped the towel and lunged towards the pile which had obviously been dropped there in a hurry. She tugged them on, wrinkling her nose at the smell of beer and cigarette smoke. She fixed her hair and makeup as best she could without a mirror.

Never seen it, never heard of it. Do I know you? It was something she'd always said to her Aunty Spider when she was a little girl and trying to get out of trouble. It had never worked, though. Aunty Spider could always see through her.

Always, Tessa thought as she remembered her great-aunt's most recent letter in her handbag. The letter she still hadn't answered.

Jasmine stumbled into the bedroom, a man's white business shirt wrapped around her like a robe. 'Well, helloooo, daaarling!' she said, her tone formal. 'Weren't you a little party animal last night!' Jaz wiggled her eyebrows up and down suggestively.

Grabbing Jaz's arm, Tessa steered her down the

4

hall and into the front room of the flat. 'Who are these two?' she whispered. 'And what did I do last night? I want to die!'

'Oh, don't worry, sweetness. I have everything under control. *Unnnderrr controllll*. Now, I believe we may need a coffee. Or another drink.'

'Are you *mad*? If I never see another drink it will be too soon! Do you know what his name is?' asked Tessa.

'John Smith. Come!' Jasmine slipped her arm through Tessa's and tried to propel her towards the tiny kitchen, but Tessa pulled away.

'You don't really believe that's his name, do you?' Tessa groaned, putting her hand to her head. 'Bloody hell, I've got to find some Panadol.' She looked around for her handbag, but couldn't see it.

She stuck her head out of the door and combed the entrance. Ah, there it was buried under her coat, which had been dumped on the mat near the front door.

Tipping the contents of her bag onto the floor, she fossicked around until she found a screwed-up packet with two tablets left in it. Throwing the tablets into her mouth she swallowed them without water, then stuffed everything back into her bag. She'd start to feel better soon. Twenty minutes and at least the edge of the headache would be gone.

'So, what's with the Queen's accent?' asked Tessa, looking up at her friend.

'I'm being impressive,' Jaz said as regally as a woman wrapped in a rumpled shirt and not much else could before heading towards the kitchen.

'What is she *on*?' Tessa muttered after her and clambered to her feet.

So-called John Smith appeared at the door. 'What a night, huh, ladies?' He grinned, his arms stretched out towards Tessa. 'What. A. Night.'

Tessa backed away. 'I'm very sorry, um, John,' she answered, emphasising his name while feigning disappointment. 'I have a meeting in . . .' She glanced at her watch. '. . . about an hour and a half and I'll need to prepare . . . I'm afraid I can't get out of it. I'll just call a cab.'

John pouted. 'You're no fun. All work and no play will make you a very dull girl. I wanted to try the, um . . . what was it? The wallaby hop again.'

'Kangaroo,' Jaz answered.

'Right, right. The kangaroo hop.'

Oh, no! 'I really am very sorry.'

Tessa tapped an app on her iPhone and asked John for the address. After she'd requested a taxi she gathered up her bag and coat and surreptitiously checked to see that her shirt wasn't inside out.

'Thanks so much for a great night,' she said.

'I'd like to do it again. Soon,' John replied.

Highly unlikely, thought Tessa, but she smiled sweetly because that was what you did when you were in marketing. After all, a girl never knew whether someone she'd met briefly might be useful in the future. 'I'd like that,' she said. 'Jazzy, I'll catch you at the office.'

'You most certainly will.' Jasmine inclined her head and turned to the man called Charlie, who had emerged dressed in a burgundy silk robe and matching slippers.

'Going already, dear lady?' he asked.

'A meeting,' John supplied.

'Ah. Well, thank you for a wonderful evening.'

'You're welcome,' Tessa answered. As she glanced around to make sure she hadn't forgotten anything, her gaze fell on a swipe ID card similar to the one she wore at work, sitting on the mantlepiece, surrounded by jars and tins.

Making out the emblem, she froze. *Oh no. No, no, no, no!*

Without another word, she turned and ran out of the flat and down the tiny stairs.

'Oh my . . . Bloody hell!' She couldn't stop, she had to keep running, had to get away. She hoped no one she knew had seen her last night, hadn't seen her leaving with John Smith because if they had, Tessa knew it would be the last work mistake she'd ever make. And it *was* his real name! She kept running, her cab forgotten.

Tessa had just slept with the manager of Soho Marketing, the biggest rival of Marketing Matters, the firm she worked for. Her boss, Darcy Anderson, would sack her without a second thought, despite their family connections, if he knew she'd done the kangaroo hop with Smith. If only she could remember *exactly* what happened last night. Obviously there had been alcohol, meeting Jaz, maybe Bar Soho on Old Compton Street . . .

She remembered the first three glasses of bubbly, which she'd drunk on an empty stomach. Then her insecurities about dancing had disappeared and the dance floor seductively beckoned. So had the bar, again and again. The dim lights, red walls and booze had given her a warm buzz. Sprinkled among the Champagnes there had been beer shooters and goodness knows what else. Then another and another. She gave up counting and trying to dredge up memories.

'Idiot! What an idiot.'

Hearing her iPhone chirping, she stopped her flight and rummaged in her handbag, cursing. She saw it was her brother. She couldn't speak to Ryan now, not until she got some more painkillers – surely there was a Boots around somewhere . . . Or maybe she should just have another drink despite what she had said to Jaz. That would certainly fix the problem. Hair of the dog and all.

She breathed deeply and shut her eyes, glad her Aunty Spider couldn't see her.

Her phone rang for a second time. Ryan again. Tessa frowned, calculating the time difference.

Wow, it's pretty early at home, she thought.

'Hello, Ryan!' Somehow she made her voice sound normal, cheery even.

'Tessa. How's it going?'

'All good here,' she said, walking on slowly. 'I'm very busy, though. Just about to go into a meeting. Can I . . .' She broke off as Ryan's tone filtered through her muddled brain. Something was wrong.

'No, Tessa, you can't call back. I need to talk to you now. Where are you?'

'Uh,' she looked around at the unfamiliar setting. 'Out on the street. What's wrong?' Fear made her voice unsteady.

'There's no easy way to tell you. I'm sorry. It's Aunty Spider. She died last night.'

Tessa stopped, her vision blurring as she tried to answer.

'Tessa? Are you there? I know how much you loved her. We all did. Tessa?'

Ryan's voice seemed to be coming from a long way away. She crumpled to the pavement and sat there, suddenly thrust back to the Nullarbor and her dear Aunty Spider. Thoughts crowded her mind, of Spider's smile, her gnarled hands, of her riding her clackety old yellow bike down the dirt roads of home.

But the most terrible thought of all was that she'd not only let her Aunty Spider down, but now she could never, ever apologise.

Chapter 2

London, three days later

'Mind the step,' said a monotone voice, but Tessa had heard the recorded message so many times she barely registered it.

Stepping off the Tube she pushed her way through the crowd. Everyone was in a hurry. She stumbled into the back of a man in a suit who turned and frowned at her, but never stopped talking into his phone. Muttering an apology she sidestepped him, hoisted her handbag over her shoulder and strode off in the direction of St James's Street, walking as quickly as her skirt would allow.

Her eyes still felt sore from all the crying she'd done last night. Spider's death had come as a huge blow. Coupled with the night spent in John Smith's company, she felt like her new life might fall apart at any moment.

It was a life Spider had helped her construct as

a means of getting away from the memories and the guilt. Spider had contacted her nephew by marriage, Darcy Anderson, in London to see if he'd take Tessa on as a junior in his marketing business. He'd been happy to – he'd even agreed to take her friend Jaz on as well. Tessa had done reasonably well since she'd arrived, winning a small promotion two months earlier.

She did love London. Sometimes she still found it difficult to believe she was living among places she'd only ever read about as a child: Piccadilly Circus, Leicester Square and Oxford Street. She hadn't just read about them but learnt about them from the songs and tales Aunty Spider had told her.

The reality, of course, was something else. None of the stories had mentioned the small corner off-licences or the litter that raced along on the wind as it blew off the Thames. There was little point, Tessa knew, in looking for a rubbish bin in London – bomb threats had put paid to those.

The city was a melting pot of garbage, history, musty transport fumes and different cultures. In comparison Perth, where Tessa had gone to boarding school and then lived for five years afterwards, was pristine. The smell of the ocean that swept over the city as the Fremantle Doctor roared up the Swan River was fresh and moist. As for the Nullarbor, where she'd lived until she was twelve, its clean, dry air shimmered in the heat of summer.

She stood waiting for the traffic lights to change. Tessa turned her face away from the bitter wind streaming up the street and recalled the previous night. Her father had phoned to let her know she had a week to get home for her aunt's funeral. After he'd hung up, she sat in her room clutching the last letter from Aunty Spider and wept. Then, overcome with guilt and sadness, she'd tried to cry silently, without her flatmates hearing.

Later, as she lay on her bed, her eyes sore and her body spent, to her relief her mobile had chirped. It was a colleague insisting she meet the new PR guy from Harrods. 'So very well connected, Tessa. You need to come. He's a bit of a dish, so it shouldn't be too hard on you!'

Another excuse, and Tessa was good at accepting them. After reapplying her makeup and quickly changing her clothes, she'd called a cab and things reeled out in their usual fashion.

Now, as she crossed the road and climbed the stairs to her workplace, she wished she hadn't gone. But it was so hard to say no. Being relatively new to London and to the job, she needed to network, make contacts and, most of all, prove her worth. It was essential for both Tessa and Jaz. There were so many marketing and PR people in the city that some Londoners could hardly believe a huge company like Marketing Matters would hire an untested Australian. Two Australians, as it happened. It was probably better that no one knew that Darcy had given her and Jaz jobs as a favour to her great-aunt.

Pushing through the glass door, Tessa licked her dry, wind-blown lips. What she wouldn't do for a drink. She stopped and glanced at her watch. How on earth could she be thinking *that* at eight-thirty in the morning? She felt for her swipe card hanging around her neck, took a deep breath and headed towards the lifts.

As the lift doors opened onto her floor Jaz was already hurrying past with a stack of files. 'Good morning, *Tessaroo*.'

Ignoring Jaz's joke, Tessa fell into step with her close friend. 'I don't suppose you know if the main man is around today?'

'He arrived about ten minutes ago. Should be in his office.' Jaz stopped at a photocopier and punched in a code before riffling through the files to select the one she needed.

'Might see if I can have a word.' Tessa headed off in the direction of Darcy's inner sanctum. Hopefully, given they were distant cousins, he'd see her. But the fact was, after an initial welcome dinner, their relationship had been strictly professional. There was never any mention of family connections or why Tessa was within the folds of Marketing Matters.

Darcy's PA strode down the hall, took up her position as guard dog at her desk and switched on her computer. Tessa groaned and altered her direction. There would be no way she could get inside the oval office now.

Instead, she detoured to the toilets and sat in a stall, feet resting on the door, her head in her lap. Eventually, she reached for her bag and pulled out the letter from Spider she'd been carrying around for two months. The letter she hadn't answered.

Oh, she had all the excuses. *I'm too busy, just racing out the door*, she'd told herself. Another meeting. Another pub. Another drink. Another man. No time to answer the letter.

But that's all they were: excuses. And now it was too late.

Unfolding the now dog-eared slip of paper, she read it one more time.

Danjar Plains, 17 October 2009
My Dear Tessa,

I guess you are very busy – it's been an age since I heard from you. Don't worry, it's not a rebuke, I'm just hoping you're all right.

I had a letter from Darcy and he says he's happy with your work, which is not surprising. I know how you put your best into everything. This is a great trait, but can also be your undoing. Try not to go overboard!

Your mum filled me in on your news yesterday, so I know you are alive! But I wonder how you are, <u>really</u>.

Tessa, please write. I am worried about you.
Much love, my darling girl,
AS

It was signed with many kisses.

The truth was, Tessa hadn't known *how* to answer Spider's letter. Because the guilt she'd hoped to throw off by moving to London still plagued her every waking moment. And no matter how settled and happy Tessa might pretend to be, Spider still knew. Her aunt was so damn intuitive, she would realise *something* was amiss. It had been easier, therefore, to stay silent.

Tessa refolded the note and put it back in her bag. Now Spider was gone, she had to go back and pay her last respects. There was no way she could *not* go to Spider's funeral. But she'd taken quite a bit of time off in the last three months, mostly because her hangovers had been so bad she couldn't even get out of bed. Tessa knew her drinking and partying had escalated as the festive season had drawn near. As much as she had promised herself that once New Year's Eve passed she would slow down, it hadn't happened. She wondered whether Darcy would know how many sick days she'd taken. It would all be on her file, but if somehow she could avoid his PA and her carefully kept records, he *might* not bother to look it up. Especially since they were family.

She still felt sick every time she thought about John Smith. That would lead her thoughts to Spider and how she had let her great-aunt down. Her heart would race and she'd break out in a sweat. Tessa was good at heaping blame on her already guilt-ridden shoulders.

More Panadol, she thought and dug through her bag. Then she stopped. *Stuff it, just this once. Or, hundredth time.* She pulled out a little bottle of vodka and took a sip. Closing her eyes, she let the drink work its magic. Instantly she relaxed. She took another sip. Warmth flooded through her and she knew she could face the day.

Tessa flushed the loo, tidied her clothes and left, only stopping to look in the mirror. The guilty reflection gazing back at her made sure she didn't stop for too long.

'Anne, I do need to speak with Mr Anderson.' Tessa tapped her pen against the papers in front of her. It was her third call to Darcy's office this morning and still the guard dog would not put her through.

'Tessa, as I have explained, Mr Anderson has asked not to be disturbed today. He's very busy. If you put your request in an email, I'll forward it to him.'

'It's of a personal nature,' Tessa said, playing her trump card.

'Personal?' Anne paused. 'Well, even so, I'm afraid you'll have to go through me. Now if you'll excuse me . . .'

Tessa was left listening to silence. She tapped the pages again, flipped through a few of them but couldn't concentrate. She was agitated. What if Darcy wouldn't let her go home? Also bothering her was the 'John Smith Incident', as she'd come to call it. The 'what if' questions. *What if someone saw me? What if I've been caught?* The answer to all of those questions was: she'd be sacked.

'I'm such an idiot,' she groaned, her head dropping forward.

Jaz's face appeared above the barrier. 'Can I come in?' she asked. 'Just need to chat about the ad campaign we want to run next week. Oh, are you okay, Tessa?'

Tessa looked up at her friend. Fear shot through her. Perhaps Jaz had found out that John Smith worked at Soho Marketing. Tessa hadn't yet been brave enough to tell her.

Jaz came around and put her hand on her friend's shoulder. 'I know Violet's death must be such a shock.'

'Shouldn't be, really,' Tessa said, relieved that Jaz hadn't mentioned John Smith. 'She was ninety-three but, you know, sometimes I feel a long way away.' She shrugged, trying to make light of it.

'Yes, it's a bloody long way away. I remember your Aunty Spider being almost frightening but exciting at the same time. And it was always obvious how much she loved you' – Jaz stopped and looked down at her friend.' You must be devastated. No wonder you're out of sorts. When's the funeral?'

'Soon. In a week. I'm trying to get hold of Mr Anderson to explain, but I can't get past the guard dog.'

Jaz smiled. 'Well, you must go! I can take care of the conference next week. And the new account! Although I don't envy you heading out to the Nullarbor in the middle of summer. You'll die! Oh, I didn't mean it like that . . .'

Tessa reached out and squeezed Jaz's hand. 'Thanks, Jaz. That would be fantastic. You know how I feel about Aunty Spider. She was . . . Well, she was everything.'

When Jaz had returned to her desk, Tessa tried to focus on the project at hand. Her client had sent through a list of tasks which, of course, all needed to be completed that second, but her brain was too fuzzy to make sense of the instructions.

Her email pinged. Glad of the distraction, she clicked on her inbox. The email was from Darcy Anderson himself, not the guard dog. With trepidation, she double clicked.

Dear Tessa,
Please be in my office in ten minutes.
D. Anderson

Eek. Fear shot through her, cold as a mountain stream. She pushed back her chair and grabbing her bag and blazer, rushed to the restroom to make sure her makeup and hair were neat. She ran her hands down her long taupe skirt and straightened her white silk top. Quickly she checked her heels for gum then shrugged on her suit jacket. She stared at herself for a moment, but the eyes that stared back were tormented. She tried to control her breathing. Panic swirled in her stomach.

Her hands shook as she fumbled in her handbag for the vodka miniature. Tessa knew this was becoming a habit and it frightened her. Every time she took a sip of that bottle she rationalised it by thinking she only took a hit when she *really* needed it – before a meeting with a big client, and after said meeting when it had gone wrong.

Two glugs later, she glanced at her watch. Screwing the lid on, she stood up, straightened her back and breathed deeply. As she felt the alcohol take hold, confidence coursed through her. What did she care, anyway, if someone found out? She hadn't known who John Smith was when she met him and it wasn't like she'd talked about any secret marketing plans. She couldn't be blamed for that. Then the wave of confidence passed: obviously she had no idea what John had done while she had been completely out to it. He could have looked at her iPhone and checked her emails.

Oh hell. She felt sick at the thought.

*

Darcy greeted her with a dry handshake and a warm smile, which threw her off balance. His auburn wavy hair looked in need of a cut and his shirt, rolled up at the sleeves, was rumpled. As she glanced quickly around the office, it was clear he was under pressure and very busy. Files and newspapers covered his desk, so she wasn't surprised when he waved her towards a small coffee table near the window.

'I was so sorry to hear about Violet's passing,' he said by way of greeting as he settled into a high-back chair. 'My PA forwarded me your email.'

Tessa swallowed. 'Thank you.'

'Hers and William's was one of the great love stories, wasn't it? A young English jackaroo meets girl on beach, they marry, he gets killed in the war and she never remarries, living out her life in the isolation of the Nullarbor.' He leaned forward and steepled his fingers. 'Family was very important to her, wasn't it? After William died, there was no need to do what she did. For her to travel over here and meet my family, bring photos and stories of his life, so they could feel a part of what he had experienced. But it was important to her and I know my lot appreciated it enormously.'

'Yes, I can't imagine ever loving anyone so much,' Tessa blurted, wondering if it were true. 'I know she enjoyed her time over here. But she never travelled overseas again. Never really left Danjar Plains for very long.'

Darcy smiled. 'How did she get the nickname of Spider? I've always wondered. I wouldn't have dared call her that, mind you. She was always Violet to us.'

'Apparently her little brother, Tom, who was my granddad, couldn't say Violet and he always called her Spider. Violet and Spider sound similar to a little kid, I guess.' She shrugged. 'It just seemed to stick. I don't think anyone called her Violet.'

Darcy nodded. 'One of those strange family traditions . . .' He looked at her carefully. 'So, you want to go back for the funeral.' It was a bald statement, not a question.

'Yes. Yes, I do.' The relief she felt knowing at last that the meeting was about compassionate leave and *not* the John Smith Incident was incredible. She gave a nervous giggle then clamped her hand over her mouth.

'I understand you have a new account and a large conference next week?'

'Yes I do but, Mr Anderson, I feel it's important for me to be with my family at this time. I can work on the new account remotely while I'm away. In fact, the time away from the office may be just what I need for that project – the space to think outside the square.'

She crossed her legs and smoothed her skirt, picking at the hem. 'The conference is a little more difficult, I admit. However, if I may suggest sending Jasmine Coulder? She's been working with me on some of the projects and has a good eye for detail.

And given we started together, she has all the experience I have, if not the promotions.'

Darcy thought for a moment before jumping up from his seat and striding over to his desk. He riffled through a pile of papers until he found the one he was looking for. Pulling a pen from behind his ear, he made a note on it.

Tessa began to wonder how much of his attention she actually had.

'Of course you need to be there,' Darcy said, still looking at his note. 'And to be honest, I should be as well. However, that isn't an option. You may take two weeks.'

Tessa shut her eyes with relief and smiled. 'Thank you,' she said softly.

'Jasmine is a good idea,' Darcy commented, his brow wrinkling in thought. 'Yes, yes. A very good idea.' He made another note on the file in front of him, then shuffled some more papers around. 'Now, one other thing, Tessa.' He opened a drawer only to slam it shut. 'It's here somewhere. Ah, yes.' Darcy took what looked like a photograph and held it out to her.

Her eyes flew between him and the picture in panic. Resisting the urge to snatch it, Tessa slowly rose and reached towards it.

'I hope you'll be able to represent my family at Violet's funeral. I'm having a plaque made, and it'll be shipped from Kalgoorlie. Something like this one in the pamphlet.'

Tessa took hold of the paper. She could have wept with relief – it was a brochure advertising memorials and plaques.

'I wonder if you wouldn't mind finding the best spot to place it? Somewhere on Danjar Plains. I only met her that once, but Violet made an impression on me.'

Tessa's voice caught as she said: 'Absolutely. Aunty Spider made an impression on everyone. She won't be forgotten easily.'

Chapter 3

Nullarbor Plains

Harrison felt his way around the fixed-wing Cessna, checking the flaps. Cally, his daughter, already a seasoned flyer at eleven, had checked the fuel and was pushing the hangar doors open wide. Light streamed in, as did the warm breeze, which had picked up in the last couple of hours. Coupled with the heat of the day, Harrison knew it might be a bit bumpy heading over to the Mathisons at Danjar Plains.

'How's the fuel looking?' he asked.

Cally turned her pixie face towards him, shoved her grubby Akubra back on her head and gave him a smile. 'It's fine, Dad. I don't ever remember you having dirty fuel.' She flicked her thick pony tail back over her shoulder.

'Better safe than sorry.' He studied her for a moment, then leaned over to brush a spider web from the shoulder of her checked shirt. As always, when he looked at her his heart tightened. The smattering of freckles across her nose and her vivid blue eyes, which were the same colour as the everlasting wildflowers of the Nullarbor, made her the spitting image of her mother. It reminded Harrison once again that Ange was no longer there.

It would be three years next month since she died. Three long years. For the first five months, Cally had pined for her mother. Then she'd realised Ange wasn't coming back and just seemed to get on with life. Harrison hadn't. He still missed his wife as keenly as the day she passed.

He'd sat holding her hand in the Kalgoorlie hospital, having taken extended leave from his manager's job on Mundranda so he could be with her every moment. The cancer had eaten her away, leaving nothing but a frail shell. She had never lost her fighting spirit, though. Until her last breath, she had fought to stay with him, with Cally. But, in the end, the cancer had won.

'Dad?'

Harrison realised his daughter was looking at him knowingly. She was too smart for her – and his – own good.

'Sorry, I was thinking. What did you say?'

'You were thinking about Mum, weren't you?'

'Guilty as charged.' He held up his hands in mock surrender. 'You just look so much like her, that's all.'

Cally cast her eyes down, but not before he saw her cheek bulge and Harrison knew she'd poked her tongue into the empty space where a molar should be. Harrison had played tooth-fairy for only the third time, two nights ago.

'I'm sorry,' she said quietly.

Harrison stood stock-still. 'What for?'

'For being like her, for reminding you all the time.' The earnest face glanced quickly at him then away.

Ah, shit. After three years, he still hadn't worked out how to handle this sort of situation.

He scratched his head, then moved over to her. 'Cally,' he said softly. 'Cally, I wouldn't have you any other way. You are part of her and she is part of you. That's what makes you so special.' He raised her head up to look at him. 'You are beautiful.'

He let his words sink in, then stepped away. 'Come on, we need to get over to Danjar Plains and see Paul and Peggy. They'll be sad about Violet.'

'Oh, Dad, it's horrible,' Cally burst out. 'Why do people have to die?'

'It's part of life, love,' he said gently. 'Come on, you know that. Violet was a fair age and although it doesn't make it any easier for the ones left behind, she had a good innings. A good life.'

'I know, but I hate it.' Cally's mouth turned downwards and her lips trembled as Harrison pulled her into a hug. Harrison felt her warm tears seep through his shirt. Finally he asked, 'Do you want to fly?'

'Oh, can I?'

'Come on then.'

They quickly finished their checks and climbed aboard.

Harrison started the engine and taxied forward onto the dirt strip. 'We'll have a squiz at the tanks out on the northern side while we're up,' he said into the headset.

Cally nodded seriously and adjusted the head-phones and microphone so they were comfortable.

They were lined up and ready to take off. Harrison pushed the throttle in and out four times as he listened to the engine and felt the machine shake.

He looked across at his daughter. 'Ready?'

She nodded again.

Harrison let out the pedals and the aircraft roared down the runway. As they left the ground, he felt exhilaration run through his body, but his expression didn't show it. He loved that moment when the wheels left the ground and quickly everything was beneath him, growing smaller and smaller. It was the only time he felt truly free – like one of the resident wedge-tailed eagles, soaring far above the land, looking at everything below. The country unrolled before him like a great map.

He levelled the plane out at five hundred feet and indicated for Cally to take the controls. Then he watched her carefully, reminding her which instruments to monitor. When he was satisfied she was okay, his gaze turned to the view out of the window.

He knew he'd get into a world of trouble if the Aviation blokes knew, but if something ever happened to him while they were flying, Cally needed to know enough to get out of any difficulty that could arise and land the plane safely. And the way he saw it, he was nurturing her love of flying. Hopefully, by the time she was sixteen, she would be getting her own licence. He couldn't see how it was different to kids driving on stations before they got their driver's licence.

Towards the south where the ocean lay, light cloud hugged the ground, but with the heat of the sun, it would soon dissipate. Looking towards the north, the vivid blue sky merged with the hazy horizon. When they drew closer to Danjar Plains, the sky would bleed into the white sand dunes and the sparkling azure of the Great Australian Bight. He could lose himself in either view.

Harrison turned his attention back to the land beneath him. A flock of galahs was coming in to land at a waterhole. He could imagine the noise. Their squawking could send a man mad. And the way they dug up new shoots and the grass, well, they were nothing short of a nuisance.

'Turn just slightly,' he instructed. 'I want to have a look at the dam in Saltbush paddock and then at the tanks on the boundary, okay?'

Cally nodded and Harrison went back to

observing the station from above. Splashed across the white limestone soil were clumps of blue bush and mallee trees.

Flying was the quickest way to check the station he managed for a large farming family who lived in the city. He flew across the whole property once a week and it only took three hours. To drive over the full 250,000 hectares would take two or three days.

'There's Joe's ute.' Harrison pointed out the old horse breaker's vehicle near the dam.

'Look, he's standing on top of the tank!' Cally pointed at a small figure not much bigger than a sheep. 'What *is* he doing?'

'Checking the float, at a guess,' he answered, peering down. 'Guess we'd better not wave, then. We don't want him falling off.'

Cally giggled.

Harrison took in the large bodies of water lying in shallow hollows. The previous fortnight's rain had cut gouges across roads and washed floodgates away.

He saw the glint of a windshield beside a fence line and was pleased to note two of his employees were doing repairs. 'Dip your wings,' he said.

Cally gently turned the steering wheel downwards then up again.

A few minutes later they were flying over the boundary tanks. Harrison spotted wires pulled away from the posts and lying on the ground. Two large strainer posts were lying across them. The weight would stop them from springing back up and laying flat. A mob of cattle were grazing towards it.

Damn! They were at it again. By hell, he wished he knew who it was, dropping fences and encouraging stock from one station to wander to another! It would have to be fixed. His eyes flicked over the instruments as he reached towards the radio mike and changed the frequency. 'Got a copy down there, Maz?'

'Gotcha, boss.'

'The fence on the top boundary has been dropped deliberately. Can you have a look when you're finished there?'

'No worries. We'll have a bit of a scout around.'

'Good on you. Cheers.'

Harrison turned back to the window and searched the landscape for anything that seemed out of place. There was nothing. It all looked normal. Who was doing this?

A few minutes later, he'd seen all he needed to. 'Righto, my aircraft,' he said.

Cally took her hands away. 'Your aircraft,' she responded the way she had been taught.

Harrison angled the plane towards Danjar Plains and twenty minutes later they were descending.

'G'day, g'day.' Harrison's neighbour Ryan Mathison nodded as they approached the ute. He looked at Cally. 'Hi, sweetie. How are you?'

'Hello,' she answered, staying close to her father.

'Sorry to hear about Violet,' Harrison said as he held out his hand.

Although Ryan was shorter than Harrison and, if you boiled him down, you'd be unlikely to get enough fat to make a cake of soap, his grip was still vice-like. Ryan never cared much about his appearance and usually his flyaway brown hair flopped over his eyes and ears. But his wife, Marni, must have cut his hair recently. It was shorter than Harrison had seen it.

'Thanks,' Ryan answered.

When he smiled, all the tension left Ryan's face. Harrison had long suspected things weren't happy within Ryan's marriage and he was sure that Violet's death wouldn't help. He knew Marni had enjoyed spending time at the old lady's home.

'Any talk of a funeral?'

'We're thinking Friday or Saturday.'

Harrison grabbed Cally under the arms and swung her onto the tray of the ute.

'Dad!' she protested.

'Sorry, force of habit. Now hold on!'

Cally rolled her eyes.

The two men climbed into the front seat and pulled the doors shut. Soon they were bumping down the two-wheel track towards the homestead.

'So what can we do to help? That's why we're here.'

Ryan shrugged. 'Better talk to Mum and Dad. They've told the cops and we're just waiting for the doctor to sign the death certificate.'

'What about getting Spider to town? I can take her in the plane if you like.'

'She had it all organised. She's going to be buried here.'

'Of course she did.' Harrison gave a rueful grin.

Peggy and Paul were standing on the verandah when the ute pulled in. Harrison sat for a heartbeat and looked at his friends, before opening the car door and climbing out.

Peggy looked tired and drawn around the eyes and Harrison suspected Paul's feelings were running high behind his cool façade. But being strong country people they would just be getting on with what had to be done, organising the funeral, running the station and looking after their own.

At the sight of Cally, Peggy held out her arms. 'Cally, darling. It's good to see you. Goodness, look how much you've grown!'

Harrison grinned as his daughter fell into Peggy's hug.

Peggy had been a godsend when Ange had died. After the funeral, she had packed a bag and driven the 150-kilometre trip to his place at Mundranda. For two weeks she'd stayed, cooking and cleaning and looking after the animals. She'd filled the freezers with enough food for six months and held Cally when she'd cried and explained the harsh realities of life in a way the young girl could understand.

In fact, with Ange gone, Peggy and Violet had been the only female influences Cally had, although Harrison had tried hard not to nod and smile in agreement when Cally had whispered one night that Aunty Spider scared her witless.

Paul was walking towards him, his hand held out. 'Nice of you to drop by.'

'Sorry to hear about Violet,' Harrison repeated.

Peggy gave Cally one last squeeze. 'Tea? Coffee?' she offered.

'Cup of tea would be great, Peggy. Thanks.' He accepted the kiss she landed on his cheek and sat down with Ryan on the verandah.

Paul joined them. 'How'd you fair with the rain?'

'We got eighty millimetres on the top part of the station, but only sixty at the homestead. Bloody lakes everywhere and a bit of fencing's underwater. Real lucky the strip has dried out, otherwise I wouldn't have been able to get off the ground. I had a quick buzz over your place but didn't see any problems.'

'Thanks for that,' Ryan said.

'I'll tell you what I did see, though. My top boundary fence has been laid down. It's still in the fence line but with enough of it on the ground to let stock walk through.'

'Is that right?' Paul said slowly.

Ryan let out an angry breath. 'Bugger me, I'd like to get hold of whoever is doing this and hang them up by their toenails,' he muttered. 'You know, we reckon we lost about eight hundred ewes last year? Thieving bastards.'

'I know it's not the time to be talking about it,' Harrison said. 'I just wanted to let you know, so you could keep an eye out here.'

'Thanks. We appreciate it, don't we, son?' Paul turned to Ryan.

'Yeah, we do.'

Conversation turned back to the rain – a popular subject in these parts. Then the men fell silent, and they sat listening to Peggy teasing Cally inside the house. Harrison knew the ritual hair brushing and French braiding would be taking place. That and food was how Peggy showed her love. Harrison suspected Peggy missed her daughter very much, but never let on.

Cally's giggle filtered through the air again and he couldn't help but smile too. He loved to hear his daughter laugh; he worried she didn't do it anywhere near often enough.

Cally appeared with a tray of cakes and biscuits. As he had suspected, her hair had been brushed and pulled back into a French braid. As she put the tray down, her shirt pulled tightly around her chest, showing the unmistakable swell of small breasts. Harrison stared in disbelief. He looked more closely at her and noticed her face had altered slightly, matured. He realised with a shock that she was not a little girl anymore. There were the definite makings of a young lady. Shit. When had that happened?

Cally noticed him staring. 'What?'

'Nothing, love,' he stammered, hoping he had hidden his shock. 'Thanks for smoko.'

'Peggy's coming with the drinks.' She grinned and almost skipped away.

Harrison's heart ached. She was still a child! A child, not an adult. He wished he could keep her the way she was forever. He really wasn't prepared for this!

Peggy deposited a tray of cups on the table and began to pour the tea.

'Thanks, Peggy,' Harrison mumbled, leaning in to take his drink and help himself to something to eat. He was still shaking off his paternal shock.

As if reading his mind, Peggy glanced over her shoulder and said quietly: 'She's growing up.'

'I know.'

'Boarding school next year?'

Harrison nodded.

The silence was filled with the cawing of crows circling over the chook pen, hoping to snatch an egg or two. Harrison watched as one landed on the ground, then, using his claws and beak, climbed up the netting and stuck his head in the gap where it met the tin of the laying shed.

'Cheeky beggar,' Ryan said.

Peggy laughed. 'He won't get in. Marni made sure of it. She's stuffed some of Ryan's old jocks down there!'

'Eeww!' Cally had reappeared, holding a cold glass of Milo.

Everyone chuckled.

'Where's Marni?' Harrison asked.

'Resting,' Ryan answered. 'Last couple of days have been a bit hard for her.'

'I bet it has. The Nullarbor's such a different world compared to other places. Even coming from a farming background, like Marni has, doesn't prepare you for the isolation, or harsh realities of life does it? It's hard to adapt to. And she loved Violet like she was her own.' He shook his head sadly.

'Hmm,' agreed Ryan, looking into the distance.

'So.' Harrison shifted in his seat. 'Can Cally and I help in anyway?' He looked around at his friends. 'Can I fly you anywhere, pick up anything? I'm here to help.'

Peggy spoke. 'I can get most of the food out on the Sands truck. It delivers every Friday. But Tessa is arriving in Kalgoorlie on Wednesday. If you were able to pick her up and grab me a few of the perishable things we'll need, I'd appreciate it.'

'Consider it done.'

Paul glanced over at Peggy. 'Guess that makes the best day Saturday, doesn't it? Pastor Allan is available and it gives us enough time to get the word out to people who need to travel to get here. And for you to get the food ready.'

Ryan and Peggy nodded in agreement.

'Saturday it is, then,' said Paul, the resignation clear in his voice.

'Won't take long for everyone to find out,' said Harrison, thinking of how quickly news got around in the small community, despite the distances. One radio call and everyone who was listening knew.

As if on cue, the phone rang.

Chapter 4

The plane journey passed in a blur of wine, broken sleep, pre-packaged food and bad movies. As Perth came into view, Tessa looked out the window, trying to place familiar landmarks. She ran her tongue around her lips and mouth, trying to summon some moisture, then shook her head gingerly. She was annoyed with herself that she'd once again forgotten the mathematics of in-flight alcohol: one glass of wine equalled two in the air. Seven glasses meant fourteen and a monumental headache. Idiot!

Goosebumps spread across her skin as she saw the jacaranda trees and the Swan River below.

She sighed. *Home*, she thought. *Home*.

But the closer she got the more her anxiety grew, hardening into a dry lump at the back of her throat. Now a quiet terror hung over her. It wasn't just the loss of Spider or her shame that she'd let her great-aunt down. And it wasn't only the fear that someone at Marketing Matters may find out about John Smith. The silent, creeping dread that had her gripping her seat as the plane descended was also caused by the same old remorse and guilt she'd been carrying around with her for the last seven years.

Even the thought of arriving in Perth terrified her, which seemed silly – Perth had been her home for years. She'd gone to boarding school there, then uni, then work. And at first, she'd loved living in the city. Boarding school had been wonderful and liberating. Her friends Jaz and Kendra had made her transition from Station Girl to City Girl easy.

Then Kendra had been killed at Danjar Plains one school holidays, and Tessa's world had turned upside down. However many times Kendra's family told Tessa it wasn't her fault, she could never quite believe she wasn't in some way culpable.

Another wave of emotions took hold. Tessa didn't know how to deal with any of it. She was certain of only one thing – that she was broken.

Breathlessly she asked a passing flight attendant, who was on her way to her seat, for a bottle of water. Then she turned to the window again. Cars snaked their way down the freeway towards the towering city offices. Tessa could pick out the St George's building where she'd interned for the first few months after she finished uni.

When the plane finally shuddered to a halt, and the passengers disembarked they were herded like a mob of sheep through Customs. After what felt like hours, she collected her luggage and gathered herself. She still had another flight ahead of her, to Kalgoorlie, and so needed to get herself across to the domestic terminal. Picking up her bags, she took a deep breath. Then she headed outside through the open sliding doors.

The heat hit her. A sweat broke instantly across her brow and she felt moisture begin to gather between her breasts. How could she have forgotten this? Familiar, but also foreign, the burning sensation was like an invasion. How little time it took to acclimatise to a different environment; to soften up! Squinting, Tessa found her sunglasses and put them on, then found her phone.

Not a minute after she'd punched in her PIN code the mobile beeped. Then again and again and again.

Puzzled, she stopped and looked at the screen.

Jaz: Honey, you might be in a bit of shit. Look at the tweets! #tessamarketingmatterswhore Call me as soon as you get this.

Alarm.
Quickly she dialled Jaz's number and, tucking the phone between her shoulder and ear, she pulled out her iPad and logged into her personal account. Her emails downloaded – there were one hundred and fifty-two.

''Lo?' Jaz's voice was sleepy.

'Jazzy, it's me, Tessa. Can you *please* tell me what's going on?'

'Tessa! About bloody time!' said Jaz, sounding like she'd been jerked awake. Have you seen the photos?'

Tentacles of dread spread from the pit of Tessa's stomach, then flooded through her arms, chest and head. One email stood out. Darcy Anderson.

'Photos? No! What's going on?'

As if in slow motion, she tapped on his email.

'Have you got your iPad? Have a look. There are heaps of photos of you going around on Facebook and Twitter. I don't know who posted them but . . .' Jaz's voice faded into nothingness as Tessa read Darcy's email.

Dear Tessa,

As you are aware, professional privacy is paramount in our business and any breach of this, as per your contract, is grounds for instant dismissal. It has come to my attention that some of your social activities have been with employees of our competitors. Due to this, it is with regret that I ask you to tender your resignation or risk the indignity of a very public termination of employment.

I am giving you the opportunity to resign only because of our family connection.

We ask that you return your work tools – iPad etc. as soon as possible.

Your passwords and account details have all been changed and if you try to log on to our system, access will be denied.

I expect to hear from you within five days of receiving this correspondence. Your failure to make contact will result in termination.

I must say, I am extremely disappointed in your behaviour, and my disappointment is compounded by the fact that you made no mention of these events when we met to discuss your aunt's passing.

Your recent time off hasn't gone unnoticed and I am well aware of your tendency to drink and socialise to excess. I had been prepared to overlook all of this, knowing you were settling in. However, the photos circulating on social media are completely inappropriate and therefore I have no choice but to insist on your immediate resignation.

Yours sincerely,
Darcy Anderson

Tessa scrolled down further, only to wish she hadn't. A photo of her and John Smith lit the screen – his hips welded to hers as they jumped forward in a drunken kangaroo hop, his hand over her shoulder and holding her breast. Tessa's eyes were closed, her mouth open, obviously whooping for joy, while her cheeks exhibited an alcohol-induced glow.

'Tessa, Tessa,' Jaz's voice called down the phone. 'Tessa, are you there, are you okay, sweetness?'

'I've been sacked,' said Tessa, feeling like she was going to cry.

'What do you mean?'

'Sacked. There's an email from Darcy Anderson. Resign or be sacked. Oh hell, Jaz, what have I done?'

They were getting closer to Kalgoorlie. In a few minutes Harrison would prepare to land.

Feeling a hand on his arm, he glanced over at his daughter.

'How're you going?' he asked above the drone of the plane engine.

'Okay. Do you think Tessa will recognise us?'

'I'm sure she will. And if she doesn't, I'll know her.' He pushed back his Akubra and a few specks of glitter landed on the maps spread out on his knee. Cally had decorated this hat for his first Father's Day after Ange had died and he rarely left home without it.

'She mightn't know you in that hat!'

'Nothing wrong with the hat.' Harrison smiled. 'I'll reintroduce myself, if she doesn't.'

'Seems ages since she left.'

'It was. You were only four when she last visited the Nullarbor.'

'Am I going to the same boarding school she did?'

Harrison lifted his sunglasses to stare at her. 'You know you are.'

Tessa held celebrity status with Cally. Whenever the older girl had been home on school holidays, she'd had cool clothes, listened to cool music and although those things hadn't meant anything to Cally, she had been so shy of her that often she'd been too afraid to talk to Tessa. However, the look on Cally's face was priceless when Tessa invited her into her bedroom to have tea parties or play dress-ups. Harrison had so much to be grateful to the Mathison family for.

'I wonder what London is like,' Cally said with a wistful look.

'Smelly, busy and too far away from me,' he answered, checking over the instruments again.

'Ha ha, Dad.' Cally rolled her eyes.

He held up his finger. 'Got to talk to the control tower. You want to take us off auto-pilot when I say so?'

'Uh huh.' Cally put her headphones back on and wiggled in her seat, getting comfortable.

'Melbourne Centre Papa November Alpha 125.75.' Harrison's voice deepened as he made the call.

'Papa November Alpha, go ahead.'

'Melbourne Centre, Papa November Alpha is thirty miles east of Kalgoorlie, ready for descent. Request traffic.'

Harrison made notes as the Control Tower confirmed there was no other traffic and gave him the air pressure. He quickly worked out how many feet per minute he should descend by and gave the sign to Cally. When he felt the nose dip he nodded his approval and called in: 'Papa November Alpha, leaving eight thousand feet on descent. No traffic.'

Moments later another call gave him the weather. Even without checking his paperwork, he knew the Two Nine was the airstrip to land on. The slight cross-breeze wouldn't worry them at all.

Within minutes, the wheels kissed the tarmac and they were on the ground. As they tethered the Cessna, Harrison noted with pride how Cally confidently moved around the plane and tied the knots exactly as he had taught her.

'So, what's first?' Cally asked as they headed towards the hire-car office.

'Reckon we'll pick up all the food Peggy has ordered, then maybe have lunch at the pub. Tessa isn't due in until one, and so long as we're in the air by two thirty, we'll be able to get home in daylight. What do you say?'

'Sounds good.'

'And maybe there'll be time for a bit of shopping for you.'

'Me? I don't need anything.'

Harrison bet she was the only eleven-year-old who didn't think she needed anything. Most girls living in towns or cities would probably be falling over themselves for the latest clothes.

'Well, I think you might. Peggy suggested I take you to this shop.' He fished in his pocket then handed Cally a piece of paper.

The colour rose in her cheeks. 'Oh.'

'I think it might be time, hey?' He was as uncomfortable with the idea of visiting Bras'n'Things as she was, but it had to be done. And sadly, he was the only one to do it.

'Whatever.' Cally turned away and stared out of the window, shutting down the conversation.

Chapter 5

Tessa boarded the flight to Kalgoorlie, feeling sick. Tossing her bag into the overhead locker she slumped into her seat and sat with her arms crossed. Now she was not only riddled with anxiety but furious with herself.

Please may no one sit next to me, she prayed. At that moment a spritely old lady sat down beside her. 'How are you, love?'

Not wanting to encourage conversation, Tessa just nodded. She couldn't face talking to anyone at the moment.

As the plane took off, her mind was still whirling. *Who had posted those photos?* From the quick look she'd been able to get at the airport, they were on a Facebook page and Twitter account that seemed fake. The person who'd opened them was without friends or followers and there was no personal information at all. It was obvious both accounts had been opened with one idea in mind. To post those photos of John . . . She had no idea how to find out who was responsible.

'Great,' she muttered audibly, twisting in her seat to try and get comfortable; the anxiety making her tense.

'Difficult day, love?' the lady asked.

'Yes, unfortunately,' said Tessa.

'Ah, well, nothing like a stint in the country to make things right.' Tessa could see the woman eyeing her linen pants, strappy sandals and low-cut blouse.

'Thank you,' said Tessa, praying the woman wouldn't keep talking to her.

A flight attendant appeared with a rattling trolley in tow. 'Can I offer you tea or coffee?'

'Do you have a white wine?' Tessa asked before the older woman had a chance to say anything.

'Certainly, ma'am. And for you?' The attendant looked at Tessa's neighbour.

'I'll have a cuppa tea, thanks, love. Geez, it musta been a bad day if you need a drink at eleven in the morning, dearie.'

'I've flown from London today, or rather, yesterday. I'm still a bit mixed up with my times,' said Tessa, before turning back towards the window.

Two glasses of wine and a little nap later she jerked her head up from where it lay against the wall of the plane. Casting a glance around her, she saw that the woman sitting next to her was engrossed in a book. Tessa glanced at her watch and listened as the captain announced their descent.

She looked out the window and down to the ground. Would she recognise the landscape, she wondered. Farming land stretched out below her. She could see the dust from the headers harvesting grain as they passed over the wheat belt and a long thin ribbon of bitumen which joined Perth to the rest of Australia. Soon enough she could see open-cut pits and the tin roofs of Kalgoorlie's untamed urban sprawl.

She remembered the day she'd left for boarding school. She and her mum, Peggy, had flown to Perth from Kal. The reflection of the rooftops had been Tessa's last image of 'home'. She wondered if it would be the same coming from the other direction. Then she thrust her thoughts back to the photos.

What on earth was she going to do? There was no reason to go back to London, but where else could she go? The consequences of what she'd done hit home. She wouldn't get another job in London. London was *done*. Finished.

But what to tell her parents? 'Oh, by the way, Mum, I've been sleeping with every man that would have me, because I've been too drunk to say no and I like it when someone pays me some attention. Oh, and I also accidentally slept with the competition's manager. Darcy found out and sacked me.'

Tessa shut her eyes and clenched her hands into fists, trying to breathe beyond the anger and frustration building inside her. What an idiot! That seemed to be her mantra these days.

'Can't be that bad, surely.'

Tessa opened her eyes and stared at her neighbour. The older woman was looking at her with concern.

Tessa frowned. 'I'm sorry?' she said.

'Your hands, your face, your shoulders. Everything about you is radiating tension. Would you like to talk about it?'

'Uh no. No, thank you, everything will be fine.'

'Comin' home for a visit?' The woman persisted.

Tessa sighed. 'Of sorts. My great-aunt died and I'm going back for her funeral.'

'Ah, you poor thing.' The lady patted her hand.

Tessa had forgotten how friendly country people were. On the Tube there was no way you'd have a conversation with anyone you didn't know, let alone let them touch you.

'Long way from home to get a call like that. I'm coming to Kal for a funeral, too. Out on the Nullarbor it is. Very old friend of mine. Violet Anderson.'

Emotion shot through Tessa. 'Really? What's your name?'

'Elsie Harlot. And no I'm not one and you don't

need to make any jokes. I've heard them all before.'
Elsie pointed her finger at Tessa in a no-nonsense
manner.

Tessa smiled despite herself. Instantly she could
see why Aunty Spider and this Elsie would have got
along. But Elsie wasn't a name she knew.

'How long did you know your friend?'

'Oh, nigh on sixty years. Met her in the
early thirties. Hell, it's probably longer. Maybe
seventy years. Gawd, we could've had a platinum
anniversary!' She roared with laughter and slapped
her hand on her knee.

Tessa closed her eyes, not sure whether to laugh
or cry.

'Tell me about her,' said Tessa.

'Ah, love, we haven't got time.' Elsie stopped
laughing, though she was still grinning. 'She was
one of a kind. Loyal, lovable, kind. But she wouldn't
take any rubbish, mind. She was wise and loved her
family and land with a passion.'

Elsie was silent for a moment, then she turned
to Tessa and said, 'I know talking about others
helps you not to think about your own problems.
But maybe you should be telling me why you're
gripping the seat like there's no tomorrow? I don't
reckon it's got anything to do with the landing.'

Tessa was surprised to realise the plane was on
the tarmac and taxiing towards the small country
terminal. She looked at Elsie and was surprised to
see how clear her eyes were. She may have looked

old, but Tessa suspected there was a young woman trapped inside that body.

'Do you mind me asking how old you are?'

'Lovie, you just ask me anything you please. I'm eighty-four next month.'

'You look amazing for eighty-four,' said Tessa, smiling for what felt like the first time in weeks. 'How are you getting to the funeral? You said it was on the Nullarbor.'

'I've got an old flame picking me up,' Elsie winked. 'He'll take me out.'

'I hope you have a very safe trip,' said Tessa, unclipping her seatbelt and putting her bag on her lap. But as she made her way down the steps and across the tarmac, she wondered why she hadn't told Elsie she was home for the same funeral.

For the fifth time, Harrison dialled Tessa's number. Again it went straight to message bank.

'Damn. Where on earth is she? She should have been here an hour ago.' He glanced down at his watch again.

'Well, if she isn't here soon, we won't get home, Dad. The light won't hold out.'

'You don't have to tell me, sweetheart.'

Cally grinned at him and poked out her tongue. As childish as it seemed, Harrison was pleased to see it. He returned the gesture. The shopping trip had been awkward for them both, but by the end of it he thought it just might have brought them even closer than before.

'I'll go for a wander through the main terminal and see if I can find her. Will you stay in case she comes?'

'No worries, Dad.'

Inside the terminal, Harrison had to walk slowly and stop to look at each person. Even though he'd told Cally he'd have no trouble recognising Tessa, he wasn't so sure. He hadn't seen her since Kendra Jackson's accident, which must have been nine years ago. He knew she had returned briefly, two years later, but the visit hadn't gone well, stirring up too many memories and much hurt. Violet had told him sadly Tessa had sworn never to come back. It seemed that Tessa wanted to cut all ties with Danjar Plains. Which was just silly, he reckoned. Home is where you *can* heal. He of all people knew that.

He gave a cursory glance over the bar then kept going. Nothing. Once again he tried to phone her mobile while checking the arrival information screen for her flight. It had definitely landed.

Looking around, he wondered if he could ask someone to check the Ladies, but the only people in sight were behind the check-in desk. He knew they wouldn't be able to help.

It was on his second round of the terminal he heard someone speaking in a voice that combined panic and agitation.

'Please, Jaz! I desperately need you to find out for me.' Silence. 'But you're still in London, I'm not. It's got to be someone we know, and you've got a much better chance of finding out than me.'

Looking around, Harrison searched for the owner. Then he did a double-take. It was Tessa, but a Tessa he barely recognised. Harrison recalled a fresh-faced girl, with shoulder length, wavy dark hair, not spikes so sharp they looked like they'd prick you. The healthy, happy glow she'd once had was buried under heavy makeup. Thin and drawn, her face was set in anger and distress as she spoke to whoever was on the end of the phone.

This was some citified version. A sharp-tongued, rude version. A type he knew instantly he wouldn't like. He'd come across these types of women in the boardroom before. They'd eat you up and spit you out as quick as look at you.

'Jaz, I so need your help . . .'

He went up to her and put his hand on her shoulder.

She started and looked up at him. But instead of happy recognition Harrison saw stress and misery.

'Sorry, I just need to finish this call,' she said and turned away and continued the conversation.

Even though he'd half-expected it, her answer took Harrison aback. He opened his mouth, then shut it again and moved a little way off. Clearly there was a problem.

Tessa lifted the phone back to her ear. 'How

54

am I supposed to know? I don't even know how long I'm going to be stuck here! But there's nowhere else to go. That's why I'm asking you to find out, Jaz. I'm not going to have any internet access, no mobile phone. I'm in the middle of nowhere and it feels like my life is falling apart what with Aunty Spider dying and now this. Bloody trolls.'

Harrison frowned at her tone. Anger had turned to desperation. This certainly wasn't the Tessa he remembered. She'd never been foul-mouthed or rude to other people. She'd been one of the sweetest kids. But then again, what the hell would he know?

Glancing at his watch, he knew that if he wasn't off the ground in forty-five minutes, he wouldn't make it home. And he had to be there tonight.

'Tessa, I'm sorry to disturb you,' he said, moving towards her.

'Hold on, Jaz,' said Tessa, turning to look at him. 'I'm sorry. This is a really important phone call.'

As her words washed over him, so did her breath, which smelt of stale booze.

'I'm sorry,' said Harrison, 'but your parents asked if I could pick you up and fly you to your great-aunt's funeral. And unfortunately we're behind schedule already.'

Tessa hesitated, clearly put out, then lifted the phone back up to her ear. 'Jaz, I have to go, but please, *please* find out for me.' She pushed the phone back into her handbag. 'Right, then. Sorry I guess we better get going.'

Harrison nodded. 'Yeah, we're late already. If we don't go now we won't make it back before dark and I won't be able to land. You may not remember, but there aren't any lights on the strip at Danjar Plains,' said Harrison, then turned away, leaving Tessa to follow with her bag.

Harrison had planned to put Tessa in the front seat of the plane. But the token 'hello' she gave to Cally annoyed him even more than her earlier behaviour so, defying all weight protocols, he put her in the back seat. She could stew there on whatever was bothering her.

Chapter 6

The familiar homestead and out-buildings came into view. Tessa felt her throat constrict and goosebumps crawl over her skin, but she couldn't contain her desire to look. What was it like now? What had changed?

She peered out the window to get a glimpse of the sheds below. There was Aunty Spider's house and the road that wound its way through the bush to the homestead. The shearing shed roof announced in large black letters that the station was Danjar Plains. She spotted the machinery shed. It was all so familiar, and yet so removed from the life she lived now. Then she saw the homestead windmill where Kendra had died, and she quickly looked away. The memories were just too frightening.

As they prepared to land she kept her eyes on the airstrip. There was the old ute – that Toyota must have driven a million kilometres by now! Her mum was in the back, doing a two-arm wave. And there was her parents' new four-wheel-drive. She could see her dad and Ryan standing by the tray, faces tilted towards the sky.

'Hello everyone,' Tessa whispered, her hands pushed against the window. 'I'm home.'

Harrison landed the plane smoothly just as the sun was about to disappear. It was the time Spider had called 'bank review hour', when the station looked its best. 'Show them around at dusk and they'll lend you the extra money you need,' her aunt had always joked. At this time of day, when the sun slowly slipped to the edge of the world, the golden rays reflected off the sheds, ground and plants and seem to hang in the air. It displaced the harshness of the land. Then the colour of the surrounding country turned deeper and the air grew still, so that even the hardest souls fell in love with the place.

For a moment Tessa wondered why she'd ever left. But then images of Kendra flashed through her mind.

The plane had come to a stop and Paul, Peggy and Ryan ran over to meet them.

'Darling!' Peggy held out her arms as Tessa clambered from the plane.

'Mum! Dad!' She raced for the comfort of their hugs and fell onto them. She felt her dad kiss her head and inhaled the smell of her mum, which, as ever, was of eucalyptus and earth.

'Hey! What about me?' Ryan pushed his way in and she turned into his embrace. 'Good to see you, kiddo. Marni isn't well, otherwise she would have been here, too.'

Surprised, but not really, by another sting of tears, Tessa tried to laugh. 'Enough with the kiddo bit! I'm a fully grown adult!'

'Man, listen to your accent. You sound English. Are you putting that on just for us?' Ryan teased.

'No! No, I'm not. It's just the way I talk.'

'Well, you sound like you should be dining with the Queen rather than hanging around a bunch of bushies in the middle of nowhere.'

Regret shot through her when she heard the phrase Ryan used. Had Harrison called ahead and told him what she'd said? She hoped not. She glanced over at him, but his face was set like stone. She didn't really remember him that well. He seemed grim and distant, a stranger. His daughter seemed nice enough, though. She smiled a lot. Harrison didn't. She remembered his wife had died when Cally was young, so maybe he was bitter and twisted. Shame really, she thought. And what was with the glittery hat!

She turned her attention back to Ryan. 'Well, the Queen was all booked up this evening, so you lot will just have to do.' Looking down the strip she noticed that her aunt's bicycle wasn't leaning against the fence post and the full ache she'd experienced in London flared as Violet's death hit her once more. Being *here* made it inescapable. Spider wasn't around anymore.

'It's really true, then?' she asked, staring at the empty spot. 'She's gone?'

Her father gripped her hands. 'She's gone. But she hasn't, really. She'll be up in the gum trees keeping an eye on us. Heaven forbid if we do something wrong. She'll probably come to haunt us!' He gave a small, sad smile. 'I'm sure she knew you'd come home.'

Tessa stood silently, looking into her father's face, searching for his meaning.

He just nodded. 'It's good to see you here.'

'Come on,' Peggy urged. 'Let's get you back to the house and settled in. You've been travelling for nearly two days. You must be exhausted! Come on, Cally, you too. I bet you're tired after your exciting day in Kalgoorlie.' She swung her arms around the two girls and helped them into the four-wheel-drive.

When the men had loaded the luggage and supplies into the back of the old Toyota the procession slowly set off through the balmy evening air.

To Tessa, it seemed that Danjar Plains hadn't changed in the whole time she had been gone. The winding track to the homestead was still bumpy. The mallee trees still looked silver in the half-light, their spindly branches stark against the darkening sky. Spinifex lined the ground, and dust hung in the air behind the vehicles.

They passed the small family cemetery and Tessa spotted the freshly dug grave and the backhoe parked discreetly behind some bushes. She quickly closed her eyes and counted slowly to twenty. It should be a safe distance behind her now.

Peggy tooted the horn as they passed Ryan and Marni's donga. Tessa waved in case her sister-in-law was looking out of the window.

When her old home came into sight her lips formed a smile. How Peggy managed to keep the garden so lush Tessa had no idea. Drifts of pink geraniums were visible, despite the evening gloom, and the lawn looked like an English meadow. The weatherboard house looked much the same but had aged. The corrugated tin was lifting slightly at the edges and the outside needed a paint.

Still, it was home.

'Wow, Mum! Everything looks fantastic!'

Peggy leaned over and patted her knee. 'It's so good to have you here, love.'

For the first time in many months, Tessa ate steak and salad. As insects committed suicide on the gas light, she laughed with her family and told stories about things that had happened in London. She didn't mention recent events, and stopped herself when her hand strayed to her phone to check her emails or Facebook.

The wine and beer flowed freely. Tessa wouldn't have to hide her drinking tonight, at least. She could just let her hair down and be free. It was a good feeling.

But there was an empty chair at the table and every time the door opened, she looked for Aunty Spider. Somehow none of the stories Tessa told felt quite complete without her aunt's probing questions or funny one-liners. Spider always seemed to get more information than Tessa ever planned to give. In which case, perhaps it was a good thing she wasn't there this time.

The wine also helped dampen the fear Tessa felt every time she looked towards the house paddock and windmill and remembered the last time she'd seen her friend Kendra.

Gradually, one by one, the family and guests headed off to bed until there was only Peggy and Tessa left. 'So how are you *really*, darling?' Peggy asked. 'It sounds like things are just wonderful over there.'

'Everything is fine, Mum,' Tessa lied. 'I'm happy and have made so many friends. Work is challenging. It tests me to my limits, but I like that. It's good to keep busy.' She fiddled with her shorts and then looked up in time to see a concerned look flash across Peggy's face.

'Yeah,' Peggy said quietly. 'Keeping busy helps keep the memories at bay.' She reached across the table and took Tessa's hand. 'When do you have to go back?'

'Um, Darcy said I could have as long as I needed.' Even though there had barely been any time to digest Darcy's email, the embarrassment of telling her parents was right up there with letting Aunty

Spider down. She'd hoped it wouldn't come up so soon, because she really hadn't given any thought to what she would say, or what excuses she would give. It was obvious she couldn't stay here indefinitely, but unfortunately there was nowhere else to go.

'Well,' her mother said, rising. 'It will be lovely to have you for as long as we can.' She yawned. 'I'd better go to bed. Such a lot to do tomorrow.'

'What time will everyone be arriving on Saturday?'

'Oh, you know what they're like. Some will turn up first thing to help; some will come just in time for the service. Ryan and Dad dug the grave this morning – you would've seen that coming in – so, really, other than cooking and setting up the chairs for afterwards, there isn't much else to do.'

Tessa smiled sadly. 'Did you have to get permission to bury her out here?'

Peggy let out a small laugh. 'It was all done. Spider had organised everything. As you'd expect. She left a letter. Would you like to read it?'

'Her will?'

'No, just telling us what she thought about us and what she'd organised.'

'What did she say about me?'

'Here, you read it.' Peggy fished around in her pocket and handed it to her. 'I thought you'd want to see it.'

With unsteady hands, Tessa unfolded the piece of paper which held Spider's last words to them all.

'My Dear Paul and Peggy,

Firstly, if you are reading this, I'm dead. Ha! I've always wanted say that. It really goes without saying, doesn't it?

I have made arrangements to be buried in the cemetery next to William's memorial. It's where I want to be. It has taken some organising, but there is nothing for you to do other than look after the service. All the necessary documents are included in here. I know that Doctor Mike will sign off on the death certificate without any concerns. He told me last time the Flying Doctor ran a clinic that I was a ticking time-bomb. My heart is nothing but a leaky old valve.

Still I won't be upset when I do go. I'm tired. Ninety-two (or whatever I am when I go) isn't a bad knock.

I'm not one for sentiment but I have to say this:

Paul, I'm proud of you. You've always been more like the son I never had, rather than my nephew. I don't think I've ever told you I love you, so I am doing it now.

Peggy, you're a fine wife and mother. Thank you for never making this grumpy old woman, who wasn't even your blood relative, feel like she wasn't welcome in your home.

Danjar Plains is in good hands with you at the helm, Paul, and Ryan next in line. Don't stay too long, though. Ryan and Marni won't thank you, if you do.

Keep a close eye on Tessa. She still hasn't completely healed.

My love to you all,
Violet

Tessa closed her eyes. *Not healed yet*, she thought. She shook her head before resting it on the back of the chair. *She knew, as she always did.*

'It doesn't seem quite real yet.'

'No, it doesn't. I'm sure she's just having a holiday and will pop over in the morning,' Peggy agreed.

'Ah, I'm so tired,' she said, handing the letter back.

'Come on, to bed with you. You're in your old room.' Peggy started to clear the table. 'Turn off the gas light, can you? You're not sleeping here!'

'I know, I know. It's comfortable, though.'

'Bed will be better.'

'Mum?'

'Hmm?'

'Where is she?'

'In the cool room, love. It was the only place to keep her cold.'

Tessa's mouth reacted before her brain. 'What! Why? Ohh. Don't worry.' She held up her hand to ward off the thoughts of decomposing and heat. 'Can I see her?'

'Oh, petal, do you want to?' Concern again crossed Peggy's face as she looked at her daughter.

'Yes. Um, I think so,' Tessa answered slowly. 'She hasn't, um, you know?'

'No. She was in the cool room within hours of it happening. She looks just like Spider. The minister will take you if you want. Or you can go by yourself.'

Tessa watched her mother walk inside then heaved herself off the chair, collected the last of the plates and turned off the gas light. As she heard the soft *pop* of the gas going out, she stood and stared. Life was just like the gas. One second it was throwing light to the darkest corners, keeping people comfortable and showing the way, and the next, there was nothing but darkness.

A heartbeat, then nothing more.

Gone.

Finished.

Dead.

In the flash of a second.

Chapter 7

Pastor Allan took Tessa's arm gently and led her away from the coffin in the cool room. He offered her tissues that seemed to appear endlessly from his pockets and patted her shoulder until her sobbing subsided. Tessa felt like every pent-up emotion from everything she'd ever done wrong was flowing from her. Kendra, her guilt at not answering Spider's letters, her excessive drinking and its latest consequences. Was there anything good left? If so, she couldn't think of one damn thing. She had stuffed up her whole life.

'It's okay to let it all out,' Pastor Allan said, although his voice was barely audible above her cries.

Tessa just shook her head and tried to control herself. 'You don't understand . . .' She gulped.

'Maybe not, but I can try if you tell me.' Allan looked around for somewhere to sit. As he swung his leg over the motorbike Tessa smiled through her tears.

'I can't. I don't know. It's all mixed up.'

The silence stretched, only broken by the scratch of birds' feet on the tin roof of the workshop. Tessa felt a need to fill it, but she just couldn't find the words.

'Do you see dead bodies all the time?' she finally asked, wiping her eyes.

'Well, it depends on whether the family want to have a viewing. I always choose to be in the room, because people have different reactions. Disbelief, anger, shock, guilt. Sadness, obviously. When someone sees their loved one lying in a coffin, it's confronting and final. They understand there isn't any turning back. Someone who's always been around has really gone. It's always different when an older person dies compared to a young person because it's the end of a long life. Most emotions then are just a sense of loss and sadness, but an underlying peace with the death because it's a natural part of the cycle. The difficult viewings are suicides, accidental and illness-related deaths. People taken young.'

Tessa nodded, understanding. She closed her eyes and leaned against the dusty, corrugated iron wall. She felt exhausted.

'Do you feel any of those things, Tessa?'

'Oh, just about every single one of them.'

'But they're not just related to Violet, are they?'

Tessa's eyes flew open. Allan was looking not at

her but out of the shed towards the horizon, in the direction of the windmill in the house paddock.

Tears sprang to Tessa's eyes but she just couldn't bring herself to unburden herself to anyone. 'No, it's not, but I'm not going there. I can't go there. I know it was a long time ago, but if I let myself think about it, I can't get away.'

Pastor Allan made calming gestures with his hands. 'It's okay, Tessa. It was just a question. I'm sorry I brought it up. It was such a long time ago . . . It was thoughtless of me. Especially today.'

'I've got to go,' said Tessa turning and walking out of the shed.

The driveway into Danjar Plains was eight kilometres long and visitors could be heard and seen long before they arrived. Now, watching from the back door of the shearing shed, Tessa saw six separate plumes of dust move towards the house. There weren't only cars, either. Since early morning she'd heard the buzz of planes overhead – most stations owned light aircraft to cover long distances. At last count there were eight Cessnas all parked at one end of the airstrip.

Already, the heat of the day was beginning to make itself felt. The ten o'clock service wasn't really convenient for people who had to travel a long way, but it was better than standing in forty-degree heat in the afternoon.

Allan's quiet questioning had left Tessa shattered, and she had retreated to the shearing shed, unable to face anyone. As she sipped from one of the duty-free bottles of vodka she'd brought in her suitcase she wondered who was in the cars and what relation they were to Aunty Spider. Perhaps Elsie was in one. Tessa had no idea what she would say to the old woman today. Like Spider, Elsie seemed to have an uncanny knack of seeing right through her.

Even though she knew she'd *had* to come home, Tessa wished she wasn't here at all. She ran her hands along the shed's worn wooden struts. Goosebumps broke out on her arms and, despite the temperature, she felt cold. 'I'm sorry,' she whispered, turning to face the empty shed. 'I'm sorry I let you down.'

She saw a bin half-full of merino fleeces, and walked towards it, the bottle swinging from her fingers. Sinking onto her knees, she buried her hands deep within and felt the soft and grainy texture against her skin.

It brought back a memory: Aunty Spider's hands guiding hers around the edge of the fleece. *No, like this. See the sweat stains here, the dark oily bits where all the burrs are? Take them. That's right. Pull gently but don't take too much.*

Violet's voice seemed so real, Tessa felt she should answer her.

'Tessa?' Ryan's call made her jump. She looked around to see where he was, then grabbed the bottle beside her and pushed it deep into the wool.

'Yes?' she called back, pulling the wool back into place. She stood up and dusted off her hands.

Her brother came into view. He was dressed in good pants and an open-neck shirt. Tessa immediately felt overdressed in her black sheath dress and high heels. The Nullarbor was casual, even when being respectful. She wished she'd remembered that.

'There you are! You hiding? Come on. It's time. We need to go.'

'Yes, of course. Sorry. I was just, um,' she looked around and gestured to the shed, 'revisiting, I guess.'

Ryan stopped and shrugged. 'All the same to me. But it's been such a long time since you were home. All seems new again, does it?'

'Not new – familiar. Comforting even. But chock-a-block full of memories.'

'Now, Tessa, today is not the day to reminisce. It'll be emotional enough.' Ryan was firm and Tessa noticed he swallowed hard.

'Maybe take your own advice.' She smiled.

'Maybe I should. Come on, kid sister. Let's go.'

Ryan held out his hand and pulled her up from the wool before he strode out of the shed purposefully. Tessa followed.

Pastor Allan had finished his address and Paul had read the eulogy, the emotion plain in his voice. Now the men were slowly lowering Aunty Spider

71

into the ground. Tessa couldn't watch. Instead, she gazed into the distance. The land was flat and the view of the horizon only interrupted by drab, grey bushes and thin-trunked mallee trees.

Nearby, a large wooden cross stood at the head of William's memorial and the gum tree that Violet had planted in his honour stood tall and leafy, casting a cool shadow over the grave. Nothing had changed much in this timeless family cemetery. Tessa could remember helping her dad make a wooden seat for Aunty Spider to sit on when she came to talk to William, her dead husband, something she'd done most days. Tessa imagined Spider was now sitting there watching the crowd and making her witty, wicked remarks.

The grave of Tom, Tessa's grandfather, was next to William's, and buried beside him was his wife, Lucy. A white steel railing bordered their final resting place.

With her eyes hidden behind her Gucci sunglasses, Tessa turned to the crowd. Some faces she recognised; others were new to her. Who was that lady sniffing into her pansy-covered hanky? Oh, she knew the face, but the name deserted her. Mrs . . . Mrs Hunter. Paula Hunter! That's right. They had a station five hundred kilometres to the north, on the other side of the trans line, where the Indian Pacific ran. Spider had never liked the woman; her aunt couldn't tolerate gossip and bad-mouthing and from the vague recollections Tessa had, she seemed to remember Mrs Hunter did both every time she took a breath.

Tessa realised the people there were mostly older – Spider's friends or neighbours. Elsie was standing next to an elderly man who was leaning on a stick. The old woman stared stoically at the coffin but Tessa thought she could see traces of tears on her cheeks.

She judged the crowd at about sixty – not a bad turn-out for someone who was ninety-three. Spider had often joked that she wouldn't have anyone at her funeral because she'd outlive them all.

Tessa continued to look from face to face. Her eyes slid past an old man, who looked uncomfortable in a shirt and tie. She stopped and went back to him. It was Joe, the old horse breaker. He'd taught her to ride, a million years ago. Of course he'd be here. He was a fixture of the Nullarbor and everyone, child and adult alike, loved him.

He caught her eye and gave a small smile and a nod. *Let's catch up later*, it said.

Tessa's eyes were drawn unwillingly towards the grave as the men stood back. She didn't want to look, but she couldn't seem to tear her gaze away. She looked, down, down, down, past the different layers of dirt, until she stopped at the coffin. There it was. And this was Tessa's final goodbye.

Allan moved forward to make the sign of the cross. 'Rest in peace, our dear Violet.' Pause. 'You are all invited to share a luncheon with the Mathison family back at the homestead.'

The crowd began to disperse. Some people came to the grave and threw in small posies of wild flowers.

Joe took off his hat and held it over his heart as he dropped in a few small sprigs of native bush. Soon salt bush, blue bush and bright blue and yellow everlastings covered the coffin. Tessa watched, angry with herself. Why hadn't she thought to do that? She knew how much her aunt loved the flowers of the Nullarbor. Was she really so self-absorbed?

Tessa felt a hand on her arm. Harrison and Cally were at her side. Cally's eyes were red from crying and she stood silent and pale next to her father.

'Do you want a ride back to the house?' Harrison's tone was still cool, she noticed. It was a reminder of her behaviour the previous day and pricked her conscience.

'Where're Mum and Dad? What happens now? Shouldn't the grave be filled in?' Tessa's questions tumbled out as she glanced around realising they were nearly the last ones left.

'She's gone to get the food ready. She knew you weren't ready to come and asked if we'd bring you. As for the grave, we'll come back after everyone has gone.'

'Oh.'

'Tessa! How lovely to see you. I knew you

wouldn't miss saying goodbye to your dear old aunt.' Mrs Hunter bustled up and gave her a hug. She was dressed all in black but for a bright pink ribbon tied around her straw hat. For a moment Tessa was smothered in the smell of lilac. Hell.

She tried to cough discreetly, but all she wanted to do was push the woman away and scream and scream and scream. Her heart suddenly began to beat very fast and Mrs Hunter's flabby face swam in front of her eyes.

'Ah.' She put her hand out as if to ward off the impending faintness.

'You okay?' Harrison asked, moving to her.

'Um, no.'

She felt him take her arm and Cally move to the other side. 'Excuse us, Paula. Tessa has had a long trip. I'll get her back to the homestead.'

'Well, she's certainly lucky to have you helping her,' sniffed Mrs Hunter, her tone envious. 'You're probably exhausted from all that travelling, dear, and it's a sad day. See you all at the house.' She patted Tessa's arm and turned to leave.

Once in the car, Tessa cleared her throat. 'Um, thank you. I'm not sure what came over me.'

'You're probably a bit tired and emotional.' His tone was short and clipped.

'If I remember correctly, that should give the gossips something to talk about.' She leaned her head against the side of the car and breathed deeply. 'I'm fine. I'm fine.'

'If I didn't know better, I'd have thought you were trying to get away from Mrs Hunter,' said Harrison to which Cally giggled. 'Still, you've just confirmed everything I already thought about city slickers. They're soft.'

His blue eyes were icy and Tessa realised he was still mad with her for being a prize bitch on Wednesday. And she deserved it really. She had been dreadful.

'Tessa, we're really pleased you're back,' said Cally, smiling at Tessa.

'Cally, I must say, it is nice to see you.' Tessa inclined her head towards the girl and didn't say another word for the rest of the short trip.

When the trio arrived back at the house there were people swarming all over the lawn. Chairs had been set up underneath the tall gum trees and on the verandah. Marni was caring for the chair-bound elderly, taking orders for tea and coffee. As Tessa went into the kitchen, her mother handed her a plate. 'Here, offer this banana cake around could you? Then come back and grab this tray of teas. Cally, you take the sandwiches.'

Tessa took the offered plate of cake and set off down the long hallway, only to find Elsie there, waiting for her.

'Why didn't you tell me who you were on the plane?' the old woman asked.

'I don't know.'

'Well, dearie, you and I need to have a chat.

I know so much about you from Violet and I can't leave here without spending some time with you.'

'If you know so much about me,' Tessa blurted, 'how come you didn't realise it was me on the plane?'

Elsie looked at her sternly. 'Love, I knew exactly who you were. How could I not? Coming home from London for your great-aunt's funeral? How many great-aunt funerals would there be on the Nullarbor?' She shook her head as she spoke. 'Like I said, we need to have a chat and I'll explain everything.' Elsie gripped Tessa's arm and stared intently into her face. Tessa saw a flicker of disappointment. Then Elsie said: 'Well, you don't look anything like her. But then again, you wouldn't, would you? Go on. Do your duty here, but I won't be leaving until we talk.'

Chapter 8

From under a tree Harrison looked on, Cally at his side. His gaze landed on Peggy, who had her eyes shut and was rubbing at her temples, as if trying to chase away a threatening headache.

'Cally, go see what you can do to help Peggy. Looks like she's just about had it.' He gave his daughter a gentle push and she ran to do his bidding.

He watched as Peggy handed Cally another plate of sandwiches to offer around.

Poor Peggy! There were so many people still left, the wake didn't look to be ending any time soon. Seeing an empty tray, he picked it up and went to collect a few dirty cups and glasses.

As he carried them inside, Peggy's friend, Diane was following close behind.

She opened her arms to Peggy, who was back in the kitchen, washing up. 'Tired?'

'Too bloody right,' Peggy answered.

She emptied the sink and wiped her hands on a tea towel. 'Harrison, get us all a beer, will you?'

He reached into the fridge, pulled out two beers and offered one to Diane and the other to Peggy.

'Don't fancy one?' Peggy inquired.

Harrison shook his head. 'Not at the moment.' It was such a hot day, and he was pacing himself.

Peggy took a sip. 'Is Tessa okay, Harrison? Paula said she had a bit of a turn at the grave.'

'She's fine. It was a bit emotional for her.' He turned to look for Tessa through the window. There she was, helping herself to another wine. It was her fourth that he knew of.

'She looks really tired. Just like you.' Diane nudged Peggy's shoulder.

'I guess you would be too if you'd travelled halfway around the world. And you know how much she thought of Spider.'

They all watched Tessa take a long drink from her glass.

'She's like her father and anyone else around here,' Peggy observed. 'Loves a drop or two to drink.'

'Right. I'll leave you to it,' Harrison said and backed out of the kitchen. He got the impression the two women wanted a chat.

Outside he talked to a few of the older people. He saw Cally, now sitting in the swing, talking to one of her School of the Air friends.

Paul was in a group, but it seemed to Harrison everyone except Paul was talking. Violet's death had hit his friend hard.

Marni was hovering over everyone, waiting to see an empty cup and offering to refill it. She rarely smiled, but was polite to everyone.

Old Joe, a man who had been breaking horses on the Nullarbor for nearly fifty years, sat by himself in a chair underneath a tree away from the crowd. Harrison started to go to him, but Tessa beat him to it. A rare, genuine smile lit her features as she sat down next to the old bloke and patted his hand. Joe seemed to get a new spark, too.

But Tessa didn't stay long. A quick chat, a peck on the cheek and she was on her way back to the Esky.

A man in a dull green shirt, loose black tie and moleskins strode passed. When his eyes settled on Tessa he made a beeline towards her.

Harrison's face set hard. Bloody Brendan McKenzie! If Tessa was the sort of girl she seemed to be, with her makeup thick as it could stick, that short black dress and swaying hips, she'd be giggling and flirting in no time. No extra thoughts for Spider.

He watched as Brendan McKenzie smiled down at Tessa and held out his hand.

Tessa smiled back and took it.

At that moment he heard a voice at his shoulder. Old Joe.

'You'd reckon Paul would run him off the place wouldn't you?' Joe said slowly.

'He's not one to make a scene,' Harrison answered.

'I've never understood why some fellas just have to be a pain in the arse,' Joe commented thoughtfully. 'And he's one of them.'

'He definitely appears to be that.'

Tessa was now holding a fresh glass of wine and in deep conversation with Brendan.

'Someone should warn that girl that his reputation with the ladies precedes him,' Joe said. His eyes stared ahead, but his meaning was clear. Harrison should.

'She's able to make her own decisions, Joe.'

Brendan's family had bought into the area four years before. In that time Ray, his father, had earned a reputation for being an alcoholic and a rogue. Brendan seemed okay even though he was widely known as a ladies' man. The girls thought him charming and devilish, but no one wanted their daughters near him in case his father's traits turned out to be his own.

Harrison noticed Pastor Allan going to Peggy, who had come outside to stand next to Paul. When Allan said he was leaving, it was the sign for others to start the exodus. Couple by couple and family by family, people said their goodbyes. There was the drone of planes overhead and dust in the drive. Within an hour most of the mourners were gone.

Peggy flopped in a chair and Harrison handed her a beer and passed another to Paul.

'Where's Tessa?' asked Peggy, looking around.

Harrison scanned the area, a feeling of unease spreading across him. Was she really so brazen? 'Not sure,' he answered.

Ryan flopped down in another chair. 'Saw her talking to McKenzie, earlier.'

Peggy's head snapped around. 'What?'

Ryan shrugged.

Paul patted her knee affectionately. 'Relax, love. Drink your beer. She's probably flaked out some-where. It's been a big day for us all.'

An elderly lady appeared. 'Excuse me, dear. I'm Elsie, a friend of Violet's. And this is Frank, an old friend of mine.'

Peggy jumped to her feet and put out her hand. 'Hello. We're Paul and Peggy. I was going to come and talk to you, but I didn't seem to quite get there. Thanks for coming. It must have been a long drive. Where have you come from?'

While Peggy talked, Harrison offered Elsie his chair, then grabbed another two from close by.

Elsie made herself comfortable and the man sat down in the chair beside her.

'Only from Balladonia, today. We left Kalgoorlie yesterday. That was the big drive.'

'Would you like to stay here tonight?' Peggy offered.

'Thank you, dear, but we'll be fine. We both know this country very well, from a long time ago.'

'Really? Did you meet Violet out here?'

'I stayed out here quite a bit in the forties. There were a few early birds out here, before the land really started to open up in the sixties. My father worked with your grandfather, Paul.'

'Is that right? Well, I never! I bet you could tell us some stories. I can't believe we haven't heard about you, Elsie. I feel very rude.' Paul looked incredulous.

'Don't feel like that.' Elsie brushed aside Paul's apology. 'But I've always kept in touch with Violet. She was such a good friend.' Her eyes misted over for a moment and Frank placed his wrinkled, sunspotted hand on her shoulder. Then she brightened as she continued. 'I really wanted to see Tessa before I left. I have something for her. Do you know where she's gone?'

Everyone looked around. Tessa was nowhere to be seen. Harrison shifted in his seat uneasily.

'I'll go and find her,' Peggy said, getting up from her chair.

'No, Peggy, I'll go,' Harrison said firmly and left the group quickly. He didn't want Peggy stumbling upon something she didn't need to see.

He walked into the house and called out, but there was no answer. He scouted around the chook shed then headed over to the shearing shed and stuck his head inside. He heard Tessa laugh and say, 'So, where is your station, Brendan?'

'To the north of here. Another drink?'

'That would be very nice.'

Harrison heard the glug of wine being poured and tossed up whether to go inside or not. The decision was made for him, when Brendan said, 'So, Miss Mathison, are you staying around Danjar Plains for long. I'd like to get to know you a bit better.'

'If I didn't know better, I'd think you were flirting with me, Mr McKenzie,' Tessa said coyly.

'What gives you that idea? Now come and sit next to me.'

For a moment all went silent. Disgusted, he turned and left. Brendan had certainly worked his charm very quickly. And Tessa had responded the way he thought she would.

Back in the garden he summoned a smile. 'I'm really sorry, Elsie, but I can't find Tessa. I suspect she may have slipped off to the shearers' quarters for a sleep. She's still a bit jetlagged, I reckon.'

Elsie looked disappointed. 'Ah well, not to worry.' Pulling a large white envelope out of her bag, she turned to Peggy. 'I wonder if you could give her this? Before Tessa opens it, though, she and I need to have a conversation.' Elsie winked.

Paul and Peggy exchanged glances. 'That sounds a bit mysterious,' Peggy said.

'It probably does, but that's the way Violet wanted it done.'

'Well, we can't argue with her, never could,' Paul said.

'Not a chance in hell,' Elsie agreed.

Peggy smiled. 'Look, are you sure you don't want to stay? I can easily make up beds. I'm sure Tessa won't be too far away.'

'No, dear, we need to go before there's any chance of driving into the sun. Getting old doesn't have many benefits.' Elsie pointed to the envelope. 'My details are on the back.'

Peggy, Paul, Ryan and Harrison followed Elsie and Frank out to their car to wish them a safe journey. When the car was nothing but a speck in the distance, Harrison turned to Paul.

'Tessa's with Brendan McKenzie.'

Chapter 9

'Mum? I don't think the internet connection is working.'

It was three days after the funeral. Tessa had been back home for nearly a week but it was the first time she'd been brave enough to go online. She was hoping above all hope the photos had disappeared and that would be the end of the horrible saga. Realistically, she knew that wouldn't have happened.

'Why's that, petal?' Peggy answered from the kitchen.

'I can't get it to open my emails. Oh wait, it's trying. I can't believe how long it takes.' Tessa swung around in the chair as she heard her mother walk into the office.

'Tessa, you've forgotten,' Peggy said gently. 'If we didn't have satellite, we wouldn't have anything.'

'I don't know how you bear it,' said Tessa jiggling her knee up and down impatiently.

'No point in getting all uptight. It's just the way it is and we can't change it. Bit like the weather, really. So just sit and enjoy the wait. It's called relaxing. See? There you go.'

'It's just as annoying as the TV,' Tessa said. 'I can't believe how different things are here.'

'I'm not sure London has done you much good if you get all wound up over a slow internet connection and some bad TV. You might need to remember what really matters, my girl.' Peggy turned and left the room.

Tessa opened her mouth to say something but nothing came out. She'd spotted two emails, one from Darcy and one from Jaz.

She clicked on Jaz's and waited what seemed like a lifetime for it to open.

Dear Tessa,

I've tried, babe. I really have. I can't find how they've been posted or who posted them. The photos are really quite funny if you look at them while you're drunk. Unfortunately, not so hilarious when you're sober. I've attached all that I can find, but I'd better warn you, your name is pretty much mud over here. Well, maybe not mud, but everyone at Marketing Matters is very disappointed with you. Apparently they're finding mistakes in your work too. And worse – one of your accounts has been hijacked by . . . yep, you guessed, John Smith and his team. They must have accessed your phone or emails or something while you were out to it.

Tessa groaned. Realistically, she knew it could have been likely. It had been sloppy of her to leave her phone unattended and, as for mistakes, well, vodka and fine details didn't mix.

And now all this just gave her a hankering for another shot of vodka.

Biting her fingernails, she read on:

So I believe you've got two choices. One, you can come back and clear your name, which is going to be pretty hard, or two, you can walk away and forget you've ever been here.

I'm really sorry to be so blunt, sweetie, but you know how cut-throat this business can be. Once you're out, well, that's where you are. Let me know what you want to do. And don't forget how much I loves ya!

Jaz

Tessa hovered her mouse over the attachment. Did she really want to see the other photos? Swivelling around on the chair, she listened for Peggy. The house had gone quiet. Maybe her mum had headed off to feed the chooks.

Tessa held her breath and double-clicked.

Bit by bit, line by line, the photo began to show. The first part she could see was her face – glazed eyes and rosy cheeks. The kangaroo ears she kept for party tricks in her handbag were on her head. John's gold chain glinted in the flash.

As the photo continued to load, Tessa watched, red-faced as her breast appeared, then her stomach. Looking more closely, she saw that her blouse was undone and John had his hand on her bare breast. Someone had taken a tablecloth and wrapped it around her waist as a kangaroo tail.

Shame flooded through her and the craving for a drink intensified. She drummed her fingers on the desk and her knee jiggled as fast as it could go. She didn't wait for the photo to finish downloading. She hit the delete button, breathing hard. She didn't need to see any more. That photo was called a Royal Stuff-Up. And the rest of them would be the same.

With trepidation, she clicked on the email from Darcy.

Dear Tessa,

As per my previous email, you have been given five days to tender your resignation. So far, you have not made your intentions known. If your resignation isn't received by 8 p.m. this evening, UK time, your employment will be terminated.

Darcy Anderson

Tessa closed that email too. Then she shut down the computer.

Outside the sky was a brilliant blue. With no destination in mind, Tessa just let her feet take her wherever. The day was stinking hot and the birds, which usually sang up a storm, were quiet, sitting in the shade of the trees or close to water.

The realisation of what she'd done hit her hard. She *knew* she had messed up big time and let down so many people in the process. She *knew* she couldn't make it right. All she could do was apologise to Darcy and tender her resignation. But she also understood what a bonus it was to be given the opportunity to resign. This way she could get another job in Sydney, or Melbourne or somewhere that had a decent internet connection, mobile phone range and shops. She didn't have to stay at Danjar Plains, she could leave.

Tessa noticed a mirage, something she hadn't seen since she left the Nullarbor. She watched the shimmering air and faux lake in the distance. As she paced towards it, the mirage became closer with each step. Closer and closer.

A story stirred somewhere in the back of her mind. Violet. Afghan cameleers, mirages and water. What was it? A story Violet had told her when she was small. But as hard as she tried, Tessa couldn't remember.

Then, as all mirages do, it disappeared.

Tessa blinked and looked around. She was at the cemetery. The freshly shovelled mound brought her to tears immediately and she sank down at the foot of the grave.

'Aunty Spider.' She sat there with her hands buried in the dirt, trying to channel her sorrow, her thoughts to Spider. Waiting for some kind of message from her aunt, knowing nothing would ever come. She stayed there until her knees hurt. Finally she shifted positions, sitting cross-legged like a kid.

'What to do? What to do?' she muttered. 'You know I completely hate myself, don't you, Aunty Spider? I'm twenty-four, I have a drinking problem and I've just buggered up the best opportunity I ever had. What would you do?'

Silence.

'You know, I've never admitted that out loud? I have a drinking problem. I. Have. A. Drinking. Problem.' She felt free as she repeated it again and again.

Tessa was sweating – the midday sun was brutal. She'd forgotten how harsh it could be and how fluorescent the landscape was. It hurt her eyes. Shading them, she wished she'd thought to put her sunglasses on before leaving the house. Then laughed out loud. *Gucci sunglasses, here, in the middle of nowhere*, she thought. Who would appreciate them? Tessa looked down at her colourful leggings and knit top with the gap at the back. They were so out of place here. Twisting on the ground, to get comfortable, she could feel her skin burning where the gaping hole in her shirt was. She'd be sunburnt later.

She got up and went over to sit on Violet's old wooden chair under the gum tree. The smell of eucalyptus from the dull green leaves and sun-baked earth swam around her. Everywhere on Danjar Plains, she was reminded of her aunt. It was as if Spider *were* Danjar Plains, herself. The sheds held her essence – the grader she had worked on, the motorbike she had bought on a trip to Esperance. The magpie, as he sang and danced along the ground, to attract his mate, held Spider's laugh. The stock held her knowledge and the land, her soul. Tessa's dad had been right – it was as if Spider was still here.

Tessa's mum had said it was lovely to have so many reminders of such a wonderful woman, such a fantastic role model. But to Tessa, all it did was throw in her face the fact that Violet wasn't here anymore. Now, Tessa had nowhere to run, nowhere to hide. She couldn't explain her connection with Aunty Spider, but her dad had it too. Ryan didn't and neither did her mum. Oh, they had respected her, loved her, thought she was an incredible person, but they just didn't have the bond, the invisible tie that seemed to link the other three together. She'd asked her dad what it was once and he'd just shrugged. 'Can't tell you, Tessie,' he'd said. 'Just something there. You find sometimes you just click with a person.'

After Kendra's death, it had been Aunty Spider who had convinced Tessa she needed to come back home and visit the spot where her best friend had died. It had been with Violet's arms around her that Tessa had finally stood at the foot of the windmill. It had been only for a few seconds, but she'd done it. Then they went back to Spider's little house and Tessa had wept hysterically.

That had been seven years ago and the final time she had set foot on Danjar Plains.

It wasn't that she didn't love her mum; she did with all her heart. But she was drawn to Spider, who seemed to know what she was thinking, what she was feeling, before Tessa realised it herself.

She clenched her fists at the pressure rising in her chest and shot up from the seat, trying to calm herself by breathing deeply and pacing.

Suddenly she turned around and screamed into the nothingness: 'I'm so confused. I'm so bloody confused!'

A crow squawked from within the depths of the tree and flew off with lazy strokes, still cawing. Tessa could hear the swish of wind as its wings pushed through the air. She turned her face upwards, her arms outstretched, tears damp on her cheeks. 'But I can make it better,' she whispered. 'I can. I just have to work out how.'

And with that, a magpie warbled its song.

Back in the office again, she opened the email from Darcy and set about replying, typing *Resignation* in the subject line.

Dear Mr Anderson,

I realise that I have broken my contract and, in turn, offer my resignation.

I apologise for any breaches that may have occurred, and I take full responsibility. I had no intention of allowing mistakes to creep into my work or compromise your business.

On a personal level, I would like to thank you for the opportunity you gave me. I understand you made many exceptions when it came to my employment and I am deeply sorry I let you and my Aunty Spider down.

Yours sincerely,

Tessa Mathison

She re-read the email, quickly, checking for errors. Just as she was about to hit send, she heard a noise behind her. Ryan was looking at her, concern creasing his brow.

'Why are you resigning?' he asked.

A wave of embarrassment and shame washed over Tessa. 'Do you always sneak up and read over people's shoulders?' She hit send and minimised the screen quickly.

'Don't get snarly with me, little sis! I don't think I'm the one hiding something.' He cocked his eyebrow and crossed his arms.

Tessa knew he was waiting for her to spill everything. Well, she wasn't ready to yet.

'You know, Ryan, I have missed you, but keep your nose out of my business,' she said quietly, trying not to cause offence but wanting to put a stop to any more questions.

'We spend our whole life wondering if you're going okay, Tessie,' Ryan said in the same tone. 'You've had to bear more than any person should in your short life. You being okay is always in the back of our minds, even when you're kicking your heels up over there in London and living a life we don't understand. So if we seemed concerned, well, pardon us, but we care.' He turned and left Tessa alone in the office, chewing her fingernails.

Chapter 10

A couple of weeks into her stay at Danjar Plains, Tessa felt herself begin to relax. She'd decided the new year would be a new beginning, a fresh start, a clean slate and every other cliché.

Walking the perimeter of the house paddock as the sun began to sink, Tessa found she was noticing things she'd long since forgotten. The animals, both wild and stock, were getting ready for the night. Birds flew back to their trees just on dark, after feasting on whatever insects or mice they could find. The sheep and cattle made the slow trek towards the troughs for their nightly drink, a cloud of dust hanging over them. Wedge-tailed eagles soared over, spying a feast, and diving towards the ground with incredible speed and grace. Tessa watched them rise into the air, their prey grasped firmly in their claws.

The sun sank lower and the shadows grew. The Nullarbor became still. From deep in the bushy undergrowth, a cricket chirped - just one - then a whole chorus started up. Simultaneously, a puff of breeze arrived from the sea, so many kilometres away. Instantly Tessa was cooler and the air had a different feel as she took a breath. Crisper, dewy, and not as dry.

Walking every evening had been her saviour. Spider's old blue heeler, Dozer, came with her, keeping her company. Though ancient, he somehow managed to go the distance. During this nightly routine, Tessa would raise her eyes to the heavens to see the red, blinking lights of jets flying from one side of Australia to the other. Were any of them heading to London?

The first night she'd done this was the day she'd achieved some clarity at the cemetery. That day she had made a decision not to drink for a week. It wouldn't be that hard.

But, so agitated by five o'clock, she'd taken herself outside again. Studiously avoiding the side of the paddock where the windmill waited, she'd paced along the fence line, hearing nothing but her own footsteps. On the busy streets in London no one in that city could imagine the space and tranquillity of her current location. When she saw the evening star for the first time in years and years, she made a wish. A wish that her life would change, that the happiness she felt when three-parts pissed

97

could be found in some other way. That somehow she could feel good about herself and get rid of the guilt that was forever inside of her. Find the real Tessa again. She'd forgotten who she had been and who she should be.

Tessa headed up the road that led into the homestead compound. Within these fences were the two houses: the large one where Paul and Peggy lived; and the smaller demountable or donga that was Ryan and Marni's. As she made her way back towards the homestead she could hear the clang of saucepans and cooking noises from Marni's kitchen. Ryan was sitting on the verandah nursing a beer. Unnoticed, Tessa stopped and observed him. Ryan was staring towards the horizon, lost in thought. He looked older than his twenty-eight years, much older than when she had seen him last. His face was burned a permanent red-brown and lined with deep creases. But there was something about his expression that made Tessa pause, a longing or wistfulness as he looked out across the flat, saltbush-covered plains. Was he happy? Was Marni? She didn't seem to be.

Tessa started to walk again, knowing if she wanted to make it back to the main house before dark, she needed to get moving. With a final glance at her brother, she kept going, skirting behind his place between the machinery and shearing sheds until she reached the homestead verandah. As her sneaker touched the bottom step, a haunting sound echoed through the dusk. The howl of a dingo.

A shiver ran through her. She looked behind, her heart racing. Of course, there was nothing. It was a wild dog, nothing else. The animal howled again, the sound lingering in the evening stillness. Without a second thought, Tessa bolted up the steps and inside, shutting the door behind her with a bang.

'That you, Tessa?' her mother called.

'Yes, it's me.' She willed her heart to slow and her hands to stop shaking. *It was a dingo. A bloody dingo and nothing else.* She held her breath for a moment before exhaling in a rush.

'Could you lock the chooks up, petal?' Peggy called from down the hall. 'Those darn chooks of Spider's won't go into the shed, so you'll have to pick them up and carry them in. They still haven't sorted out their pecking order. I haven't had a chance to get out there.'

It was the last thing Tessa wanted to do. 'Um, Mum? I think there's a dingo out there.'

Peggy's face appeared in the doorway. 'There probably is, my girl! I hear one every night about this time. If we don't get the chooks away, we won't have them or any eggs! Don't tell me it frightened you?' Her mother gave her an inquisitive look. 'Goodness me, Tessa, you must have gone soft over there.' She bustled back into the kitchen. 'Here,' she said, handing over the scrap bucket and a torch.

Tessa unwillingly took what her mother offered and turned back to the door. Why was she afraid? She knew it was only a dingo. Only a dingo. Not

Aunty Spider's soul, not Kendra's soul. It was a damn dingo.

But she knew what dingoes could do. They were hunters and she'd seen them stalk and attack in packs. She shivered.

Angry now, she yanked open the door and raced out into the darkness. The lights from the porch gave a few metres of illumination before she had to rely on the torch. She walked purposefully towards the chook run. She soon established that Spider's chooks had managed to get themselves into the shed, but were not sleeping near the others. The chooks clucked and stirred as she flashed the light over them. Back out in the pen, she up-ended the bucket then, without stopping, she yanked the gate shut behind her, latched it, and ran back towards the comfort of the well-lit verandah.

Just before she reached the house she turned and flashed the torch behind her. Something glinted. She stopped, and pointed the beam into the darkness. Yep. There. A pair of yellow eyes.

Giving a strangled scream, she flew up the steps and into the house. The slamming of the door ricocheted through the night.

Peggy threw a couple of chops onto a plate already covered with mashed potato and vegies. Tessa tried not to screw up her nose – she wasn't sure how she would manage to eat so much protein and carbs in one hit. In London, mostly she ate salads, chicken and fish.

She picked up a plate and handed it to her father, then reached across for her own.

'Thanks, Mum.'

There was silence while everyone started to eat. Then Paul put down his knife and fork and rested his elbows on the table.

'So, Tessa,' he said slowly. 'What are your plans?'

Tessa pretended to chew; it gave her time to deliberate. 'Oh well, I should think about heading back, but Mr Anderson gave me as long as I needed.' She shrugged carelessly. 'I'm enjoying being here so I might as well spend a bit of time,' she lied. 'And I've got to wait until the plaque he ordered comes from Kal. He wanted to have something in the cemetery that linked back to his family.'

'That's nice of him. And we're enjoying having you home.' Paul smiled at her. 'I see you met Brendan McKenzie at Spider's funeral?'

Tessa's chewing slowed. 'Mmm, yes, I did. He seemed lovely.'

'Lovely being the operative word,' Peggy muttered.

'Well, he seemed nice to me.' Tessa's tone sounded defensive, even to her own ears.

'You need to be careful of him,' Paul said gently. 'He's got a bit of a reputation for being, well, a ladies' man. I'm sure he comes across as nice and charming. But he's mixed up with a bad lot, Tessa. Just be mindful of that.'

'Right.' Leaving her chops alone, Tessa shovelled in another mouthful of vegies. 'I doubt I'll see him again, anyhow.'

'Probably not,' Paul agreed. He glanced across at Peggy and Tessa caught the look.

'What?'

'There was a lady at Spider's funeral. Her name was Elsie,' Peggy started.

'Yes. I met her on the plane coming to Kalgoorlie and talked to her briefly on the day.'

'Did you? We weren't sure, but figured you must have known her somehow, because she left an envelope for you the day of the funeral. We wanted to give you a bit of time before we handed it over. Just to make sure you were strong enough . . .'

Annoyance rushed through her. 'You don't need to protect me, Mum. I'm *fine*.' Tessa threw down her knife and fork and stared defiantly at her mother.

'Fine is the most overused word in all of the English language,' Peggy retorted. 'I'm fine usually means I'm *not*.'

'Peggy,' Paul said mildly. He turned to Tessa. 'We know you're okay,' he said. 'But we also know what Spider meant to you. We're assuming whatever is in the envelope has something to do with her. If so, it may upset you.' He left the words hanging.

What Tessa knew he meant was, it might tip you over the edge again. Like with Kendra.

'Maybe we're wrong. If we are, we're sorry, but we love you, Tessa. We want you to be fine.' He used his fingers to make speech marks around the word 'fine'.

Tessa looked down. Her reaction had been over the top. 'Sorry. But what is all this about? I know as much about Elsie as you can find out in a fifteen-minute conversation.'

Peggy and Paul exchanged glances.

Peggy shrugged 'It's got to be about Spider. Can't be anything else. Elsie left instructions that you must speak to her before you open it.'

'I can't imagine why. Would it be Spider's will? And if it is, why leave the letter to me? It should be with a solicitor.'

'Spider didn't have much, really – just what's in her house – and she left her instructions with Paul. Maybe you should give Elsie a call tomorrow.'

The rest of dinner was eaten in silence. After the plates were collected, Peggy passed on the envelope. Tessa's name was scrawled on the front in a hand she didn't recognise. Elsie's details were clearly written on the back.

Tessa weighed it in her hand, turning it over and over. 'I guess I can't open it until I speak to Elsie. Do you know anything about her?'

Paul shook his head. 'We only recognise her name. Spider wrote heaps of letters – it was the only way she communicated, as you know.'

A shot of guilt went through Tessa and she couldn't hide it any longer. 'I never answered her last letter,' she blurted. 'I had it for at least two months and I never answered it.'

There was a pause. 'There's not always time to do everything we want to do,' Peggy said finally.

'I could have made time! I just didn't want to. I thought she'd see through what I wrote – she always could.'

'Oh, Tessa, what would she see through? You've done so well over there. There was nothing for her to disapprove of. She wasn't supernatural. You've got to get over thinking she knew everything. She was just human, and you weren't doing anything wrong for her to see!' Peggy leaned forward and put her hand on her daughter's arm.

'But I was. I was,' Tessa moaned, tears in her eyes. 'I don't have to go back. I wasn't doing the job up to their standard.' Yes, better to tell them that than the truth. There were just things parents didn't need to know. 'So I resigned.'

'Oh, love! Why didn't you tell us?'

Tessa wiped the tears away. 'I don't know. Everything was just too hard with Aunty Spider dying and coming back here. You know how difficult it has been for me to come home since Kendra's accident, but Aunty Spider left me no choice when she died. She probably knew that too.'

She got out of her chair and paced the room. 'If I hadn't come home, then I probably wouldn't have resigned, but maybe I would have. I'm so confused.' Once she'd finished, she sank back into her chair, relieved some of her secrets were finally out in the open. The others would always stay hidden.

'Well, sometimes home is the best place to sort those feelings out,' Paul said. 'And you know you're welcome to stay here as long as you need.'

Tessa gave a watery smile. 'I've really stuffed everything up.'

Peggy looked at her daughter thoughtfully. 'I read something somewhere – can't remember exactly how it goes: "Never regret anything you've done, because at one stage that was exactly what you wanted." It's true. So don't regret or feel guilty about anything you've done so far. It's about turning your life around from this moment onwards. And we'll help if you need us.' Peggy reached across and picked up Paul's plate and held out her hand for Tessa's. 'Come on, help me with these dishes then go and get a good night's sleep. Everything always seems better when the sun's up.'

I doubt things will look better for me, thought Tessa. Her mother was just like all station people: no-nonsense, practical and couldn't see the point in dwelling on things that can't be fixed. Still, maybe home was a good place to be at the moment, even if it did mean doing the dishes.

Later that night as Tessa heard her father leave the house to turn off the generator, she went to the window and stared into the darkness. The eerie sound of the dingo's howl was still in her head and she wondered whether, if she swung her torch around outside again, she would see those evil eyes.

Chapter 11

Tessa picked up the phone and dialled Elsie's number. Her curiosity was piqued and she had wanted to call last night, but thought it may have been too late. Older people went to bed early, didn't they?

'Hello?'

'Um, hello . . .'

'Ah, Tessa. You've finally called. I was beginning to wonder if you would.'

'How did you know it was me?'

A chuckle sounded down the phone line. 'Not too many young women ring me these days, dear,' Elsie answered. 'You got the letter, then. Have you opened it?'

'No. I'm dying to, though. I'm not sure why she's left it with you instead of just posting it to me.'

'No, well, at the time I wasn't, either. But then, you didn't answer her last few letters and she was worried. Violet trusted me, completely and utterly. She knew I'd make you see reason.'

See reason? Tessa decided to ignore that for a moment or two, since it didn't make any sense.

'How did you meet Spider?'

'We were kids together. The country was just opening up out there. It was the thirties and Dad had decided to try and find work in the west. We were taking the train across the Nullarbor and we stopped at a siding – I can't remember where it was. Might have been Jalinda or somewhere similar. We all got off to stretch our legs. You can imagine how difficult it was for kids to be cooped up in a small carriage. My brothers just about went mad. Poor old Mum, she'd exhausted her repertoire of games and stories by the end of the first day!

'Dad got talking to Len Mathison. Now he would have been your great-uncle . . . Violet's oldest brother—'

'I haven't heard of him,' Tessa interrupted.

'He was sort of the black sheep of the family. Bit of a con man – oh, that makes him sound like he did things illegally. He didn't – he was a lovable rogue, could talk the birds out of the trees. Charming. Pushed the boundaries. And somehow he managed to convince a family man with three children and a wife to get off that train and go help him open up a stretch of land that was south of what's now the Eyre Highway.'

'Danjar Plains,' Tessa murmured.

'That's right. Even though Violet was much older than I, being the only two girls out there we seemed to just move together. Between Violet and my mother we always had lessons, reading and writing, but there were days when Violet didn't want to teach so she helped us sneak away instead. Such a wicked sense of humour! We rode horses, learned to cook over fires and muster sheep.'

'How do I not know about Len?' Tessa wondered aloud.

'Well, it was many years ago. Families seem to know of their immediate relatives but not so much about the brothers and sisters of their grandparents or great-grandparents. Not unless they're particularly interested in researching their family history.' Elsie paused. 'Len was a hard worker when he was here. As were her other brothers. Violet's Uncle Sam and Aunty Margaret brought them out here, you know? They ended up loving it and stayed.'

'Did she have many? Brothers, I mean. And where were her parents?'

'Well, on the brother front, there was Len, Edward and George. She had an older sister, Grace. Then there was gorgeous Tom. They were already out here by the time I met Violet, so I don't know anything about her parents except what she told me, which was that her mother was pregnant again and not well enough to look after all the children. Things were tight in the city so she sent them to live on a farm with Margaret and Sam. Sam saw potential here and the rest is history. Anyway, Tessa, that's all by-the-by now. I'm sure you'll find out more about the family over the next little while.'

Elsie then took a breath. 'In that letter are some instructions. It's not a will – she always said what was in that house went to whoever wanted it. So ask your family if they would like any of the furniture or books – I think there might be some early works by Henry Lawson and Banjo Paterson in the bookshelves somewhere. They might be worth quite a tidy amount, by gawd.'

'How on earth would have she gotten those?'

'Just because we lived in the wild west didn't mean we didn't have access to nice things. There were the Afghan cameleers, the Tea and Sugar Train – and we didn't know they were going to be first editions back then, did we? You've got to remember, we're quite old!'

Tessa was unable to control the laugh that slipped from her.

'Now listen, child. I can't sugar-coat this. What Violet has asked you to do won't suit you. But it has to be you. There is no one else. Open the envelope while I'm on the phone.'

'I'm not sure I can face it,' said Tessa.

'Just open it,' Elsie said gently.

Tessa tore at the envelope and her stomach did a little tumble turn as she saw her great-aunt's familiar handwriting.

"'My Dear Tessa,'" she read out loud. "'I do hope you come back from England for my funeral. Your continuing silence is worrying me and I wonder if it's time for you to start on something fresh. And I have just the thing for you. My house will need cleaning out and guess what, my darling? You're it.'"

Tessa was silent as she re-read the sentence over and over. *Clean out her house?* As the words sunk in, she began to shake her head.

'No!' The word erupted from her. 'No way. She can't keep me here. No, that should be Dad's job or Mum's. Not mine!' Tears formed. Her hands began to shake. A movie of images spun in front of her eyes; Spider's house, her bedroom, the kitchen. The Story Telling Chair.

'Read on,' Elsie urged.

Tessa wiped her eyes, still shaking. How could Spider ask her to do that?

'Um . . . "Cleaning out. Please take what you wish and ask the others what they would like. But the things I want you to take care of are the letters and history of our family. I'm entrusting this to you. Yes! Our family has a few skeletons and secrets.

"'You can squawk all you like, my dear, and curse just as much. Don't worry; I know you're doing it! But I have a reason for doing this. As I said, your silence is bothering me. When you don't write to me, I know something isn't right. You need to come home, which, if you remember, I suggested you do before you left for England. You need to face your fears, get back to your roots, and heal properly – something you've never done.

"'And you don't know it yet, but your whole family needs you. Ryan isn't happy – maybe that's something you can help him with. Peggy is tired – she needs another pair of hands. And Marni needs a friend.

"'I know you aren't the answer to all these problems and I don't want you to try and fix everyone's issues, because you need fixing, too, but you being on Danjar Plains, even just for a short while, will make a difference. To everyone.

"'I love you, my darling girl. You were the daughter I never had – corny I know, but it's the only way I know how to express my love enough. Now make me proud and do as I ask. Love, Spider.'"

Tessa's tears fell onto Spider's last letter.

Tessa was staring intently at the computer screen when Ryan's LandCruiser pulled up at the homestead in a cloud of dust. She quickly shoved the letter, which she'd been carrying with her constantly, into her pocket and exited Facebook.

Her mind was all over the place. One moment she was thinking about Spider and her request. The next, she was trying to track where those bloody photos had come from, but she always ended up in the same place – a Troll account, just as Jaz had said, and which had since been deleted.

Leaning back in her chair she contemplated the options. It didn't take long. Really, the only one was to forget about it. So what if the photos had appeared on the 'Drunk at a Nightclub' photos page. And did it really matter if friends had left comments about them on her Facebook wall? After all, she didn't have to face any of these people. She wasn't in London. She was here, on Danjar Plains, with the world's worst job hanging over her head.

Spider's letter had left her in shock. She had never once thought about cleaning out a dead relative's house. How would she feel when she pulled out Spider's favourite pair of pants and shirt? And then there was this hinting at family skeletons. Well, obviously there was nothing too much there! Tessa thought the Mathisons might well be the most boring family in the history of the universe.

'Want to come for a drive?' Ryan was at the office door. He looked worn out.

'Didn't you sleep? You look terrible.'

'I went for a drive last night. Didn't get home until after midnight. Bit too hot last night to get any decent rest after that. The bloody mozzies gave us hell, too. Noisy, annoying little buggers.'

Tessa's face lit up with a smile. 'I hate it when they just buzz round and around your head and wake you up. I'd forgotten that!'

'I wish I could. There was more than one in the room last night and fly spray doesn't seem to kill them anymore. I reckon Marni's sprayed them so much they've become resistant!'

'Why were you out driving last night?' Tessa asked, curious.

'Someone's dropping fences and pinching stock. I was out driving the boundary to see if I could find anything. Spider and I used to do it together some nights. Anyway, I'm heading out to Deep Bore. Thought we could swing past Aunty Spider's place if you want to. You haven't been there since you arrived home.'

'I'll come for a drive, but I don't know that I want to go into her house. It would feel like trespassing or something.' Tessa held out her hands like she was warding off something.

'Yeah, I know, but there's no one there. We should at least check on it.'

As they drove out to the bore, Tessa saw many places full of memories. The spot where they used to have family picnics in the rocky outcrop; and the place where she had fallen off the ute and broken her wrist during the last muster she'd ever been involved in.

'You know my wrist still aches, from when I broke it on that muster,' Tessa said, gently rubbing her arm.

'That was all *your* fault,' Ryan said with a grin. 'If you hadn't been yelling into the wind, I wouldn't have stuck my head out the window to hear you and not seen the trough.'

'I still can't believe you hit it!' Tessa laughed. 'Remember how cross Dad was?'

'I remember how sore my bloody pride was.'

'So was my wrist.'

'And we didn't get the sheep in for shearing, so we were both in the shit! Fun times.'

Tessa thought for a moment. 'Yeah,' she answered, nodding. 'Yeah they were.'

'And the pool comp we used to have!'

Tessa grinned. 'Yes! That was the one thing I could beat you at.'

'Bit of a shame Mum and Dad sold the table. I could've tried to redeem myself.'

'In your dreams!'

They wound their way through the bush and it wasn't long before Tessa thought of another childhood memory.

'Do you remember the way we used to race? You on the motorbike and me in the ute? Up the airstrip? It was so much fun!'

'I always won,' Ryan said matter-of-factly.

'Could have had something to do with the fact that you could take off from a standing start and get to sixty clicks in no time at all. I had to change up through all the gears!' She whacked Ryan's arm and giggled.

'It's nice to hear you laugh, little sis,' he said.

'I like laughing.'

'Good to know. So, you gonna spill on the whole story about why you resigned?'

The question took Tessa by surprise, although it probably shouldn't have. 'Only if you tell me why you're really so tired and looking not particularly happy with life,' she shot back as quickly as she could.

Ryan glanced across at her.

'Watch where you're going.' Tessa pointed as the LandCruiser hit a pothole and bounced a couple of times. 'Don't think Dad would forgive us if we stuffed something at our age!'

Ryan didn't answer, but a wry smile played on his lips.

They drove in silence until they reached the bore. Ryan stopped the ute and they both jumped out. A windmill towered above, the blades creaking as it turned. Water gushed into the cement tank, the sound resonating across the flat ground. There wasn't any stock Tessa could see, but a magpie was sitting on the edge of the tank and further out in the sun two galahs were pulling up grass for the roots. White limestone rocks littered the ground. The stock tracks wound in between the clumps of bushes and low trees, all the way to the water.

'Gotta check the oil in the head,' Ryan said. 'Can't wait until we replace all these bloody mills with solar pumps.' He began to climb the tower. 'Can you look in the tank? Needs to be at least three-quarters full. Better if it's only about a foot from the top.'

Tessa gingerly picked her way through the ankle-high bushes. Her Converse sneakers were now much worse for wear – she'd have to get some proper boots if she was going to stay. Not that she'd made up her mind.

She watched as Ryan shimmied up the ladder of the mill.

Flashback: Kendra climbing up the house windmill.

She squeezed her eyes shut.

Flashback: Jaz at the top of the ladder.

Tessa rubbed her eyes, trying to rub away the images.

'No,' she muttered. 'No. He does this all the time.' Slamming the door shut on her memories, she reached the ladder that was leaning up against the cement tank.

She swung herself up onto the first rung.

It fell backwards and she let out an ear-piercing shriek as she fell and landed on her bum. 'It's not attached!'

Ryan looked down from halfway up the windmill and started to laugh. 'You are so citified. I wish you could see yourself.'

Heart thumping, Tessa got to her feet and put her hands to her chest for a moment. She took a few deep breaths and then dusted off her shorts. 'Ouch!' She looked down at her hands and saw four bindi-eye prickles stuck in one palm. She pulled them out, her eyes smarting.

'You could have told me.'

'Wouldn't have been as much fun.'

Ryan made his way to the top of the windmill, checked the oil and started to climb down.

Tessa stood the ladder up and leaned it back against the tank, carefully putting her foot on the first rung.

'Don't worry,' Ryan said. 'I can see it from here. It's full.'

'Did you just want to see me fall?' asked Tessa standing with her arms folded as Ryan jumped the last few feet and landed lightly on the ground.

'I'm just catching up on all the brotherly tricks I should have been able to play when you weren't here. Don't be so uptight. Live a little! Laugh a lot.'

I've lived more than you know, Tessa thought as she opened the door to the ute.

'Don't get back in there. Come and sit in the shade,' Ryan said as he opened a tucker box. 'It's smoko time.'

'You're not going to light a fire and boil the billy, are you? Surely not today? It's as hot as Hades! What about fires?'

'We have a new invention called a Thermos,' Ryan quipped.

He poured a pannikin of tea and handed it to her. 'Milk and sugar is here,' he said, handing her a tube of condensed milk.

'What?'

'That's the milk and sugar – bloody hell, Tessie, it hasn't been that long. We did this when we were kids. Saves taking real milk out with us. It would go rotten in the heat. Have you purposely forgotten everything to do with the station?'

Tessa squeezed the milk into her tea. 'Possibly,' she said quietly and took a sip. 'So you said something earlier about dropped fences and Aunty Spider?'

Ryan crouched down, resting his pannikin on one knee and scraped the ground with a stick. 'It's a bit unclear really. Someone is dropping fences and encouraging stock across into holding yards on the neighbour's place. It's happening everywhere out here. Every so often, I go for a nightly drive, just to see what's what. Especially on moonlit nights, when it's more likely that whoever's doing it would be operating. Aunty Spider loved coming with me. There was a mystery to be solved and she wanted to be a part of it. Anyway,' he flicked his hand, 'let's not talk about that. Let's talk about London.'

'Let's not,' Tessa said firmly. 'How's Marni? I've hardly seen her since the funeral.' She hoped the swift change of subject would deflect any more questions.

'She's fine. It's not unusual to not see her around much. She stays in the house a lot.'

'She seems unhappy,' Tessa ventured.

'Yeah, I think she is.' Ryan finished off the last of his tea and threw the cup and spoon into the tucker box. They landed with a clang and Tessa figured that was the end of the conversation, so she did the same.

'I'll tell you a secret,' Tessa said as they climbed back into the ute. 'Spider asked me to stay and clean out her house.'

'Like that's a secret!' Ryan scoffed. 'Who else was going to do it?'

'Not me! How on earth did she think I would get time off work to do that? I'm always so . . .'

'Busy, yeah, we know.'

Tessa threw him a look. 'I never really gave it any thought, I guess.'

Ryan started the ute and put it into gear. 'So, you going to stay and do it or what?'

'I'm not sure I have a choice.'

'Well, if you haven't got a job, you might as well hang around. You could stay at Spider's – get out from under the olds. Must be difficult to stay with them when you've been living by yourself for a while.'

Tessa pretended to give it some thought.

'Even if it's only for a month or two,' Ryan continued. 'The Nullarbor Muster is coming up. It's got to have been seven years since you've been to one of them. We used to live for it when we were kids. You'd get to see a few of your old School of the Air friends, too.'

'Well, I guess I could,' Tessa mused. She thought for a little while then glanced across at Ryan. 'So are we going to Spider's?'

'Yeah. Be there in about half an hour. You know, her house was always just far enough away from all the homesteads and yards that it was private for her, but close enough for us kids to walk if we wanted.'

'Yeah. That's just how she liked it.' She shivered and noticed Ryan glancing at her. 'What?'

'You'll be okay. It's just a house that holds some memories. Mostly good ones. You'll probably enjoy seeing it again.'

Tessa wasn't so sure.

Finally, Ryan said: 'Look over there.' He pointed to the left. 'You'll see the shine of the roof any minute.'

There it was, the roof glinting in the sun and then the familiar gate. As they drove up the driveway, Tessa tensed automatically in preparation for the pothole that had been there ever since she could remember. They hit it. Her body knew this land, even if her mind didn't anymore.

Slowly she got out of the ute and stood, staring, little tickles of emotion running up and down her spine.

The small stone-walled house looked empty and sad, almost as if it knew its owner had gone. The lawn had started to brown off without water but the geraniums and succulents that Spider had been so fond of were not bothered by her absence or lack of water. The wrought-iron outside table was where it had always been, under the kitchen window, and pots of plants lined the wall of the house and hung from the roof.

The windows were small. Inside, Tessa knew, the walls were a fresh white and the floors covered with lino instead of carpet – easier to keep clean, Spider said. The furniture had always been minimal, except for her two extravagances, a sapphire-blue rocker that Spider always sat in and a large king-size bed.

The rocker would be next to a blue Smoker's Bow chair – it was an antique handed down from who knew where, but it was where all the Claytons grandkids had sat, while she had told them stories. The Story Telling Chair.

Tessa was aware of Ryan talking to her, as they walked down the dirt path to the front verandah, but she didn't hear what he was saying. Her memories were too loud, shouting at her, reminding her of times when she'd felt whole.

Her foot touched the outside mat and she waited a beat, expecting Spider to fling open the door, with a wide smile. But she didn't.

Tessa reached for the door handle. She pulled it down and the door swung open. Tessa stood in the entry way. A coldness spread over her. She was here. After all this time, she was back.

But Aunty Spider wasn't here.

Chapter 12

Adjusting her earplugs, Tessa increased the volume on her iPod and changed up a gear. She'd borrowed her parents' LandCruiser, only to discover there wasn't Bluetooth for her iPod, nor a charger to channel the music from her iPod through the FM stations and speakers.

Ah well, at least she could listen to the smoky voice of Amy Winehouse through her earplugs.

Her heart beat a little faster with anticipation. It was good to get away from the constraints of her parents for a night. Not that they were difficult to live with, but it had been many, many years since she had been under their roof for this long. It was a fact of life that she and her parents would do and see things differently.

Three weeks and two days she'd been there. Waking up every morning without a purpose, after living such a highly geared life in London had been difficult. Hiding her drinking even more so.

A night at Balladonia would do the trick. It wasn't exactly the Soho Bar – it was just a roadhouse with a motel, a bar and a camping ground – but it was better than nothing. Even if the likelihood of her knowing anyone was zilch.

Tessa had decided that one glass of wine wouldn't hurt – she'd been four days without a drink and she felt good. The second day, she'd woken with a headache that was akin to a hangover. But not having to get up, she'd taken a Panadol and gone back to bed. The next morning, the headache was still there but nowhere near as bad. This morning it had been non-existent.

Withdrawals? Nah, she wasn't that hooked on the wine – she'd just proved that to herself.

Tessa came to the ramp on the boundary of their station and slowly drove across it. She could remember the time she'd driven so fast over it she'd nose-dived the car into the ground. Her father had not been impressed!

Flicking her blinker, she turned onto the Eyre Highway and headed west. Balladonia was about forty kilometres away.

A heavily loaded road train passed her. Tessa watched as the back trailers swayed dangerously towards the edge of the road. Holding her breath to see if it hit the gravel, she suddenly felt her own front wheels leave the bitumen. Instinct kicked in and she slowly corrected the steering wheel back to right. 'Gently does it,' she muttered. Feeling all four tyres back on the road, she breathed a sigh of relief, then shook her head angrily.

It was difficult driving into the sinking sun. She slowed down, and pulled the car back a gear. Everything was so different to how she remembered it, which just showed how childhood memories weren't always right. The country was so wide, so spacious and there was so much nothingness. In London she'd be lucky to find a side alley without people in it. The Nullarbor seemed to have an intense loneliness about it, but Tessa hadn't worked out if it was just her. Her parents certainly didn't seem to notice it.

Still, they had each other and Ryan and Marni. Harrison and Cally seemed to spend a lot of time at Danjar Plains too. They were all seasoned to it, she told herself.

The silence, for Tessa, was disconcerting at times and the need to do something was strong. After all, during the past few years she'd spent every waking moment hurrying. Answering emails, making phone calls, networking. Socialising. Drinking. Now there was nothing to do. She wasn't ready for Spider's house yet.

Tessa tapped her fingers on the steering wheel, partly out of agitation and partly in time with the music. Spotlights blinded her for a moment as another truck flew by, the trailers rocking from side to side. Despite being such a busy highway, the main link between the west and east, there was just a million miles of nothing. Of emptiness.

As Tessa peered forward, looking for kangaroos and the lights of the roadhouse, her headlights picked up a dark shape on the road. Instinctively she lifted her foot off the accelerator. A dead roo? A tyre? Neither.

Slamming on the brakes, she pulled over. She fumbled for her phone but her earbuds tangled, so she yanked them out and tossed them onto the passenger's seat. Then, checking for traffic, she clambered out of the car. She hadn't seen a wombat for years! They were elusive creatures and, even though there were many signs on the Eyre Highway saying to watch for them, the only confirmed colony was at Balladonia.

The sun had slid below the horizon, but the heat rose from the road and she began to sweat. Juggling her phone she found the camera and, keeping her distance, snapped a few photos of the wombat to post on Facebook and Twitter then snarled as she realised she didn't have mobile range. She would have to get to civilisation to fix that, she realised. Still, she could post them later.

The grey-haired wombat ignored her clicking and continued to waddle across the road. Halfway across it stopped and shook itself like a dog. White dust drifted from its coat. Then it was on its way again. Tessa watched until it had disappeared into the undergrowth. She heard the grumble of another engine. With one last glance, she got back into the car and went on her way.

Tessa had to laugh at her antics. There was no way, at the beginning of January, she had thought she would be following a wombat across the Eyre Highway in her London clothes. She presumed she'd stand out in the roadhouse with her halter-neck black top, tight silvery leggings and strappy high-heeled sandals, but at this point, she really didn't care.

She ran her hand across her hair. She'd spent some time teasing the curls to make them straight then moussed it all up into spikes before she left. Her hair was longer than when she'd first arrived and she'd thought about getting it cut again but there wasn't much chance of a cut out here, so she'd have to be content to let it grow.

Finally, she saw wide beams of light in the distance. Ah, she could almost taste the wine!

She swung the LandCruiser into a parking spot and killed the engine. Would she know anyone and if so would they recognise her? Did Harrison bring Cally here for a meal he didn't have to cook? Did Ryan ever bring Marni here on a 'date'?

Would Brendan be here? Now *that* was an interesting thought.

She walked towards the roadhouse. The plain-looking building was covered in signs and coloured lights. No traveller passing could miss it.

As she approached the entrance she heard splashing and the high-pitched giggles of children. They must have put in a pool since she'd been here last.

The door was heavy. Pulling it open, she was hit with the full force of cold air. How lovely! Air-conditioning!

She looked around. So much had changed. She could see a sign pointing to a museum – parts of Skylab, the American space station, were on display. The history of Balladonia was there, too. In the other direction, was the bar. Without stopping, her feet took her there.

'What can I get you?' a young man with an English accent asked.

'What sort of white wines do you have?'

He indicated towards the fridge. 'You best look in here. What's on the menu isn't always in stock.'

Tessa glanced over. 'A bottle of unwooded chardonnay if you have it.'

'Sure.'

Tessa paid him and waited while he poured the drink. She told him her name and watched as he wrote it on the bottle before returning it to the fridge.

She took a sip – exquisite. She took another sip, and another. *Eat something*, her head said. Good idea.

'Do you think I could order a snack?'

'Course you can.' He passed her a menu.

'Just a chicken salad, please.' No chops tonight!

She took another sip and found a table near the TV. The tennis was playing, but she didn't take much notice.

'Well, well, fancy seeing you here,' a familiar voice said. She turned, wondering who it was. A tall, dark-haired man was standing behind her, beer in hand and a lopsided smile on his face. Oh, the night was just about to get better.

'Hello, Brendan.' She smiled. 'What are you doing here?'

'I could ask you the same thing. You'd be the last person I'd have expected to see!'

'Just needed a night away from the parents,' Tessa answered. 'What about you? Here for dinner?'

'Thought I'd get a drink or two. Can I join you?'

'If you like.' She tried not to sound too keen.

He pulled out the chair next to her and sat down. 'So, tell me, what on earth made you come here? Thought Kalgoorlie would have been more your style.'

'There's the problem of distance and not having a car. Otherwise, yes, I would love to have a weekend there! But here's the next best thing. Wish I'd known there was a pool though. I would have brought my bathers.' She stared wistfully through the windows at the kids diving and bombing each other under the lights.

'Think it went in a couple of years ago. Good for the tourists, apparently.'

'Yes, I imagine it's a great drawcard.'

There was a silence, and Tessa started to feel uncomfortable. It was one thing to flirt and share some playful kisses in the shearing shed when you've had a few drinks, but to have to hold a conversation with someone she barely knew, was, well, weird. She snuck a glance at him. Brendan seemed anything but awkward, with his arm linked over the back of the chair, looking up at the TV screen.

'Yes!' He thumped the table, startling Tessa.

'What?'

'Game, set and match to Lleyton Hewitt! You little ripper! Poor bugger, he's been struggling for a while, so it's good to see him get up.' Brendan turned back to her. 'So . . . how long are you going to be around for? Or are you heading straight back to London?'

Tessa shook her head. 'No, I'll be around for a bit. Aunty Spider wanted me to clean out her house. Not something I'm looking forward to and I've got no idea how long it will take.'

'That's bloody good news!' He winked at her. 'Can I get you another drink?' Wordlessly Tessa held out her glass and tried not to blush as his fingers brushed hers.

Over the next few hours, the bar and dining room slowly filled. Tessa could tell the travellers from the locals, and it seemed there was a gang of road workers too.

The laughter and beer were flowing freely.

Finally, Tessa began to relax. Brendan introduced her to a couple of his mates. Then Tessa realised that an old School of the Air friend, Jemima, was working in the kitchen. She snuck in to say hello, but in the steamy kitchen, Jemima was red-faced and busy, so Tessa didn't stay long.

'Challenge you to a game of pool,' said Brendan, appearing at her side.

'I haven't played in years!'

'Heads, you break; tails, I do.' He flicked a twenty-cent piece into the air.

'Tails,' she called.

'Tails it is.' Brendan handed her a pool cue. 'I'll rack 'em.'

Tessa rubbed some chalk over the end of her cue as she tried to remember the rules – they didn't take long to come back. Lining up, she shot the white ball down the centre of the table and into the point of the triangle. Balls went everywhere. An orange one was sunk.

'Yes!' She punched the air, then leaned forward to line up the next one.

'Beginner's luck,' Brendan moaned, leaning against the side of the table.

Tessa glanced up. 'What I didn't tell you was that I used to kick my brother's arse at pool. It may have been a while, but you're looking at the Danjar Plains champion.' She smiled sweetly and sank another two.

Brendan watched with an amused smile.

'You're toast, McKenzie,' one of his mates called from the bar.

'Gonna get beat,' another agreed.

Brendan shrugged and raised his hands. 'She's only potted three balls!'

'I can tell a good 'un when I see it,' said an old man who was leaning against the stone wall. 'And you're done, Macca.'

'Winner buys another round,' Brendan said as Tessa sent yet another ball spinning towards its hole, and then lined up the black eight.

'What? You can't change the rules halfway through!'

'We didn't have any rules! Best of three, then.'

'You're on.' They shook hands.

'Last drinks,' called the English lad about an hour past closing. While the roadhouse operated twenty-four hours a day and weary travellers could order takeaway day and night, the bar had to shut, as did the dining room.

Tessa ordered another bottle of wine and a six-pack for Brendan.

'Come on, let's get outta here,' Brendan said, grabbing his beer. 'I need to redeem my reputation since you've whipped me every game we've played.'

'Ha! Not just you, but anyone who was brave enough to play me,' Tessa said smugly.

'Let's go out to the pool. I'll teach you all about the stars. Unless of course you already know about them, too?'

'I used to be able to recognise most of the constellations but now I can find the Saucepan and that's about all. Not much call for star gazing in night clubs.' She followed him through the door and out into the open.

A pool lounge beckoned. She sat down and looked up into the clear night sky. The stars began to swim in all directions and she blinked, trying to clear the alcohol from her system, all the while knowing it was futile.

'Done it again,' she muttered.

'Done what?'

Brendan was beside her on another lounge he'd pulled up close.

'Been an idiot and drunk too much.'

'I thought you were here to let your hair down.'

'Hmm. Think I might pay for it tomorrow. Or today, as the case may be.' She let out a giggle. Then she felt his hand on her thigh. She opened her eyes and turned towards him.

'So, you're gonna be around for a while.' It was a statement.

'Not sure how long,' she answered.

He leaned towards her, his eyes reflecting in the soft orange light that lit the grounds.

'Just a warning,' he murmured, his lips only millimetres away from hers. 'I'm a bad boy. You should think about that.'

'I like bad boys,' Tessa answered. 'I seem to attract them.'

She felt his grin. 'Should be good together, then.'

As he kissed her, Tessa discovered that, in contrast to his hot and rushed kisses in the shearing shed, Brendan was slow and gentle.

Chapter 13

The thunder roared overhead and lightning split the sky into segments. Tessa gritted her teeth and drove on. She needed to get home before the heavens opened. If the rain came in heavy, the road back into Danjar Plains would become as slippery as ice and she could slide off the road and get bogged. This sort of land didn't take the water well and would transform from hard as hell to slippery as hell in a matter of about five millimetres.

She tightened her fingers around the steering wheel as one drop of rain splashed onto the windshield. 'Come on,' she urged.

Storms out here could be dangerous and unpredictable. She almost wished she'd taken up Brendan's offer to drive her home. They'd watched the storm build while eating lunch by the pool at Balladonia. The enormous, vivid white rollers looked like skyscrapers in the sky.

'Better watch them,' Brendan had said, nodding towards the north.

'Look nasty, don't they?' she had agreed.

'I don't want to cut this short, but it will take me longer to get home than you. I'd better push off. Not keen on getting halfway home and then getting stuck. But if you're worried, I can drive you home.'

'No, no, I'll be fine,' she said, hiding her disappointment. Not only was Brendan gorgeous, he was knowledgeable and smart. They'd had long conversations about the world financial crisis and where things were headed. She had been surprised at how switched on he was.

'You thought I was just some country hick, didn't you?' he'd said at one point, poking her with his toe.

She'd had the grace to blush, wishing she hadn't stumbled into her rented unit by herself last night. He was alluring.

Now, she focused on the road ahead and watched as another crack of lightning burst above. It was only four p.m. but it was as dark as night. She switched on her lights and drove hard.

Ten minutes after the rain had started with a fury she stopped at Ryan and Marni's house. They were sitting outside, nursing drinks as they watched the spectacle. Shutting the engine off, she listened to the water belt onto the tin roof. It was deafening. As she got out and ran to the verandah, lightning once again lit the sky. Seconds later, she felt the ground tremble with the force of the thunder. It sounded like it was right overhead.

'Far out!' she said, shaking the droplets out of her hair.

'Do you remember these, little sister?' Ryan asked with a grin.

'They're a bit hard to forget. Just happy I made it home before it got serious,' she answered, breathlessly. 'How are you, Marni?'

'Fine, thanks. Would you like a drink?'

'Something soft, if you've got it. I think I may have overdone it last night!'

'Now there's a surprise,' Ryan commented with a grin. 'Our Tessa is never one to do something by halves. And let me tell you, you look like it. Your eyes are like piss holes in the snow.'

'Well, thank you very bloody much,' she said. She sighed and flopped into a spare chair, rubbing her temple. 'Yep, definitely overdid it.'

Ryan went to the fridge at the end of the verandah. 'Coke, Fanta or lemonade?' he asked.

'Lemonade, please.'

There was another crack of thunder and the rain seemed to get heavier. Ryan looked out towards the sheds. 'Of course, we can't do anything about it. It could stop anytime soon. But we might end up with a small flood!'

'I imagine we won't be going anywhere for a while,' Marni added. 'Good thing we picked up extra food when we shopped for Spider's funeral. Still I guess the delivery truck will be out as it always is.'

'At least it runs on the bitumen. It never gets stopped, no matter the weather. The Flying Doctor is due to do its run some time next week, too. Have to hope everything will be dried out enough by then, otherwise he won't be able to land.' Ryan touched Marni's shoulder as he passed her.

He returned with a can of lemonade and handed it to Tessa. 'Hey, guess what I found yesterday?'

'What?'

'A photo. Wait here. I'll get it.'

'I'm not going anywhere in this rain,' Tessa answered. Although, as she looked out across the waterlogged yard, it did seem to be easing slightly.

She turned her attention to her sister-in-law. 'So, Marni, I've hardly had a chance to catch up with you since Aunty Spider's funeral. What's your news? Seen your family lately?'

'No, not for a while. I had hoped they might be able to come to the funeral, but Mum said it was too far. It's a long drive from Esperance.'

'I guess they'd find the drive hard at their age.'

'Yes.'

'So.' Tessa searched for something to say. It seemed that all of her good social skills had deserted her since she'd been back. Or maybe it was because she didn't always have wine and vodka inside her, making her bold. 'Are you thinking of kids yet? I'd love to be an aunty!'

Instantly Tessa knew she had said the wrong thing. Marni turned away and stared into the rain that had become a drizzle. The thunder seemed to have passed, too.

'Life doesn't always go according to plan,' Marni said. She got up and walked inside, leaving Tessa embarrassed and perplexed.

'Here it is,' Ryan said as he came out and handed the photo to Tessa.

She took it without looking at it. 'I may have just upset, Marni,' she confessed. 'I asked about kids.'

'Oh.' His face lost its life.

'I'm sorry, I didn't know there was a problem.'

'There's not. No problem.' Silence. 'So, do you remember when that photo was taken?'

Tessa glanced down and felt herself smile. There she was astride a misty grey mare called Sooty. Ryan was behind her, holding on to her waist, and Spider stood beside them, twisting the reins in a tight grip. In the background there were acres of low, grey, shrubby saltbush. She had been about five years old and Ryan was nine. Spider had taken them on a day-long picnic while their parents worked in the sheep yards, getting ready for shearing.

'We ate butterfly cakes that had strawberry jam in them, and mutton sandwiches with chutney for lunch,' Tessa said, feeling her throat tighten.

'Yeah, and do you remember how I kicked Sooty in the guts, hoping to make her canter faster, and she just stopped and you and I went tumbling over her head?'

'Oh, yeah, I do! Was that the day I got that horrendous bruise on my thigh? I think it was.'

'You were always covered in bruises. You used to be a regular tomboy.'

'So were you! Covered in bruises, I mean. I did used to be a bit of tomboy, didn't I? I wonder when makeup and fashion changed all of that?' she mused.

'When you went to school.'

'Really? Was it so noticeable?'

'It's to be expected you'd be different after hanging around with city girls. I know I changed when I went to boarding school. Just a fact of life.' He shrugged.

'You know, we should head up to Spider's tomorrow, with Mum and Dad and Marni. You guys could take the things you wanted and that would give me a bit of room to start cleaning it out.'

'You're going to do it, then?'

'I don't really have a choice. She knew I'd do what she asked. I don't want to. I can't think of anything worse than going through her things, but, in a way, I'm super curious, too. She said something about a family mystery, so you never know what I might find!'

'Mystery? What, that she had a secret child or

something like that?' Ryan lowered his voice and cast his eyes around him. 'What if we're not the only heirs? What if there is someone who could come in and snatch it all away?'

Tessa laughed. 'God forbid! Or there's a million-dollar inheritance stuffed in a mattress!'

'Bloody hell, if you find that, I'm definitely claiming half,' Ryan said. 'I could use it.'

Tessa cocked her head. 'Things a bit tight?' She'd never considered the idea.

'No more than usual. But if it's buried on my land, I'm entitled to half!'

'Of course. Anyway, I'd better go and see Mum and Dad. I'm sorry if I upset Marni.'

Ryan snorted as he walked her out to the ute. 'Unfortunately, it's not hard to do these days. No, don't ask. I'll tell you sometime.' He ended the conversation.

Over tea, Tessa told her parents she wanted to shift some of the bigger furniture from Spider's house. 'I just need a bit of room if I'm going to start clearing things out. Have you got any idea what you'll do with the house once I've gone through everything? Or is it just going to sit there empty?'

'We always assumed that after you came home you'd stay and live in it,' Peggy answered.

Tessa looked up from piling vegies onto her plate. 'What?'

'I'm joking, Tessa.' Her mother reached across and patted Tessa's hand, but there was something in Peggy's eyes that made Tessa wonder if it really had been said in jest. Was it a hint? Was that what her parents wanted her to do?

Tessa decided to ignore the comment and spoke on. 'It said in the letter she left me that the family could take what they wanted, so as long as you leave me the spare bed and kitchen table, it might be time to do just that. When I was there with Ryan, we had a bit of a look around and all the cupboards and drawers are full of newspapers and files. So I might need some extra floor space.'

'That's a great idea, Tessa,' Peggy said, looking at Paul.

'Did you want some of the pieces?' Paul asked his wife.

'If it's okay, I'd really love that sideboard she had in the lounge. Good Lord, I feel rather morbid, asking for the things of a dead lady!'

'It feels very strange,' Paul said looking forlorn.

Peggy covered his hand with her own. 'We can leave it for longer if you want, love.'

'No, you're right. It needs to be done. And I guess you want to get it done, Tessa? Not have it hanging over your head.'

'Yes, I would. But if you need more time?'

'Nah.'

'I also had another idea. I'd like to move down there while I'm cleaning it out. Ryan suggested it and at the time I didn't think there was a chance I would want to do it, but the more I think about it, it's a good idea. It's not that I don't want to stay here,' she hurried on, seeing her mother about to say something. 'It's just that I can do a better job and just get on with it any time of the day or night if I'm there. I'll take Dozer with me so I'll have company.'

'What I was about to say, Tessa,' said Peggy, looking at her with raised eyebrows, 'was that it was a good idea.'

Tessa laughed.

'Right, that's settled then,' Paul said and started to eat again.

Peggy held her daughter's gaze. 'Harrison rang over the weekend. He has to go to Adelaide late next week, just as the school term is starting.'

'Yeah?'

'Hmm, he's got a meeting with the owners – his annual board meeting, so it's not something he can get out of. Do you think you could pop over and look after Cally while he's away? It'll only be for three days.'

'What do I know about looking after a kid, Mum? I don't think that's a good idea.'

'Tessa, all you have to do is make sure she has three meals a day and fronts up at the computer on time for School of the Air. It's not hard, and you'd be doing him a favour. I would usually go, but I'm needed here. We're going to have to start bringing the sheep in closer to the yards – after this heavy rain the flies will be around and we'll probably have to jet them.'

'I don't think Harrison would want me there. We didn't start off very well. I'd feel rather uncomfortable.'

'Oh for goodness sake. Who is the adult here?'

'Come on, Tessie,' Paul said quietly. 'We won't be able to start until it dries out a bit and by then it will be about the time he goes. You can do it. Be good for you. And he did us a big favour, picking you up from Kalgoorlie.'

Tessa pushed her mashed potatoes and peas around her plate. She'd rather have nothing to do with that sullen man, who seemed to completely dislike her. Still, Cally was lovely. And she knew her parents thought the world of him. She felt the obligation close in on her. 'Fine,' she said shortly.

The next day dawned clear and sunny and the whole Mathison family travelled in three separate vehicles to Aunty Spider's house. Tessa had Dozer with her, along with clean bed linen and enough food for two days.

The heat that had been present before the storm wasn't as fierce but the humidity made up for it. Marni was first out of the car and into the garden. 'I'd really like to get some cuttings if that's okay?' she asked.

'Spider would love you to take anything at all,' Peggy said, smiling. 'I'm going to grab a few too. Petal,' she turned to Tessa, 'Ryan will have to show you how the garden pump works and when to refill the tank. Okay, Ryan?'

Tessa grinned as her brother put two fingers to his forehead.

'At your service,' he answered.

Tessa turned to share a laugh with Marni at Ryan's expense but caught an impatient look aimed at Ryan as her sister-in-law bent down to snap off a frond from the geranium bush she was standing near. Worried now, Tessa was sure she could see a great distance between Marni and Ryan and she hoped it was just her imagination. She knew Marni was perfect for her brother but, reading between the lines, if they were having trouble falling pregnant Tessa knew that could create tension.

'Should we go in?' she asked trying to defuse the situation and pushed open the door.

The house had begun to look and smell like no one lived there. Cobwebs hung in the corners and dust had settled on the furniture and surfaces. Yesterday's rain had come in underneath the front window and there was a damp patch on the carpet. Tessa was surprised that a house could look so unloved within a matter of five weeks.

She looked at her parents. 'Where do we start?' she asked, feeling suddenly very sad.

'We've just got to get on,' Paul said. 'If no one has any objections I'd like to take that.' He pointed at an antique chair covered in blue fabric. 'The Story Telling Chair,' he said. 'Do you know it's a Smoker's

Bow? I spent ages sitting in it while she spun tales sometimes too far-fetched to believe!'

'Yeah, I did too. Remember that story she used to tell about a kid called Spindles and his pet goanna?' Ryan said.

Peggy nodded. 'Oh, do I ever. You wanted one and were forever fossicking about in the scrub looking for a baby goanna you could train up as your own.' She shuddered, but with a smile.

Tessa knew she had sat there, too, when Spider told her tales of the cameleers, but she didn't say anything. Her emotions were running high and, as always when that happened, the cravings for a drink came in spades. She tuned back into the conversation.

'Since I never found one you would let me keep, I was happy with the string of geckos I had!' Ryan picked up the chair. 'So this goes to Dad. Mum?'

'The sideboard.' Peggy went over to it and ran her hand over the top, leaving fingerprints in the dust. She pulled open a drawer. It was full of papers. 'But maybe I won't be taking it today,' she said with a smile.

'That will be the first thing I sort, Mum,' Tessa said, bending down and opening a cupboard door in the dresser. 'Oh, wow, look at these photo albums!' She pulled one out and opened it. Three pictures of Spider and her family were on the front page. Spider had a baby on her hip. 'Imagine the history in these,' Tessa said in wonder, carefully turning the pages.

'Don't get rid of any of that,' Paul said. 'That's our history.'

'I'd never do that, Dad. How cool would it be to dedicate a room at home to the history of the family? I might try and do that once I've finished here.' She continued to look through the album, while everyone went in and out of the other rooms, looking at what was there.

Ryan came in holding a painting of a camel train pulling a load of wool. 'I'd really like this.'

Tessa looked up. 'Great! What about you, Marni, have you found something?' She smiled at her sister-in-law, hoping her friendliness might encourage Marni to smile back.

'It's not really my place to take anything,' Marni said quietly.

'You take what you want. Mum said that at the beginning.'

'Do you really mean that? Could I—' she stopped and Tessa smiled in what she hoped was an encouraging way. 'Could I have the spinning wheel? I love to spin.'

'Wow! That's something I didn't know. It's yours. I don't think any of us even know how to use it! It's almost a lost art.' Tessa was rewarded with a grin from Marni.

'And I'd like to lay claim to Aunty Spider's writing desk,' she said. She unlatched it and folded down the front to reveal pigeon holes on the inside. This was where Spider would have penned her letters. Sitting at it, she knew she would feel close to her aunt.

'Oh, my goodness me! Do you remember this?'

Tessa looked up and saw Peggy holding a photo of the four of them. 'Spider took this after the big rains back in '88! Look at you two. We were hunting for yabbies in the dam. You were both as quick as sticks on your feet. I was trying to keep you at least half-clean and look at you! Covered in mud from head to toe. She thought it was a scream.'

Tessa giggled. It was bittersweet, but there were lots of good memories here.

Chapter 14

It was dark when the others left Spider's house. The thunder clouds had begun to build again at lunch time, but thankfully they'd stayed to the north of the highway.

From the garden Tessa watched the cars' tail-lights disappear as her family drove away. When she could hear nothing but silence she walked back into the house and switched on the kitchen light.

'Well, Dozer, it's just you and me,' she said to the old mutt. He seemed to understand and puffed loudly. Tessa knew he'd been pleased to come home, although he had spent most of the time wandering from room to room as if he were looking for Spider. She wished she could explain to him what was happening. Instead, she bent down and fondled his ears.

'I'd love a glass of wine, old fella,' she muttered.

But she'd made a pact with herself after the night at Balladonia: she would come to Aunty Spider's, where it was difficult to get in and out of, and wouldn't take anything alcoholic – Tessa would just have to do without. It was obvious that if she had it with her, she'd drink it. Stuck out here in a lonely cottage, twenty minutes from the homestead, would do her good.

Tessa poured herself a glass of lemonade and wandered out to the verandah, though she wasn't sure it could be called that – it was more of a roof over a dirt path. Still, Spider had done it up prettily with painted white pots full of flowering red geraniums. There was a heavy cast-iron table with chairs set up underneath the kitchen window, also painted white, in the middle of which sat a clay pot. Tessa knew it was for plants because there had been times Spider had grown small succulents in it, but there wasn't anything shooting up in it at the moment.

Tessa sat there and took a sip of her drink before picking up the pot and looking inside it. It felt heavy, but there was nothing inside but cobwebs and dirt, as far as she could see. She put it back and sighed. Dozer sighed too and curled up at her feet.

'Did she do this most nights?' Tessa asked the dog. Dozer didn't even look up.

She turned her attention back to the night. Across the plains, she could see the rich glow of the moon just below the horizon. A full silver moon. It sent shivers through her. It had been a full moon when Kendra had died. *Don't even go there*, she thought angrily and slugged at her drink wishing it were wine. If only there was something to take away this guilt, fear and need for a drink. These things wound around her, leaving her agitated and disturbed.

Not even the chorus of crickets and frogs, competing for best vocalist, calmed her. She heard a fox bark and shivered again. 'Come on, I don't think I should be out here tonight,' she said and encouraged Dozer back inside.

Cranking up her iPod, she let the music block any outside noises as she prepared a meal. She'd bought some chicken breasts from Jemima, her friend in the kitchen at Balladonia – she didn't think she could stomach another chop. After so long eating fish and fowl, all the red meat she had been consuming wasn't agreeing with her.

Tessa rummaged around in the cupboard and found the frying pan and spices. After dicing the meat she threw it into the pan, added the vegies and spices, and put a pot of water on to boil for the rice. Everything was where it had always been kept and Tessa added what Aunty Spider had taught her to. Saffron and coriander plus many other spices. They were all there. Considering Spider had never travelled further than England, Tessa had always thought it interesting that she had a love for Afghan food. Her signature dish had been Qorma Lawand, an onion-based dish of lamb or chicken. Yoghurt, turmeric and coriander were the other ingredients and that was what Tessa was going to cook tonight. She'd cooked it many times back in London, so well, in fact, that some of her friends had asked if she'd been taught by a chef. What a hoot that was!

While dinner was simmering, she went into the spare bedroom and made up the bed. She turned on the hot water in the shower and stood there, waiting for it to change from cold to hot. It didn't. She frowned as she remembered there was a chip heater she had to light. The chip heater was a filthy piece of equipment – a large rectangular cistern kept in the laundry, with a section down the bottom to light a fire and heat the water. Old-fashioned and a terrible waste of time, but frugal, just as Aunty Spider had been.

Tessa swore. She might have to wait until tomorrow for a shower but, looking down at her clothes, she knew she was too grubby to stand herself.

'Come on, Dozer, you'll have to come with me. I don't fancy going out to the wood pile by myself.'

She turned on the outside light and walked across to the tank, where small fist-size stumps were kept out of the weather. She quickly gathered an armful, then raced back across the lawn and into the house. She shut the door and tried to suppress a shudder. *Idiot*, she thought.

After lighting the hot-water system and checking on her meal, there was really nothing else to do but wait. She was itching for a glass of wine. Was there any here? She opened the sideboard where Spider had always kept the sherry. Nothing. Maybe the pantry? Nothing.

'*Spider,*' Tessa groaned. It was almost like she'd known not to have anything in the house!

Muting the iPod, Tessa turned on the TV, only to become instantly annoyed at the primitive ad for some second-hand car yard. 'Stuff that,' she muttered angrily and switched it off.

Tessa turned her thoughts to the night ahead. She might need a torch after she went to bed, so she went hunting for one, all the while knowing it would be on Spider's bedside table. She really had been hoping that she didn't have to go into her bedroom for a little while. Not until she had settled in, anyway.

Tessa stood at the door of the bedroom for a long time. Finally she turned the handle and walked in slowly. The smell hit her instantly. Sandalwood. Spider had always loved the smell. Choking back tears, Tessa went in and grabbed the torch before backing out and shutting the door again.

In the lounge room she curled up on the couch and cried – the cauldron of emotions had finally bubbled to the surface. She'd tried to be brave in coming back, but it was so hard. Kendra's accident had just about wrecked Danjar Plains for her.

As a young girl, some small part inside thought she could be happy here in Spider's house, living the rest of her days out in peace and solitude. But then she'd left for school in Perth. Saw how the city lights could be much more fun than an isolated stretch of land. It had been great coming home for holidays – she got to fill her lungs with clean, fresh air, ride the motorbikes and horses and spend time with her great-aunt. Jaz often came with her. But not Kendra, even though Tessa had been to Kendra's many times – it was so much easier to get to Narrogin than to the Nullarbor.

But at last, in Year 12, during the mid-term school holidays, Tessa had convinced Kendra to visit the station. Kendra, her best friend. The one who had wiped her tears when she'd been homesick, laughed with her over stupid teachers, and talked until all hours of the night when the boarding house mistresses weren't within earshot.

Opening her eyes, Tessa stared at the crushed tissue in her hand. All she could see was the windmill, Kendra's lifeless body and the dingoes circling. *No! No, you bastards! Get away from her.* The dingoes would have thought Kendra was nothing but a meal, not a loved person.

Tessa couldn't leave her. She'd tried to grab Kendra's body, to hold it up, make her start breathing again. 'Kendra,' she'd screamed. 'Kendra. Oh,

Kendra. Jaz, help! Jaz.' But Kendra was dead and Jaz was sound asleep by the fire.

Tessa could still remember the weight of her friend as she dragged her towards the homestead. Kendra's trailing legs had haunted her for years afterwards.

She'd sobbed and screamed all the way, calling for Jaz and swearing she wouldn't leave her friend until she was safe. But Kendra would never be safe because Tessa hadn't watched her closely enough and this is what had happened. Danjar Plains was her home, not Kendra's, so that made her responsible.

No one had heard her until she was within fifty metres of the house. She'd seen the ute lights go on and the white of the spotties as the vehicle backed out of the garage. *Thank God they were home!* She'd seen her dad drive in an arc, trying to work out where she was. She had nothing to signal him with, so she just kept up an ear-piercing scream. And all the while, the dingoes followed her . . .

A rap on the bedroom door woke Tessa with a start. 'Piss off,' she muttered, pushing her hair back from her face and squinting at her brother.

'You never were a morning person,' said Ryan, handing her a mug of coffee.

'Have you been here for a while?' she asked, accepting it gratefully.

'Long enough to hear you snoring.'

'Thanks. I think.'

'Welcome.' He sat on the side of the bed. 'So, how'd you go last night?'

'Fine.'

'Yeah, right. Burnt dinner, tissues across the floor. Yep, that makes me think everything went just hunky-dory.'

'Oh, just piss off, would you? You and your high and mighty attitude!'

'Steady on, steady on, I was just joking,' Ryan answered, sounding injured.

'Well, take your jokes and leave.'

'Sorry.' Ryan looked suitably chastised. 'Sorry, I was just trying to get you to open up. Tessa, you've been clamped up like a bloody safe since you got home.' He got up. 'How about I come back in a couple of hours? I just wanted to see if you were okay.'

'You can stay if you stop asking me how I am,' said Tessa.

'Fine.'

'I forgot I had to light the chip heater to get hot water,' Tessa admitted.

Ryan laughed. 'I said to Marns on the way home I thought that would happen.'

'But I managed.'

'Of course you did. You're a Nullarbor girl. It never leaves you, no matter how much you try to push it away.'

'And it was a full moon last night.'

'So it was.'

There was a silence.

'Have you had breakfast?' asked Tessa.

'Mate, I've been up for the last four hours. It's nine-thirty, you slacker! Come on, get up and I'll see if I can find a tin of spaghetti for you.'

'No! No thanks. That won't be necessary. Now get out of here so I can get dressed, then I'll make *you* a coffee.'

'Deal.'

In the kitchen they sat facing each other, silent, so many things unsaid.

Not knowing how to clear the air, Tessa finally spoke. 'I thought about Kendra last night.'

'Yeah, thought you might've. And I'm sure there will be nights you think about nothing but Aunty Spider.'

'I guess.'

Ryan leaned back in his chair. 'She knew you were struggling in the UK,' he said. 'I didn't think you were. All I heard about were these great parties and how busy you were. I didn't think there were any problems at all, but she knew.'

'Did she tell you what they were?'

'Not exactly, but when her letters started to go unanswered, she knew things weren't right. And now you're back, I'm guessing you might be drinking a bit much?'

Tessa looked down at the tablecloth, her face aflame with embarrassment. 'Bloody hell, has she passed the all-seeing gene on to you since she died?'

He snorted. 'Well, you're in the right place to fix it. There's a long drive in front of you if you want any booze here,' Ryan said, putting his hand on her arm. 'Now, which room are you going to start on today?'

Chapter 15

One week and more trailer loads of rubbish than Tessa could believe later, she had managed to get the bathroom, laundry and hallway cupboards all cleaned out. She'd started with places that weren't going to upset her, leaving the spare room, lounge, kitchen and Spider's bedroom. She knew that would be last.

The contents of the bathroom had consisted mainly of half-empty containers of powders and lotions. Tessa had giggled when she found five bottles of bubble bath and three gift boxes – all the same brand – filled with a hand-cream, shampoo and conditioner. None had been opened and were obviously presents from someone who didn't know Spider at all well.

Dozer lay in the doorway, head on his paws, watching every movement and pricking up his ears when Tessa spoke.

The lounge room was full of piles - keeping; to go through; family history; and rubbish. There was also a family pile; things Tessa didn't need, but Ryan, Marni, Paul or Peggy might like.

Music played in the background continually, thanks to the docking station Ryan had lent her. The music not only helped her work but was company of sorts. Occasionally Dozer joined in with a howl when Pink hit a high note or Tessa's singing wobbled off-key, causing her to roll about in fits of laughter. It felt good.

And there was the scent of sandalwood flowing through the house.

The days had been punctuated with visits from Ryan and her parents. Marni stayed away, keeping to herself. Maybe it was time she visited her, tried to open the lines of communication and be a friend, like Spider had mentioned.

She stood up from the piles of papers she was sorting and stretched. 'Your mistress obviously liked to keep every tiny thing,' she said, looking towards Dozer.

He answered by yawning. She grinned. 'Yeah, I've been repeating myself a lot lately, haven't I?'

The sun was beginning to set. It was time for their evening walk. 'Come on, let's go,' she said and they started off at a quick pace, Dozer climbing behind. One and a half kilometres down the track then she'd turn around and head back. She'd gone from a slow amble to a power walk. Without the

grog, she was feeling the best she'd felt in ages –
strong, clear-headed and alive.

Tessa was back on the verandah with a glass of
lemonade within twenty minutes. She heard the
vehicle before she saw the lights.

'Hi, Dad,' she called from the comfort of the chair.
She'd been around long enough now to recognise
the station cars by the sound of the engine or the
squeaky brakes.

Paul got out of the ute and shut the door. 'G'day,
Tessie. How you going?'

'Really well, thanks. I've got another trailer-load
of rubbish ready for you to take away.'

'Is that all your old man is good for these days?
Getting rid of the rubbish?'

Tessa grinned as he eased himself into the other
seat. She noticed the grey streaks through his hair
and a few extra lines around his eyes and her smile
faded as she felt a sense of sadness. Everyone was
changing. Getting older. The people she had always
thought to be indestructible were now the opposite.

'Drink? Only soft things here, I'm afraid.'

'Lemon squash?'

'Sure.'

The can fizzed as he opened it and took a long
drink. 'So how far have you got?'

'Not far enough. She had so much stuff crammed
into such a little area. The linen cupboards are full
of old papers – nothing exciting as far as I can tell.
I can't even see her reasoning for keeping them.

Old newspapers from the early fifties, things like that. I think she may have even kept her first-ever set of sheets. I've found fifteen sets!'

'You've got to remember that things were hard to come by out here. Always had to be prepared and she'd come through the Depression. She knew what it was like to have nothing. Sometimes it's hard to give up things when you haven't had them before and you don't know where the next one will come from.'

'Some of the newspapers have been used for cupboard liners, just laid on top of one another. I'm sure she couldn't have kept all these papers just for that, but I'm loathe to throw any of them out until I've had a really good look at them. According to Elsie, I'm looking for a huge family secret, so I don't want to throw them out if there's some chance it's in there!'

Paul smiled wryly then took a sip of his drink. 'I don't think it will be life-changing, Tessa. Maybe someone married a man the family didn't approve of or ran away, but I wouldn't get too excited about it.'

'I know,' Tessa agreed. 'Our family is *very* boring! Well, this generation is. Aunty Spider wasn't, though. She always had a part of her that was shut away and she wouldn't let anyone in.'

'Yeah, she did, didn't she? Had a bit of a mysterious air about her. And it wasn't even that, was it? More like part of her life she just never wanted to share. She loved us to the end of the world and back, was a wonderful support and steadying influence in our lives, but I always felt there was a small part of her life that she didn't want to share. I really always thought it was William and losing him so young that made her put a wall around herself and she was never going to let anyone get through it.'

'Yeah, that's exactly how I felt. I miss her.'

'I do too.'

They sat companionably for a while then Paul stretched. 'Well, I'd best be off. Your mother will be wondering where I am.'

'Oh, before I forget. I've got a pile of bed linen for Marni – would you take it back to her? I don't reckon I need fifteen sets of sheets here.'

'No probably not.'

Tessa went to get them. 'How's Mum?' she asked when she returned with an armful of thick cotton sheets. 'Did she help shift the sheep today?'

'Yep. She's fine.' Paul opened the door into the ute and Tessa piled the linen onto the front seat.

'Just going back to Spider for a moment, Dad. One thing I've noticed as I've been looking through the photos is that there's such an age difference between her and your dad – Grandpa. I started to draw up a family tree. Her oldest sister was Grace – she was born in 1912; then Len – who started out here on the Nullarbor – in 1914; George, 1915; Edward, who was born in 1920; and Spider in 1921. Then there's this baby who appears years later. Like in 1931. That's your dad, Tom. Such a gap. Quite curious, really.'

'Not that odd. Don't forget the war was in the middle of that. It was a bit hard to have babies when the men were fighting on overseas. Also, back then more babies died. There wasn't the same level of medical intervention as there is now. A miscarriage is another thought. And there's always the good old mistake.'

'Good point, I hadn't thought of that. So your grandfather fought in the Great War then?'

'He did. He was on the Western Front but was injured and sent home in 1917, I think. It took him a long time to recover – I can't remember what was wrong with him. Must have taken a bullet somewhere, or some shrapnel, I guess. Grandma and Mum helped nurse him in Adelaide. That's where we were originally from. South Australia.'

'Really? I didn't know that.' Tessa was intrigued. 'I guess I don't really know much about your grandparents. I know more about Spider and Grandpa's life out here than anything.'

'They all helped here. It's because of them Danjar Plains is what it is. Len was a bit of an old drifter – he never seemed to stick at much, from what I can remember, but the others, they were salt of the earth, hard-working and dependable men. They all died close together, but I'm not sure how. Spider never talked about it, so I didn't pry.'

Tessa looked to the sky. 'I wonder what stories the land would tell us if it could speak.'

'Many we wouldn't want to hear, I'm sure,' he

answered. 'Night, Tessa, sleep well.' He leaned over and kissed her cheek and she put her arms around him in a brief hug.

'Night, Dad. Thanks for the visit.'

From the verandah she listened as the sound of the ute grew distant, until she could hear nothing but silence. Feeling restless, she picked up the pot that sat in the centre of the table and tossed it from hand to hand.

Something moved inside and clunked against the side of the pot. Tessa stopped and shook it. This time, Tessa could feel something hitting the inside walls.

She upended it onto the table. A shower of dirt fell out and through the cracks in the table. She peered inside the pot and saw a small box covered in dust. At first she tried to fish it out, but the bottom was too deep for her fingers to reach and she didn't want to be bitten by a red-back spider, so she tapped it gently on the table.

A dirt-encrusted jewellery box clunked softly onto the iron. Tessa stared at it, not sure what to think. Her thoughts flew back to the letter she had from Spider.

Mystery . . . skeletons, she'd written.

Finally Tessa opened the filthy box. Nestled on fawn-coloured silken bedding were two gold wedding rings, looking as new as could be. Tessa stared at them, trying to remember if Spider had ever worn a wedding ring. She had. But it was thick and old. Scratched and dull. These rings were shiny. There didn't seem to be a blemish on either of them.

Taking one, she went over to the light to see it better. There was writing on the inside, but it was hard to read. Tessa raced inside to grab a torch.

'Forever mine, forever yours.'

She checked the second one. The same.

How strange! And why hide them in the pot? Tessa kept the rings in her hand, inspecting them, thinking. She went into her bedroom to find the final letter from Aunty Spider. As she opened it, she felt a tingling sensation.

'Our family has a few skeletons and secrets!'

Huh, won't make it easy for me? Well, Spider, I've just had two rings literally fall into my hands. It can't be that hard from here on in, she thought. But where to start? The obvious thing would be to work out who the rings were intended for.

Back to the photos.

Pouring another glass of lemonade, she went into the lounge. From their spot on the bookshelves she pulled out four photo albums and started to flick through.

In Spider's familiar handwriting there were labels against them all. One showed a young family of three standing in front of a horse and carriage. 'Grace, Len, George. Adelaide 1917.' Tessa looked more closely and realised the family were standing in a wide open street.

'Grace, Len, George, Edward. Mummy and Daddy', said the next one. Tessa looked at the tall imposing man who was her great-grandfather. He wore a bowler hat and a belted overcoat, while the children wore dark clothes, with collars high to the neck. It looked like Great-Grandma was pregnant again. Tessa checked the date on the photo and worked out that the baby would be Spider. Why were they always so serious in photos back then, she wondered as she studied each unsmiling face.

Turning page after page, she saw the children grow until Grace wasn't in one photo and neither was Len.

The dog whined and Tessa realised she'd been lost in the past for too long. If she was going to head over to Harrison's tomorrow to look after Cally, she needed to pack and get ready.

After a quick tea of eggs on toast, she packed her bag and set it at the front door.

Then she went back to the rings. Carefully she pulled out the lining of the box, looking for some sign of ownership, but there wasn't even the name of a jeweller.

In the laundry she found a cardboard box, in which she neatly stacked three photo albums from the shelves. Tessa hadn't touched the writing desk yet – she hadn't felt strong enough to go there – but if she had something to look for it might help. Were there diaries, letters, anything?

She pulled out the drawers and had a quick look through. The first one looked like it held nothing but bills; the second, recipes. The long one across the top contained writing pads, envelopes and stamps, plus letters that needed answering.

Other than that, nothing useful.

She didn't really want to spend much time in Spider's bedroom yet, so she hurried in, yanked open the top drawer in the bedside table and riffled through. There was nothing there either, so she made a quick escape.

She would just have to make do with the photo albums and see what she could come up with.

A bit annoyed but very curious, Tessa stopped and looked around the lounge room. 'Who were you keeping secrets for, Aunty Spider, and why were you the secret keeper?' she whispered.

Chapter 16

The two-wheel track that led towards Danjar Plains' boundary and on to Harrison's was rough and full of potholes. Deep puddles lay across their path, but Ryan handled the ute with ease.

It was the second week in February and Tessa's babysitting job was about to start.

Tessa was silent, watching, one moment sure she recognised places from childhood, then doubting herself. It all looked the same and she couldn't be certain that the places she remembered were what she was actually staring at.

'I want to head up to the northern part of the place,' Ryan had said when he'd arrived to pick Tessa up. 'Haven't been up there for a week or so. Got a few waters and fences I can check on the way.'

'I haven't been up there for years!'

'You haven't been home for years,' said Ryan simply, then changed the subject. 'You can get to Harrison's from the back of our place – do you remember? We butt up against his side boundary.'

'I may not remember the names of paddocks and things of that sort, but I do know who our neighbours are,' said Tessa. 'Be a good way to see some of the countryside. Although,' she conceded, 'I'm having trouble working out where we are.'

The ute hit a pothole and Tessa felt the box in her pocket containing the rings press into her thigh. Even with the hours she'd spent the previous evening poring over the pages of the photo albums, she was still no closer to finding out who the rings belonged to.

She wondered whether she should tell Ryan about them, but there was really nothing to tell. It wasn't in her nature to say something unless she could back it up or there was reasoning behind it. She'd learned that quickly in her job.

As she opened the third gate, she looked about her. There was nothing but vivid blue sky and shrubby bushes, the land stretching on and on until it merged with the sky at the horizon. She'd first thought there weren't any changes, but the soil colour had transformed from white to apricot and the trees were slightly smaller than the ones closer to the homestead. So isolated, so much space. It had taken a bit of getting used to after the busyness of London, but getting used to it she seemed to be.

She could feel the land beginning to get under her skin and it was unlike any feeling she had ever experienced. She knew she was changing too. Waking in the mornings, Tessa didn't crave the rush and adrenalin she had when she was working. She had slipped into the relaxed way of life quickly. There were times when she wondered if she might have never left Danjar Plains, but for Kendra's accident. But she'd pushed it away. She knew what she was experiencing now was akin to a holiday and nothing else. The moment she hit the city, her blood would begin to buzz again.

Tessa shook her head as she latched the wire around the fence post and made sure the gate was secured. She didn't want to stay. She was here to do a job, and once Aunty Spider's house was done and the mystery solved, she'd be moving back to the city. There were some jobs she wanted to research on the net and she planned to do that while she was at Harrison's – hopefully his internet connection was better than the one on Danjar.

Jumping back in the ute, she opened her mouth to ask Ryan about the stock stealing, but he spoke first.

'Tessa, I've been wanting to tell you this for a while. Marni is acting like she is because we're having trouble falling pregnant. You probably worked it out when she rushed off like she did the other night, but I wanted you to know that's the reason.'

The quiet inside the cab was broken only by the jarring rattle of the ute tray as they drove over rough ground.

'Oh, Ryan,' was all Tessa could think to say for a moment. 'I did think something was up, when she reacted so badly after I talked about becoming an aunty.'

'She's been through a bit of a rough time. She miscarried three months ago and we'd been trying for over a year before that happened.'

Sympathy for her sister-in-law hit Tessa hard. She didn't understand the craving for a child but she had heard from friends it was the worst kind of yearning – enough to change personalities. Obviously it had done so with Marni, because the carefree, quick-with-a-smile-and-a-laugh young woman who had married her brother was now a closed-off, quiet, almost haunted woman. She was nothing like how Tessa remembered her. When she'd first arrived home, she'd wondered if the isolation had eaten away at Marni during the previous couple of years, but with Spider's cryptic clues in her letter and Marni's recent behaviour, clearly it wasn't that at all.

'I'm sorry, Ryan. It sounds like you've had a terrible time.' She chewed the inside of her cheek as she tried to work out what to say. 'Um, so, what can you do? Have you been to the doctor? Don't feel like you need to answer if you don't want to,' she stumbled.

'Doctor Mike from the Flying Doctor thinks we should go to Kal for some tests, but he's talking IVF.' Ryan sounded disgusted.

'From what I know that's a very good option.'

'What do you know then?' Ryan shot her a curious look.

'Not very much, just what I've heard girls in the office say,' Tessa admitted, watching Ryan's shoulders slump slightly. 'But, I do know it can take over your life, that the desire for a child can overshadow everyday life. It can become an obsession.'

'That's what it is! Exactly,' Ryan burst out. 'The thermometer lives in her pocket and if her temperature is slightly raised, she calls me on the radio. "It's time to come home, honey," she says. On the bloody radio! She monitors everything she eats and getting pregnant is all she talks about. We used to laugh and chat; she'd come out in the ute and we'd have fun. Now she's constantly anxious.' Frustrated, he ran his fingers over his head. 'Anyway, I just wanted you to know, in case you thought you'd offended her or something. She's just easily upset these days, so don't take it personally.'

Tessa felt her heart squeeze at the defeated look on his face.

'It's easy enough to get sheep and cattle pregnant,' he continued. 'We cull the ones who don't, so our flocks are fertile. It's not something I ever really thought about or imagined we'd have trouble with. She blames me – thinks I drink too much, don't eat the right things, it's too hot out here. Apparently high temperatures affect the sperm count, but it doesn't seem to do that with the stock! It's warmer out there in the paddock than it is in my bedroom, I can tell you. She's got me in these bloody boxer shorts to make sure things – circulate! I don't know who has the problem but I can't see the point in blaming each other. It's just one of those things.' He sighed. 'I feel like a bloody failure.'

'You can't feel like that! Neither of you can! It's just nature.' Tessa was trying to sound wise. She hoped what she said was true.

Ryan looked at her and missed seeing the pothole ahead. The ute jarred as it ploughed into the deep rut. Tessa hit her head on the window as the vehicle veered off into the bush. 'Ow!'

The scratching of the brush against the ute sounded like fingernails down a blackboard and she wanted to put her fingers in her ears.

'Sorry, sis.' Ryan gunned the accelerator and Tessa felt the back end of the ute swing to the side. She squealed and lunged for the handrail.

Ryan let out a laugh. He turned the wheel and got the ute back onto the track. 'Awesome!'

'If you think so,' Tessa said, rubbing her head. 'Oh my ears. That's a terrible noise!'

'Ripping it up makes me think I'm a young bloke again. It's fun, and fun, dear sister, is like coffee in the morning. Essential!'

Tessa laughed, then became serious. 'So can I do anything to help?'

'Nah, I don't think so. Just somehow gotta get a bit of time away from here, get to Kal and then up to Perth, I guess. Bloody hell, would you look at that?'

Tessa followed his line of sight. 'What?'

'The fence. It's down.'

She peered out, searching the bush. She couldn't even see a fence, let alone one that was down.

Ryan drove off the track and into the scrub, picking the path of least resistance. They bumped over clumps of grasses and avoided large sticks and piles of rocks.

Then Tessa spotted it. 'How the hell did you see that from the road?' she wondered aloud. The fence seemed the same colour as the bush to her and was about twenty metres from the road.

'I'm going to know where my fences are. I run the joint!' Ryan killed the engine. 'Can you grab me the pliers? They're in the toolbox in the back.'

They got out. Tessa retrieved the pliers then watched as Ryan inspected the fence.

He pulled a couple of wires and tested the tension on the top one. 'Look at this,' he said. 'The top two are fine. They haven't been touched. But the lower ones have all been pulled away from the posts. It's been done so you have a quick glance at the fence, see the top wires and think everything is okay. But if there are any stock grazing along here, which they do to get to the tank, they can go under the fence and into next door's place.'

'What are you saying? The neighbour has deliberately done this? Why?' Tessa asked innocently.

'Not a neighbour. I think it's someone who has local knowledge, but I don't think it's a neighbour.' He shook his head. 'We haven't got any proof who's doing this. This is the whole reason I've been driving around at night. I'm trying to see if we can catch them at their own game. We've got theories about who it might be, but no firm proof. It started four years ago. Stock counts were down, and when the Hunters came to muster the cattle for calf marking the number of calves was right down. It took a while to work out someone was deliberately dropping fences and turning off bores, because it doesn't happen often. Whoever is doing it isn't doing it all the time.'

He tugged on the wire again. 'Grab me the wire strainers from the toolbox, will you? I've got to fix this now.'

Tessa did as Ryan asked then looked on as her brother fixed the strainers onto the fence and started to jack the handle. The slack wire seemed to take on a life of its own, rising from the ground into a tight line.

'Far out,' she said, looking around her. 'That's terrible. We're in the country. Everyone is supposed to be honest.'

Ryan lined up the wire on the post then grabbed his hammer and stapled it firmly into the wood. He then cut a piece of wire as a tie and poked it through the hole in the steel post. Deftly he tightened it until it held firm. He did the same for the next three strands then stood to view his handiwork.

"Ha! Don't let where we live fool you. Farms and stations are often targeted for theft. People drive in off the road and fill up their fuel tanks from ours. We've found slaughtered cattle with the prime cuts taken. The list goes on, let me tell you. It really used to get up Spider's nose. She'd come with me sometimes when I'd go out at night.' He looked up from his work with a grin. 'She wanted to be there when the perpetrator was caught so she could roast them. You can imagine it, can't you?'

Tessa knew it wasn't a laughing matter but she couldn't help but giggle at the thought of Spider, hands on hips, dressing down the thief. She sat down on a rocky outcrop. 'How did you find out?'

'We figured it out when all the owners and managers caught up for our annual meeting about wild dogs at the last Nullarbor Muster,' he said. 'It turned out we'd all had the same sort of experiences.' He walked down to the next post and tested the ties. They were firm.

'Anyway, the sheep just walk under the fence and into next door. I suspect what's happening is, whoever is doing it keeps an eye on the fence line, and when he sees the stock, he drops the fence and maybe even encourages them through. Not sure how he does that, 'cos no one has ever noticed car tracks on our side of the fence and, believe me, we've looked. Spider thought she'd tracked someone one day, but it turned out to be Joe riding a horse he'd been breaking.'

Tessa took the hammer he handed her. 'Someone is stealing them? Tell me how?'

'That's what we think,' he answered grimly, turning to face her. 'Like this. There is someone dropping the fence and once the stock - cattle or sheep - cross that boundary, someone collects them. See, if you turn off the water this side of the fence and have water on the other side, the stock will just walk through to the next watering point. They don't care whose land they're on.' He pushed his hat back and scratched his head. 'They must keep them in some sort of yard and take them away from here. Personally? I'm guessing they're ripping our tags out and replacing them so they can be sold. It's not hard to change an earmark with a pocket knife. All hearsay, mind you.'

'Are you certain?' Tessa was stunned. 'I mean, come on, this is the Nullarbor. You all know each other, you're neighbours, friends. You socialise together. It doesn't seem realistic.'

'Like I said, locality doesn't make people honest. And it's happened enough times for me to know that someone is stealing them,' Ryan confirmed.

'Who do you think it is?'

Ryan looked straight at her. 'I won't accuse anyone until I have proof. The gossip mill has gone into overdrive, suspecting this one or that. So-and-so had a dodgy station hand or Joe Bloggs from over the back had three horses taken when his jillaroo shot through.' He shook his head. 'Innuendo and rumours are all we have. All these so-called suspects have left and it still keeps happening.'

'Bloody hell!' Tessa was bewildered. 'So do you think any stock have gone under here?'

'Nope. Look at this.' He pointed to the ground.

It just looked like dirt to her.

'There hasn't been any activity here since it rained. You can still see where the water has lain, whereas here—' he walked several metres away from the fence into the bush and pointed '—here you can see tracks. Do you know how to tell which are sheep or cattle?'

'The smaller ones will be the sheep, obviously.'

'Yeah, but depending on the time of the year, they could be calves too. See here? These are sheep – see the squareness of the hoof? If it was a cow, it would be sort of like a horse's hoof. But these are split in two. The inside of the hoof has straight sides. They're called claws.' He spread his fingers for emphasis. 'Get it?'

'Funny, I sort of remember all this, but there is no way I would have known the proper terminology for it. I think I'll trust whatever you say,' Tessa said, straightening. 'And, I might just look for big tracks compared to small ones.'

'Or you can do that,' agreed Ryan with a grin. 'Come on, we've saved our sheep today, so let's get going over to Harrison's. I've still got to get back home tonight.'

Chapter 17

The dogs barked. Harrison looked through the window of the Mundranda homestead. Ah, here they were. He hoped he'd done the right thing when he'd asked Tessa to look after Cally. He felt his little girl needed some female company other than Peggy and although Tessa wasn't exactly ideal, there wasn't a lot of choice around.

Briefly he wondered what the five-bedroom transportable house would look like to her, before deciding he didn't care. He knew it was probably obvious there wasn't a woman in residence – the garden was uncared for – but he did his best. There were pockets of green lawn as you walked towards the front door and the line of bushes by the edge of the deck that Ange had planted just two weeks before her diagnosis, Harrison would have kept alive at any cost.

Ryan was just shutting off the ute by the time Harrison walked out onto the deck and started down the steps.

'G'day, mate.'

'Ryan, good to see you. Tessa.' He nodded in her direction.

'Hello,' she answered.

He thought she sounded unsure of herself.

Footsteps clattered along the wooden passage-way and Cally came hurtling out of the door, letting it slam behind her.

'Hi,' she called. 'Hello!'

'Hi, Cally,' Ryan and Tessa answered together.

'Offer you a cup of tea?' Harrison asked.

Tessa nodded.

'Mate, I'd love one,' Ryan said, 'then I'd better make a mile. Long way back.'

Cally served the tea with bought biscuits. When everyone was sitting around the big old table Tessa quickly engaged her charge in conversation, asking her about the photos covering the wall.

Harrison talked with Ryan while keeping one ear on the talk between Cally and Tessa.

'And this one,' Cally said, pointing to one of her sitting astride a horse, 'was taken at the end of last year's Nullarbor Muster. So it's nearly a year old.'

'I can see how much you've grown up,' Tessa said. 'Did you win anything?'

'Nah, Gracie Pike from two stations across won. But I'm going to beat her this year.' Harrison felt his heart constrict as Cally thumped her fist into her palm with a quiet air of determination.

He watched Tessa interact with Cally and thought there was probably some good inside her somewhere. Despite her earlier rudeness, maybe the young Tessa was still in there. He was heartened by the thought. And he had to admit she looked better too. The thick makeup that had caked her face was gone. Her skin and eyes were clearer and the dreadful haircut she'd had seemed to be growing out, with the harsh blonde colour gradually being taken over by her natural dark brown.

Ryan interrupted Harrison's thoughts. 'Well, suppose I should get going.' He pushed back his chair and got to his feet.

They all stood to see him out. As Tessa hugged her brother goodbye, Harrison caught a look of loneliness cross her face. Guess it must all be a bit daunting for her, he figured. Then he thought about the shearing shed and felt an angry protectiveness of the Mathisons. Tessa could cause some trouble by hanging out with Brendan McKenzie, he thought as he stalked back into the house.

When Ryan had gone Tessa washed up the cups while Cally and Harrison wiped. Knowing he had to make an effort, he cleared his throat. 'Thanks for coming,' he said when the table had been wiped down and everything put away. 'Come on. I'll take you to your room and show you where everything is. Then Cally can tell you about School of the Air. It's probably changed a bit since your day!'

'I appreciate this, Tessa,' Harrison said, as they stood outside the hangar the next morning. During the previous evening and after observing Tessa's warmth towards Cally, he'd decided to make an effort with her. Cally hung onto her every word and it was the first time he'd seen her enjoy another woman's company other than Peggy and Violet's. As much as he hated to admit it, Tessa might be good for Cally.

'It's fine. I'm happy to do it. We'll get along great, won't we?' Tessa called to Cally.

'Yeah, Dad, don't worry.' Cally was under the wing of the plane, once again checking the fuel.

Harrison turned back to Tessa. 'Have you got any more questions? Anything you need to know?'

'No, I think you went through everything last night. Anyway, Cally knows the run of the place. Honestly, we'll be okay.'

'Okay, then.' Harrison reached out to pat her shoulder, but she leaned to one direction and his arm went around her shoulders.

'Ah, sorry,' she mumbled and her face flushed. Harrison grinned, dipping his glittery hat before turning to Cally.

'So I'll see you in a few days, Squirt.' He hugged her, not wanting to let go of this little body who made his life worth living. 'I've left all my numbers on the notepad by the fridge.' With that he climbed into the plane and started the engine.

Cally and Tessa stood at the airstrip and watched until Harrison's 182 Cessna was nothing but a shining silver glint in the sky. Out of the corner of her eye, Tessa could see Cally was holding back tears. She wondered if she should put her arm around the girl, but didn't feel she knew her well enough to show such an obvious sign of affection.

What would Aunty Spider have done? What would her mum have done? If she were Cally, what would Tessa have wanted? The answer was simple: hug Cally. She awkwardly put her hand on Cally's shoulder. 'Come on, let's go and do something. Why don't you show me your horses?'

Cally nodded. She swallowed and threw her shoulders back. 'They're in the house paddock. Come and meet Megs.' As they strolled over, Cally waved to a couple of men who were slowly driving out of the shed in a battered ute. 'That's Robby and Pete – they work for Dad, or at least, they work for the company and Dad is their boss. There's another couple of old guys around, too.' She turned to Tessa. 'Do you remember old Joe, the horse breaker?'

'Yeah I do. I talked to him briefly at Aunty Spider's funeral. Old Joe is almost like a fixture of the Nullarbor! I can remember loving it when he came over to Danjar Plains. He always had a pocketful of lollies and he'd spend ages with us, telling horse stories. But we got rid of the last of the horses just before I went away to school. Except for Bonnie – she belonged to us kids – but she's dead now. Anyway, once we did that, Joe stopped coming.'

'He's still got lollies. Dad tells him not to give them to me, but he sneaks me some now and then.' Cally smiled. 'Joe's working for Dad. Just doing odd jobs, I think, 'cos he's getting too old to break horses.'

Tessa waved to the men as they drove past. She was slightly relieved there would be other adults around. Otherwise it would be just Cally and a million miles of no one.

'It would be nice to see Joe again. Now, tell me about Megs. That's a lovely name for a horse.'

'She was my mum's. Mum named her after her mum, my nana.'

'Well, she must be pretty special, then. Is she a chestnut?'

'Palomino. Dad looked for ages to find the perfect horse for Mum after I was born. She always told the story of a palomino she had when she was a kid – they were best friends, always out in the paddocks, getting up to mischief. Well, that was what Dad told me. I don't actually remember the story.'

'Oh! I think I remember Megs! Is she the one your mum used to ride when she was competing at the Muster? She used to ride in the barrel races, didn't she, your mum?'

'You remember Mum?' Cally stopped and faced Tessa with an odd expression.

'Yeah, I do. I used to ride, too. Been a few too many years for me to want to get back in the saddle, though. Haven't got the right boots, either.' She grinned wryly, sticking out her foot to display her muddy sneaker.

'We've probably got some boots here you could borrow. I'll have a look when we get back to the house. Can you tell me about Mum?'

Hunger, Tessa thought. *That's what it is – a hunger to hear about her mother.*

'Well, I can tell you vague recollections. It's been a long time. Yeah, I can, but let's see Megs first. See if I remember her as well as I think I do.'

Cally grinned. She began to skip a little. 'Ay-up, Ay-up,' she called.

Tessa looked across the paddock. She couldn't see anything. 'Lord, that's another thing I'd forgotten about. I feel like I'm learning everything all over again. I used to do that too; call them in. Dad taught us a different call. Something like, "Way-yoy, Way-yoy."'

'Doesn't matter what you use,' Cally said. She looked into the rubbish bin near the fence. 'Just so long as the sound carries a long way and the animal knows it's going to get a treat when it gets here. It's a training thing,' she added knowledgeably before calling again, a saucepan full of oats now in her hand. 'Look, here they come.'

Tessa heard the horses before she saw them. The snorts and whinnies gave them away, but the first animal she saw was a young Hereford heifer. The calf pushed her way out of the bush and came running towards Cally, tossing her head.

Cally laughed. 'This is Rusty. She was rusty-red when she was born. Her mum didn't want her, so I fed her from when she was a baby.'

Rusty thrust her head towards Cally and bellowed again.

The noise was so loud Tessa felt the ground vibrate under her feet. 'Oh Rusty, I think you've just about deafened me!' She reached out to rub Rusty's head and then spied the horses coming behind. It was easy to pick out Megs.

The three mounts nodded their heads, trying to get their share of oats. All the time, Cally talked softly to them, showering two of the animals with kisses and pats.

'So this is Megs. Dad gave her to me when Mum died. She's my best friend. And this one is Whiskey.' She kissed Megs and Whiskey again on the nose as she introduced them and then held out her hand to the piebald. 'This one is a bad-tempered little so-and-so, and only Dad can handle him. Got to watch him 'cos he bites, even when you're feeding him. Dad called him Snickers 'cos he's a little bit nutty.'

Tessa burst out laughing. 'Well, Snickers, I'm pleased to meet you. But you should never bite the hand that feeds you!' She reached out and patted the other two. Rusty bellowed again.

'Oh, settle, petal,' Cally said, rubbing her cheek. 'You just want all the attention.'

'Do you ride often?'

'Every day, if there's time. But there are heaps of other jobs to do - and school work.' She screwed up her nose. 'I like to get tea for Dad. He works so hard and it's not fair if he has to do all the work outside as well as the housework. I try and help as much as I can.'

'I'm sure you do. But now you've mentioned that school work, we should probably think about starting it. Your dad told me you'd try to get out of it, if I let you.' She looked at her watch. 'Come on, it's almost nine. You'd better go and fire up that computer or whatever it is you do to learn.'

'Only if I have to,' Cally groaned.

'You have to,' Tessa confirmed. 'We'll do the fun stuff and talk about your mum later.'

Here it was the end of three days. Harrison was due back first thing in the morning - he'd rung to say he was in Kalgoorlie and was leaving at first light. Cally was excited and Tessa had to admit she was looking forward to seeing him, too. She wasn't sure why. Especially when she had Brendan to daydream about.

Tessa set the table as Cally put some sausages on a plate and mashed the potatoes. Tessa thought they had got along well; she'd told the girl everything she could remember about her mum and Cally had hung on every word. When she'd gone to bed, Tessa had made sure she'd kept herself busy, to try to keep the longing for a drink at bay, so she had jumped onto the computer and researched IVF treatment. She had a heap of information for when she saw Ryan next.

She'd also spent hours trawling through the photo albums and newspapers she'd brought with her, but to no avail. There was nothing to help her identify the jewellery.

Now she felt she had Ryan and Marni sorted, the two rings had taken over her thoughts. She'd looked at them every night, holding them and turning them over and over, willing them to talk, to tell her who they belonged to, what their story was. Had Aunty Spider had another love? Or did they relate back to 'the secret'?

Apart from the family shots, the photo albums had contained only pictures showing the opening up of the station land on the Nullarbor. And as interesting as it was to read about the Afghan camel trains carting supplies and equipment to help develop the land, the newspapers hadn't contained any more information, other than a history. Spider's name hadn't been mentioned in any of the papers she'd looked through, nor the family name or that of the station. Zilch.

Tessa now knew that the cameleers had carted wool from the stations – all the stations, so that would have included her family's – down to the coast, near Esperance. The wool was floated out on barges to the ships and went to market by sea.

It made shifting wool by road train look fairly easy. People's ingenuity was amazing back then, she'd decided.

The previous night, Tessa had sat outside after Cally had gone to bed and watched the moon rise, trying to imagine what it would be like to be a pioneer of the Nullarbor or a cameleer. The newspapers had said the camel was the best vehicle for carting things. Their humps and long necks created all sorts of spots to tie the goods down and they could carry up to eight hundredweight. Not knowing how much that was, she'd looked it up and found it was more than four hundred kilos in today's measurements. It seemed the camels were really nothing but a walking road train! They were easy to teach and majestic – if slightly bad-tempered.

'Tessa,' Cally's cautious tone interrupted her thoughts.

'Hmm?'

'You know the Muster is coming up in April?'

'Sure do. If I remember correctly, you've talked about not much else since I've been here. There's only two more months to wait!'

Cally slid into her seat and squeezed tomato sauce onto her sausages.

'I don't know how you can eat that when you could have gravy,' Tessa teased.

'You know what I think?' Cally asked, looking serious.

'Nope, but I'm sure you'll tell me. You're not exactly shy about speaking your mind.' She grinned, remembering Cally's yelled instructions about keeping her heels down and relaxing while Tessa attempted a slow walk around the yard on Whiskey's back. She'd tried to remember everything she'd learned as a child about riding horses but, afterwards, Tessa had to disagree with the old saying 'It's like riding a bike – you never forget how to do it'. She'd felt nervous, like she was a million miles from the ground and completely out of control. She hadn't stayed on the mare's back for long. There was something just too scary about sitting on a moving mountain of muscle with a mind of its own.

'I think you're running away from something.'

Tessa stiffened, amazed that an eleven-year-old kid could be so intuitive.

She took a sip of water. 'You know what I think?'

A small smile played around Cally's lips. 'Nope, but I'm sure you'll tell me!'

'Cheeky. I think you wanted to ask me something about the Muster, so you should.'

Cally turned serious again.

'I haven't got anything to wear.'

'Ah.' Tessa took a scoop of the mashed potato. 'But why do you need to wear something flash? It's just the Muster. From what I remember, everyone wears jeans and shirts.'

191

'None of my shirts fit.' Cally flushed as she indicated to her chest.

'Oh. Got you. Right. Well, that obviously means a shopping trip is in order, yeah? How about we check out the internet tonight and see if we can find something that suits. I'm sure some of the clothing companies mail out.'

'Dad usually gets Peggy to take me shopping when we're in Kal or he'll take me and sit outside until I'm finished.'

'Sounds like a dad! Well, eat up! Then we'll see if we can find some clothes that will make you Princess Cowgirl of the Nullarbor Muster. Thank goodness your internet is faster than the one at Danjar Plains!'

Cally giggled.

Two hours later, printed-out pages covered the table. There was a look of excitement on Cally's face.

'Don't move,' said Tessa as she ran the measuring tape under Cally's armpits and fastened it just under her breasts.

'Don't tickle!'

Tessa wrote down the measurement and checked the sizing on the printout. 'Okay, I think you're a size eight in this shirt and you could probably get a size ten in that fleecy jumper, because you've still got heaps to grow. What colour did you want?'

'I love that purple check shirt and white jumper, but the colour isn't very practical for out here.'

'What about the dark pink one? It will go beautifully against your dark hair.'

'Will that go with the shirt?'

'Of course. Trust me! You've got the best fashionista on the Nullarbor helping you. You should see my wardrobe! I wanted to shop at Harrods when I was in London, but it was too expensive. That's one of the places where Princess Mary shops, you know.'

Cally made the appropriate noises and turned back to the computer screen and looked again at what they were going to purchase. She drew in a breath and smiled. 'Wow,' she said softly. 'I don't need to shop at wherever you just said. These are gorgeous.'

'Come on you. You'd better get to bed otherwise your father will be very cranky with me when he gets home.'

'I've missed him.'

'I bet you have. You'll be the first one to hear the plane tomorrow! But it will be nice to have him back. Night, Cally.'

'Night, Tessa. And thanks.' She stooped and gave Tessa a hug.

She hugged her back tightly.

Tessa watched as a kid on the brink of adulthood padded off in her teddy-bear pyjamas. Still so innocent. She hoped that the innocence was never touched, never broken. She sighed and went to turn the kettle on for a cup of tea before bed.

*

Sitting on the edge of the mattress, Tessa once again took out the rings.

There was a soft knock on the door. 'Can I come in?' Cally asked.

'Sure.'

'Oh, wow! They're beautiful!' Cally sat down beside Tessa.

'Mmm, they are. There's a story behind them, but I don't know what it is.'

'Were they Aunty Spider's?'

'I wish I knew. I found them at her house.'

'Aunty Spider was so cool. She was like a really tough old outback lady with a bit of gypsy in her.'

Tessa stopped as she thought about that. 'You know,' she said slowly, 'you're right. Gypsy. That's a really good word. Not that she ever went anywhere. But it was like she travelled to heaps of places in her mind and never told any of us about it.' Tessa talked softly to herself while Cally waited without interrupting.

'Anyway,' Cally said after a moment, 'I just wanted to say thanks again.'

'Oh, sweetie, you're very welcome. I hope you like the clothes as much, when they get here.'

'Night.'

'Night.' She looked back down at the rings. Gently tossing them in her palm, she walked to the window and looked out on the moonlit landscape. She thought again about the word 'gypsy' then stared once more at the two gold bands.

Chapter 18

Twenty minutes earlier, Cally had heard the noise of a faraway engine and had rushed from the school room to scan the sky. Tessa had gone after her but was still searching for the plane when Cally had pointed and yelled: 'There he is!' Following Cally's line of sight Tessa spotted a minute speck. Slowly it grew bigger and bigger.

Now, the wings wiggled from side to side and a beautiful giggle erupted from Cally. She put her arms above her head and waved them from side to side. The plane wings wobbled even more frantically. 'See, Dad's saying hello!' she called above the noise.

The Cessna swooped towards the end of the runway and came in to land, throwing up a cloud of dust. Tessa glanced over at Cally, who was still jumping up and down and waving in excitement.

Harrison taxied over to the parking bay in front of the hangar and shut down the engine. The propeller jerked to a halt.

Cally rushed over to the plane. 'Hi, Dad,' she shouted and threw her arms around Harrison before his feet had even touched the ground.

Tessa couldn't hear what he said, but his tone was tender. She slung her overnight bag over her shoulder then picked up the box of newspapers and photo albums. It was much lighter – the papers that hadn't held any clues were now in Cally's chook shed, making nests for the layers.

'Hi, Tessa,' Harrison called. 'Ready for home?'

'Hi, Harrison! Where do you want these?' she said, gesturing towards her luggage.

'I'll stick them in the hold. Cally, you going to come for a fly?' he asked.

'Yeah! Do you need to refuel?'

'Nope, I've still got three-quarters of a tank. Let Tessa in the front – I'll take her for a quick sightsee as a thank you. In you hop.'

Cally climbed over the front chair and settled in the back, clipping her seatbelt on like a pro. Tessa felt irrationally pleased to be promoted to the front seat, and found herself blushing, just a little.

'Everyone right?' called Harrison, shutting his door, and checking Tessa's side and her seatbelt. When the chorus of 'yes' came back, he hit the key and the plane shook as the engine kicked into life.

The warmth of Harrison's body as he leaned close made Tessa react without thinking. He smelled so good and, really, he was quite handsome, if you ignored the fact he was forty – sixteen years older than her, practically ancient and wearing a ridiculous sparkly hat.

His eyes caught her, this time, as he made contact to check she was okay. They were a sapphire blue and had a hypnotic feel to them. Tessa found it hard to look away.

Oh, for fuck's sake, Tessa, she berated herself. *It's not so long since you've been in male company that you need to go weak at the knees just because some old fart might give good cuddles and smells nice!* She reddened, hoping no one could read her mind. Sometimes it felt as though your innermost thoughts could be heard in these little planes.

Harrison turned them towards Balladonia and Danjar Plains to the south-east. With her nose pushed against the plastic, Tessa drank in the sights. She couldn't help but smile because she felt so free.

'See over there?' Harrison leaned towards her, shouting over the noise of the engine and pointing out the window. 'That's Newman's Rocks.'

She looked where he was indicating but was distracted by his hands. Rough, calloused hands with dirt ingrained in the skin, but she was sure they were gentle. *Stop it, NOW.*

She concentrated on looking to where he was pointing. A large granite rock jutting out of the otherwise flat landscape came into view. She could see water in the crevices and a couple of camper trailers parked under some trees.

'Are they allowed to camp there?' she asked.

'Yeah, it's pretty popular 'cos of the water and scenery. On dusk you can see wedge-tailed eagles and kangaroos, emus and all sorts of wildlife coming in to drink. Brumbies come and without a doubt a dingo or two will be hovering in the background looking for some easy pickings. Whether or not the campers ever see them depends on how observant they are.'

Tessa shuddered at the mention of the dingo.

Harrison talked on. 'The Nullarbor seems to be a wild frontier that the grey nomads need to cross and see. Once they've done it, it's almost like they get a feather in their cap or something.' He sounded half-disgusted and half-amused that his backyard was seen as the wild frontier.

A little while on, he spoke again. 'Down there to the right? That's Afghan Rocks. You know the story?'

Tessa looked down. Tall trees surrounded a pool of water. She racked her brains. She couldn't think of any stories about Afghans other than what she'd read in Spider's newspapers. She didn't think she'd even been to the spot. She shook her head. 'I know I might seem ignorant, but even though I spent all my primary school years here, once I left, I only came back on holidays. I wasn't into doing things with the family, more listening to music and stuff. Maybe I missed out on a lot the Nullarbor had to offer.'

'I think it was in 1894, there was a pack train of camels camped at the water hole. Even though it's seasonal, everyone knew they could get water there and so, as the Nullarbor opened up, it was a popular camping spot for all the camel trains and other explorers. Anyway, this camel man wanted to have a bath and went for a dip. But the waterhole was beginning to dry up and the Australian blokes who had pulled up with a bullock team knew it was important to keep the water as clean as they could for the coming summer. Of course, the Afghan bloke had every right to wash himself – as everyone did! But instead of taking a bucket, scooping some water out and then using it, he actually went out into the pool. There of course was some talk it was a religious rite, but the others didn't see it that way.

'One of the bullockers told him to get out, that he was contaminating the water. The Afghan told him to get nicked.

'There was a bit of yelling and what not, then the Afghan threw a stone that hit the other fella in the face. He didn't like that so he took out his gun and shot the bloke. Killed him.'

'Oh yeah, I think I remember Spider telling me something like that. But . . .' She stopped to think. 'Weren't there other Afghans there? And they threw the stones? I seem to remember they were the ones who were killed, but the one who'd gone into the pool was wounded.'

'There's that version too, only he died later.'

Tessa looked back down at the coffee-coloured rocks. They stretched over a large area, acting as a catchment. The plane was so low she could see the reflections of the trees in the water and the small bushes that poked up from little pods of dirt in the middle of the rocks. It was a beautiful area but with a haunted past.

After one more circuit they headed towards Danjar Plains. From the air, Tessa could see the Eyre Highway stretching out into the misty haze of both horizons. She knew that this section of the highway was called the 90-mile straight – a driver didn't have to turn his steering wheel once as he drove the ribbon of blue through seemingly endless low scrubby bush. Tessa could see road trains thundering along and cars pulling caravans.

'So how did you get on with Cally?' Harrison asked.

It seemed the tourist lap was over. Tessa glanced over her shoulder. Cally was sleeping. 'Really well. She's a delight, Harrison. I think we both had fun.'

'That's good.'

'She looks like you.'

'You reckon? Not really, she's so much like Ange.' He turned to check his instruments, but not before pain flickered across his face. There was more to Harrison than met the eye, she decided.

Tessa saw Harrison check his instruments again. He tapped at one of the gauges and she felt her stomach constrict. She was really in a very small plane! He adjusted a couple of things then sat back.

Tessa continued to scan the horizon, then realised she hadn't told Harrison about the clothes.

'Cally really needs some new clothes, Harrison,' she said.

'Does she?'

'Most of her shirts were too small. I've left the website details and what she wants to buy on the fridge in the kitchen. Could you order them when you get home? All you need to do is put your credit-card details in and the company will put them in the mail. But you'll have to do it soon because she'll need them for the Muster.'

'No worries.'

Harrison looked over at her. 'Seems like you've relaxed since you got home. All those lines around your eyes have gone – makes you look younger. Danjar Plains must be good for you, Tessa,' he said, grinning wickedly and patting her knee. Tessa felt a thrill shoot through her. Desperately trying to hide it, she turned back towards the window and stared down at the ground below.

A short time later, they began the descent to Danjar Plains. Harrison turned to look at Tessa. 'Thanks for organising the clothes,' he said quietly. 'She really needs someone to do it with her. I'm not much good at that. I didn't even know.' He turned back to the business of landing, before Tessa could say anything.

The laughter around the kitchen table was how Tessa remembered it when she was a child. Ryan was animatedly telling a story he'd heard on ABC radio and her mother was laughing at his antics. Her dad was leaning back with a bit of a grin – even Marni cracked a smile.

Yes, it was good to be home, even if it was only for a short time.

'I don't believe a word you're saying,' Tessa interjected. Ryan's story had got completely out of control.

'Oh, don't you? Well, next time you're on the computer, you get onto the Regional Drive WA's website and have a listen – they said they'd put it up as a podcast.'

'I'll probably die waiting with the download speed here! Oh, now that reminds me, how come Cally's internet for school work is so much quicker than ours?' Tessa asked.

'Probably got something to do with funding for School of the Air.'

'But what about checking stock or wool prices, using it as a marketing tool to get the best sales and that sort of thing?'

'Tessa, love,' her mother said, shaking her head. 'We are simple farmers. We grow wool and meat. As farmers, it doesn't matter how much we try, we are price takers, not setters. We're always going to be at the whim of world market prices for wool, the Australian dollar and what the abattoirs are paying for meat. We are at the bottom of the food chain, so to speak.'

Tessa felt indignant. Her hard-working family wasn't able to have choices? That seemed so very wrong. Not able to think of anything to say, she reverted to one of the sayings she'd always used as a child when trying to shock her parents. 'Well, that sucks!'

The table erupted into laughter again.

Tessa pulled the sheets back on her childhood bed and slipped between them. It was hot again and the mozzies were buzzing at her window. She hoped none had managed to penetrate the flyscreen. Whoever thought station nights were silent had obviously never slept with a single mosquito buzzing in their ear.

A book open on her lap, she leaned back against the bedhead and tried to read. The words weren't making sense. She was conflicted. Harrison had showed a different side today. It was clear he loved his child to distraction and for some reason she assumed he would be like that with a wife.

This has to stop. Now. Think about Brendan.

That didn't work either, so she looked around for another diversion. The bookshelf above her desk – she got out of bed to take a closer look. Running her fingers across the spines of the books, she stopped at one and tapped it. It was a thick glossy book about Australian native animals. She'd won it in Year 7 for the most improved in her School of the Air class. She could still remember how excited she'd been when it had come in the mail and how reverently she had turned each page, marvelling at the beautiful photos and information on animals she saw almost daily.

Spider had been so proud of her.

But all of that was before Kendra. Before her world crumbled. Lord, what a fuck-up she was.

Pulling the book from the shelf, she cracked it open. Inside, just where she'd left it on the day that Kendra had been killed, was a hand-written page of lyrics. She'd put them in this book because of the contradiction. How she could achieve so highly, but how her life had slumped to such a low.

When she'd written these words out, she had truly believed Slim Dusty had written them for her.

Slim's music had been such a presence in her childhood. She remembered singing along to his songs as she drove around the station or travelled to Norseman or Kalgoorlie with her parents. And the shearers were always playing Slim on their tape deck in the shed.

The lyrics of his songs had struck a chord deep within her, none more so than 'The Biggest Disappointment'. Tessa related to every word in that song. In her mind, she could still hear the opening guitar twang and Slim's gravelly voice reaching into her soul, singing about her and what she already knew. She knew she was the biggest disappointment to her family. She didn't seem to fit in, just like that twisted branch Slim Dusty sang about, and she certainly hadn't been the girl Aunty Spider had hoped she'd be. There. It was clear. The song had been written for her.

As Tessa traced those words with her fingers and replayed the song in her head, she reflected on all her failures. All her mistakes came flooding back and the light-heartedness of the evening left her. Slim had been right or, at least, the song had. Did she really think she could get away from the ghosts of her past out here? This is where they mostly were, for goodness sake!

Tessa slumped down to the floor, staring.

'The biggest disappointment in the family was me,' she whispered.

Chapter 19

The smell of sandalwood hit Tessa as soon as she opened the door of Aunty Spider's house. Her throat tightened and her eyes filled with tears. She hadn't slept the night before - not after recalling what a failure she was. She had gone over and over every single mistake she had ever made. From tiny ones, like leaving the gate of the chook yard open so a fox or dingo got in, to hanging out with the wrong crowd at school. Then there were the London mistakes. Tessa knew she was going to have to keep herself very busy today - she was too fragile for her own good. And that's why she felt Brendan was more her style. He was like her. Bad and good all mixed in. There was no way in the world Harrison would want to touch tarnished goods like her. He was a kind, caring person. One with values. Best to banish any thoughts she had, because Harrison wouldn't be thinking along the same lines.

Last night, she'd thrown herself onto the bed and wept quietly, so she didn't alert her parents. But once the crying had subsided, the craving for a drink had been so intense that she'd paced the perimeter of the room as if it was a prison cell. She couldn't go out and grab a beer from the fridge or pour herself a glass of wine, no matter how much she wanted to. She'd worked too hard to keep away from it. But she'd had to keep moving so she didn't succumb.

Realistically, she knew she should be celebrating today – she hadn't given in to the desire for alcohol. She'd stayed strong. But Tessa knew her demons were too close to the surface to allow for anything as frivolous as celebration. A 'celebration' always pulled her back towards the booze. This whole sorry saga started with alcohol and it just always seemed natural to return to it. Yes, that was something else she'd worked out while she'd been here.

She dumped her overnight bag on the floor. Ryan was behind her, carrying a box and some frozen meals Peggy had cooked – care packages.

'Would you like a coffee?' she asked, remembering she had the info on IVF in her bag.

'That would be good,' he answered, his eyes sweeping over the lounge room.

Tessa could almost hear him thinking: *What's changed since I was here last? Has she moved anything, got rid of something that reminded me of Aunty Spider?* But she knew it was without malice. If the shoe was on the other foot, she'd be doing exactly the same thing – looking for what had changed.

Instead of asking, Ryan just said: 'I'll put the jug on if you want. You can throw your bag in the bedroom.'

'Okay.' Tessa moved slowly through the house, peering into each room. What she was checking for she wasn't sure – it was not like anything would have moved in the few days she'd been gone. Maybe she was reacquainting herself, trying to get the feel of the house again. And she was stalling: she wanted control of her emotions before she sat down to talk to Ryan.

The shrill sound of the telephone cut through the quiet and made Tessa jump. Two rings, three, four.

Ryan stuck his head out of the kitchen. 'You going to get that?'

She went to answer it. 'Who would be ringing me here?'

'Ah, Mum and Dad, maybe?' Ryan looked at her strangely as she lifted the receiver. 'Not that unusual to get a phone call out here, you dag!'

'Hello?'

'Tessa, it's Brendan.'

A thrill shot through her. Of course! She'd given him Aunty Spider's phone number the weekend they'd met up in Balladonia.

'Hello! How are you?' She glanced sideways to see if Ryan was still watching, but he'd disappeared back into the kitchen. She was sure he'd be listening, though. He'd be sure to notice the change in her voice from wary to . . . what? Sultry?

Tessa! She laughed at herself, feeling the black mood begin to lift.

'Been trying to call you for a few days. Wondered if you'd shot through.'

'No, not at all! I've been looking after Cally for Harrison, over at their place. He was in Adelaide for a few days.'

'Right. Well, I'm pleased you haven't gone. I'm heading over your way tomorrow. Can I come and say g'day?'

'Of course you can. It would be lovely to see you.' She tried to keep the excitement out of her voice. There. A visit from Brendan would banish any unwanted thoughts of older men and their hugs.

'Righto. See you in the afternoon sometime.'

'Do you know how to get to Violet's place?'

'Yep. Been there once or twice. I'll catch you tomorrow.'

'See you then.' Tessa replaced the receiver, a bubble of nerves in her tummy.

'Who was that?' Ryan called, trying and failing to sound nonchalant.

'Brendan. He's coming to visit.'

From the kitchen there was only the sound of a spoon hitting something ceramic as it stirred coffee. Then Ryan appeared with two mugs. 'Here you are.'

'Thanks.'

Ryan made himself comfortable on the couch. 'You know, there're a few people around here who would say Brendan's bad news.'

Tessa closed her eyes and held up her hand. 'Dad has already told me. I'm old enough to make my own mistakes, Ryan. Goodness knows, I've made enough already.'

He talked over the top of her. 'I haven't made up my mind about him yet. He *seems* okay, but I don't know him well. His family are a bit strange, though.'

Tessa digested this. She nodded to show she'd heard him then changed the subject. 'I did a bit of research on IVF treatment while I was over with Cally,' she said, handing him the envelope. 'I hope you don't think I'm interfering. I just want to try to help somehow.'

Tessa watched as Ryan's expression became neutral. She hurried on. 'There are heaps of forums on the net for people in a similar situation to you guys. Marni might find them good to read, to help her understand she's not alone. One of the things I learned was that couples can feel really isolated, like they're the only ones going through it. I've put the best web addresses in there, along with the name of which doctor I think might be the best. She's got glowing reviews and is based at Hollywood Hospital, up in Perth. They've got a fertility clinic there.'

Ryan looked at the envelope and stuffed it in his back pocket. 'Thanks,' was all he said.

'Anyway, it may or may not be of some help.'

'Thanks.'

They finished their coffee and Ryan headed back out to work. But half an hour later, Tessa noticed Ryan's ute parked a little way down the track under a tree. The glare of white paper reflected in the sunlight. It looked like he was reading the information. She allowed herself a small smile.

Later, she wanted to curl into a ball and sleep forever. The initial excitement of Brendan's impending visit had worn off, as had her pleasure at helping her brother. Once again, all she could hear reverberating in her head was Slim Dusty's voice.

She stomped through the house and went outside. The sun was shining, and even though the day was hot and most of the wildlife was still and silent, the magpies were warbling. Maybe a walk and some fresh air would help.

Tessa called to Dozer then set off down the track without waiting to see if he appeared. Shortly, she heard his soft padding and the occasional puff, and knew he was just behind.

So many conflicting thoughts were colliding in her brain, it was hard to work out which to focus on first. The rings, her future, Brendan, Aunty Spider's house. They were all meshing together. But after walking about a kilometre she had made a decision. She would tackle Aunty Spider's writing desk today – that would keep her mind active and focused. And it would get her closer to finishing the task her aunt had set. Then she could leave.

She turned and headed towards home.

On top of the desk, Tessa placed the two rings. She looked at them for a long time. Taking a deep breath, she opened the fold-down lid before seating herself in front of the desk. She wriggled to get comfortable, knowing it was unlikely to happen. She'd spent hours sitting on the hard, vinyl chairs, talking with Aunty Spider. This one would be just as uncomfortable as its mates that were gathered around the kitchen table.

Tessa took in the row of eight pigeonholes. They were filled with envelopes, some yellowing, some crisp and new. She took a deep breath and started on the first pigeonhole.

She sorted and filed into piles: bills from stores in Kalgoorlie, Norseman and Esperance. Some dated back to 1934. Why on earth had Spider kept them?

The second pigeonhole was full of old letters. Tessa put them to one side to read later.

The third pigeonhole was as boring as the first. But the fourth one made Tessa stop for a moment. It was full of birthday cards Spider had received from Tessa.

Slowly she opened the first one and saw her own childish writing tracing over her mother's dots, wishing Aunty Spider a very happy birthday.

It was dated 1988. She would have been two! The next was from 1989, and so on right up until the present day.

The last one she had sent was still in its envelope. Tessa read the words and felt her stomach curl.

Dear Aunty Spider,
Happy birthday from the UK! I hope you have a great day.
Love Tessa.

Bloody hell! She hadn't even been bothered to write a decent letter to her favourite aunt on her birthday! 'What a selfish bitch,' she muttered, throwing the card onto the rubbish pile.

When she'd finished cleaning out the pigeonholes she started on the drawers. The first one held pens and pencils, erasers, notebooks, and all the normal paraphernalia needed to run a small office. The second was full of telephone books and cheque books. She put them aside – they'd be needed by the executor, whoever that was.

The third drawer was empty. Tessa shut it with a bang. As she did so she realised it felt heavier than it should. She pulled it open again, right to the end of the runners. A small book lay up against its back wall.

Embossed on the front was '2010'. A diary. From last year.

A diary! She flicked to the first page. A mixture of excitement and hesitation made her tremble. It was one thing to clean out someone's house but something else altogether to read their diary. She glanced at the rings. *How else am I going to find out?* she thought. She began to read.

1 January 2009

Well, well, another year is finished and the new one has started. It's 2 a.m. as I write this and I wonder what the year will hold. The moon is full tonight, so I can see out across the plains. The outlines of the trees, the bushes and road. I can hear the party at the hut beginning to wind down. It's great for Ryan and Marni to be able to invite their friends over and let their hair down. For Marni in particular; I'm sure she finds it lonely out here even though she was brought up on a farm. Being fifty kilometres from town is very different to having to drive four hours to the closest shopping centre. And it's good for them to have friends their own age – not socialising all the time with their parents.

It's so nice to hear fun being had, because sometimes, it seems this station has seen nothing but heartbreak.

I wish I could have convinced Tessa to come home for tonight. To be with us all before she leaves. All I can do is hope that this England phase will be the right move for her. I suspect it will be. But only for a time.

Paul and Peggy seem tired. I wonder how many more years they will have out here? And I wonder how many I will have? Dr Mike told me on the last visit my heart could go at any time. I'm prepared, even though there is so much unfinished business for me here, but as usual I will set things in place – I will get it done, even if I'm not here.

It will be wonderful to see my William again. It's been a long and lonely life without him.

Tessa sat back. This melancholy writing didn't sound at all like her practical, no-nonsense aunty! It unsettled her to think of Spider out here, looking over her home, wondering if she was going to die soon. Wishing for her husband. How lonely.

February 2009

A dry thunderstorm really rattled the countryside tonight. I can smell smoke, but it's coming in on the northerly breeze, so I think it's probably north of the highway.

The days have been unbearably hot – I've found that, as I've got older, the heat bothers me more. I wonder if I should have moved to Esperance like Elsie suggested, or even to Perth to be near her, but I'm sure that would have killed me quicker than living on the land I know. This property runs through my veins and I don't belong anywhere else. And William

*is here, as are Len, George, Edward and Uncle
Sam. I don't think I would like to leave them.*

Tessa found herself nodding as she read that
entry – Spider wouldn't have been happy unless she
was on Danjar Plains.

March 2009

*Tessa rang today. She is leaving for the UK
in two days. I wish she'd have come back to
Danjar Plains before leaving. I'm sure it would
have helped her. I have my reservations about
her going now – not that I would ever tell her.
I wonder if I did the right thing in contacting
Darcy and organising this job for her and Jaz.
Maybe they needed some time apart? I don't
know. But what I do know is she hasn't healed.
I know she relives that night over and over, still,
even all these years later. But to be fair, don't
we all? My Godfather! No one could walk away
from that scene and not have nightmares. But,
Tessa, oh Tessa, you've got to be strong, my love.
You're going to face challenges that will break
down those fragile walls you've built. Don't fall
in with people just because they shower you
with their attention. You are so much better
than that, but I fear you don't realise it yet.*

Tessa sat back, tears rolling down her face. Aunty
Spider knew her better than she knew herself. Just
look at the John Smith incident.

Chapter 20

Tessa heard a car door slam. She ran her hands through her hair, before moving quickly to the door and pulling it open. Brendan smiled at her and she felt her knees go a bit soft.

'Hi,' she said.

'Hi, yourself,' he answered. Tessa felt herself being drawn towards him and by the time she landed at his chest, his mouth was on hers. 'I think I might have missed you,' he growled.

'What? Only might have?' She pulled away and looked up at him coyly. 'What sort of a way is that to greet a girl?'

'Oh, so you don't like my greeting? Well, how about this?' He swung her up into his arms and carried her into the house. Tessa's words became muffled as he pressed her to him. She was distracted by his muscles beneath her hands. She opened her eyes just for a moment and saw his black hair and tanned face. Lord, he was gorgeous.

The dog, perplexed, watched them for a moment then wandered out of the room.

Brendan seemed quite comfortable in the kitchen as he cooked dinner. Tessa had made up the spare bed and was now sitting in the kitchen watching him cook the steak he'd brought. 'Surprisingly she found the smell enticing. After weeks now of eating mostly chops and sausages, she honestly felt that if she never ate red meat again it would be too soon. But somehow her childhood eating habits seemed to be reasserting themselves.

Sipping on her lemonade, she wondered whether she should explain why she wasn't drinking. She decided against it. She really didn't know Brendan that well and who knew if this was just a fling or something more. If it went on for much longer, she would think about telling him.

'Got any bread?' Brendan asked.

'I'll get it.' She went into the laundry where the freezer was, found the hard-frozen loaf and brought it back.

'Spider used to make her own bread,' Brendan noted.

'Yeah, she did. Her bread rolls were to die for,' Tessa agreed. She looked at him. 'How did you know that?'

'I spent a bit of time with her. Met her at the

Muster two years ago and thought she was a bit of a cool chick, so I called in to see her most times I was heading into Balladonia. Think she liked the visits. Old Joe introduced us.'

'Really? Good old Joe!' Tessa thought for a moment. 'But, she never mentioned you in any of her letters?'

Brendan was quiet for a moment, digesting this. 'Oh, well I was definitely here.'

Tessa wondered if he could shed any light on the rings. Had Spider talked to him at all? It would be just like her to pick up a stray, someone who most of the community thought was bad, and befriend them. Spider had a thing about the underdog.

'I've got something to show you,' she said. 'Be back in a moment.'

'Be quick, this steak is almost done. Can't not eat it when it's ready.'

'I found these before I went over to Harrison's,' she called from the lounge.

Back in the kitchen, she opened the box and held it out to him.

'What's this?'

'Well, I assume they're wedding rings, but I don't know who they belong to.'

Brendan took them out and looked at the rings closely. 'They're hand-crafted, I reckon. And old. I can't tell you a date. But they're definitely before the fifties.'

'How do you know that?'

'I've got lots of talents you don't know about yet.'

She let the 'yet' bit pass. 'I thought they were old, too. I mean, they're new in that they've never been worn, and yet someone loved someone else enough to have them made and engraved. Got to be a story there. Did you see this?' She pointed to the inside of one of the bands.

'That's a lot of letters for such a small space – would have taken someone a long time to engrave them,' Brendan agreed. 'Now put them down, this steak isn't going to wait.'

They sat at the table and Tessa told him all about Spider's letter, and how she had to clean out the house and unravel a mystery. 'That's why I feel these rings are so important,' she finally finished. 'And the steak is just divine, by the way. It's melting in my mouth!'

Brendan smiled. 'The amount you've been talking I didn't think you would have had time to taste it.'

Tessa sat back in her chair.

'You're an interesting study, Brendan McKenzie,' she said, narrowing her eyes to examine him. 'A mix of country boy, bad boy and international man of mystery. What *is* your story?'

He laughed loudly. 'That's the first time I've ever been described like that! What can I say? I went to a good boarding school. The house mistresses taught me my manners, my mother taught me to cook and all sorts of other good habits, and I'm an adrenalin junkie And the mystery? Well, a bit of mystery is healthy, don't you think? Wouldn't want you getting bored too soon.' His wink was like an exclamation mark.

In the middle of the night, Tessa got up to go to the toilet and saw the kitchen light was on. Too sleepy to see clearly, she padded towards the glow and pushed open the door.

Brendan glanced up from the table and the book he was reading. 'Sorry, did I wake you?'

'Nah. Wondered where you were. Night.' She stumbled back to bed. As she was settling down she thought she heard the click of the writing desk opening, but was asleep before it registered.

The next morning, Brendan kissed her goodbye. 'I won't be around for a month or so,' he said through the window of the ute. 'I've got some jobs to do in the city. Then I'm heading over east to see my Aunty. Mum's sister. She's turning seventy and I want to be there. But,' he said tapping her nose, 'I'll be back in time for the Muster.'

'Of course you can.' Tessa gathered all of her strength to hide her disappointment. A month? She wasn't sure if they had an 'arrangement' or not!

'So I'll see you there?'

'Absolutely.'

'And I'll ring if I can, but I might be off-air for the first part of the trip.'

She wanted to ask him what he'd be doing, but was wary of sounding too much like a prying wife, so she just smiled and nodded, even though she could feel loneliness building up inside her. *He hasn't even gone yet*, she chided herself.

'Well, I'll see you at the Muster, then.'

He left in a cloud of dust, Tessa staring after him. That was just the Nullarbor way, she thought, as she went back inside. No designated meeting time, just 'be there and I'll find you'. *Well*, she thought huffily. *I might find someone else first.*

Then she cried.

Tessa stood at the writing desk, looking for any signs something had moved. As she'd opened it after Brendan left, the click had jogged her memory. She was sure she'd heard it last night, but why would Brendan be looking in here? And nothing seemed to be missing or disturbed. It was a good thing Tessa had finished clearing it out because otherwise there would have been no way of knowing. With the writing desk cleaned out, Tessa was sitting on the floor, reading over some of the letters between Elsie and Spider. And the diaries! She'd laughed so much her cheekbones hurt and once, when Spider was describing a shearing time antic, Tessa had actually cried tears of amusement. Spider really had a way with words.

A knock on the door startled Tessa. 'Come in,' she called from the lounge room.

The door opened and her sister-in-law entered. Surprised, Tessa shot to her feet. 'Marni, hi! What a nice surprise. Would you like a cup of tea?'

'Hello, Tessa. No, I won't stop, I just wanted to thank you for all the information you sent home with Ryan.' Marni twisted her hands and Tessa felt she had to relieve the tension somehow.

'Come in and sit down. I'll put the kettle on anyway.' She walked out, not giving the other woman a chance to answer.

'I looked at some of those websites,' her sister-in-law called through the doorway.

'That's great. Were they helpful?'

The silence stretched so long that Tessa stuck her head back into the lounge and saw the poor girl with tears on her cheeks. 'Oh, crap.'

She held Marni while she cried.

'I didn't know anyone else could feel the same way,' Marni hiccupped. 'It was such a relief to find out I wasn't crazy – I thought I was, you know. Mad with envy, mad with desire and failure all at the same time. I don't know why I never thought to use the internet and look it up. It just never occurred to me.'

'Well, I guess I'm so used to using it for work and everything, to me it was the obvious place to start,' Tessa said gently. 'The online world isn't a huge thing out here and I understand that. I'm pleased I was able to help in a little way.'

'I've talked to a couple of girls on those forums who have been in the same situation. It's been good to hear about their experiences. It's almost like a whole new world has opened up.'

'Has Ryan read any of the forums?'

'Yeah, and I think it's done him some good too. It's like we both understand each other's feelings a bit more. Finally.'

'That's great news, Marni. Really it is.'

There was a lull for a while, while Marni wiped her eyes, then Tessa said: 'Now, how about that cup of tea?'

Marni laughed weakly. 'That was always Spider's cure for tears or emotion of any sort, so I guess we'd better.'

Cups of tea made, they went and sat out on the verandah. 'To Aunty Spider,' Tessa said, raising her mug.

'To Aunty Spider,' Marni echoed.

'Isn't it funny that this house is still hearing the innermost thoughts of others, even though she's not here? I wonder what these walls would tell us if they could,' Tessa mused as she sipped her drink.

'Too many things and probably things we wouldn't want to know.'

'Yeah, you're probably right.' Tessa smiled, thinking that Marni's words were almost identical to Paul's a few nights back. Her hand strayed to pat the dog, who'd slipped beneath her chair the moment she'd sat down. 'But I've just got a feeling that there's something here, some story about Aunty Spider that we all need to know.'

Marni raised her eyebrows. 'If she wanted us to know, she would have told us. Don't you remember how straight down the line she was?'

Tessa felt a surge of jealousy rise up as she realised for seven whole years, while Tessa had been studying, working and refusing to return to Danjar Plains, Marni had had Aunty Spider to herself. Well, Marni hadn't been here that long, but whoever had wanted Spider, could have had her. *It's your own fault. You never wanted to come home*, the soft rational voice said. Not after the accident. Until now. Not for Christmas, not for anything. Imagine how that would have felt for everyone else.

The demon voice never spoke. It just *felt*. Irrationally.

Anger.

Envy.

Rage.

Loss.

Tessa almost didn't hear Marni talking. 'I remember a CWA Household Hints book gave me the idea to soak old tea bags in metho and use them as firelighters. I was so happy with myself, thinking Spider would be pleased with my thrifty ways. That was the sort of thing she was into – you know, boiling the kettle and pouring the hot water into a Thermos, so she didn't have to boil it again for the rest of the day.'

Marni grinned. 'But she just looked at me with a bit of a smile and said: "Oh, fiddlesticks, girl. This is how you light a fire." Then she got paper, leaves and some kindling and showed me how I should light a fire. She wasn't having a bar of the tea bags and metho!'

In spite of her jealousy, Tessa laughed. She could hear the conversation and imagine the self-consciousness Marni would have felt.

But in the end her envy got the better of her. She didn't want to talk about Aunty Spider with her sister-in-law anymore. Without looking at Marni, she got up. 'Well, I'd better get on and keep cleaning this house out. I've hardly done a thing since I got back from Harrison's.'

Marni looked surprised, then wary as she put down her cup. 'Of course. I'm sorry I've held you up.'

'No no, not at all. But the quicker I get this done, the sooner I'll be out of here,' Tessa said, her expression deadpan.

Marni tried to smile as she made her way down the steps towards the car. 'See you later.'

'Bye,' Tessa answered. Then she stomped inside, furious with Marni for causing new feelings to surface. She certainly hadn't felt like that when Brendan had mentioned he'd popped in to visit her aunty.

But Tessa was even angrier with herself for letting something so trivial upset her. She was sure her rudeness had just destroyed whatever good she'd done for her relationship with Marni by helping out with the IVF information.

'I'm so bloody illogical at the moment,' she muttered. 'What is my problem?'

The soft rational voice spoke again: *Aren't the living more important?*

'Oh shut up.' Tessa threw the mug she was holding. It smashed against the kitchen wall.

Chapter 21

Tessa flicked over another page of a newspaper dated 1944, but there was nothing except stories of World War Two woe and sadness. With a sigh she tossed the paper on the pile to go into the rubbish. Just what was she looking for? She had no idea.

It had been two weeks since Brendan had left and, true to his word, he'd called a couple of times. The conversations had flowed easily and Tessa found herself missing him more after each call. She'd put the desk incident down to being so tired.

Cally had rung too. Her new clothes had arrived in the post and she was beyond excited. 'Take a photo!' Tessa had encouraged her. 'Email it to Mum and Dad and I'll see it when I go up there.'

The photo had duly arrived and now Tessa had it pinned on the fridge door. Making a small difference to Cally's world left her feeling satisfied.

She'd wanted to ask how Harrison was but, having already made up her mind he was off limits, she wouldn't let herself.

'What do you think, Dozer?' she asked, getting up.

There was no response. Tessa watched him for a moment. He was breathing, so she knew he was alive. He just hadn't heard her, poor deaf old sod.

She flitted from one room to the next, knowing she would have to tackle the last one pretty soon. Aunty Spider's bedroom. She'd run out of ways to procrastinate. This would be the most emotional clear-out of all for her. Once she had finished it, the house would be done and there would be no reason for her to stay. But there was also nowhere for her to go, and she wasn't sure she was quite ready to leave. The developing relationship with Brendan felt good to her and she didn't want it to stop yet. Even if he had disappeared for a month.

Rather than think about anything else, she went back to the newspapers. She started on one dated 15 September 2006. This was a farm paper, not a city one. Its headline read: 'Government to spend $19 million on camel cull'. Tessa knew that camels on the northern part of Danjar Plains had caused her dad more fencing problems than anything else, so that policy seemed like a good one.

'Bounty for foxes announced'. That too seemed like an excellent idea.

She turned the pages and her eyes were drawn to a small article that had been ringed in red. 'Horse thefts across the Nullarbor cost station owners'.

She read on:

Twenty-seven stock horses were reported stolen last week, 17 from Jimantra Station on the trans-rail line. Another ten horses were reported stolen from Nickel Downs, 350 kilometres north-west of Norseman.

The theft of the horses, which were worth nearly $20,000, has delayed shearing for the stations affected. Some of the terrain is only accessible by horse and will now have to be mustered on foot with dogs.

Anyone knowing the whereabouts of the horses or with information please contact Dave Burrows at the Stock Squad or Crime Stoppers.

Phone numbers were listed. Tessa tore out the page and placed it on the couch next to her, a small buzz of excitement building. She grabbed the next paper and whipped through it, looking for any marked articles. There was nothing in that one or the next three. She began to think her idea of Aunty Spider leaving newsworthy breadcrumbs was totally off-base.

'Argh!' She threw her head back against the back of the couch and thumped her hands down. It frightened the dog, who whined then slowly got up to come and sit next to her.

'Sorry, Dozer. It's just so bloody frustrating. I'm looking for a needle in a haystack! It would have been better if she'd left a pile of diaries with the answer in each and every one of them.' Then she stopped. Diaries. Of course! She'd seen one already, so there must be more.

She had already searched through the cupboards in the hall and in the small makeshift office in the corner of the lounge, but found nothing. Then she tried the shed outside, but other than a cobweb and dust collection and some rusty old gardening tools, there was nothing of interest there, either.

There wasn't an attic, so that left Spider's bedroom.

As Tessa pushed the door open and stood on the threshold, she shivered. Everything was just the same. There were photos of William on the wall and on the side table. The bed was neatly made, just the way Spider had left it the day she died. A floral blanket was folded at the end.

Tessa hadn't noticed last time she'd raced in, but Spider's slippers were tucked under the bed.

'I feel like I'm invading your space,' she muttered, before moving to the bedside table. There was a half-read novel with a bookmark, and a photo that Tessa hadn't seen before. She picked it up: it was a photo of herself, at her graduation. She looked relaxed, but for the torment in her eyes. She had no idea that Aunty Spider had this in her room but, then again, why would she?

Not wanting to look at it anymore, Tessa quickly put it down and pulled open the first drawer. She carefully checked its contents before moving to the second drawer. Then on she went, to the third, and the fourth. From the bedside table she moved to the dressing table, the wardrobe and then the bookshelves. But they were all bereft of what she was looking for; nothing looked like a diary at all.

After a time she glanced at her watch: she'd been searching Spider's room for almost an hour and there was nowhere else to look.

Then she had an idea.

'Mum! Mum, are you here?' Tessa burst into Peggy's kitchen.

'In the office, petal.'

Tessa jogged down the passage towards her mother's voice. 'Mum!'

'What's wrong?' Peggy turned and shot out of her chair as she saw Tessa's red face.

'Nothing. It's all fine. I just walked from Aunty Spider's.'

'Good Lord, child! In this heat? You must have gone mad.'

'Maybe.' She grinned. 'I found a diary of Aunty Spider's when I was cleaning out. It was for last year. I haven't been able to find any more. Do you know if there are any here? I thought she might have given them to Dad.'

'Yeah, there are some – I think we've got about twenty years' worth. There's not much in them, though. They record the history of Danjar Plains. There's nothing personal.'

'Oh.' For a moment, Tessa was disappointed. 'Can I have a look at them anyway?'

'Sure. I've got them archived in the cellar.'

'Lovely. I'll be down there if you're looking for me.'

Tessa held herself together as she stepped into the darkness. There were forty-three steps she remembered from when she was a kid. Made from stone and wood, she ran down them to below the surface of the earth and into a world of cool, if rather musty, air.

When she reached the bottom, she felt for the light switch. Her fingers found it and she flicked it on. As her eyes adjusted she automatically looked for the bullet hole where, years ago, her dad had shot a massive king brown snake that had managed to get into the cellar. A bit of investigation showed it had come in through the vent, which went up into the garage. It hadn't been sealed properly, giving the snake just enough room to squeeze through. Ryan had seen it trying to slither up the stairs. Tessa could laugh, now, at the circus that followed, but at the time she had climbed onto the kitchen table and stayed there, screaming. Ryan and her mum had rushed around trying to keep an eye on the frantic and deadly serpent while her Dad went to get the gun. Ever since, she had felt a certain amount of apprehension regarding the cellar and she couldn't quite believe she had willingly gone down there.

It wasn't a big room – about five metres by four. In one corner stood wide shelves lined with old newspapers and covered with jars of preserved fruit and vegies that her mother had bottled. There were oranges laid out on newspaper and eggs in cartons stacked on top of one another.

In the other corner was a cupboard full of folders and papers to do with the farm. And Aunty Spider's diaries.

Tessa opened the door of the cupboard. There they were, stacked into shelves. What secrets did they hold? Tessa felt apprehension as she took the first book in her hands and opened it, almost reverently.

It was the earliest one, written in a woman's hand, the firmer, steadier script of a younger Spider.

Tuesday, 24 April 1928

Well, it's finally happened. We've been granted a Water Lease. Over the last four months, we've been droving our stock slowly towards Balladonia, where we know there is a good water supply. I'm riding my push bike, while my brothers Len, George and Edward are all on horseback.

Grace will come on the train next month.

Once we find a place that looks like a good spot for a homestead we will start to build.

Aunty Margaret and Uncle Sam have given the journal-keeping responsibility to me. I am to record the events such as weather, temperatures and the developing of the land. Aunty Margaret is helping me and it is part of my schooling. I feel very important.

Today it was one hundred and ten and the wind blew strongly from the west. Soft clouds scuttled across the sky and Uncle Sam thinks there is rain coming. The ants have been very busy scuttling around.

Uncle Sam killed a wether today so we will have fresh meat for tonight's tea, but we'll have to be very careful with the meat that is left. A dingo followed him the whole way back to the camp afterwards, attracted by the smell of the blood. They seem to be in large numbers at the moment.

. . .

Monday, 14 May 1928

We have started to build a homestead but more importantly, a shearing shed. Our chosen place is about thirty miles south of the road that goes to South Australia. The walls are made from limestone and at the moment we are trying to get the roof on. The cameleers will replenish our supplies when they come by.

We're expecting a boring plant within the next twelve months – it would be nice to sink

*some bores so we don't have to move the stock
further north each time we head out.*

*The rain seems to be taking its time in
coming this year. We had about half an inch
last month but nothing more. We are being
teased with large rain clouds to the south, but
they aren't coming this far up.*

*The weather has been cold at night but
lovely during the day.*

. . .

Wednesday, 5 September 1928

*There was great excitement today when a
cloud of dust appeared in the distance. It was
the first Afghan cameleer train we have seen
since we moved out here.*

*The camels snorted and some even spat –
they seemed very cranky creatures, but their
brown eyes are beautiful. Ali, the man who
walks alongside them, uses a nose peg and
rope to direct them.*

*The camels carry everything from timber to
household needs. They are camped over at the
small crater of water we call the house dam.
It's not a dam at all, but rocks that hold water.
There were other men with Mr Ali. Three, I
think and what looked like a young boy a bit
older than me.*

*Oh, I forgot to record the weather. It was
ninety-two today and sunny, and for once*

there wasn't any sign of dingo tracks around
our camp this morning.

Tessa ran through the dates and worked out
Spider would have been seven at the time these
entries were written. She flicked through a few
more pages and didn't see anything of interest, so
she chose another later one.

Saturday, 1 January 1955
We've been here for many years, on this
piece of land, but it seems that the rest of
Australia has only just realised the potential
of the Nullarbor. People have come and gone
since we arrived. Not many stay long – it takes
a special type of person to be able to handle
the isolation and remoteness. But recently
we have started to get neighbours who are
settling.
A big company has bought the stretch of
land next to us and installed a manager who
is going to 'develop the country'. They've been
sinking bores, searching for water.
I believe they have brought stock from South
Australia across the telegraph line.
If they haven't already, they will soon realise
the hardship of this land and how unwilling it
is to be tamed.
In the years we have been here, the weather
plays the most important role in our lives. It

dictates when we fence, when we muster, even what we eat.

The last three weeks have been unbearably hot, but the nights have been cool. The breeze off the ocean comes in around eight in the evening and later, as the sun sets, it really is quite pleasant.

For the first day of the year, it was one hundred and four in the shade of the verandah. But it would be much hotter 'in the waterbag', as the stockmen say. As I write this by the light of the lamp, it's a nice eighty-six.

Len has brought us a kero fridge! We feel very rich and spoilt to have somewhere to keep our supplies cold. He had to show Uncle Sam where to put the fuel and as they shuffled it into the corner of the kitchen, it spilt on the floor. Such a waste!

We have had word that our water lease has changed to a pastoral lease. We now have to fence the 782,000 acres that are ours. We started on the boundary, but Uncle Sam says it will take us many years to fence the paddocks the way he wants them done. He tells us he and Len have surveyed the whole of the station and says there will have to be at least fifty paddocks!

Today we managed to get in about half a mile of posts and tomorrow, George, Edward and I will run the wire. We're going to use rabbit-proof netting, which Len brought back *from his last trip to the railway line. The Tea and Sugar Train is a godsend when it comes to getting supplies, as were the cameleer trains.*

I miss Ali and his team of camels. Neither he nor any others have been through here in many years. When they upgraded the road in the 1940s so vehicles and trucks could access the route it really put these kindly men and their animals out of business. I guess these new trucks are making it easier and quicker to cart supplies. Maybe they are not even using camels anywhere anymore.

It was a grand sight to see those stately animals pull our wool on flatbed trailers down to the coast. I know it took them many days and I can only imagine what it looked like when the bales were floated on barges out across the sea and loaded onto ships. They would then sail to Fremantle, where the wool would be sold.

This is something these new neighbours will have to get used to. Markets are a long way away and we have to use other means of transport to get our produce there. Maybe I sound cynical, but having lived here for so many years, I know it isn't a life or land for the faint-hearted.

'Tessa? Do you want a cup of tea?' Peggy's voice floated down the stairs.

Tessa glanced at her watch. She would have to head home soon.

'Yes, please. Just a quick one, Mum.' She flicked through the books again. The first few were in date order, then it seemed some were missing. She went back to the cupboard to see if she'd missed some, but she hadn't. There must have been some missing.

'Can I take these back to Aunty Spider's, Mum?' she asked when she was back in the kitchen upstairs. 'I'd like to read them.'

'Course you can. I've hardly ever looked at them other than to have a quick flick through.' Peggy grabbed a couple of potatoes out of the pantry and started to peel them. 'Do you want to stay for tea, petal?'

'Uh, no, thanks. I've got something defrosting already.' Potatoes could only mean meat! 'You know, I'm not sure they interest me, either, but I'd like to have a read. But there's one from 1930, then nothing again until 1945. Are there any other diaries somewhere else, Mum? There are a few years missing.

'No. I shifted them all from the office down to the cellar when Dad and I moved in. They're not over at Spider's?'

'I haven't seen any diaries except for the 2009 one. And she didn't write in it every day, like she has in these ones.' She paused. 'Do you know why Aunty Spider's family came out here?'

Peggy was busy pouring the tea. 'Not really. I had a brief conversation with her years ago. Spider's mother got pregnant with one of the boys – Edward,

I think. It was just before the Depression while they were living in Adelaide. There wasn't any food and her mother was very ill. Spider said she remembered a train journey to Ceduna, where her uncle met her and two of the older boys – George and Len – and took them to live on their station. They sort of gravitated out here. There seemed more opportunity, I guess. I have some idea her mother may have died during childbirth – or maybe not.'

'Can't have – there was Tom a whole lot later,' Tessa pointed out.

'That's true. Maybe during Tom's birth? I honestly don't know. I certainly don't have any idea where her dad ended up.'

Tessa watched her mum run water over the potatoes and set them on the stove to boil. 'It must have been horrible for kids in the Depression,' she said.

'Horrible for anyone, I'd think,' Peggy answered.

'Yeah, but imagine being so young and being sent away from your parents.'

'Did that happen much? Kids being sent away to other family members like Spider was?'

'Good Lord, how would I know? But it does seem to make sense. When you live on a farm there's always food – eggs, chooks, rabbits, sheep, cattle. Even when things are pretty desperate, as they were during the Depression.

'Anyway, I would have thought if Spider's mum died, then her dad would have come out here, too. But he didn't as far as I know. Your dad might know.'

'Or, maybe I could check with Elsie.'

'Oh, now, while I think about it, Elsie rang to see how you were getting on. She's left her number again, even though you've already got it. I think that was a hint.'

Now that was an idea.

Elsie.

Chapter 22

Tuesday, 1 March 1955

I'm so glad we know this land like the back of our hands. When Uncle Sam and Aunty Margaret first brought us out here, there weren't any roads or tracks, but as time went on, rabbit trappers, gold hunters and ordinary travellers have made a criss-cross of tracks which, to the untrained eye, might look like one huge cobweb. The trails don't all lead to the same place or even to anywhere. Just into the open bush.

We had a tracker arrive today looking for two blokes who have become lost 'out there, somewhere'. Len was here, so he's joined the search party on horseback. I pray they find them. This terrain can be merciless.

There won't be any point looking for tracks now, because the winds have been so strong from the south. Any footprint or bike or horse tracks will have been filled by the drifting sand. They will have to rely on looking for broken branches and scrub. Not the easiest way to find someone.

I still have George, Edward and Tom here. Even though I'm perfectly capable of handling everything on my own, I prefer it when my brothers are around. And, of course, Uncle Sam and Aunty Margaret.

Thankfully the weather is kind. Cool, today, with no sign of rain, even though it's overcast.

. . .

Tuesday, 24 April 1956

The boundary fence was finally completed today. We've been working on it for twelve months. Our pastoral lease is at last clear to everyone. We celebrated by trapping some rabbits and killing a wether. Because Len had just arrived back from the Tea and Sugar Train, we had fresh vegetables for a stew and a bottle of port. Such a luxury!

It's taken a lot of blood, sweat and tears to get these fences erected. Len and George started them, with Uncle Sam helping, but we found the limestone and rock was too hard for us to get through just by digging or with a crowbar. Len decided we needed help so, about six months ago, he went to Kalgoorlie to find someone who would be able to spare the time. The fencers he brought back have gelignite, and they blast out the post-holes much more easily and faster than we could have ever done. The fence just appeared in no time!

The nights are beginning to get cold now but the days are still lovely and warm.

. . .

Friday, 6 December 1957

I have neglected the diary for some time. What is left of our family is only three and it's taken some while to become used to that. The deaths of my uncle and three brothers left Aunty Margaret, Tom and me grief-stricken, but after so many months, we are beginning to come out of the fog that has surrounded us and Danjar Plains.

In April, Uncle Sam was mustering ewes in the home paddock. He hadn't returned by dark, so Len and Tom went looking for him. They found him dead, underneath his horse, Buck, who had obviously stepped in a rabbit hole and thrown him. The horse had snapped his leg so he also had to be put down. Uncle Sam was the reason we came here, the reason we have become one with this land. And now he is gone. Aunty Margaret won't stay. She's asked to go back to Adelaide, so I will go with her next month and get her settled, then return.

245

Next Len, the golden-tongued and charis-
matic Len. He went in June. Our property is
dirty with rocks and limestone and we were
very impatient to get three more fences up so
we could keep the sheep close to our house.
The dingoes had been taking lambs – a loss
we couldn't afford. Len and George had started
to help the fencers again, instead of dedicating
their time to putting in windmills and troughs.
They were getting ready to blow a post-hole and
the dynamite went off while Len was holding
the charge. He was killed instantly.

Thinking nothing more could go wrong, we
started to muster for crutching. August had
been a good month – enough rains to make
the grasses abundant and make us confident
of a good wool clip. The shearing team who
came was short of a presser, so George filled
in. He spent hours at the Ajax press, pumping
the arms up and down and pushing the pins
through to hold the wool down.

Somehow, God only knows how, he was on
the inside of the press, jumping the wool down
and was speared through the chest with a pin.
I have my suspicions about this, especially
after a couple of the other blokes made it clear
there had been an argument between George
and Dan, one of the shearers. Something to do
with revenge, but I don't understand how Dan
could have known. Of course, it doesn't do any

*good to think about these things. The death has
already happened and we've got no proof. It
will just make us afraid of our own shadows.
And of the shearing team.*

*And Edward, cheeky, fun-loving Edward?
He fell from the windmill in the house paddock.*

*Our boys are buried not with my William but
under the grove of mallee trees we always joked
would become the cemetery. Uncle Sam picked
the spot when we first came out here, saying it
was the coolest and most peaceful place on the
station. We've always known and been prepared
for death out here, but we never thought we
would bury so many there so quickly.*

*It could have weakened a lesser family,
but their deaths have made Tom's and my
resolve stronger than ever to make this stretch
of land into one of the best stations on the
Nullarbor.*

*Yes, tonight, sitting in front of our fire, we
are a lot more solemn and sad, but we won't
fail, because that is not a word either Tom or
I understand.*

Tessa drew a sharp breath. She'd had no idea
what Aunty Spider had faced – such disaster and
sorrow! Spider had never spoken about it, never
mentioned those losses. In fact, she'd rarely talked
of early times, except to recall what year they'd had
a good clip, or bad rains.

This must have been why she was so under-standing, so sympathetic, when Kendra had been killed. Because she understood loss by accident. Lord, it made the things Tessa had faced seem insignificant by comparison.

Nine words, in particular, had jumped off the page for Tessa: 'He fell from the windmill in the house paddock'. So Kendra's death wasn't the first one on Danjar Plains! The local Aborigines might have said the place was cursed but, really, accidents were nothing but bad luck or bad management. At least, that was what Spider would have said, but it was not necessarily what Tessa believed.

Restlessly, she got up and paced. What a horrendous year for them all, but it was just like Aunty Spider to not give up, the tough old bird. Obviously she'd gone on to do what she had promised 'the boys', because Danjar Plains, although a small station, was a good one.

Tessa placed the 1957 diary on the pile next to her and opened another.

Tuesday, 8 July 1958

It is going to be a good season – the grass is long and the bush green (or rather a bluey-silver) with new shoots. We have started to see the budgerigars in large flocks. The noise they make is just deafening and when they fly together they seem like one green cloud moving across the sky. I rode my bike out to

Jackman's paddock yesterday and there they were lining the trees. From a distance it looked like the branches had some kind of growth all over them! It really was an incredible sight. I've been here now since 1928 and while the birds come every year, I don't believe I have seen so many. Dear Uncle Sam would have told an old wives' tale about why they are here in such numbers, I'm sure.

They drink from the puddles and the dams we have dug. Even though there are heaps of live ones, there seems to be many dead ones too. Who knows why, but I am continually scooping them out of my house water tank. This impresses me no end. Tom says he'll bring me back a gas cannon next time he goes to Kalgoorlie. It will keep them away from my fruit trees, which I've so carefully looked after and which these pesky birds love to eat!

. . .

Sunday, 13 December 1959

We are celebrating tonight. It is the biggest wool clip we have ever sent off. And it went by truck. Yes, I know, we've been doing that for a few years now, but I still find it strange seeing the bales loaded one by one onto motorised machinery, rather than the trailers pulled by the camels down to the sea.

. . .

Thursday, 14 January 1960

Well, well, isn't Tom a dark horse? He has arrived home from his annual break in Kalgoorlie with a bride in tow. Always to be expected, I guess, but at 29, I did wonder if marriage would pass him by. Lucy is a station girl from further north of Kalgoorlie and is a good worker. We will get along fine.

. . .

Monday, 28 March 1960

Fires have been bad throughout the summer – the dry storms and lightning strikes have kept everyone alert. But tonight there is soft and steady rain from a cyclone on the north-west coast. It should put paid to any wildfires still burning.

. . .

Sunday, 22 December 1963

I think the most exciting news I have is I am an aunty to a sweet, dark-haired child. His nose is tiny and his mouth seems to open all the time. His skin is like his father's, a dark olive, which means he won't get burnt!

Lucy is well and the birth seemed easy – but how terrible of me to say so when I haven't had a child. What I mean is, there weren't any difficulties. Thank goodness. I had been terrified there may be.

They have named the boy Paul.

I am going to tell Tom I will move out of the homestead. What way is it really, to have a family when you have a sister living with you. I will move to the little hut we first built when we arrived. It is plenty big enough for me and won't require too much fixing. Lucy will need a house and amenities. It will help, too, if she's near the house windmill – much easier for the vegie patch.

Tessa stopped reading. That baby was her dad. She'd just read about the birth of her dad out here on the Nullarbor. And obviously the house Aunty Spider was referring to was where Tessa had been raised. She tried to imagine what it would have been like, alone except for a doting family. No friends outside of the station. What a lonely existence.

She flicked back through the rest of the books and opened up 1967's diary.

Thursday, 19 January 1967

The wool market is very much in the doldrums at the moment. The money we should have received for the last clip isn't what we'd budgeted on and it means we will have to put on hold some of the water development we wanted to do. We also found the cull ewe price wasn't what we were hoping for, either. I'm thinking we need to diversify. Perhaps buy

some cattle. Our neighbours have some cows
for sale and we could buy a bull easily enough.
It would help alleviate the money pressure for
a year or two. I hope.

Tessa found herself not just wanting, but also
needing to know what happened in the early years,
when there weren't any diaries. But there had to
be! Spider wouldn't just stop writing them.

And then she remembered she hadn't returned
Elsie's call.

Tessa picked up the phone.

'Hello, Elsie. It's Tessa.'

'Tessa dear.' The joy in Elsie's voice shocked
Tessa. The old lady must have been waiting to hear
from her.

'Yes, it's me. How are you, Elsie?'

'I'm getting along just fine. I keep myself busy.'

'What do you do?' Tessa asked out of politeness,
when what she really wanted to do was ask a
million other questions.

'Oh, you know, the usual sort of things. I help
out at the museum once a week, visit all the old
people in the hospital who haven't got anyone else.
That sort of thing.'

'All the old people? Elsie, you're eighty-four! How
old are the old people you visit?'

'Some of them are younger than me, but they're
ill. Unfortunate for them, really. But there are some
as old as ninety, you know!'

Tessa laughed. 'I think you and Aunty Spider may have been hellraisers when you were younger.'

'Ah yes, my dear. We could well have been. But no different to you or Ryan or any other young person.'

'Elsie, I'm wondering if I could ask you something?'

'Of course dear. Anything.'

'I've been reading Aunty Spider's diaries. I've found quite a few but there are some years missing. I would've thought there should have been others around, but I can't seem to find them. Have you got any idea where they'd be?'

'Here in my spare room.'

'Beg your pardon?' It was the last answer she expected.

'She gave them to me for safe-keeping. There was a time, although I'm not sure why, that she felt the place for these wasn't on Danjar Plains, so she sent them to me. One's family history is very important. It shows later generations where you've come from and why your family is the way it is today. I don't mean just yours, Tessa, I mean anyone's. Everyone has a right to know about his or her heritage. But for some reason she told me I had to wait until the time was right before handing them on. But without any other instructions from her, I do believe that time is now. I've got them all packaged up ready to send.'

'Wasn't safe?' Tessa was still back at Elsie's first sentence. 'Why?'

'I can't tell you.'

'Can't or won't?'

'Can't. I don't know why, other than she wanted them off the place. But I happily took them.'

'Have you read any of them? Can you give me a clue?'

'Tessa!' Elsie sounded shocked. 'Never would I have broken my dearest friend's trust like that. Never.'

'Sorry.' Tessa felt suitably chastised. 'Sorry. I was only joking.'

'Trust is something to never joke about.'

There was a pause while Tessa tried to work out what to say next. 'She had a pretty hard life, didn't she?'

'We all did back then, but we never saw it that way,' Elsie said. 'It was the way life was. Everyone experienced the same things. There was death, you accepted it. There were fun times, you enjoyed them. No point in moaning or whining. Life was just there to be lived the best we could.'

'Did you tell her that when her uncle and brothers died?' It was a loaded question. Tessa still wasn't convinced that Elsie had spent as much time with Spider as she claimed. After all, her aunt had made no mention of her. But still, she seemed to know so much.

'I didn't have to tell her, dear. She already knew that.'

'The diaries are very scarce with info, especially

personal stuff. I thought that was what they were for, to record your deepest thoughts.'

'Ah, but that's where you're wrong, Tessa. Diaries back then were for historical reference. That's how most people wrote them – so younger generations would know what we did. Letters were for personal thoughts. Even if you wrote them to yourself.'

Tessa's desire to read those diaries and whatever letters she could get her hands on was so strong she wanted to jump down the phone and grab them that very moment. 'Are there any letters you can send me?' she asked.

'No, dear, I don't have them.'

Disappointed, she said: 'So, I'm assuming I won't get anything much out of these diaries? If it's all just historical recounts?'

'It depends on what you do with the information you read. Sorry to be so cryptic!' Elsie let out a chuckle as if she wasn't sorry at all and Tessa snorted at the absurdity. It was almost like talking to Aunty Spider all over again.

'She knew she would send me mad, trying to figure this out, didn't she?'

Elsie chuckled again. 'I don't think it was her intention, but she wouldn't have been surprised! Goodbye, Tessa, dear. I'll take the parcel to the post office tomorrow.'

'Thanks, Elsie. Take care.'

Tessa hung up and jiggled her knee in agitation. There was something hidden in this family, a secret of some sort. Elsie knew what it was, but she was a bloody vault.

Tessa would find it, she was determined. Then she realised: she'd forgotten to ask Elsie about the rings.

Chapter 23

Tessa rummaged through the storeroom at the homestead trying to find an old sleeping bag and tarpaulin she could use as a swag. There were heaps of blankets at Spider's and she had a couple of those, but she needed something waterproof in case there was a dew.

The Muster was only days away and with the planning and helping her mother to get everything ready, the family investigation had been put on hold. She couldn't help but wonder when Brendan would get there. She was very keen to see him – the spasmodic phone calls had only whetted her appetite.

She wasn't sure how she felt about her first Muster since Kendra had died. It was too long ago for anyone to bring it up, but the fact remained, she'd only come back once after the accident. Her presence was sure to stir some interest from the locals who knew her story.

'What'd you find, love?' Peggy was standing in the doorway.

'I've got a holey sleeping bag, but I can't find anything else I can use as a swag.'

Tessa turned around. Dust freckled her nose. Her mother gave a little chuckle. 'You look like the Tessa of old,' she said, reaching out to pick a cobweb off her daughter's fringe. 'And your hair has grown. Thank goodness for that. I must say, petal, you look much better. Fresher. I'm so pleased you've stayed for a while. Now, did you see anything in the cellar when you were down there?'

'No, not that I remember.'

'Well, there's probably something in the shearers' quarters. Head over and have a look there.' Her mother paused. 'Actually there's a chance Spider's swag is over there with all of ours. Why don't you see if you can find it.'

Uncomfortable at the thought of sharing her great-aunt's sleeping space, she wrinkled her nose. 'I'll see what I can find,' she answered.

The shearers' quarters were probably seventy years old. They were made from limestone, with walls nearly twenty-five centimetres thick. Tessa had never thought about how much effort would have gone into building them, but as she placed her hands on their coolness, she knew it must have taken years and much man power. How they could have managed to get the ceilings as high as they did was beyond her.

She cautiously stuck her head through the door and looked around. Snakes and all sorts of creatures might be found here, so she wouldn't be setting a foot inside until she'd carefully surveyed the room.

The small kitchen was neat and tidy, but empty. A little bedroom opened straight off it. Years ago it would have been the cook's bedroom, but Spider had always refused to let a cook in here while she was able to keep up with the huge hunger demands shearers had. She would vault from the shearing shed to the kitchen and back again. Tessa never knew how she managed such a workload.

For a moment, Tessa stopped and thought about the days she had spent here, sitting on the bench watching Spider. That was where she had learned to cook cakes and pies – apple and rhubarb had been one of the shearers' favourites. For lunches there had been large servings of roast mutton, potatoes and pumpkin, all washed down with mugs of hot tea. Dinner was the eastern dishes that Spider had been known for.

All those skills Spider had taught her, and Tessa was blowed if she could remember the last time she'd baked a cake. Maybe next time she went to Cally's she could make one. She bet there wasn't too much of that sort of thing over there with Harrison in charge. And Brendan would probably like one too, she thought, pushing Harrison out of her mind.

She set off down the passageway. It was narrow, cool and brilliantly light, thanks to the white-washed walls. Off it were five bedrooms behind heavy wooden doors. Each room contained a fireplace and two single beds.

Tessa was rewarded in the second room she looked. There were five swags already rolled up and placed beside each other on one of the narrow beds. At first glance she knew the large double one belonged to her parents. There were three smaller ones, which were singles. One had been used recently and was the only one not covered in dust. She stared at it, knowing it was Spider's but wondering why it wasn't like the others. Surely the old lady hadn't been camping recently! With unpractised fingers she loosened the buckles of the straps and unrolled it. She removed the inside of the swag to take back to the homestead and wash and dragged the tarp onto the floor. Then she half-carried, half-dragged it to the kitchen. There she quickly had a look for holes. It would be fine. Tessa started to roll it back up when she felt a bulge at the bottom. Frowning, she unzipped it further and felt for what it was. Her fingers touched on something hard. She brought it out and stared at the bulky camera. It was an old-fashioned wind-on film camera. How strange. Tessa hadn't known Spider liked taking photos. She checked the display panel and saw there were twenty-four photos on the film and twenty of them had been used. 'Wonder what these shots are of?' she said out loud, before placing the camera carefully on the bench.

She turned and went back down the hallway, and popped her head into the other three rooms. All empty and clean, except for the layers of dust. It would be another seven months before these rooms rang with voices and energy again.

Back at the homestead, she laid everything out on the front lawn and started assembling the swag. First, the tarp was laid out flat and then on top she placed a thin mattress. Next was the sleeping bag and three blankets then everything was wrapped in a silver space blanket, which looked like nothing more than alfoil. Then she folded the tarp in all around the lot, zipped it all in and rolled it as tight as she could.

'You look like you did that only last week.' Marni was walking up the path, an overnight bag in her hand.

Tessa looked up. 'Oh ha, ha,' she said, smiling. She turned back to survey her handiwork. 'It's a bit rough, but it'll keep out any nasties. What's with the bag? You packing for the Muster?'

Marni's face broke into a huge smile. 'Ryan and I are going to Perth after the Muster. We've made an appointment to see that fertility doctor you suggested. I've come to borrow a couple of things from Peggy.'

'Oh, that's fantastic!' Without thinking she threw her arms around her sister-in-law and held her. 'I hope it turns out the way you want it to.'

'I'm reckoning it will. We just need a bit of help, and we should get it there. We'll go and see Dr Mike in Kal before we go, but the first appointment, at least, is set up. We'll work out a plan from there.'

'I think that's just great! Mum and Dad obviously know then?'

'Yeah, Ryan told them yesterday. I think he's hoping you might stick around for a little while, until we get back in case they need another pair of hands.'

'Don't think I'll be much use,' Tessa said, making a face. 'But Marni, I would honestly love to do that, if it will help you guys relax while you're away.'

'Thanks, Tessa.'

'And I owe you an apology. I was so nasty to you when you came to visit. I'm very sorry. For some reason, you talking about Spider made me jealous. I felt I just had to hurt you. Sorry, I'm so fucked up.' Tessa looked at the ground but jerked her head up when Marni started to laugh and laugh. 'What's so funny?' she asked, frowning.

'Oh, Tessa, I never thought I'd hear you say the word "fuck"! You're too much of a city person! I'm so nervous around you, 'cos I think I come across as such a country hick!'

'What? City people don't say fuck? Oh you are sooo wrong! Come on inside and have a cup of tea with Mum. We'd better rectify this problem!'

'Well, I'll take you up on the cuppa, but it's okay. I know you've only been here three months, but you've mellowed, Tessa. You don't scare me as much now.'

'You're right, Marni.' Peggy was standing in the doorway. 'We're beginning to see the real you, Tessa, not the one you want us to see. And that makes me so glad.'

Tessa looked at them both, thinking about their words. They were spot-on, if you disregarded all the meltdowns she'd had since she'd arrived. She was feeling calmer, more peaceful and more at home. Her thoughts were clearer, as was her whole body. Was it possible that she was putting her ghosts to rest, even though she kept thinking about them?

'I think you're all a bit heavy for me this morning,' she finally said. 'I need that cup of tea.'

Inside, the three women chatted happily together as they drank their tea. Tessa and her mum were relieved and pleased for Marni, and they were all excited about the upcoming Muster.

'Do you have to do anything at the Muster, Mum? We've cooked all the little cupcakes for the food stall. Is there anything else?' Tessa asked. She had vague memories of all the food being provided by locals.

'Yeah, I'll help Diane and Pastor Allen to cook doughnuts on the first day. He's raising money for the Frontier Services and the Flying Doctor. But now, all of the catering is done by Kalgoorlie folks. There're too many people coming for just us "Nullarborians".' She made quotation marks with her fingers. 'Your Dad's job, as the treasurer, is a fair bit bigger than mine.'

'Is he really? I can't see Dad doing that.'

'He's been doing it for a couple of years, hasn't he, Peg?' Marni commented.

'Mmm, yep.' Peggy collected the cups and took them to the sink. 'Harrison will be dropping off the float for the till tomorrow and then the next day we'll go and help set up. There's always a bit to do beforehand.'

'I hope Cally rides well in the barrel races. She has her heart set on winning.'

'Oh, she's a great barrel racer, just like her mother was,' Peggy said. 'Did you know Ryan judges that?'

'Really? Well, I'm actually quite excited about it all. Nothing like a good party.' Grinning, Tessa did a couple of dance moves across the kitchen.

Marni laughed. 'Oh yeah, it's the event of the year!'

'I just hope there aren't any problems,' Peggy said. 'Organising it is a huge job these days, because so many people come. In the last few years, we've had over eight hundred visitors come through the gate. It's amazing to think people will come from as far as Perth to compete with their horses and for the bull riding!'

'That many? Wow! Still, it's for a good cause – we all know how much you depend on the Flying Doctor out here.' Tessa rinsed the cups her mother had put on the sink and turned back towards them.

'Now, can I change the subject?' Tessa asked. She motioned for Peggy to sit down next to Marni.

'I found something at Aunty Spider's that I need some help with.'

'Sure.'

Tessa dug into her pocket and pulled out the box holding the rings. She opened it and placed them on the table. The two gold bands lay glittering on their bed. Instinctively, all three women leaned forward.

'Whose are they?' Marni asked quietly.

'I have no idea. I was hoping someone here might know.'

'I've never seen them before. Where did you find them?'

'Spider had hidden them well. I'm not sure I was meant to find them. They were in that little clay pot on the outside table.'

'Why did you go looking in there?'

'Sounds weird, doesn't it? I was holding it, tossing it from hand to hand and I felt something clunk inside it. I turned it over and they fell out.'

Peggy gently picked one up and held it up to the window. '"Forever mine, forever yours",' she read. 'I've heard that somewhere before.'

'Really?' Tessa looked at her eagerly.

'But I'm buggered if I can remember where. I'll ask Paul when he gets home.'

'Ask me what?' Paul and Ryan came in, covered in dust and grease.

'What have you two been doing?' asked Peggy.

'The bloody grader shat itself. Had to pull out the fuel pump.'

Ryan washed his hands in the kitchen sink then sat down next to Marni. 'They're a bit flash. Where'd you get them, Tessie? Someone want to marry you?'

'Found them at Aunty Spider's.'

'Where have we heard the saying "Forever mine, forever yours", Pauly?' asked Peggy. 'I know I've heard it somewhere.'

'Hmm, yeah. You're right.' His brow wrinkled as he thought. 'Not a hundred per cent sure, but I wonder if it's down at the old cemetery on one of the graves. We can have a look later, if you want.'

'Old cemetery? Is there another one, other than where Aunty Spider is?'

'Yeah, it's where they first camped when they first came out here. Near a grove of mallee trees. It wasn't used until the fifties. I can't rightly say why her other family is buried over there and William is in this one nearer to her house.' He reached for the teapot and swished it around, before pouring it into his cup. 'That might be it, because she wanted William closer to her.'

'Oh! That's what she meant about another cemetery.' Tessa's eyes flashed with recognition. 'Her brothers and uncle? I read about them dying, in the diaries! So tragic. Can we go and have a look?' She leapt up from the table.

'Hold your horses! You're always so impatient.' Paul smiled. 'We'll have to knock that out of you! Let me have my tea, then I can take you.'

'Yeah, Tessie.' Ryan chimed in as he lifted his cup. 'Us hardworking fellas need our sustenance. How'd you go with a swag?'

'Smart-arse,' she muttered, passing him a plate of biscuits. 'Oh, I forgot! Yeah, I got the swag done, but when I opened it all up to check for creepy crawlies and things, there was an old camera in it. Right at the bottom of it.'

Ryan straightened up. 'Was there?'

'In the swag?' Peggy asked.

'Yep. It's an old wind-on one.'

'What did you do with it?' her brother asked.

'I couldn't carry it back with everything else, so I left it on the bench.'

'Weird.' Marnie shrugged. 'I didn't know she took photos.'

'Can't say I did either,' Paul entered the conversation. 'But I think there were plenty of things we didn't know.' He put down his cup and stretched. 'Come on then, Miss Impatient. I'll drive you out to the plot.' Paul and Tessa climbed into the ute and drove about thirty minutes to where three of Tessa's great-uncles plus her great-great uncle were buried.

Under the shade of the mallee trees, everything was silent, almost reverently still. Tessa took in the old gravesites, the handmade wooden crosses and headstones. Clumps of grass grew out from in between the rocks which covered the hard-working pioneers' final resting places – unless you looked hard, you wouldn't have known they were there. The land they had loved had claimed them.

She shivered, knowing the rocks had been placed there so the dingoes and foxes wouldn't dig up their remains.

Paul stopped to read the inscriptions, all of which were carved by hand.

'Len Mathison, died, 30 June 1957,' Paul said softly. 'And over here, Sam Mathison killed in a horse fall, April 1957.'

'Edward Mathison,' Tessa continued, her fingers tracing the letters. 'George Mathison.' Tessa could only imagine the grief felt by Spider and what was left of her family when they lay to rest these men who had played such a large role in their lives. She suddenly remembered the words of Aunty Spider in one of the diaries: '. . . sometimes it seems this station has seen nothing but heartbreak'. Tessa repeated it out loud for Paul.

'Danjar Plains has definitely had its moments,' he agreed.

Tessa took one last look at the four graves and turned away, looking to see if there were any more. Nothing leapt out at her.

Disappointed that she hadn't found the words she was looking for inscribed anywhere, she walked further out into the trees and glanced around. Hidden in the middle of a cluster of bushes she saw part of a little rusty white fence poking out. It corralled off an area that was small enough to be a child's grave. Beside it was another one, not much larger. The two seemed to be joined together with the fences connected.

As she looked carefully, Tessa realised there was something scratched into the fence. She leaned closer.

'"Forever mine, forever yours",' she read. 'Dad! Dad, here it is!' she called.

Paul came to stand beside her.

'You found it.'

'Yes, but whose grave is it? There's nothing to say whose it is.' She ran her finger across some marks in the stone. 'But I can't read it. Only the words "Forever mine, forever yours".'

'I have no idea.'

Chapter 24

Harrison put the parcel on the step and raised his fist to knock on Violet's front door. He paused. He wondered what sort of a reception he'd get.

He had instantly disliked Tessa at the airport, and hadn't warmed to her at the wake. On both occasions she seemed shallow and selfish.

But he hadn't seen that when she was with Cally. Watching from a distance, he noticed her smiles had been kind and genuine. Cally was besotted, as only a child could be – it had been her idea to get Tessa a thank-you gift. Remembering his promise to himself to make an effort with her for Cally's benefit, he'd agreed.

Ange had always said kids were the best judge of people, but there was still something that made him wary. He knew she was involved with Brendan McKenzie and, in his eyes, that wasn't to her credit.

Even if his body had responded to her closeness in the plane on the trip home.

The door was ajar and he peeked through the gap. Tessa was hanging photos of her family in the lounge room. He wondered if she was going to live here after she'd finished clearing everything out. Was she going to stay?

He adjusted his hat and knocked. 'Special delivery!' he called, pushing the door open further.

'Oh! Hello!' Tessa said, smiling. 'This is a surprise.' Then she must have seen the parcel in his hands. 'Oh, they're here already? The diaries!' She rushed towards him, her hands outstretched.

'Well, that's a nice hello and I don't mind if I do.' Harrison grinned, holding open his arms and closing them around her briefly.

'Uh. Oh. Um.' Tessa was red-faced. 'Sorry. I meant the parcel. I thought it was from Elsie.'

Harrison laughed and handed it to her. 'I think it is, if she's "E. Harlot, sender".'

'Oh, it is! They're finally here!'

He grinned, finding it hard not to get caught up in her enthusiasm and he watched as Tessa plonked the package on the chair and ripped it open. Inside the box were eight books with black covers.

'What are they? They seem very important.' Harrison leaned over her shoulder.

'Aunty Spider's diaries from the early years.' She flicked through them. 'Yeah, see, here's 1932, 1933 and 1934. Oh, there are still some missing,' she sounded disappointed.

'Why are you interested in them?'

'I found these rings,' she pointed to the open box on the table, 'and I'm a bit keen to find out who they belong to. They're engraved, and Dad remembered that he'd seen the same words on an old family grave. So we went up and had a look. Sure enough, there're two unmarked plots up there, with this scratched into the paint on the fence.' She showed Harrison the engravings.

'Yeah, right,' he said, bemused. 'Sounds like a bit of a mystery. So you want to find out who owns the rings?'

'Absolutely!'

'Hopefully there'll be some answers in the diaries then.'

'Can't wait to start reading them! And look at what I'm doing.'

Tessa reached for his hand and, without thinking he held it out to her. 'Show me,' he said. 'Looks like you've done a lot of work.' As he let himself be dragged over to the first photo he noticed her hair was touching her collar. The harsh peroxide blonde was growing out and he could see her natural dark brown and gentle curls starting to take shape again. She turned to look at him and the excitement in her face reminded him of Cally when she had achieved something special. Suddenly, he wanted to stay with Tessa longer. He looked at the grainy black and white photo trying to think of a question that would keep her close to him but she spoke first.

'I'm going to do our family history and the history of Danjar Plains. I guess they're sort of one and the same, really. But look, here's a photo of Violet with her parents, her sister and brothers. I think I've worked out who is who by their ages. This is Grace.' She pointed at a solemn teenager in the photo. 'Here's Len, George, Edward and Violet. Tom couldn't have been born then. I'm not sure if the adults were their parents or Spider's Aunty Margaret and Uncle Sam. So far I haven't found any records of them.'

'Don't know how you'd tell, but I would imagine they are the parents. Didn't Spider's Aunty and Uncle live near Ceduna and then gravitate out here when seasons were bad? I'm sure that's what I remember Violet telling me. There wouldn't be many professional photographers roaming the Nullarbor in those days – even these days. Look here.' He pointed to a small logo at the bottom of the photo.

Tessa stopped. 'That's a really good point.' She grabbed a note pad and jotted down 'parents'. 'You're good at this.' She flashed him a brilliant smile. He nodded his acceptance of her thanks.

'And look at this next one. All the same except a couple of years older. And then I think we get to Danjar Plains. But we're missing the parents, which makes sense because they didn't come out here. Mum told me Aunty Spider and Edward were sent

273

to Margaret and Sam's just before the Depression. Things were tight for them in Adelaide. Their mum was pregnant and they didn't have enough food for everyone. I guess the older boys followed after them. I wondered why they never went back to Adelaide.'

'Can't answer that.' He caught her eye and tried to hold it for a moment, but Tessa quickly turned back to the wall.

'This is the second to last one, I promise. Sorry, I'm probably holding you up.'

'You're all right.'

'All five of them. Grace, Len, Edward, George and Spider. I don't know where the photo was taken, but it looks a bit like where the shearing shed is now.'

Harrison peered closer. 'Reckon you could be right. See here? I bet that's the edge of the old wooden yards Paul doesn't use anymore.'

'Yes! That's what I thought. And last one, except here, Grace is missing and there is a young Tom. Dad's dad,' Tess clarified. 'I'd love to know where Grace is.'

'She probably got married to another station owner. Or moved back to town. Wouldn't have thought that would be too much of a mystery or hard to track down. Why don't you ask some of the older people at the Muster? I'm sure they'll remember stories about her. Actually,' he paused, thinking. 'I tell you who'd probably know. Old Joe. He's been around forever and spent a bit of the time with Spider. Or if worst comes to the worst, you could always try the Births, Deaths and Marriages Registry.'

'That's a fantastic idea! Why hadn't I thought of that? Will Joe be at the Muster? Or can I come across to your place and talk to him?'

'Either, or.' Harrison watched as her fingers twirled around the pen she was holding.

She jotted down more notes then pointed to another image. 'Anyway, I've found the photos I'm going to hang next: this one of the camel trains hauling out bales of wool, and then here's a cheeky one of Len on a horse with Tom sitting in front of him. There's such history here.'

'Looks like you're doing a great job. History is really important. The people who own Mundranda have heaps of photos and paintings of back when they were developing the land. The way they used to put up windmills would have WorkSafe cringing these days! It's amazing there weren't more people killed. Most of the blokes who have worked on windmills are missing a finger, though. Even in this day and age, if something goes wrong when you're pulling a bore you'll get your fingers chopped off. Solar pumps are much friendlier to work with.'

A shadow quickly passed across Tessa's face then was gone. She grimaced. 'Oh, gross!'

'I think Violet would be proud of what you're up to,' Harrison said. 'What are you going to do with the house once you've finished?'

Tessa looked thoughtful. 'You know, I hadn't given that any consideration. I don't know. I just felt I wanted to get the family history up here. Anyway, it's not really my house to make the decision. It's Mum and Dad's. I couldn't stay here – how would I earn a living? Marketing is my thing, not chasing woolly sheep. Anyway, I hope Spider would approve. And I hope these books have got some answers for me!

'Hey, doesn't Cally look gorgeous in those new clothes? Look, I've got the photos she sent up on the fridge.' She pointed towards the kitchen and Harrison stuck his head through the doorway.

'I'll tell her that. I don't know where the time has gone. It only seems like a moment ago she was in a cot. Now she's in the last year of primary school. I'll miss her next year.' Just the thought of Cally leaving made him feel sick, so he quickly moved on. 'Oh, while I remember, Cally asked me to pick you up something. They're just outside.'

He ducked out the door to grab the parcel he'd left on the step. On his return he held it out to her. It was gift-wrapped. 'Cally promises me you'll love them and they'll be the right size.'

Tessa glanced at him quizzically. She took it, tore off the paper and opened the box. 'Boots!'

'Cally said you didn't have any.'

'No, no, I don't. Thank you. I guess I can't go to the Muster in a pair of tatty sneakers.'

'Nope.' He smiled. 'Better get on. I'll see you tomorrow.'

'Thanks, Harrison. For the boots and the diaries. And for all the other things I've forgotten to thank you for.'

'It's my pleasure,' he answered and found he meant it.

Harrison had said goodbye and left, but Tessa was still standing in Spider's lounge room with the boots in her hand. What a mixed package he was! Of course the boots were just a thank you for looking after Cally, but his interest in what she was doing made her feel like she was doing something of value.

Anyway, she had the diaries to focus on now. She put the boots down and made herself a cup of tea before settling into the lounge chair and picking up the last diary she had taken from the cellar. She couldn't wait to start on the rest.

Saturday, 9 February 1929

It's very dry and Uncle Sam and Len think we need to cull some of the kangaroos and rabbits because they are eating all the bushes and grasses. There's not enough for them and the sheep. The blokes have been going out at night and killing as many as they can, but it doesn't seem to make any difference to the numbers I see.

One of the water sources has dried up and

Len is keen to get the stock on the move again, to look for more feed and water.

The good thing about the water lease is we can roam as far and wide as we want to, although we have our favourite spots.

. . .

Thursday, 28 March 1929

A camel train came through yesterday. It wasn't one we've seen before. Usually the camel train drivers are quiet, lovely and gentle. These men weren't. Uncle Sam and Len weren't here – they were on the hunt for water, but Edward and George were around. I'm pleased because I don't know how I would have handled their surliness and anger.

We bought some soap, flour and many of the other household items we would usually get from the Tea and Sugar Train. It was easier to buy it all from these men than make the long journey to the railway line. Because we didn't have the correct amount of money, the younger man yelled and made threats. I suspect they had been drinking, even though it was early in the day. It was a very odd incident.

. . .

Tuesday, 28 May 1929

We have had little rain since the beginning of the year and Uncle Sam is starting to get worried.

The boys have been droving the sheep daily, but Aunty Margaret, Grace and I have stayed in one spot. It's much easier than packing up the camp every couple of days. Grace seems unwell, as she has for the last month or so. But then again, Aunty Margaret is finding everything very tiring at the moment, too. I hope it's just the weariness of the dry and that once it rains, everyone will be 'right as rain'. Pardon the pun.

We met three Aboriginals droving a mob of cattle today. Len was taken with the hardiness of the stock and is now trying to convince Uncle Sam we should buy some.

. . .

Monday, 17 June 1929
It's rained! The land is awash with puddles and water. And everyone is smiling.

Tessa closed the book with a snap and picked up her cold cup of tea. She'd been swept away for the last few hours. Standing up, she stretched and picked up the next diary. She was impatient, wanting information to jump out at her, but it was all just bald historical stuff. Just as Elsie had told her. The 1934 diary seemed much the same. Although she had to admit, she felt like she was gaining a better understanding of her family.

'Bugger it,' she swore. 'There just have to be letters somewhere.' Her mind was whirling. She went back and looked at the photos, trying to glean something from them.

Then she noticed something sparkling on the wooden floor and bent down to look. It was a piece of glitter from Harrison's hat. For a moment, she was lost in thought. Could she even entertain the idea of him?

Don't be ridiculous. She shook her head. *You're lonely because you haven't seen Brendan. And once again, when some bloke pays attention to you, you fall into his arms. Just* stop *it!*

'Who knows, Dozer,' she finally said to the dog, who was sleeping on the floor. Without his eyes opening, Dozer thumped his tail. 'Come on, it's time for a walk. Maybe I should christen my new boots! My head's crammed with history, men and diaries!'

Chapter 25

Tessa pulled the ute door shut. When she'd made herself comfortable, Ryan started the engine and put the LandCruiser into gear. Slowly they drove away from Spider's house.

They were heading for the Nullarbor Muster at Rawlinna Station, and Tessa could barely contain her excitement. Brendan would be there! It felt like years, not just a month since she'd seen him.

She was conflicted when she thought about Harrison, especially knowing she would see a lot of him because of Cally, so she tried not to think of him at all.

'You look a bit try-hard in all that new gear,' Ryan said, catching her eye in the rear vision mirror.

'I know,' she moaned. 'But I think it's better than wearing clothes that would be just so out of place.'

'I'm gonna step on those boots and christen them as soon as we stop,' he threatened.

'That's something I think of every time I buy new shoes.' Tessa laughed. 'We always did that as kids. Did you Marni?'

'Um, nope.'

'We loved jumping on whatever new shoes we'd been given – while our feet were still in them, mind you. I'd end up with some horrible bruises from Ryan.'

'You weren't bad at it yourself,' he answered.

They swung onto the highway. In three hours they would join the queues of utes and other four-wheel-drives making their way to the annual rodeo.

She remembered from her childhood that the trip could be very different from one year to the next. Sometimes they drove through massive potholes and down two-wheel tracks full of mud. They'd laugh as they slid around the road. Others, bogged to the axles, had not been so fortunate. In some years, though, the dust had been so thick it was hard to see three feet in front of the bullbar and the holes filled with bull dust would make for an uncomfortable ride.

Ryan cranked up the stereo and Marni began humming to a country artist Tessa had never heard before.

'Who's singing?'

'Beccy Cole,' Marni answered. 'She's good. If you like her, you'll like Sara Storer and Gina Jeffreys.

They're all solo artists but they sing together. Call themselves the Songbirds. I could listen to them sing the bills on Ryan's desk!'

For the rest of the trip, Marni introduced Tessa to new country music singers. The three of them sang and laughed together. Tessa was thrilled to see Marni and Ryan so much more relaxed, now they had a plan in place to try to get pregnant. Even though Tessa assumed there would still be tough times ahead, she was sure they'd be okay.

As they drew closer, the traffic increased until there was one long line of vehicles. Some were towing horse floats and some hauled trailers. Most of the cars had their windows down, country music blaring from the speakers. People who were travelling together kept the airwaves busy, calling each other to warn of deep bogs or to agree on a good spot to stop and have a break.

Tessa noticed that many of the vehicles had spotlights and aerials on the roof and were loaded up with swags. The atmosphere was electric and they hadn't even reached the grounds yet!

Finally they pulled up in the camping bays. Tessa helped Ryan and Marni unload and they began work on setting up their site. They'd brought their own wood to burn in the large iron rings supplied for small fires. Ryan expertly lit the kindling while Marni unpacked the chairs and food. Tessa threw the swags onto the ground and made sure there was room for Peggy and Paul to join them later.

She could hear music coming from the main arena and bulls bellowing from their pens.

Straightening, she gazed around, trying to see if she could catch a glimpse of Brendan. Everywhere she looked people were setting up camp. Shouts and expectation filled the air. A group of young lads ~~was~~ were hanging out the back of a stationary ute, all with cans of rum'n'Coke in hand, yelling encouragement to a group of girls who were dancing to their own music.

The smell of woodfire smoke and food wafted through the camps and there was the sound of children laughing everywhere.

Tessa smiled. She had missed this.

'Tessa! Tessa!'

She turned towards the voice. Cally was running, waving at her.

'Look at you!' Tessa exclaimed as the girl twirled in front of her. 'You look beautiful.'

'Everything fits perfectly,' Cally said with a grin. 'I feel amazing.'

'So you should. When did you get here?'

'A couple of hours ago. I came with old Joe. Dad came early 'cos he had some stuff to organise.'

'Joe's here? Fantastic! I've got some questions to ask him.'

'He's around somewhere, probably checking out all the horses.'

'Cool, I'll find him a bit later. So, tell me, when do you ride? I don't want to miss it.'

'This afternoon.' Cally tugged at Tessa's hand. 'Come on. I'll show you around.'

Tessa laughed. But thinking it might be a good chance to find Brendan, she agreed.

'I'll catch up with you somewhere, sometime?' she said to Ryan and Marni.

'Yeah, well, you won't get lost. We'll find you, or you'll find us. See you later.' Ryan waved as he slipped his arm around Marni's shoulder. Tessa saw her look up at him and smile. The tension between her brother and his wife had definitely dissipated.

Tessa focused on Cally. 'So where do we start?'

'The horses,' Cally stated firmly.

'Naturally.'

Weaving their way through the other camps, Cally stopped occasionally to say hello to people she knew. Finally they made it to Cally and Harrison's horses. They were tethered next to their float, happily chewing on hay. Big plastic buckets of water lay within reach. Cally pressed her face against Megs' shoulder and the horse nuzzled her. 'We're gonna try really hard to win today, aren't we, beautiful girl?'

'Give it your best shot, Cally. But it doesn't matter if you don't win.'

Maybe I should take my own advice, Tessa thought as soon as she said it. She'd always wanted to be the best, and had strived to do everything better than anyone else. She'd always sought everyone's approval, and if she didn't get it she'd tried to make

Gromover . 7

285

herself into what other people wanted her to be. She didn't want to see Cally become like that. That sort of process destroyed you. It spun you around until you didn't know who you were or who you had been.

'I want to, though. For Mum. She always won.'

'She may have done, but all she would've wanted from you is to do your best. And be yourself.' She hoped it's what Spider would have said to this girl.

Cally didn't answer – she was too busy crooning to Megs. Then she turned. 'Come on, there's more to show you.'

They wandered over to the main arena, where transportable cattle yards had been set up.

'Bull riding.' Cally waved towards the ring. 'That's where they hold the horse and barrel races. And over here,' she indicated a large shed, 'food, dancing, drinking. All that sort of stuff. And the arm-wrestling competition. Did you know Ryan won it last year?'

'What? My Ryan? Are you serious?' Tessa looked at the girl. 'He's puny!'

'Dad says he wiry and strong.'

'There seem to be many things I don't know about my family! Next you'll be telling me Mum won a dancing competition!'

'Nope, but she cooks the best doughnuts.'

As they wound their way through the crowd, Tessa could see people were gathering in the shed where the bar was.

She was on constant lookout for Brendan but

so far she'd not sighted him. What she did notice was the sea of hats and checked shirts, faded jeans and belts with large buckles. It was almost like a uniform.

'I'd better go and get Megs,' Cally said an hour or so later, after she'd shown Tessa through all of the sights. 'I want to get her ready.'

'Do you need any help?'

'I'll be fine. But don't forget to come and watch me, will you?'

'I won't, I promise. Good luck!'

Suddenly on her own in the crowd, Tessa didn't know what to do. Feeling self-conscious she decided to head back to the camp. As she pushed her way through the masses she willed Brendan to appear, but he didn't.

There's plenty of time, she thought. *It goes for the whole weekend. He said he'd be here.*

Finding herself in an open area, she stopped and watched the hustle and bustle, the flow of bodies. She was listening to the laughter and rumble of voices when she felt a hand on her shoulder and spun around.

'It's good to see you, Tessa.' A stooped old man with watery eyes stood before her. Tessa broke into a smile.

'Joe! Cally said you were here!' She grasped his hand tightly. 'It's so good to see you again.'

'The yarn we had at Violet's funeral was too short, missy. I want to catch up with all of your latest news.'

'And I've got a heap of questions for you. So we'd better make time for a chat.'

'How long you staying 'round?'

'For as long as it takes to clean Aunty Spider's house out, at least. She left a letter asking me to do it.'

'There's no one else who woulda done it right. Now, how about you make an old man happy and have a drink with him. I was just on me way to the watering hole.'

'I'd really love to, Joe, but it will have to be something soft.'

Together they ambled across to the bar and ordered some drinks. Then they sat on a bench against the wall and talked of old times.

'Cally says you're not breaking horses anymore?'

'Nah, mate. I like to go easy these days. Getting a bit doddery on me feet to be in the yards. 'Specially with those young, flighty things that come in from the bush.'

'Are there still brumbies around?'

'Too right, there are. Not as many, but they're there. Some bloody good stock horses in amongst em, but it'll take a better man 'n me to get 'em.'

'You need to cut that out, Joe! You sound like you've put one of your own feet in the grave already!'

'You'll understand when you get to my age. Now, tell me about you.'

'Not much to tell, really. I'm not going back to

England. I'll stay out here until I've finished Aunty Spider's house, then make a decision about where to go from there.' She cocked her head to the side. 'How long have you been out here, Joe?'

'On the Nullarbor? Too long to remember. It seems like forever.'

'Do you remember Violet as a girl?' She saw his puzzled expression and explained. 'I'm trying to solve a bit of a mystery but I'm not really sure what I'm looking for. Found a couple of wedding rings and Spider left a note saying there're a few family secrets in the closet. Any ideas?' She looked at him hopefully.

'Reckon you're asking the wrong person there, Tessa. Never been around enough to hear any rumours. Spend it out on the fences by meself these days. Even when I was breakin' horses, I never stayed around long enough to hear. Plus me memory ain't what it used to be.'

'Oh well, it was a long shot, but I thought I'd ask anyway.'

'Tessa! Come on! You're gonna miss my ride.' Cally appeared at her side. 'Hi, Joe, are you coming to watch me too?'

'Yes, Miss Cally. I'll be there.' Joe touched a finger to his battered hat and smiled at her.

'Cool! Now I just gotta find Dad.'

'You go and get Megs,' Tessa said. 'I'll find Harrison.' She turned to Joe. 'I'll see you over there.'

*

Tessa hung over the rails, standing so close to Harrison they were touching. She felt so proud of Cally. The horse and girl blended with each other, and Megs' hooves kicked up dirt as she wove around the forty-four gallon drums. Cally's only obvious movement was her arms pushing forward, urging Megs to go faster. She and the horse blended as one.

Harrison's eyes never shifted from his daughter and her mount. 'Come on,' he muttered. 'Come on.'

'Is she going fast enough?'

'She's not doing too bad.'

As Cally reeled her mount around and galloped towards the finish line, Harrison leaned further over the fence and yelled encouragement. The rest of the crowd whistled and applauded. Tessa couldn't help but get caught up and she started yelling, too. But by the time she'd found her voice, Cally had crossed the finish line and started to slow.

'Good girl!' Harrison said, clapping loudly. 'Now we'll have to wait and see how the others do to find out who wins.' He turned to Tessa. 'She was so much more confident today. That was because of you.' He gave her a warm grin. 'Thanks again for what you did with the clothes. It's made a big difference to her.'

'You're welcome,' Tessa answered, aware her cheeks had flamed under Harrison's gaze.

At that moment she realised someone was shouting. They both looked towards the noise. Two men were in a scuffle. One had the other in a headlock and was trying to get a punch into the other's face.

'Bloody hell, Ray McKenzie. He couldn't have had too much to drink already. Trouble just follows that bloke.' Harrison strode off to break up the fight.

Ray McKenzie? Tessa followed Harrison at a distance and watched as he skilfully got in between the feuding males and gave them a dressing down. She could see both offenders were older – in their late sixties, she guessed. That could make Ray McKenzie Brendan's dad. In fact, she was certain she could see a resemblance, despite the dirt and sweat covering his face.

Even though Tessa was thinking about Brendan, she found she was watching Harrison.

'If you want to be fucking idiots and kill each other, get outside of the arena and go where there aren't any kids watching,' she heard him say angrily.

Thank goodness they weren't so cut they didn't listen to him. Sheepishly the pair wandered off in different directions, but not before she heard Ray mutter: 'This isn't finished, Hunter. Not by a long shot. You can't go spreading rumours about me without any evidence and get away with it.'

Harrison shooed them away and Tessa watched, feeling that anyone under Harrison's protection would be safe indeed. She shook herself. *Geez, stop daydreaming about Harrison!* For goodness sake, she obviously needed to find Brendan.

Chapter 26

Outside the shed, roaring fires lit up the darkening night. Smells of cooking made Tessa realise she hadn't eaten since mid-morning.

Pushing her way through the dancers who were cutting up the cement floor, she joined everyone who was queuing for food. She looked for someone she knew, but there was such a throng of people, she just couldn't find anyone local.

A drunken man fell against her as he tried to negotiate the macarena and a line started snaking its way around the shed. Tessa smiled, but for once felt no urge to join it.

She collected a heaped plate, thanked the caterer and manoeuvred her way back over to the wall, where she could eat, hopefully without interruption. Cally would be off with her friends and the bull riding was due to start in half an hour.

The crowds in the food hall would start to thin as they made their way over to the arena to watch. Tessa thought she might give it a glance, but she was more intent on finding Brendan.

With the growling of her belly silenced, it was time to find a loo. She'd been putting it off, knowing it would be a port-a-loo. Might be easier to go out into the scrub and find a bush. Still, that could be embarrassing too. As she made her way out the door, she saw Joe again, sitting by himself nursing a beer. He'd been there since she had left him and she'd seen a string of locals come and sit, chat and then move on. Joe was definitely in seventh heaven.

'Hi, Joe,' she said and walked on.

'Tessa,' he said. 'Pleased I seen ya. Come and sit over here.'

'Got to run to the loo,'

'Won't take a minute.' He patted the bench next to him. She sat down.

'Been thinking about your question about Spider. A million years ago, there was a rumour going around. I just can't remember if it involved your aunt's family or another local lot. Course, it happened long before I got here, so it was sorta a folk story.'

'Sounds interesting.' Tessa smiled encouragingly, hanging onto her bladder.

'Not many would recollect the story now. Not unless you'd been here a long time.'

'No,' Tessa agreed, willing him to hurry.

'You'd know there used to be lots of camel trains?'

'Yes, I've read about them and seen some photos and paintings.'

'Now, this ain't gospel, girl. You understand me?' He didn't wait for her to nod. 'I seem ta think there was a local woman who ran off with one of them camel drivers.'

Tessa sat still.

Okay.

She hadn't expected that. What a scandal it would have caused back then.

She quickly reviewed her scant knowledge of family history but couldn't see how that would apply to the Mathisons. Oh, but what a wonderful tale it would make!

'That's pretty interesting. Do you know what year it was?'

'Nah, the rumour mill is the best I can do. Now you run along.'

'Thanks, Joe.' Tessa kissed his cheek and bolted for the loo.

'Tessa! There you are, I've been looking everywhere for you.' Cally rushed up to her, breathless. 'Come on, the DJ is starting the proper music. We've finished everything for the night. Come and dance!'

'I was going to go to bed!'

'You can't! Come on!' The girl grabbed her by the hand and pulled her back towards the dance floor, where the music was thumping. Laughter reverberated around the shed and Tessa was surprised at how noisy she found it.

Cally started to move. Tessa did too, but then Cally stopped.

'Show me how to do that move,' she instructed. Tessa showed her the dance move and a couple of others.

'Jackie,' Cally called to one of her friends. 'Come and try this!'

Before she knew it, Tessa was holding a small dance class in the middle of the Nullarbor Muster.

Peggy tapped her on the shoulder. 'Looks like you've got a following,' she shouted and smiled. Paul spun his wife around and they danced away. Further over, Tessa caught sight of her brother, swaying with Marni.

The hot burn in her eyes took her by surprise as happiness bubbled to the surface. She was here and she was loved. And she felt like she was really, truly at home.

Feeling a tap on her shoulder she turned to see Harrison standing close. Tessa drew in a sharp breath as her stomach and heart reacted of their own accord. What was it about this man?

'Dance?' he asked, holding out his hand.

'S-s-sure,' she stammered and cursed silently as the music changed to a slow song.

Harrison slipped his arms around her and they swayed in time to the music. Tessa was sure he would be able to feel her heart beating through her chest or at least her quick, sharp breaths.

Go with it, her inner voice urged.

She shut her eyes and let the music and Harrison's dancing take her away.

'Geez, didn't take you long to move on.'

The loud voice cut across her reverie. Brendan! Tessa jerked away from Harrison and tried not to look guilty. *You haven't done anything wrong*, the voice inside told her.

'I've been looking for you!' she exclaimed and threw her arms around him.

'I thought I'd been replaced,' he said, sounding churlish.

'Not on your life,' she responded. 'Come on, let's go outside.' She turned around to apologise to Harrison, only to find he'd disappeared. Then she spotted him leaning against the wall, looking unhappy.

Feeling a small amount of regret, she linked arms with Brendan and they walked out into the night.

'Haven't got much time,' he said as he backed her up against the outside wall of the shed and kissed her. 'Gotta unload some fresh bulls for tomorrow.'

'I'm just glad to know you're here,' Tessa answered, looking up into his face and smiling, trying to placate him. 'I've missed you.'

'I've missed *you*.' His charm was back and he kissed her again.

'So can I catch up with you later?' she asked, when she pulled away.

'Yeah. Not sure when I'll be finished, but I'll come and find you. Look, I better go. I just needed to clap eyes on you after all this time.'

'It's okay. I know everyone's got their jobs to do.'

He leaned forward and kissed her again then disappeared into the glare of the spotlights.

She stood there a moment, savouring the sensation of his arms around her. Then, turning, she looked inside the shed. Tessa threw her head back and laughed loudly. But no one heard because that blasted macarena line had started up again.

'Night all.' Tessa waved and stepped out into darkness. Except it wasn't dark. Spotlight towers lit the way back to the camp and the glow of fires made her feel safe.

Grabbing a torch from the glove box of Ryan's ute, she headed off in search of a small piece of quietness and stars. She had to walk a fair way to find it, but she did, and with a happy sigh she sank to the ground. Sitting cross-legged she thought about the evening. It had been so much fun, but the best bit was that she had got through it without even thinking about a drink. Knowing that, the stars appeared to shine a little brighter. She nodded. Yes, that was cause for celebration.

And it had been so good to see Brendan. Now, surely, she could lay aside those thoughts about Harrison.

She turned her head slightly, thinking she could hear something. Faint shouts were coming from the toilet area. She shrugged. Probably a few drunken blokes having a bit of a punch-up.

Then she heard running.

And puffing.

Tessa jumped to her feet and flashed her torch around, but she couldn't see anything. She frowned and walked towards the toilet blocks. The yelling was still going on. Then she saw Brendan.

She opened her mouth to call out to him, but then stopped. There was something wrong here. Then she realised there was someone else with him, on the ground. As she came closer, she realised it was Joe.

Brendan must have been yelling for assistance. 'What's wrong? Do you need help?' she called as she started to run.

Brendan turned at the sound of her voice, a worried look on his face. It cleared the moment he saw her.

'Babe.' His grin was as wide as the sky, then he dropped to his knees alongside Joe. 'Yep, you'd better get someone. I found him like this.'

'I've got a first-aid certificate. Let me look. You want to get the ambos?'

Bustling in, she squatted down and looked into Joe's face, before taking his wrist and feeling for a pulse. He had blood seeping from his nose and a bruise starting on his cheek already. 'Joe! Joe, it's Tessa. Can you hear me?'

His eyelids flickered, then his eyes opened and he groaned. 'What happened?'

Brendan loomed over them and Tessa saw an emotion she couldn't read enter Joe's eyes.

'It's okay, Joe, I'm here,' she said quickly. 'What happened?'

'Yeah, mate, what happened? I came for a slash and found you here. You have a turn or something?' Brendan sounded concerned.

'Get away from me!' Joe struggled to his feet. 'I'm fine,' he muttered. 'Fine, I tell you.' He tried to walk away but staggered. Tessa moved to catch him.

'You're not going anywhere,' she said. 'Brendan, can you get the ambos?'

'Yeah, sure, babe.' Tessa heard him run.

'You look to me like you've been punched,' Tessa said quietly. 'You've got blood coming from your nose. You didn't have a turn, did you?'

The expression on Joe's face was one of complete defeat. 'Wrong choices,' was all he said. 'Made some wrong choices.'

She didn't push it any further. Instead, she made sure he was comfortable and sat with him until help arrived.

*

Brendan slipped his arm around her shoulders as they watched Joe being loaded into the back of the ambulance. Tessa did her best not to pull away. She wasn't sure what she had seen, but something didn't feel quite right about Brendan's account.

Joe'd be fine, they'd been told, just a few scratches and a horribly bruised cheek. He was an old man, he'd had a few too many, he could have fallen.

'Never many fights at the Muster,' said Lizzie, one of the medics. 'Probably bashed his head on the ground.'

Joe remained silent as he was settled in.

Tessa watched him, feeling whatever fight he had left in him was gone.

'Poor bugger,' Brendan said with feeling. 'Geez, I'm pleased I came along.'

'Yeah, that was lucky,' Tessa agreed.

'You coming for a drink?'

'Oh Lordy, I don't think so!' Tessa pressed her fingers to her forehead, trying to ward off a headache. 'I was just on my way back to camp when I saw you. I know we organised to catch up, but I'm wrecked. Can I catch you in the morning?' She was unsettled after everything that had happened.

'Going to find Harrison?' Brendan snapped, a look of jealousy crossing his face.

'What? No.' Tessa was stunned at the venom in his voice. 'I really just need to have a sleep.' And I'm not sure about you, she thought.

She turned her back on him but felt his hand on her shoulder. 'Sorry, babe. I just wanted to spend a night with you.'

Tessa stared up at him. 'And you can, just not tonight.' Not wanting to start a fight, she reached up and kissed him, before starting back to the camp. She resisted the urge to glance over her shoulder as she got further away. She knew Brendan was watching her.

Once she was comfortable in her swag, she lay on her back, staring at the stars. There was something wrong with what she had just seen, but what was it? Tossing and turning, she relived the moment, trying to work out what it was.

Then she got it. Brendan had his fist clenched. Had he hit Joe? But why?

A voice whispered in her memory. *I'm a bad boy.*

Surely not so bad as to hit an old man? What cause would he have? And with that thought, she drifted off to sleep.

'Tessa, wake up!'

She opened her eyes. Paul was standing over her. Behind him, the sun was high in the sky.

She struggled to sit up under the weight of the tarp.

'Come on, we need you to come and help us clean up,' Paul said seriously. 'We're shutting down early this year.'

'Why? What's happened?'

'Old Joe died last night. Had a stroke in the ambulance.'

'No!' The word sprang from her lips without thought. 'He was only hurt. Roughed up a bit from a fall or punch.'

'Probably brought on by that,' Paul confirmed. 'Anyway, let's get packed up and help Harrison. He'll have a bit on his hands today, being Joe's boss and all. We don't think Joe had any other family, so everything will fall on Harrison's shoulders.'

Tessa wriggled out of her swag and found some water to splash on her face. The place was strangely quiet. People were speaking in low voices as they rolled their swags and packed their cars.

Most people had known and liked Joe, even the tourists who came year after year. He'd been around for so long. To close early was a sign of respect.

Tessa blinked back tears, reliving her last conversation with him, seeing the beaten look on the old man's face and the funny expression that had flickered in his eyes when he saw Brendan. Was it fear? She couldn't be sure.

She didn't really know what had happened last night and it would be wrong to make assumptions, she decided. But she did remember Peggy's comments about the McKenzies at Spider's funeral.

And the angry jealousy that had radiated momentarily from Brendan last night made her feel he wasn't the person she thought he might have been.

Chapter 27

As the news sank in, Tessa's heart began to thud like a drum.

Dead! Poor Joe was dead.

Her only thought was to find Brendan. She *had* to know what happened last night.

She ran a brush through her hair and cleaned her teeth. Then she quickly helped Marni pack the car.

'I'll go and find Harrison, see what I can do for him,' she said when they were done.

The atmosphere had changed since the night before. The blow-ins, those who hadn't known Joe, were still drinking and partying, but the locals were grim-faced and quiet.

An announcement from the MC came over the PA. With only a half-day left of the Muster, the bar would close early and the last race was cancelled out of respect for Joe. There would be a minute's silence to remember the old horse breaker at three p.m.

Tessa's eyes filled with tears. The Nullarbor people might be few, but their hearts were big and they would miss the old man as one of their own.

She set off in search of Brendan. She tried the bull yards – nothing. Then the horses. Still nothing.

The food area was crammed with the hungry and hungover, and she elbowed her way across the room, scanning the crowd. Nothing.

Next she tried the car park. It was filled with trucks waiting to take the animals back to their stations. There she saw him, leaning up against a float, talking to his father.

At first glance it looked like a normal conversation. But Tessa knew that first impressions weren't all they seemed. She watched carefully and noticed the tension in Brendan's shoulders and how his head was pushed forward towards Ray.

She strained, trying to hear what they were saying, but their voices were a low buzz.

Taking a deep breath, she ducked behind a trailer and walked nonchalantly towards them, keeping vehicles between her and them.

'It was the wrong thing to do. Poor old bugger.' Brendan's voice was filled with anger.

'Ah, piss off. You should have dealt with this long before now. You're just gutless.'

'It was in hand. I kept telling you that.'

'Well, it's done now. Finished.'

'Bastard,' Brendan hissed.

'Yeah, mate.' Ray's voice sounded carefree. 'That's me. And you're my son, so you know what it makes you. Now 'cos I've fixed your last fuck-up, you make sure you get what you need out of that girl. That bloody old Violet definitely had something on me – you know she did. Get it and fix it.'

'You know I've been trying. I searched last time I was there.'

'Not good enough.'

There was the sound of boots on gravel. Tessa ducked down and peered through the wheels of the trailer. What? Tessa's mind whirled with confusion. At the same time, after hearing the anger between the two men, she was convinced Brendan had something to do with Joe's death. If he didn't, Ray must have.

Ray stalked past her hiding place. Now was her moment. She wished her heart wasn't pounding quite as fast. As she stood up she felt a wave of dizziness, but she took a breath and her head cleared. Nervously she started towards him.

'Hi, Brendan,' she said, when she was within a couple of metres of him. The vehicle looked like it was the only thing holding Brendan upright. He had his head in his hands.

He looked up and saw her. A wave of conflicting emotions passed over his face before he settled on coldness.

'What can I do for you, Tessa?'

'Do you know Joe is dead?' she asked, facing him straight on.

'Course I do. What about it?'

'I just want to know what happened last night, Brendan. I don't think he fell.' Tessa felt the urge to take a step back from him, but she knew she had to hold her ground.

'Are you saying you don't believe me?' said Brendan raising his voice as he drew himself up straight and looked her in the eye. 'You reckon I hurt him?'

Tessa felt fear rush through her, but she couldn't stop now. She crossed her arms to hide her shaking hands. 'I don't know, but I do know what I saw last night. I'm not stupid.'

'Mate, you know fuck all. You know *nothing*!' he said moving towards her, his fist clenched. Fury was written all over his face. 'You reckon you know what happened last night?'

This time, Tessa did take a step backwards. And another, and another, as Brendan advanced towards her. She felt her back run into the edge of the bullbar – she was trapped. Her stomach constricted, but she knew not to let the apprehension show on her face.

'No, I don't know!' she said calmly, trying to pacify him. 'I want you to tell me. I'm not doubting you, Brendan. I'm not, but I think you know more than what you told everyone last night.'

As Brendan came closer she smelt his sour breath, noticed his bloodshot eyes and felt the anger radiating from him.

'It was pretty clear you doubted me last night. You couldn't wait to get away from me. I warned you. I *told* you I was a bad boy.'

Tessa's mouth fell open. 'You *did* do something to Joe. I don't believe you. I thought you knew more than you were telling.'

'I did nothing to the old man. You hear me? Nothing.' He grabbed hold of her arm.

At that moment Harrison appeared from around the corner. 'What's going on here?' he shouted as he grabbed Tessa by the other arm and pulled her behind him. 'Got a problem, mate?' he said to Brendan.

Brendan blinked. His focus changed. 'No problem here, mate.'

'Didn't look that way to me. What is it with you bloody McKenzies? Just can't resist picking on a woman? Like father, like son. Get some fucking manners.'

'And who made you king?' Brendan spat. 'Anyone would think you're a bit keen on "the lady". Or do you always play "knight in shining armour" when something's none of your business?'

'Listen here,' Harrison said quietly. 'I never knew what Violet saw in you and I don't know what Tessa sees in you. What I do know is, she was your only friend out here. You don't try to fit in, so you

307

never will. Neither does your father. Your family's reputation goes before you, McKenzie, so you might as well leave now. And so help me, if I ever catch you or your bloody father terrifying another woman, I won't be responsible for what I do. Now go on, piss off.' He jerked his head towards the vehicles and stared Brendan down, until the younger man shook his head and moved off.

Harrison kept an eye on him until he was out of sight. Then he turned to Tessa. 'Come on, let's go.' He gently took her by the arm and they strode back towards the camp.

'Did you actually see Brendan do something to Joe?' Peggy looked hard at Tessa.

'No, I didn't, Mum. I've told you all I saw. It's nothing other than a feeling I have. It's more that I think he knows more than he's saying. Maybe he knows who did it.'

'Well you need to tell the police. Let them judge whether the information is important or not. They've been asking questions of people all day. So after we've packed up here and said goodbye to Ryan and Marni, we'll go and tell them everything you saw.'

Tessa fiddled with the hem of her shirt, feeling torn. 'I, um . . .'

'Tessa, no matter what your relationship with him was, you need to talk to the police.' Paul's tone was no-nonsense. 'And you should tell them what he did to you. It's clear he's a nasty piece of work and you'll just have to avoid him. I'm sorry, Tessa.'

'I don't want to accuse him of anything. I just think there's more to Joe's death than a fall!'

'If there is, I'm sure the police or the coroner or whoever will work it out. But that's why they need any information, no matter how small. After all, you loved Joe as much as the rest of us.' He patted her shoulder. 'Thank goodness Harrison was close by.' He went back to packing up the transportable yards with Ryan.

Paul shook Ryan's hand as the women kissed goodbye.

'Wishing you all the luck in the world, Marni,' Tessa said as they hugged. 'I hope everything goes just the way you want it to.'

'Thanks, Tessa.' Marni brushed away a tear and got into the car.

'Take care.'

Ryan and Marni would drive to Kalgoorlie that night, then on to Perth the next day. They had no idea how long they'd be gone – a week or two, or three. The drive itself would take longer than a day.

Tessa couldn't help but feel, after everything that had happened, that a little baby would be a wonderful thing for the whole Mathison clan. She only hoped that if they ended up trying IVF that it would work.

It was dusk by the time Tessa and her parents left, joining the long line of car after car, and ute after ute, all leaving the Muster for another year.

She still felt sick, thinking she might have got Brendan into trouble. She hoped she'd been wrong. She tried to push it to the back of her mind.

Tessa, seated in the backseat, turned and looked behind her at the empty arena. Goosebumps crawled over her skin. The place was beautiful in the late sunlight, shrouded in dust. Beautiful and sad all at once.

Goodbye Joe, she thought. Then, with conviction, she turned around and looked out of the front windscreen. Because no matter what had happened at the Muster – the sad things, the scary things, the fun things – she had found herself. She hadn't gotten drunk, she hadn't slept with anyone, she'd stood up to Brendan and helped Cally. All of these small things amounted to something big.

Violet had been right. Home was where you could heal.

Chapter 28

A week later, Tessa sat staring at the simple wooden coffin in the Kalgoorlie funeral home chapel. She brushed away a tear as Harrison spoke.

'In closing, I'd have to say there was no one better with a horse. Joe's heart belonged to those creatures.' He turned to the coffin. 'Mate, the place just won't be the same without you.'

Before making his way back to his seat, he stopped just for a moment to place his hand on the coffin.

As he sat down, Tessa, sitting in the pew behind, felt the urge to reach out and touch him, to offer some comfort. He had no one. Cally was conspicuous by her absence.

Harrison's face was more lined than she'd seen it in the short time she'd been reacquainted with him. Joe's death had affected many but, by the look of it, none more than him.

Finally the celebrant concluded the service and everyone moved to the outer room for morning tea. Tessa stood with her parents and one or two others, all Nullarbor locals. Many others milled around, talking.

'Good old CWA ladies,' one man said as he bit into a piece of cake.

'Yes, they know how to put on a top spread,' Tessa agreed.

'Peggy! Paul! How are you both? Looking well as usual.' A man Tessa didn't know shook Paul's hand and took over the conversation.

Tessa wandered away to look at the photos on the wall. The low hum of voices and clinking of spoons against coffee cups soothed her sadness.

Harrison appeared with a coffee in hand. 'Thought you might want to know the police haven't come up with anything. They can't charge anyone, can't prove anything. Joe had a stroke and that's the end of it.'

Tessa sighed. 'I wish I got there just a minute or two earlier.'

Harrison shrugged. 'But you didn't. Don't dwell on it. Maybe you weren't meant to.'

'Rather profound of you, Harrison.' Tessa looked up into his face. She noticed for the first time the grey hairs at his brow line, but other than that, you wouldn't be able to guess his age.

'Yeah, well. One of those sorts of days.' He took a sip of coffee then put it down on a side table and faced Tessa. 'I've got an idea and I'm wondering if you'll help me with it.'

'Really? Sounds interesting. Something for Cally?' Tessa hoped it wasn't shopping. She was itching to get home and stay there for a while. The last few weeks had had their fair share of excitement. 'Where is she, by the way?'

'At the School of the Air with her teachers. They're leaving in a couple of hours for a school trip. Going to Perth.'

'Oh, she didn't mention anything.'

'I think the Muster had been taking up most of her thoughts recently. And I didn't want her at the funeral, just when she was about to go away for a week. Thought it might be too unsettling.' He rubbed his face.

'So, this thing you wanted help with?' Tessa asked curiously, shifting her weight from one foot to the other and adjusting her handbag.

'I wanted to discuss it with you at the Muster, then Joe died and things just went downhill from there,' he explained. 'Then I was going to organise to catch up a bit later, but I saw you with Brendan and, well, you know . . .' They hadn't spoken about the confrontation with Brendan McKenzie since it had happened.

Tessa screwed up her face. 'Don't want to even be reminded,' she said, holding up her hand as if to ward off his words.

Harrison shrugged. 'You're good at marketing?'

'It's what I'm trained in,' she answered.

'Do you think you could market something you didn't know much about?'

Tessa was puzzled. 'I'm not sure what you mean. I mean, the principles of marketing are the same, whether you're selling cheese or pens. You have to make people want to buy whatever you're advertising.'

'So you don't have to have an intimate knowledge of any industry to be able to promote it?' He handed his empty cup to the CWA lady who had come around with a tray. 'Thanks,' he said and turned back towards Tessa.

'No, it's all about research. If Fred Bloggs wanted me to sell his civil celebrant services, theoretically, I'd be able to.'

'Right. That's what I was hoping to hear. Would you be able to come up with a marketing plan for our lambs?'

The request stopped Tessa in her tracks. It had been months since she'd even thought about marketing. On top of that, she sure as hell didn't know anything about selling wool.

She hedged. 'That might be a little out of my league. There's been a lot of changes since I left the Nullarbor. I don't know anything about the wool industry these days.'

'Not wool. Lambs. Meat.' Harrison looked disappointed. 'I thought you'd like the challenge.'

'I do!' She knew he was trying to appeal to her

competitive side, but lambs? 'I'll need a bit more information than just "lambs"!'

'I want to sell the meat for the best price. It's that simple.' He shrugged.

'Tell you what. I'll do a bit of research when I get home and try to come up with some information. If I think it's worth going on with I'll let you know.' She smiled. 'But aren't you locked into selling them all at one time and that sort of thing?'

'Yeah, because of the freight, mainly. But, see, I had this idea about our meat being organically grown. Load of shit, really, but the fact is, we don't use chemicals on our pastures. Everything they eat is natural. Thought we might be able to find a niche market or something.'

He looked so hopeful, Tessa couldn't say no, even if she wanted to. It would be a reason to spend some more time with him. To impress him with her skills.

'That's thinking outside the square! I'll give it some thought and see what I can come up with.'

'Why don't I fly over and pick you up the day after tomorrow? You can spend the weekend and we can mull over it together.'

Tessa felt a thrill run through her. 'No worries. I'll try and do a bit of investigation before then.'

'Great.' He glanced at his watch and sighed. 'Right, I'd better be off and see Cally before she leaves. Imagine, fifteen kids and three teachers on a bus for seven hours. That's how long it'll take them to get to Perth! Probably longer in a bus.'

Tessa screwed up her nose. 'Couldn't think of anything worse. Give her a hug from me.'

Harrison nodded. 'Sure. And I'll see you in a couple of days.' He winked as he turned away, leaving Tessa smiling like a clown.

Get a grip! she thought silently, watching him move through the crowd. Her eyes strayed to his shoulders and down further. She blushed and turned away.

Tessa leapt from the car. 'I'm back, Dozer!' She ran to pat the dog, who was doing a kind of arthritic hokey-pokey as he attempted to jump up on her. 'Don't jump, you silly thing. You'll hurt yourself. Did you miss me?' She gave him another pat then opened the front door and looked around.

There was the sandalwood smell again. The diaries lay where she had left them.

Tantalised, she picked one up and let it fall open.

Sunday, 7 December 1930

Ali and his team are here to load the wool. They have towed a flatbed trailer with them. One by one, the men have loaded fifty-two bales onto it. Then they will tow it down towards Esperance. Tagon Harbour is where they'll meet the ship. The market is buoyant, we are told. So, once again, we are hoping for high prices.

Ali has stayed longer than usual this year.
The unseasonal rain has prevented him from
leaving. They are camped a little way away
from us, but they are all so quiet, you'd never
know they were here.

She snapped the book shut. *First, a cup of tea,*
then *you can start reading them*, she told herself.

In the kitchen she put on the kettle. Opening
the pantry, she reached up to grab the sugar. But
her fingers didn't grasp the jar firmly enough and
it tumbled down. With a crash, the glass shattered.

'Oh shit!' Grabbing the dustpan and brush, she
got onto her knees and began to sweep the sugar and
glass into a mound. She flicked the brush in under
the bottom shelf of the pantry. It hit something hard
and unyielding. She tried again, but the same thing
happened. This time there was a dull *thwack*.

She bent down and peered under. It was an old,
rusty tucker box about the size of a laptop computer
but bigger. It was what everyone used to pack their
food into in the old days. She dragged it out, cursing
as it spread the mess further, and lifted it onto the
table. Then she went back to cleaning up.

Dozer tried to nuzzle under her arm and lick at
the sweet treat.

'Get out of it, Dozer. Sugar isn't good for dogs.'

He lay back down and sighed.

When the floor was clean she returned to the
tucker box. 'I hope Aunty Spider cleaned this out

317

last time she used it. Otherwise it's going to be gross,' she told the dog, wrinkling her nose.

The latch was stuck, so she got a knife and wiggled it around, hoping to dislodge the rust. It finally came loose and she pulled up the lid.

'Oh, bloody hell, more papers! Aunty Spider, you were the biggest hoarder I've ever known! I thought I'd found everything there was to find.'

She reached in and grabbed a handful. How many more places had Spider hidden things? But as she started to read, she almost dropped the pile.

16 June 1942

My darling Violet,

I can't tell you where I am, because the censors will just cross it out. I am overseas, though. It is the first time we've been able to post letters since we left home, but I have written to you every day.

How are things on Danjar Plains? Has it rained?

Do you remember how we walked down the road, just before I left? The wildflowers were beginning to bloom and the kangaroos were grazing under the mallees. I think of that, all the time.

The smell here is putrid. We smell like rotting bodies, even though we are alive. The sound of gunfire is all around and the cries of the wounded are eerie.

I crave the quietness of the plains and your soft touch.

I often think about how we met. It was fate. You on holidays and me, a young English jackaroo, hoping to make my fortune in Australia. I was too shy to speak to you the first time I saw you, shoes in hand, walking along the sand staring out to sea. Fancy, our first time ever on the beach and we fall in love!

Violet, if I don't make it back, I want you to know I have never once regretted leaving England to be with you. I may have lived at Danjar Plains for only a couple of years, but it is my life. I love it the way you do. And I don't want to be anywhere other than where you are.

All my love, forever,
William

Tessa's eyes widened as she flicked through the rest of the pile. Something personal! This was the sort of thing she'd been so desperate to discover – and had despaired of finding. *Oh, my goodness!*

She went on to the next letter, realising they were in no particular order. The dates were higgledy-piggledy.

18 June 1942
Dearest Violet,
We've been moved, on a [the censor had struck out this line]. We are going into action

*[again, blacked out]. I love you, my darling. I
can't tell you how much.*

   *Keep the memories close, in case I don't
return.*

   All my love,
   William

23 July 1943
   Dear Mrs Anderson,
   *We regret to inform you that Second Lieu-
tenant William Anderson was killed in action
on 19 June 1943.*
   *The Australian Government sends its deep-
est sympathy.*
   Signed,

The signature was illegible.

Tessa kept flicking:
Dear Violet.
Dear Violet.
Dear Violet.
Dear Grace.
What? Dear Grace? It was Violet's handwriting.

Dear Grace,
   *My darling William is dead. Gone. Killed on
foreign shores. My darling, darling man.*
   I am heartbroken.
   Violet.

September 1941

Dear Grace,

Tom turned ten today. I must say he is such a strapping lad. There's none better on a horse and his ability to muster a paddock and bring in every animal is almost legendary!

I am recovering from William's death. I guess I always knew it was possible he wouldn't come home, but it doesn't stop the ache in my chest. I can function and keep going and that is what is important.

I thought I would find it lonely without him, but Tom keeps me company. He has a wicked sense of humour. The tricks he plays can just about stop my heart, but he has a kind and thoughtful side, too. Yesterday I came home after sheep work and found a pot of freshly picked wildflowers on the outside table.

I miss you, dear sister,

V x

Tessa's tea had gone stone-cold on the bench. When she finally tore herself away from the letters she found it was late afternoon.

Unwillingly, she put the pages down and went to light the hot-water system. Her mind was in a tangle. She was desperate to keep going, to unwind this family mystery. But she was keen to get on and research Harrison's scheme, too. And of course there was the weird conversation between Brendan and his father, back at the muster, when Spider's name was mentioned. Oh, the webs.

She decided to focus on the letters for today. On the one hand, she felt she was intruding upon her aunt's private world but, on the other, it was *her* heritage too – and if you don't have a history, then who are you?

But why were the letters to Grace not posted? It was a mystery.

Back inside, she spread out the letters and sorted them into piles. There were missives from Elsie, William, Ali. *Ali?* Now that was strange. The handwriting in Ali's letters was printed and careful. Perhaps they were from the camel-train man? Why would he be writing to Violet? But the biggest bundle was made up of the ones Violet had written to Grace.

Fetching the diaries and a piece of paper, Tessa began to make a timeline, trying to cross-match the letters to the diaries. Hopefully then she'd have a clearer picture of what was going on.

Something was fizzing inside her – excitement, perhaps. Or was it fear of what she might find? Either way, she was almost certain that if there *was* a family secret, it was within her grasp. She wanted to jump up and down and jiggle all at once, but she needed to stay calm and be methodical. Otherwise, she might miss some small clue.

Tessa started with the smallest pile.

9 March 1933

Dear Violet,

Here is the recipe you asked for when I passed your way last. It will work well with mutton.

Dripping for the pan

Mutton

Onion

Turmeric

Nutmeg

Cinnamon

Cayenne pepper

Water

Simmer all together for about two hours. We wouldn't usually add potatoes but it does help to fill out the meal.

We are travelling towards Ceduna and then I have managed to win a contract to cart supplies to Alice Springs. I won't be back your way for a long time.

Ali

. . .

1935

Dear Violet,

I am writing to let you know I am going home. I will travel by ship in three months. As much as I would like to see you, Tom and the rest of your family before I leave, it will be impossible. I am making my way towards Adelaide now.

Thank you for all your love and support,
dear friend.
    Ali

Tessa was confused. Why were they so friendly? Still, Violet had been a warm person and would have made sure she greeted and treated them all as family, if they allowed her to.

At least this solved the mystery of how Spider learned to cook her famous qorma!

Think, Tessa, think! Ali carted supplies to Danjar Plains and back-loaded wool to the coast. He must have done this for many years to forge such a friendship.

Joe's words came back to her. *A woman ran off with a camel driver.* Spider? Surely not. It was obvious she was too much in love with William. But wait! She checked the dates. It was 1935. Violet wouldn't have met William yet.

Did Violet have a lover before William? The questions! Tessa scratched down her thoughts so as not to forget, then laughed out loud. That was ridiculous. Spider would have been all of fourteen.

She stretched and looked at the clock. Midnight! Where on earth had the time gone? Barely able to keep her eyes open, she left the letters on the table and headed to bed.

Although she wasn't sure she'd be able to sleep, she needed to rest her eyes and clear her mind. She was agitated, as she thought through the different scenarios. Something she couldn't put her finger on was bothering her. Maybe if she lay quietly it would come to her.

She dozed, dreaming of Afghan trains, Violet and Ali. The smell of spices and sandalwood permeated her imaginings.

She awoke with a start. That was it!

She raced out to the lounge, switched on the light and looked at the photos. All of the brothers and Violet lined up in a row.

Yes! She could see it now. She'd never noticed it before. He wasn't just younger by years, but different. The colour of his skin was different to the rest of the family.

Something else jumped out at her. Every time Violet wrote in the diary, she had said 'my brothers and Tom'.

Tom wasn't a brother.

Was he the son of an Afghan? Of this Ali?

Did he even belong to the Mathison family? And if he didn't, then neither did her Dad, Ryan or herself.

Tessa's world tipped slightly sideways.

Chapter 29

The plane thundered along the airstrip then lifted off gracefully. Tessa watched her mum, who was standing by the ute waving, grow smaller. She glanced across to Harrison. He was stern-faced, concentrating on the instruments.

It would take only half an hour to get back to Mundranda, so instead of talking shop, she waited. She would try to enjoy the flight and look at the view.

Since her discovery two nights earlier, the letters had dominated her thoughts. But she had steadfastly left them on the bench, not looking at them. Even when her hand strayed of its own accord and picked up the top-most letter, she had willed her eyes not to look, and had finally convinced herself to put it down. To leave things as they were, to let sleeping dogs – or secrets – lie. If she was honest with herself, the truth was she was frightened.

Instead, she'd told herself she had research to do. Then she braved the slow internet connection at the homestead to get as much information about organic lamb as she could. She was keen to impress Harrison, suspecting he thought her a bit of an idiot for getting involved with Brendan. She couldn't say she would blame him, or hadn't thought that herself.

Now she looked at him out of the corner of her eye and was embarrassed to find he was watching her from under the brim of his sparkly hat. Quickly, she looked down at the folder on her lap and busied herself with sorting her notes. For an older bloke, Harrison was handsome, she'd decided. The flecks of grey at the sides weren't too obvious – distinguished, really – and although sadness still lined his face, it disappeared when he smiled.

Then Tessa scolded herself. *He's forty, for good-ness sake. You are twenty-four. Why are you thinking like this? You have to learn to stop running after the first bloke who looks at you. Bloody hell, woman, I thought we'd already been through this.*

The sun had begun to sink. Something glinted in the scrub below. 'What's that?' She tried to lean out the window but only succeeded in bumping her head.

Harrison twisted in his seat and leaned over her to look. Tessa pushed herself further back in the seat, not wanting to touch him.

'Don't know.' He glanced at his watch. 'Let's have a look, eh? We've got time before the light runs out.'

He turned the rudder and the plane gently tipped downwards towards the reflection. It instantly disappeared.

As they flew low over the area Tessa tried to spot the reflection again, but it never reappeared.

'Whatever it was, we've lost it,' Harrison said.

Tessa nodded. Then she saw a clearing just below them. 'What's that?' She pointed.

'An old emergency airstrip. We use it for mustering. There's a few around. Otherwise, if someone gets hurt out in the paddock, the closest airstrip can be hours away. A few landholders got together and decided to put 'em down. Do you remember Harry Barlow?' Tessa shook her head. 'He was a bloke who fell from his motorbike and ended up with a mallee stick through his leg. He was in so much pain it was difficult to shift him. That was what made us decide to do it.'

'So you can land there?'

'Yep. Once every year or so, when the grader is around, we get the drivers to give them a bit of a tickle and take any of the bushes off that have grown. All good to land on.'

Soon Tessa felt the plane begin to descend and saw Harrison's place in the distance. Taking a deep breath she pinched her nose together and blew gently, trying to unblock her ears, but it didn't work. She knew she would be hopelessly deaf when they landed.

The sun disappeared from view just as the

wheels touched down. When Harrison steadied the plane as it careened down the dirt strip, Tessa tried not to notice his flexing muscles.

They taxied then stopped and Harrison indicated she could open the door.

'I bet it's quiet without Cally?' she said as she got out and stretched.

'The house is very empty,' Harrison said simply, as he pulled out her bags. 'But it's something I need to get used to. She won't be here next year. Now, have you got everything out? I need a hand to push the plane back into the hangar.'

They left their bags in the corner of the shed, pushed the Cessna in backwards and started towards the house.

The dogs heard them coming and reached the ends of their chains in excitement. A barked welcome went up. As Harrison hit the steps leading up on the deck, Tessa was trying not to think about being alone in the house with him.

'You know where the guest room is?' he asked, as if he'd read her mind.

'Yeah. I'll throw my bag in there and we can get started.' She was suddenly nervous. *Stick to business and you'll be fine*, she told herself.

On the kitchen table she dumped the folder containing all the information she'd collected.

'That looks pretty thick. You must have done your homework,' Harrison called as she headed off down the hallway.

'You can make that call after I've been through it with you,' she shouted back.

'Beer?' he asked when she returned.

Tessa took a breath. He was leaning against the kitchen bench, about to open a can of beer. He looked relaxed and content. And he was smiling at her.

'No, thanks. I don't drink anymore.' She looked down. 'But I'll have a lemonade if there's one.'

'Really? Why not?' He pulled open the fridge door and handed her a cold can.

'I can't control it,' she said, surprising herself with her honesty. 'That's been one of the good things about being holed up at Aunty Spider's. If there's nothing there, I can't drink it.'

'Oh. Does it make it hard when someone else drinks? I don't have to.'

'Not now. It did at first. I was really proud I got through the Muster without any problems. If I was going to muck up, it would have been there.' She was touched by his offer, though.

'I'll slip out and feed the dogs and horses,' he said, returning the unopened beer to the fridge. 'I won't be long.'

'I can start getting some dinner, if you like.'

'That'd be great.'

The back door shut with a bang – Tessa was all alone. But she knew the house well after her previous visit, so she busied herself putting the shopping away then started on a salad.

When she was finished, she took a sip of her lemonade and looked about her. A photo of Harrison and his late wife was on the sideboard. Harrison was looking at Ange and, judging by the expression on his face, it was clear he adored her. She picked up the photo and stared at it. Did he still miss Ange, she wondered. Could there even be room in his heart for anyone else? She sighed. *Business*, she reminded herself.

She heard the clunking of his boots on the verandah. Quickly she put the photo back and sat down at the table. She spread her notes in front of her.

The door opened. Harrison appeared and gave her a grin. He went to the fridge and pulled out a can of lemon squash. 'So, tell me what you've found out?' he said, sitting down. He opened his drink and took a sip.

'Well, I think the best place to start is for you to tell me your vision,' Tessa said, pleased her business voice hadn't deserted her.

'Right, it's like this. We grow wool and sell cull ewes and lambs for meat. But I'm wondering if there's a way we can change the *way* we sell. As I see it, we've actually got a product people are screaming for. Isn't the next big thing organically grown meat and vegies?'

'There does seem to be a leaning towards that,' Tessa agreed.

'So if we could supply a consistent product to, say, a restaurant, we should be able to increase the amount of money we get for each animal.'

'Sure. And that's what you want to achieve? Higher dollar value per head?'

'Yep.' Harrison sat back and linked his hands over his knees. He looked at her expectantly.

'Okay, I see it like this. One, you need a quality product.' She counted off her little finger. 'Two, you need consistent supply.' She tapped her ring finger. 'And three, you need to offer a guarantee that is so fantastic, people actually believe what you're saying.'

'What do you mean?'

'So, if you send a truckload of lambs to a five-star restaurant and it isn't the same product you've supplied them before, you'll give them the next shipment free, or something like that.'

'Ouch. You'd have to be certain, then?'

'Absolutely. Now, I see some problems. First off, the freight, the distance. Second, the fact you are only going to be supplying these lambs for a small part of the year, not for the whole time. And lastly, do you use a drench or fly preventative or anything like that?'

'Only jet the sheep with a chemical if we have flies or lice. Nothing else.'

'From what I've read, that would still be enough to stop you being able to call them "organic". So we would have to find another drawcard. Maybe the name. Something like "Desert Lamb".'

Harrison looked at her blankly. 'Would anyone go for that? It sounds a bit dry!'

'But see, it can work the other way, too. "Lamb" has the lovely warm and fuzzy connotation of fluffy babies jumping everywhere. The word "desert" makes me think of red dust, blue skies and vast plains. Just like the Nullarbor. Who would have thought those two words could go together. It's worth trying. See?'

'Yeah.' Harrison drew the word out.

Tessa could tell he wasn't convinced. 'Going back to the freight, I thought that if we can sell into a few top restaurants with seasonal menus, it won't matter if you can't supply the product all year round.'

Tessa could see that Harrison's brain was running at a million miles. She smiled.

He threw another couple of questions at her, which she answered with ease. She'd been prepared and was happy with her work. She hadn't lost it. She would be able to find another job when it came time to leave.

'Geez, you're amazing!' Tessa could see the new respect in Harrison's eyes and it felt good.

Over dinner they talked through it all again. Harrison seemed to grow more and more excited about the possibilities.

'Bring your cup of tea onto the verandah,' he said after they'd washed up and boiled the kettle.

'It's a beautiful night.' He took a box of chocolates out of the fridge and went outside.

Tessa followed him. She walked over to the verandah railing and looked up at the stars. 'It's so lovely out here,' she said, breathing the night air in. 'Peaceful.'

'Yep. But it's easy to forget how good it is when you're busy and you live here. So it's nice when some-one comes in and reminds you.' Harrison put his cup down and came to stand beside her. He leaned over the rails and his hands dangled close to hers.

'You've come at a fairly slow time of the year. In a couple of weeks, there'll be lambing, then lamb marking. We'll have calves to mark and later wean. The first few months of the year are reasonably quiet, except for bore runs and fencing. It's usually too hot to do anything with the stock. But then you'd know that.' He turned around and leaned against the railing, looking at her.

'I guess so, but I've sort of forgotten a lot of it. I really haven't spent much time here since primary school. School holidays, in high school, were more about what music I could listen to or books I could read. And study, especially in those later years.'

He handed her a chocolate, his fingers brushing hers. Accidental or not? Tessa couldn't tell.

She sipped her tea and said nothing until she had finished her cup.

'Well, I'd better get off to bed.' She was still standing, gazing out at the stars.

'Don't go yet.' Harrison leaned over and put his hand on her hip. 'Sit down. Tell me about you, Tessa. There are quite a few gaps in your story. What have you been doing, all the way over there in England?'

'You don't want to know,' Tessa said, meaning every word.

She sat down and thought for a moment before answering. 'I worked hard, played a bit harder, then Aunty Spider died and I came home. That's pretty much the executive summary.'

'Do you miss it?' He leaned forward, intent on her answer.

'I thought I did. I always loved the adrenalin of a great marketing campaign. Seeing the sales results come in and that sort of thing. But I'm not sure now. I've started to get my head in order since I've been back. Oh, I still want to work in marketing, absolutely, but not at the level I was over there.' She sighed and stretched her legs. 'I don't know.'

'So you don't think you'll stay out here?'

She noticed he looked down as he asked her the question. She cocked her head, wondering why he wanted to know, then shrugged. 'How can I? I have to work, I have to live. And once I've solved this bloody mystery of Aunty Spider's, apart from visiting family, I don't really have anything to do out here, do I?' She looked him straight in the eye. 'Unless there was a reason to stay.'

Harrison stared back and something passed between them. Tessa wasn't sure what it was. She broke the contact as she shot to her feet. She had to protect herself.

'Bed time, I think,' she said and walked past him.

Harrison grabbed her hand and stopped her. He stood up, still holding her hand.

Tessa swallowed, but held his eyes.

'Good night, Tessa,' he said softly. 'Thanks for everything.' He kissed her cheek.

Chapter 30

Harrison was certain that if he talked to Tessa he could get her to stay. He knew she liked Cally, and he loved how he saw another side of his little girl when Tessa was around. She'd really intrigued him with her bundles of insecurities. He knew how much she'd changed in the four months she'd been home – the plastered makeup was gone, she laughed more, and any rudeness had all but disappeared. It seemed the old proverb of 'train a child in the way they should go and when they are older they will not turn from it,' was right with Tessa. The way she had been brought up hadn't deserted her – she'd just strayed a little.

Harrison knew with love and constant support she would never become the person she'd been when she first arrived home. He was also discovering that he liked female company again. He hadn't thought about Ange as much as he usually did, and for the first time in a long time, Harrison was actually looking forward to the future.

But he knew he'd have to be careful how he approached her. Tessa was like a frightened calf. She'd watch him with those beautiful brown eyes, let him get close then, at the hint of trouble, flee back to the safety of Danjar Plains.

He stacked two cups into the Esky, along with sugar and teabags. It had been a long time since he'd packed a picnic. Harrison wondered what it would feel like to kiss her. Would he feel he was betraying Ange? He hoped not.

But he wanted to protect Tessa. Keep her away from all the things that hurt her, that haunted her eyes. And that bloody Brendan McKenzie.

He was instantly mad when he thought of that name. Prick. He wished he could have punched him at the Muster. Would have made him feel so much better. *Good one, Harrison*, he thought. *Very mature of you.*

He knew Brendan was only keeping company with Tessa so he could find out what Violet had on his family. Well he was too late. The information had already been passed on and was being investigated. He wouldn't find it.

He boiled the kettle and filled the Thermos with hot water. He stacked biscuits and sandwiches into the cooler and placed ice around them.

He had a plan. Take her on a drive. See if he

could get her as enthusiastic for this project as he was. It was the only way he could see of keeping her here, for the time being.

Tessa had been awake for hours, reading and keeping herself busy. She didn't want to think about anything. Not about Violet and the rings or Harrison and these ridiculous feelings she was trying to quell. And even if her feelings could possibly be reciprocated, she was tarnished goods. Shit, just look at her history with men. What would a man like Harrison want with a woman like her? And did she really belong out here, on the Nullarbor?

Argh! She wanted to scream. She lay back on the bed, hands behind her head and stared at the ceiling. She tried to imagine Spider sitting her down, asking those probing questions of hers.

Let's start with the easy bits, her aunt would have said. *You're attracted to Harrison.*

Tessa would have nodded. *But then I was attracted to Brendan, too. Made another stuff-up there. And even if I am attracted to Harrison, what's the point of it? I'm not sure I'm ready for happy-ever-afters yet.*

Could you see yourself with him in a year's time?

She turned over and hit her pillow. *Maybe.* She remembered his arms around her, the gentleness he had, the way he loved Cally. The way he'd acted at the Muster.

She sat up. 'Damn,' she whispered. 'I want some of that. I want to feel loved and wanted. Safe. He'd do all of that. Damn.'

Spider's voice was ringing in her ears, almost as if she was sitting right beside her. *Well then, dear, this takes out most of the variables, doesn't it? If you want Harrison, you'll have to stay out here, 'cos you won't shift him from the Nullarbor.*

Tessa could almost hear Spider cackle the way she always did when something turned out the way she knew it would.

Who's to say he wants me? But she was sure there had been signs that he might.

Tessa knew she was at a crossroads in her life and that was why she had to go. It was what she was good at – leaving, avoiding anything that might put her in touch with her feelings or drag up memories from long ago. She built walls and ran. That's how she dealt with things and this was to be no different.

A voice called through the door. 'Wake up, Tessa, we're off for a drive,' called Harrison, knocking so loud she jumped.

'Just a minute.' She took a breath. Did she? Didn't she? Would she? Could she? She thought frantically then opened the bedroom door.

'Mornin'.' He smiled and rested his hand on the door frame above her head. 'I'd like to show you some of the paddocks I thought we could dedicate to this lamb project.'

He looked fresh and relaxed and the crinkle lines around his eyes and his rumpled hair made Tessa want to fall into his arms. But no, she couldn't. She couldn't take the risk. 'Actually, Harrison, I'm not feeling very well. Would you be able to take me home when you've finished whatever you have to do today?'

Harrison frowned. 'What's wrong?'

'Nothing much, but I need to go home.' She avoided his stare.

'Right.' He frowned and his face settled into an unreadable deadpan expression. 'No problems. Give me half an hour to get the plane ready and we'll go.' He turned and left.

Tessa sagged against the door and shut her eyes. It was done.

They were both silent as they set out for Danjar Plains. *Uncomfortably silent*, Tessa thought sadly, as she snuck a glance at Harrison, when he wasn't looking. Then, about fifteen minutes into the flight, Tessa saw Harrison do a double-take as he looked out of the windscreen.

'Shit,' she heard him mutter.

Her stomach lurched. 'What?' She tried to keep the panic from her voice.

'The screws from the engine cowling flap have come loose.' He pointed to the front bonnet of the plane. 'Don't panic, it happens sometimes when you're using rough bush strips. They bump out. I'll have to land and screw them back in.'

He turned to her. 'Seatbelt on?' he asked, his face solemn.

'Yes.'

'Okay, we're going to land. There's no need to worry. It'll take me five minutes to get them back where they should be and you'll be home before you know it.'

'Right.' Tessa really meant *Shit*! Her hands began to tremble.

But the landing was smooth. When they'd come to a standstill, Harrison leapt out of the plane and opened the back door. Tessa watched as he pulled a small toolbox out and went to the front of the plane.

'You can get out if you want,' he called, before burying his head under the cowl flap.

Tessa climbed out. 'I might just stretch my legs.'

Harrison looked up. 'Just don't get lost. I don't need to be looking for you as well as fixing a bloody plane.'

Tessa tossed her head, indignant. 'Unlikely.'

She set off, but she was shaking. In all of the times she'd flown overseas, she had never once been in an air emergency. She wasn't even sure if this was really classed as one but, in her fragile state, it felt like it. Still, a walk would calm her nerves.

She spotted a glow of pink off to the side of the strip. Everlasting wildflowers. Tessa admired them for a moment, breathing deeply to stop her jitters. Then she walked a little further to see if she could find more.

She noticed a two-wheel track heading into the scrub. It looked like there were fresh wheel tracks going in. Remembering the glint she had seen the previous day and Ryan's stories of stolen stock, she followed it.

Not far in, she found a square metal frame covered in shade cloth. Outside there was a table, chair and a billy.

Someone's camp. 'Hello?' she called. 'Anyone around?'

Silence. Then she heard Harrison shouting in the distance.

'Tessa! Tessa, where are you?'

'Coming,' she yelled and followed the track back out onto the strip.

'We're right to go,' Harrison said.

'Someone has got a camp in the bush there.' She pointed. 'Are people allowed to camp on your land without you knowing?'

'We prefer if they ask,' he answered shortly. 'Just so long as they leave everything the way they found it, gates included. This isn't my land, though. It's Ray McKenzie's.'

Tessa squirmed at the mention of the name. 'This one looks a bit more permanent,' she said.

'Better have a look.'

Tessa led the way.

Harrison froze when he saw the camp. 'Holy hell.' He started to have a look around. 'This looks like some of Joe's stuff,' he said. 'I didn't know he had a camp out here.'

He lifted up the flap of shadecloth and let go a low whistle. 'Have a look at this.' He held the flap up higher. Tessa stuck her head inside. Steel shelves held trays of small seedlings. It took a moment for Tessa to register what they were.

'Oh Lordy, that's marijuana,' she said, shocked. 'This can't be Joe's camp.' As she looked closer, she realised there were larger plants further in and a thin reticulation hose ran from tray to tray. A timer sat on a folding table. To her scant knowledge, it looked like a sophisticated set-up.

'Bet it is. I always knew he smoked a bit because of his aches and pains. Never worried me because he did it out of work hours.' He stepped into the hide. Tessa followed.

'Pretty complex set-up by the look,' Harrison said, glancing around.

'What makes you think it's Joe's? Maybe it's Ray's. Or Brendan's.'

Harrison picked up a bag that had been lying on the floor and peered inside. He pulled out an envelope. '"Mr Joe Jenkins,"' he read. 'It's his place all right.' He looked at the address in the corner. 'Looks like a hospital bill.'

'Was he sick?'

'Not that I know of.'

'What do we do?'

Harrison was too busy looking through the rest of the gear to answer.

Well, she'd certainly got more than she'd bargained for on this trip, Tessa thought as she went back outside and looked around.

Harrison came out. 'I think we should just get rid of it. No one is going to believe Joe was growing anything. The cops won't know, so we could just pull out the plants and dump all this gear. No one would be any the wiser.'

'Good idea.' Tessa was pleased to have something to do, because even though they were both trying to act normally, their easy friendship had dissolved with Tessa's request to go home.

'I'll come back in the ute and collect it all.'

'Right.'

They threw themselves into pulling out the plants, Harrison seeming to use more force than was necessary as he upended the steel trays and dragged them outside. Then they dismantled the steel frame.

All the while, Tessa was aware of Harrison and she was sure he was aware of her, even with the heavy handedness. She caught him looking at her when she glanced over towards him. What was going on inside that gorgeous head of his, she wondered. Whatever it was, she couldn't let him close to her. She couldn't risk changing her mind.

They stopped for a breather, and Tessa opened some of Joe's mail. It was all bills. Large ones. For a hospice in Perth.

'Far out! Looks like Joe was paying for someone's care – look here.' She handed Harrison the bills. As she did so her fingers accidentally brushed his and she pulled back in a hurry. Harrison didn't seem to notice – he took the envelopes and read through them.

'If that's the case, someone is going to miss him,' said Harrison, frowning. 'I guess we'd better find out who it is. I always thought he didn't have any family. When he died, I put a notice in the paper, but haven't yet heard from anyone. Still, I guess it's early days.'

'It's so sad,' Tessa said quietly. 'Fancy dying with no family. With no one loving you.' She looked at Harrison, her eyes misty. 'I couldn't think of anything worse.'

Harrison stared at her, the inner turmoil showing on his face, and Tessa took a step forward. Then retreated.

'You would never have to,' Harrison said. 'Tessa, I . . .' He stopped. 'I really want you to stay,' he finally managed. He ran his fingers through his hair. 'I enjoy your company and want to get to know you better. Do you think you could consider being with a bloke who's an old git?' He looked at her solemnly, then touched her cheek very gently.

Neither of them moved.

'What?' she whispered finally. 'I've been telling myself you wouldn't be interested. Where the hell has that come from?'

'Tessa, can't you see? You make me laugh, you intrigue me. I like spending time with you. Yeah, you were a materialistic, self-absorbed little cow when you first came back, but you've changed. The real you has come out since you've been home. When you were so good to Cally I realised how lonely I was. How much I looked forward to seeing you.'

Tessa clamped her hand over her mouth, tears brimming. 'No,' she said, holding up the other hand to ward him away. 'No, Harrison. It won't work. I'm no good for you.'

'But why? Tell me why you think that? There's got to be a reason. And shouldn't I be able to decide that?'

Tessa thought of how safe she had felt with him. The feelings she had for him refused to go away, and she craved his arms around her. But there was no way she was going to start something unless there was a chance it might last. He needed to know about the photos.

She opened her mouth. There in a small camp, in the middle of nowhere, among the blue and grey bush of the Nullarbor, she told Harrison why she went overseas and what had happened while she was there.

'I've never found out who posted the photos,' she said finally, staring at the ground. 'But I was given the choice to resign or be sacked. I resigned. See? You don't want to be with me.' She smiled through her tears. 'And you're too old for me.'

Harrison leaned forward and touched his lips to hers. 'Yes, I do.'

Kiss.

'And no, I'm not.'

Kiss.

'Come on, let's go home. We've got some talking to do.'

The flight seemed to take no time at all, but all the while Tessa was chewing the inside of her cheek. Harrison couldn't have meant what he said. After all, he hadn't touched her since that second kiss. Nor tried to hold her hand. She tried not to get her hopes up.

Somehow they ended up back at his place with a cup of tea, sitting around the kitchen table. That was when he finally reached out and took her hand.

Tessa closed her eyes.

'I've been trying to work out,' Harrison said softly, 'if you will stay. You made it pretty clear last night, you wouldn't. Can I change your mind, 'cos I don't want to start something if you're gonna leave?'

'I'd like to. But how can it work? What if Cally hates me? Or she doesn't want me? She's craving for someone to talk to her about her mum. That was what bonded us to begin with. If she comes home and the situation has changed, her feelings might, too.'

'Do you always look for every negative?' Harrison chided. 'Do you reckon you could just give it a go?'

'I'm terrified,' Tessa confessed.

'I am too.'

'Is love enough? Do I love you? I know I like you, and there are times you just pop into my head when I least expect it.'

'Tessa, think back over what we've been talking about for one moment. I'm trying to keep you here. I'm giving you a job to do. You don't have to come and live here. Stay at Danjar Plains, see how it pans out. We don't have to get married tomorrow. There are ways to get to know each other, even if we are a couple of hundred k's apart.'

Tessa hadn't thought about that. She'd been worried Harrison would want her to move in, to act as Cally's mum. Things she definitely wasn't ready for.

Far out. There was nothing to lose and everything to gain. She'd told him the whole story and he still wanted her. *Yes!* she thought, starting to smile. *Yes, yes, yes!*

'Harrison.' She reached up to touch his face. 'Yes. Yes to everything.'

'But?' he asked with raised eyebrows and a half-smile.

'But,' she said, trying not to squirm, 'I can't start this relationship with secrets. For it to work, you need to see those photos.'

Harrison's smile faded and he sat there for a moment. 'I don't see the need.'

'No, but I don't want anything to come back and haunt me.'

He took a deep breath. 'Okay, if that's what you want, that's what you get. Let's have a look.'

Chapter 31

While Harrison looked through the photos Tessa paced the kitchen floor, her arms folded tightly over her chest. She couldn't bear to see them or his face while he looked at what she'd done, what she'd been. *If he doesn't want you afterwards, you can't be upset*, she kept telling herself.

When she heard his footsteps on the floorboards in the passageway, she froze. She badly wanted to be sick. Somehow, though, she summoned the courage to stand tall and face him, even if her face was lined with unease and fear.

He gave her a lopsided smile as he came in then held open his arms.

Tessa closed her eyes and swallowed, took the final two steps towards him and let herself be swept up in his comfort.

'You were a bit of a party girl, weren't you?' he said against her hair.

'Something I'm not particularly proud of.'

'Come on, I'll make you a cup of tea.'

'Another one?' Tessa giggled as relief bubbled up. 'You're as bad as Spider!'

Harrison laughed as he gathered up the used mugs and took them to the sink to rinse. Then he busied himself in the kitchen.

He returned with the refilled mugs and placed them on the table in front of her. 'So you don't know who posted them?'

Tessa shook her head as she blew on the steaming liquid.

He sat down beside her. 'Do you think someone has a vendetta against you? Were they trying to discredit you?'

'Who knows?' Tessa shrugged. 'It probably doesn't matter now. But if they were trying to make me look bad, then they did a bloody good job of it. I reckon the moment they pressed "publish", everyone in the office knew.' She took a sip and licked her lips. 'Do you understand why you had to see them, Harrison? Once that sort of thing is on the internet, it stays there forever. If you'd seen them in six months' time, you wouldn't be happy. Or what if Cally saw them?'

'Yeah, I understand where you're coming from. Anyway, let's forget about that. Finish your tea then we've got work to do!'

Tessa turned to him and he put both arms around her and kissed her. She closed her eyes and thought of nothing but this strong man, his arms encircling her, and how good he made her feel. She smiled against his lips.

'What?' He pulled away and looked down at her. 'Am I doing something wrong?'

'Nope, I'm just very happy.'

He hugged her tight. 'So am I.'

They flew back to Danjar Plains that afternoon. From the air, Tessa spotted the small scar on the landscape where Joe's camp had been. If she hadn't known it was there, she doubted she would have picked it out. She leaned over to Harrison. 'We need to find out who is in that hospice,' she called above the noise of the engine. 'I'd hate to think some poor person had been kicked out because the bill hadn't been paid.'

'Yeah, we do. Did you bring the bills with you?'

'Yes. I can make some phone calls when we land, if you think it's okay to.'

'At the very least, we need to let the accounts department know what's happened. They can make the decisions from there.'

The plane began to descend.

'Look, there's Mum waiting for us.' Tessa pointed to the tiny ute below.

Harrison ran his fingers over her cheek. 'It'll be fine. Don't panic!'

'I'm not!'

'As Cally would say: "Yeah right."'

Tessa laughed and kissed him.

They landed and taxied to the end of the runway. Harrison leaned over and opened her door. 'Out you get!' He gave her a quick tap on the bum as she scrambled out.

'Hi, Mum.' Tessa waved.

'Hello, you two. Harrison, I've made the bed up in the quarters. I assumed it would be too late for you to fly back tonight.'

'Thanks, Peggy, I'll take you up on the offer.'

Harrison passed Tessa's bag and folder to her. She could barely contain her smile as she glanced sideways at him, wanting to say something. He avoided her gaze.

'Actually, Mum. Harrison will probably come and stay with me at Aunty Violet's,' she said, a spark in her eye challenging her mother to say something.

Peggy paused for a moment then continued walking towards the ute. 'Sure, petal.'

Tessa took Harrison's hand. This time Harrison did look at her. A broad smile lit up his face.

Tessa came out of the office, a worried look on her face.

'What's wrong, love?' Peggy asked, wiping her hands on a tea towel.

'Did Harrison tell you Joe was paying for someone in a hospice?'

Peggy shook her head. 'Sounds like you two were rather busy over there for twenty-four hours!' she said in an undertone. 'You still haven't told me what happened.'

Tessa blushed. 'I'm still amazed anything has happened. I've noticed him a few times since I've been home, but never thought . . . It's obviously very new and we'll take things really slowly. I didn't think he could possibly be interested in me. I thought the age gap at the very least would be a stumbling block.' She shrugged. 'But Harrison didn't see it that way. He's very persuasive!'

'He's a good man, Tessa. He's been a friend of the family's for a long time and he's very important to us. If it works, you'll be a very happy girl. And we'd be so happy to have you out here. You know he won't leave the station, don't you?'

'I know. I feel safe with him. I feel, I don't know, alive or something!'

'I think you'd be very good for each other. I was only saying to your father a couple of weeks ago that you'd make a good match.'

Tessa stared at her mum. 'Good on you! And what did Dad say?'

'He said,' she made quotation marks, '"Leave them to work it out, Peg. They'll get to it when they're ready. *Do not,*" and he gave me that stare only he can give, "Do not interfere!"'

'So you guys had it all worked out before Harrison and I did? Oh, great!'

'Did they?' Harrison walked in with a quizzical look on his face.

'Old folk's intuition,' Peggy said with a smile.

Tessa grinned at Harrison as he put his arm around her shoulders. "Steady with the "old" bit,' he grinned good-naturedly. 'Next time you've got a good idea like that, maybe you should tell us a little sooner. We could have got our act together much more quickly!'

Tessa turned to Harrison. 'I spoke to the hospice – it's so sad.'

'What is?'

'Joe's got a disabled sister. Her name's Susannah and she's had brain damage since she was a child. When their parents couldn't manage her anymore, they put her into a hospice and once they died, Joe took on making the payments. I bet that's why he was growing all the marijuana. To help pay the bills, because it's really expensive.'

Shock crossed Peggy's face. 'Growing what?'

'Oh, we haven't told you that bit yet.' Tessa slapped her forehead. She told the story, with Harrison adding small pieces.

Peggy's disbelief was evident.

'Anyway, he would never have been able to afford those fees on his station hand's wage,' Harrison finished. 'But what I want to know is, how did he get it to the buyer? He never went off the place.'

Tessa shrugged. 'Trucks? Gave it to someone? Who knows, but he obviously managed it. The lady said there is a trust fund set up, so if something happened to Joe, Susannah would be cared for until she died. She's nearly seventy-eight, so,' Tessa left the word hanging in the air. Maybe there wouldn't be too much longer.

Paul clattered up the steps.

'Evening all,' he said then did a double-take as he saw Harrison with his arm around Tessa's shoulder. 'About bloody time. I'm just going to wash my hands. Who wants a beer?' He walked out of the room before anyone had a chance to say a word.

Tessa and her mother exchanged wide grins.

That night, as Harrison and Tessa lay in bed, she told him all about Spider's letters and diaries and what she had discovered about Tom and her suspicions.

'Do you think Violet could have been in love with Ali?' Harrison asked.

'No, I'm sure she wasn't. She would have been, what? Fourteen? She might have had a crush or something, but nothing would have been acted on. Tom can't have been her child.' Tessa ran her fingers over the outside of the diaries. 'Maybe he was Ali's child and for some reason he left him with Violet?'

'I think you're clutching at straws,' Harrison said, his fingers circling her bare shoulder. 'Why don't you get the rest of the letters and we'll have a look at them together.'

Tessa jumped out of bed. She ran into the kitchen, grabbed the letters then ran back again. Her body was covered with goosebumps. 'Brrr. It's getting cold at night now,' she said.

Harrison grabbed the doona and wrapped her up in it. Then they sat together and read out loud.

'This is from Elsie to Violet in 1937, so she would have been – Elsie – I mean . . . twelve? Somewhere around that, anyway.' Tessa cleared her throat.

Dear Violet,

We made it to Perth on the train. There are people everywhere and they all seem in such a hurry. Quite strange after the stillness of Danjar Plains. Still, I guess it was busy there, too, a different type of rush. Building and making things better.

The cars whip down the streets and people run across the roads to catch trams. You must bring Tom to the city and see these things – they're electric! They make such a noise, clattering and banging all the time, but they are fun to ride on.

I miss reading to you, Violet, and doing the lessons you had me do. It was a lot more fun learning out there than it is here, in a classroom.

Love,

Elsie

'Okay, so we know Elsie had been here in 1937,' Harrison said and made a note.

Dear Violet,

Mum told me tonight that Dad is coming back out to help Len on the station. I'm really sad we couldn't come too. But Mum says I must do proper lessons. I miss the horses and the sheep. Did you buy any cattle?

Love,

Elsie

'And another from Elsie, but it really doesn't say very much,' Tessa said, scanning it quickly. 'Neither does the next one, just stuff about living in Perth. Okay, so there isn't any info there.'

She riffled through the pages and read a few more out. After ten minutes, Harrison had had enough.

'Righto,' he said, taking the lead. 'Let's leave it for now.' He took the letters out of her hands and put them on the floor. Then he gently pushed her back against the pillows. 'Whatever the secret is, Violet kept it hidden for a long time. A few more hours isn't going to hurt. We'll solve it tomorrow. What do you say?'

'Kiss me,' she answered, and gave herself up to him.

Chapter 32

'I'm going back to the start,' Tessa said as she spread Violet's letters to Grace across the lounge room floor. 'Got to get them all lined up in date sequence.'

Harrison looked at her, bemused. 'I reckon I might go for a drive with Paul,' he said. 'I'm happy to help you, Tessa, but I gotta get out of the house. I don't do very well inside for long periods of time.'

Tessa looked up. 'Shit, I'm sorry! I didn't think. I've been making you deal with my stuff, and ignored all the things you've got to do.'

'It's not a chore, but while we're on the subject, I need to head home tomorrow. My employees will be wondering what the hell is going on! I've hardly been there since the Muster. Good thing we can talk on the radio.' He reached for his sparkly hat and put it on his head. 'And Cally gets back at the end of the week so I'll have to go into Kal and pick her up.'

'Did you want me to come?'

He shook his head. 'I think I need to tell her about us by myself. I don't think she'll react badly, but I need to make sure she is fine with it all before you guys catch up.'

'Oh. Well, whatever you think.' Tessa turned away to hide her hurt.

'Tessa, Tessa, Tessa! You're such an open book! I'm not shutting you out, but it's been just me and Cally for a long time. She'll need a while to get used to it. You guys can chew the fat when she's been home for a bit and you come over.'

'Okay.' She rubbed her face, but when her hands came away, she was smiling. 'I know, I know.' She held her hands up in defeat. 'It makes sense, but I'm going to miss you!'

Harrison held out his hand and pulled her up. 'Make no mistake, Tessie, I want you with me all the time.' He kissed her, spun her around and let go.

'I guess we've got things to get in place, haven't we? Once I've wound all of this up.' She waved her hand at the house. 'And you've got your blokes to organise and work to do.' She nodded her head. 'But we'll make it work, won't we?'

'Too right. And you don't have to hurry,' Harrison pointed out. 'Mundranda and I aren't going anywhere. Stay here as long as you like, there is no pressure from me. In fact, I'm sure Violet would have wanted you to live here until it's time to move on.' He wiggled his eyebrows at her.

They heard the rumble of the ute as Paul pulled up and beeped the horn.

'How did Dad know to come and get you?' Tessa asked, her hands on her hips. 'Did you ask him last night?'

'Ah, maybe! See you soon, darlin'.' Harrison headed out the door, stopping only to pull on his boots.

After he'd gone, Tessa sat on the floor with a silly smile on her face, thinking about all that had happened. The she shook herself. 'Come on, girl,' she chastised. 'Pull yourself together.'

She turned back to the letters.

September 1947
  Dear Grace,
  Today it's been sixteen years since you left. When it first happened, I kept thinking you'd walk back in the door, pick up Tom and laugh at my tears. But you haven't and I know you won't. He's such a strapping lad now. And he loves the land with his whole being.
  V

  . . .

January 1948
  Dear Grace,
  Tom has been working so hard over the last few months, I decided it was time for him to have a holiday. I took him to Esperance. He

loved the sea, although he has been there before. The last time we went, I had William with me. He adored taking Tom swimming near the jetty and he fixed up a fishing rod for him to use.

This time I took him fishing, but I can't abide swimming. There is always seaweed tugging at my ankles and I'm frightened something will grab me and pull me under. Now you must promise never to tell anyone that! I have never once admitted to being scared and I never will – except to you!

Love,

V

. . .

February 1948

Dear Grace,

The fires have started – our first dry thunderstorm was three days ago. Uncle Sam has ridden out to see how far away the fire is, but I can smell the smoke. Len isn't here – he's off on one of his excursions but the other brothers are all fine. Aunty Margaret is looking much older. I don't think the sun agrees with her.

Love,

V

Tessa put down the letter. 'Aunty Violet,' she spoke out loud. 'This is boring. What are you trying to tell me?' Frustrated, she got up and walked around the room. She stopped and looked out of the window. Dozer was sleeping in the sun and there was a gentle breeze blowing. The blue skies beckoned her so she pulled on her boots and went out into the sunshine.

Her feet took her to the cemetery where she stopped at the foot of Aunty Spider's grave. The clouds scurried across the sky, carried by the brisk southerly winds. As Tessa looked up, she realised the light wasn't as harsh as it had been when she'd first arrived. The seasons were definitely changing.

As was she.

'I know you can't hear me, but I wish you could. I found the letters and I haven't finished reading them yet. I still can't work out what you're trying to tell me.'

She sat down. Dozer, who had finally caught up with her, nosed in under her arm. 'And I've got some other news, Spider. Harrison and I, well, we're sort of together.' Tessa looked up as a magpie burst into song. It was loud and melodic, and she sat as still as she could so as not to frighten the bird away. Finally it stopped singing and Tessa watched as it flew down from the tree and hopped over towards her. Its brown eyes watched curiously then, without warning, it spread its wings and flew away.

Tessa sat peacefully, enjoying the sun on her skin, then she turned back to the grave. 'If I didn't know better, Spider, I would have thought you'd just given your blessing.'

She stayed there a moment or two longer, then got up, dusted off the seat of her shorts and headed home again.

November, 1957

> *Dear Grace,*
>
> *They're all gone. All the brothers and Uncle Sam. All killed before their time. All accidents on the station. Aunty Margaret has gone to live in Perth, now – she didn't want to be out here anymore. She wanted to go to Adelaide at first, but with a little persuasion, she decided on Perth. It's a much better place for her. Elsie goes to visit and Aunty's letters, although still full of sadness, contain hints that she will be all right. If you can believe this, she's joined a bowling club! And Dad is there too. He visits Aunty Margaret often, as he should, since she's his sister!*
>
> *Grace, do you ever get angry with what happened to you? And Mum. After all, her death was the whole reason we came out here in the first place. It was the start of our lives out here. If she hadn't become pregnant, hadn't died, we'd probably all still be in Adelaide, still be alive.*
>
> *Have you ever asked, why me? Because I'm finding myself doing that more and more, in the early hours of the morning when there*

is no one awake except me and the howling dingoes.

Why was William slain, fighting a war we didn't start? Why were our brothers killed by the land they loved and worked so hard for?

Tom never seems to question anything. He is accepting and takes everything that happens with a shrug of his shoulders. He asks about you, though. He always has, especially when he was younger – nine or ten. And I tell him as much as I dare.

Love,

V

. . .

February, 1960

Dear Grace,

Tom has been on holidays to Kalgoorlie. Oh how happy I was when I finally saw his Vanguard ute trundling down the driveway, for I missed him. But it wasn't only him who came back. He has brought a wife! Her name is Lucy and she's a dear thing. Her family have stations much further north than we've ever been, so she is used to the lifestyle and work. She has dark hair and the prettiest smile. Hopefully before long there will be another baby in our midst.

I wish I had known Tom had these plans. I can't say I'm not slightly hurt he married without me there to see it, but I must be *practical. If I wasn't here, who would have looked after the waters? As you know, the summer is unrelenting and if a trough went dry, well, it doesn't bear thinking about.*

I guess the main reason I was so sad not to have known was because I had always intended to give the rings to him when he wanted to marry. They are his.

But then it opens a whole new can of worms. How much should I tell him? I can't decide, and you're not here to guide me. So, for the moment, I'll be quiet, until I see a different way. Of course that means the rings will still stay with me.

Love,
V

Tessa found herself breathing hard. The rings! Finally there was a link. Frantically she turned over the page.

December, 1960
Dear Grace,
Right in the middle of shearing, baby Paul arrived. Oh, he looks so much like Tom did when he was born.

But there is much to do. I must shed up and take the shorn ewes away. And, of course, get the shearers their tea. I never did like anyone else in the kitchen.

But I just had to tell you, darling sister, you are a grandmother.

Whoa. What?

'Hi, darlin'. I'm back!' Harrison walked through the door, a smile on his dirty face. 'What's wrong?' He rushed over to her.

Tessa's face was pale.

'Grace,' she managed. 'Grace.' She shook the letters at him. 'I don't know it all, but it's got something to do with Grace. Look here.' Her hands trembled as she turned back through the letters, desperate to find the pages she was looking for. 'See here, a mention of the rings. And here, she can't work out how much to tell Tom and down here, oh Lordy, down here, Harrison, read this! Read it.' She thrust the page at him.

Taking it with one hand, he kept the other firm on her shoulder, and read the letter.

'Okay, so Grace was Tom's mother,' he said finally. 'I don't get it, Tessa. What's the problem with that?'

'It means we *are* who we thought we were. I was so frightened we weren't! I'd imagined that Tom had just been raised with the Mathisons but wasn't their child. Which would have meant we weren't who we thought we were. But we *are*!'

Harrison stayed quiet. Waiting for her to go on.

'I knew Tom wasn't one of the brothers. I think I told you, in all the diaries she always said "the

368

brothers and Tom". So I worked that bit out. Then I realised he was darker than the rest of them and this Ali, the cameleer, started to come into it. So I'm putting two and two together here. If Grace was Tom's mum, I'm betting everything that Ali was his dad. So it still means Dad, Ryan and I are who we thought we were, sort of. I mean, we're not completely Mathisons because of the Afghan link, but we're still Mathisons! Am I making any sense?' She looked up at him.

'I think I've got you,' Harrison said, grinning at her excitement and shock.

'And I reckon I've worked out why it would have been such a big secret. This was in the days of the White Australia policy. If people found out Grace was having a relationship with a man who wasn't white, she may well have been made an outcast.'

'Yeah, that would have caused a big kerfuffle,' Harrison agreed. 'I remember Violet saying once it upset her how anyone who wasn't white was so badly treated. She obviously had actual experience of it.'

'Have I shown you the rings?'

'No.'

Tessa raced into the bedroom to get them. When she came back, Harrison was holding another letter.

'See?' she said, opening the box to show him. 'Aren't they beautiful? And look at the engraving inside.' She took out one of the rings and held it up to the light. It sparkled like new. 'What a history behind them! What a love there must have been!'

'So what happened to Grace, though, Tessa? She hasn't been around for a long time.'

'I don't know. I'll have to keep looking, but this must have been what Aunty Spider had wanted me to find. I wish she could confirm it, though. I'm still only guessing, really.'

'I think this probably does,' said Harrison, handing her another letter he'd been reading.

Dearest Grace,

I will be returning in six weeks. Until then, keep these safe, for we will become husband and wife when I return.

Never forget: forever mine, forever yours,
Ali

Chapter 33

Tessa watched until the Cessna was just a tiny speck in the air. Loneliness hit her as she turned to go back to the house.

She hoped above all that Cally wouldn't be upset about this new relationship, especially because Tessa knew it was the best thing that had happened in her whole life. If Harrison broke it off because Cally wasn't happy, she wasn't sure she could bear it. And there was no doubt he would do so - his daughter meant everything to him.

Instead of driving straight back to Aunty Spider's in the ute her parents had lent her, she veered down the overgrown track to the resting place of the early Mathisons. The lonely graves needed tending and Tessa needed distracting. Especially now she knew the inscription on the rings was also on the fence. She wanted to sit and think about what she'd learned.

Tessa had talked to Harrison before he left, about whether she should tell Paul what she had found. He saw no reason not to, whereas she was nervous about her father's reaction. It was one thing to find out you weren't who you thought you were but another entirely to find out before the mystery was completely solved.

Tessa still didn't know who was in the bush grave. She suspected it was Grace, but how she died, Tessa had no idea.

She pulled up and sat there for a while, watching the birds flit from tree to tree and pick at the grass. She noticed a movement to her right and turned her head just in time to see a huge kangaroo flop down in the shade of the mallee tree. His paws scratched at his tummy and Tessa thought how long and fierce-looking they were.

Not wanting to disturb him, Tessa slipped out of the ute and walked slowly over to the plots. As she sat, the 'roo's ears flicked around and he watched her. She sat down at the two unmarked graves and surveyed them. A hundred questions ran through her mind. Grabbing a handful of dirt and letting it drift through her fingers, she tried to piece together what she knew. An idea was forming, but it just wasn't clear enough, yet. She would have to check some things when she got back.

Impatient, she jumped up and climbed over the fence. She wanted to clear some of the grasses away, make the plots seem as if they were loved and cared for. Even if she hadn't known Grace, Violet had undoubtedly loved her.

As she came within sight of Spider's house, Tessa noticed a white Toyota LandCruiser parked out the front. Even though she knew it couldn't be Harrison, her heart leapt with anticipation.

It wasn't him.

She weighed up her options, then squared her shoulders and drove on.

Brendan was sitting at the outside table, his arms crossed and a fierce look on his face. When he saw her, he broke into a huge smile, got up and held out his arms. Tessa remained in the ute with the engine still running. Her hand was on the CB radio mike, just in case.

'Babe! I'm sorry,' he said. 'Got a huge apology to make to you.'

'Is that right?'

'That day at the Muster, I was a bit overwrought. Dad had given me a hard time and I took it out on you. I'm really sorry.'

'Took you a while to come and say that.'

'I know. I had some stuff I had to take care of for Dad.'

'I'm not interested, Brendan. I won't be with someone who behaves like that. I don't need to be.'

Brendan's smile faded. 'What do you mean? We're good together. I'm apologising.' He shrugged his shoulders and threw her a puzzled look as if to say, *What more do you want?*

'Don't bother with the charm.' Tessa held up her hand. 'It won't work. You might as well leave, because nothing you say will make me change my mind.'

Brendan's face hardened. 'You'll regret it,' he warned.

'I don't think so.'

'Violet said she'd leave me something,' he said.

The change of tack threw Tessa.

'Look, I overheard your father at the Muster. I know you seem to think Spider had something of yours, or something on you. But I've turned this place upside down and apparently you have too.' She cut off Brendan's protest. 'I heard the click of the writing desk on the night you stayed over, Brendan. Believe it or not, I'm far from an idiot. I have no doubt you've been with me so you can get your hands on whatever it is, but it's not here. There's nothing here about you or your family. I don't know what activities outside of station work you're involved in, but the fact that I haven't found anything should make you happy, shouldn't it? Cos I'm guessing whatever you're doing isn't good. Now leave.'

'She said it was a crate of things,' he whined.

'There isn't. Leave.'

He took a step towards the ute. Tessa's hand shot up. She was still holding the microphone. She waved it at him. 'Leave before I call Dad.'

Brendan stood for a moment, undecided, then swore and moved towards his ute. 'We were good together,' he said once more.

'That may be so, but I'm better without you.'

'You reckon you'll be better off with Harrison? You want to be mum to a kid and not be free? And you'd better understand, we know what you both did to the drugs.' He sounded threatening.

Fear crept into her stomach. 'Is this to do with Joe? What are you saying?'

'You're so clever, you work it out. Bitch.'

Tessa waited until the dust in the distance had faded. When she was sure Brendan wasn't coming back she got out of the ute and ran inside. She looked around to see if anything had been disturbed. She couldn't be sure, but she thought the diaries might have been moved, and she was convinced the letters had been riffled through and read because they were spread across the table.

Brendan had also tracked in dust with his boots and left a trail across the floor.

Bastard!

Big bloody help Dozer was. Worst watchdog ever. She spun around the lounge room, trying to see what else might be out of place, then went from room to room.

In the bedroom Harrison's distinctive blue sparkly hat was still on the chair. That explained how Brendan knew he'd been ousted from her affections, she thought.

She tried to control her breathing as she went into the kitchen and switched on the kettle. Well there was nothing she could do about it. All she could hope was that he didn't come back.

'Fat lot of good you are,' she said to Dozer as he limped into the room and flopped on the floor. 'One, you wouldn't hear him arrive, and two, you're too friendly!'

Dozer huffed as if he were offended, and got up and went off to sleep in the sun.

Tessa decided she would tidy everything up and stow things somewhere more secure. If Brendan did return, she wanted things safe.

Heaving out the tucker box, she packed away the letters and diaries in date order, shut it and pushed it back underneath the bottom shelf in the pantry. If she hadn't found it while she was clearing out the house, she didn't think anyone else would.

Maybe now it was time to go through all the books in the lounge. She could pack them into cardboard boxes, and when she went to Kalgoorlie next, she would take what they didn't want to the second-hand shop. She must stay busy.

One by one, she pulled them out, and was excited to see some of her old favourites. *What Katy Did* and *What Katy Did Next* went on the 'keeping' pile: Tessa would never forget Aunty Spider reading to her from the red-covered books. She hadn't been allowed to touch them, because they were 1924 editions. Oh, how Tessa had loved those stories. She wondered if Cally would like to read them.

There were books on land management and sheep husbandry – they went on the 'Dad, maybe' pile. And then there were novels that held no meaning for Tessa – they were the ones she would give away.

Before she packed a box, she flicked through the pages of each book to make sure there was nothing in it. Then, one by one, she stacked them neatly inside.

She picked up an old faded edition of *The Washer Woman's Dream* by Hilarie Lindsay. As she grabbed it, she noticed it felt different to the other books. She turned it over and read the back. It sounded interesting, a story about Winifred, an Australian white woman who met Ali, an Indian Muslim while she was working at a bar.

Tessa opened the book and began to read, searching for the part about the camel train. Was this Grace? Or was this what her life was like? When she came to chapter seventeen, she realised that some pages were missing. Someone, no guesses who, had cut the text from the pages but left the margins. And nestled within the pages was a folded piece of paper.

Reverently, Tessa took it out and opened it.

At the top of the page were two words: 'Grace's Story'.

Chapter 34

The camels walked slowly, raising little dust. One step, next one, next one, next one. The same steady pace that they began at first light was the same one they finished with in the evening.

A man walked next to the leader's shoulder. Sometimes he would talk to him but, for the most part, it was a silent trip. Other men were employed on the camel train: some rode the beasts while the rest walked alongside. The camels were heavily loaded with not an inch to spare, covered in bedrolls, boxes and goods that were piled to twice the animals' width.

Water bags hung around their necks and a thick rope linked one camel to the next, keeping them in a line. One step, two, they each followed their leader.

The man at the front was dark-skinned with kind brown eyes. He was quick to smile and had a gentleness about him that drew the customer in. Even though he couldn't speak English particularly well, he was always able to make himself understood.

All the men wore turbans and traditional Afghan clothes, which seemed to flow freely and let the air circulate.

The first time we saw these camel trains, we stopped and watched in awe. The camels seemed to haul such heavy weights effortlessly. And I can still remember the first time they carted out wool for us. Each animal was loaded with great bales, two on each side. It was incredible. Uncle Sam told me that each camel could carry almost six hundred pounds on its back.

The nose pegs fascinated me as well. Just a gentle tug and the animal would go in whatever direction Ali wanted.

They seemed to love him and he loved them. Even though, when I got closer to them, I found the camels (especially the bulls) could snarl and spit and try to bite. But it was only when they were upset or didn't want to do something Ali had asked of them. They were stubborn, and there were times he had to tug harder or remonstrate with them. In the end, he always got them to do what he wanted, even if they were disgruntled and you'd be able to see they were! Camels are such expressive creatures!

I'm not sure how Ali and I fell in love. We talked a lot – I helped him with his English, especially with the slang we Australians use. He would come to the camp at night and ask if I would like to go for a walk. Of course, Uncle Sam wasn't pleased to begin with, but I think he knew how lonely and harsh I found the Nullarbor and, no matter what, he loved all of us. His main desire was for us to be happy. I'm sure he realised I'd found that happiness.

Ali had to keep travelling and he never stayed long at Danjar Plains. His camel train was full of supplies to keep all of the settlers going. He carted tea, flour, rice and even clothes. He also had a box full of books that kept me entertained during the nights. It was like an Aladdin's cave on the back of those camels – you just never knew what was going to come out next!

The third time he came, he asked if I would travel with him. Of course, it was such a huge request – so many different problems to weigh up. But I didn't see any of them. My head had been full of this man since our first walk out in the bush, when he so gently took my hand and held it to his lips. He brought posies of wildflowers whenever he arrived and always left a little treat for the rest of the family – maybe an extra length of calico or a pound of flour.

Ali wove his way into all of our hearts.

Aunty Margaret was concerned about the backlash from the rest of the whites out here. I couldn't have cared less. So long as I was with this man, I knew I would be happy.

So I left Danjar Plains. Of course, we were never able to marry because of his religion. We never wore the rings he bought because of that. But we knew we had them as our symbol of marriage.

We travelled to Norseman and up to Kalgoorlie. On the way we saw many sights. Even though there were large distances between the settlements, they were bustling hives of activity. People were building dams and fences. There were wood cutters as we came closer to Kalgoorlie. And camels seemed to be the most popular choice of transport.

Ali told me that proper cameleers walked alongside their camels and didn't ride them. So I walked too. Not alongside him, but further back.

In early 1931 I realised I was with child. I can't tell you how excited I was, but I did ask Ali if we could return to Danjar Plains for the birth. It took some time, but I managed to convince him.

I was barely showing when we began the trek home. I was excited at the prospect of seeing familiar country and even more excited to be seeing my family.

The night before we arrived home, we stopped at a near-empty water hole. As usual, we set up camp, unloaded the animals and tethered them. I prepared the evening meal while Ali and the other men did their jobs.

There was another camp of men within hearing distance. They were obviously white because I could hear their loud and raucous voices – it sounded like they had been drinking whisky.

I saw their camp as I was trying to find a private spot to bathe. And they saw me.

I can still feel their hands on me and smell their foul breath. I fought as hard as I could. I tried to call for Ali because he would have saved me if he could have. They pinned my hands down, and as hard as I tried to kick, they dodged and laughed. I heard as they unbuckled their belts and, at that point, I stayed still. I couldn't fight in case I hurt the child within me, a child that was conceived in love.

These men knew of me – I heard them say they had seen Ali's camel train. 'Us whites not good enough for you, ay?' they jeered. 'We'll show you how good we can be.'

They laughed and talked the whole time and when the three of them had finished, they just walked off.

I couldn't tell anyone. Imagine the disgrace. Just so long as my baby was all right and I could get back to Ali.

Bruises I kept hidden under long skirts – they were clever enough not to touch my face.

But from the moment I arrived at Danjar Plains, I cried. I sobbed and sobbed. Aunty Margaret and Violet had such kind arms and very slowly I told them what had happened, making them promise not to tell Ali. He wouldn't want me after that.

But they must have told Uncle Sam and my brothers.

I read a newspaper article, later. Three men had been found slaughtered in their camp. Their throats had been cut.

The police searched for the murderers, but they hadn't been found.

Chapter 35

'So have I got it all right?' Tessa asked Elsie on the other end of the line. 'Grace lived and travelled with Ali and she was raped on their way back to Danjar Plains to give birth to a baby. She wasn't just raped – she was pack-raped.' Tessa took a steadying breath. 'Ali never knew but Sam, Len, Edward and George went and found the men and murdered them.' Tessa paced the floor as she talked, stopping only to look at the photos of Tom on the wall.

'Grace gave birth to not one baby, but twins. The first delivered was stillborn, and Grace had so much trouble getting Tom out, she died, too. That's not just a family secret, it's a friggin' massacre!'

Down the line, Elsie's voice was clear. 'I didn't know about the murders or the rape, Tessa. Although, in hindsight, the killings make sense. The diaries Violet sent to me for safekeeping obviously had incriminating things written in them.'

'There wasn't anything obvious from what I've read,' Tessa answered. 'But of course I didn't know the story.'

'I imagine Violet wouldn't have known about the murders until after the fact. It sounds like Len's hotheadedness to me, and egging the other boys on. I'm almost positive Sam wouldn't have had anything to do with it. But Len? He was a charmer and a hothead all in one.'

'Sounds like Brendan,' Tessa said.

'Yes, well, I believe there are some similarities,' Elsie chuckled. 'Violet bet me fifty dollars you'd hook up with Brendan when you first came back. "She won't be able to resist his charms," she said. It's a bugger she's not here for me to pay up!'

'Are you serious? I sometimes think that woman had a crystal ball.'

'You wouldn't be far wrong there.'

'Did she also guess I'd end up with Harrison?' Tessa heard a swift intake of breath. She giggled. 'What? Have I shocked you? After all this time, something has shocked you, Elsie?'

'No, dear, not at all. I'd just love it if she were here now. It was her dearest wish that you and Harrison would be together. She swore to me he would help you heal and you would help heal him. Oh, Tessa, it's great news!' Elsie gave a little sniffle. 'Now, promise me, you will invite me to the wedding. Please.'

'Oh hell. Let's not get ahead of ourselves. We're taking things really slowly.'

'Piffle! No point in taking it slowly. Get married and work it out from there.'

'What?' Tessa's voice rose into a girly high-pitched squeal. 'Geez, I'm really pleased you're not a marriage counsellor, Elsie. Bloody hell!' She shook her head.

'When you get a good man, don't let him go. I'll tell you something you don't know. I was engaged to Violet's brother, Edward, for a time. I didn't want to let him go and I would have loved living out there, but when he died we hadn't got any further than getting engaged. The wedding never happened. He was the salt-of-the-earth type. Trouble is, he got away, in a different sense of the word.'

'Yeah, I guess dying sort of puts a stop to getting married.' Tessa tried to make light of it. 'But I didn't know. There's nothing in the diaries or letters about that.'

'Ah well. Guess it wasn't worth recording. Anyway, that's enough of that. But heed my advice, dear girl, and don't let Harrison get away.'

'I hear you, but we're both a bit gun-shy, I think. Anyway, I'll invite you to the wedding if there is one!' Tessa smiled. 'But going back to what we were talking about: out of all of this, it's the rape that bothers me the most. Grace "marrying" a cameleer doesn't upset me in the slightest. It was obvious they were in love and no matter what people thought

386

about interracial marriages, her family was going to support her. It's what she went through because of being with Ali. I bet it would have killed him if he'd known.'

'Oh, absolutely. No question. And, you know, those boys did Ali a favour by doing what they did. Not that I agree with an eye for an eye, but imagine the outcry if an Afghan man had killed three white men while they were sleeping. Quite simply, he would have been hanged.'

Tessa could almost hear Elsie shaking her finger at the phone. 'But three white men against three white men would just as likely not be followed up out there. You've got to remember, the police were few and far between.'

Tessa was quiet for a moment, thinking about that. Yes, times were different and it had probably been survival of the fittest back then.

'The one comforting fact in all of this is that Tom was born into a relationship that was loving. Imagine if she'd got pregnant when she'd been raped.'

'Didn't happen. Not worth thinking about.'

'And the small grave that's out here, it's her other baby, the twin. From reading the diaries, Violet said she laboured for three days after the first one was born. It was a girl and they had to bury her before Grace had Tom. You know, what our pioneers had to go through was incredible. There would be a massive outcry if something like that happened now. In fact, it wouldn't happen. The mum would be whipped into surgery and given a Caesarean. It just wouldn't happen. The more I think about it, the more distressing it is. I can't think of a word strong enough.'

'Life, my dear. It's just life. Yes, horrible, yucky, hell-I-wish-it-didn't-happen stuff. But it's still life,' Elsie said gently. 'Now, are you going to tell the rest of the family? I think Spider was leaving that decision to you.'

'I talked to Harrison about this before he left yesterday. I didn't want to spill the beans until I had the full story. He didn't see anything wrong with telling everyone, then, but I wanted to wait until I had as much information as I could get. I reckon I've got that now. So help me, if something else pops up! But I think it's the right thing to do. We should be proud of our heritage, especially because our line was born from love. I know I keep harping on about it, but it's important.'

'Yes, you're right, but also understand this: it doesn't really affect you in the way it would have caused problems back then. You, Ryan and Paul aren't going to have to deal with the kind of ostracism they would have had to put up with. I see no point in hiding it anymore.'

'I'm with you,' Tessa said with conviction.

There was a bang on her door. 'Oh, someone's here, Elsie, I have to go. Come in!' she called out then turned back to the phone. 'Did you know Ryan and Marni are up in Perth?'

'Oh that's good news, too. Which hospital are they at?'

Tessa's face lit up in a huge smile as she saw Harrison and Cally walk in the door. 'Hi, you both! Sorry, Elsie, Harrison and Cally have just arrived. Um, I think they're seeing a doctor at Hollywood Hospital. There's a fertility clinic there. But how did you know that? Oh, don't bother answering. I don't think there's anything about us you don't know.' She accepted a kiss on the cheek from Harrison and said goodbye.

'Hello, hello!' she cried as she hung up. 'Cally, how was your trip? I didn't hear the plane.'

'Good, thanks.' The young girl smiled tentatively.

Tessa turned and searched Harrison's face for some sort of hint that everything had gone all right. Cally certainly wasn't rushing over and giving out hugs.

'Excellent. Where did you go? What did you do?'

'Oh, you know, just stuff.'

'Okay, well I'm pleased you had fun. How was your flight?' She turned to Harrison.

'Beautiful. Smooth, no issues,' he said.

'Lovely.' She forced a smile. *Spider, where are you when I need you?* 'This is uncomfortable,' she finally blurted out. 'Are there rules about this sort of thing?'

Harrison laughed and Cally smiled slightly.

'Cup of tea anyone? Bloody hell, now *I'm* turning into Spider. She always said a cup of tea could fix anything.'

'I'll have a cup,' Harrison answered. 'What about you, Cally?'

'No thanks, but I'll help you get it, Tessa.'

'That would be lovely.'

Tessa's mind was churning. She hadn't given any thought about what she would say to Cally. She imagined she'd have days to sort through all of that. 'Milk's in the fridge and there are some biscuits in the pantry, if you want.'

Cally silently got out the milk carton and looked for the biscuits.

'Cally,' said Tessa, deciding honesty was the best policy. 'I don't really know what to say to you. I can't begin to know what you're thinking. But we did have fun together before your dad dropped our news on you. I hope we can still do that.'

Cally put the milk on the bench and, casting a quick glance over her shoulder, faced Tessa. 'Ages ago, Aunty Spider told me Dad might remarry. I never believed her because there could be no one more special than my mum.'

Tessa wisely said nothing.

'She said that Dad might get lonely without me when I went away to boarding school and I'm going there next year.'

Tessa nodded. 'Yes, I know.'

'I can't pretend I don't feel funny about it. I mean, I've never seen Dad with a girlfriend before. But Aunty Spider told me it wouldn't change how much Mum loved me or how much Dad still does.

She *promised* me there would be enough love to go around. She also said I wouldn't always get along with whoever he chose. So I guess that means we'll have arguments and fights. But I will get used to it and, besides, I like you. I can talk to you.' She gave a grin and a shrug. 'I just don't know how to act around you now.'

'For starters you can give me a hug, because you were giving me them before your dad was.'

The girl moved towards her. She stroked Cally's hair. 'You're a very grown-up young lady and I appreciate your honesty and everything you have said. I'd love it if you could act the same as before, because I was friends with your dad before and I'm still friends with him, so not too much will change. How's that?'

'We'll give it a go.'

Tessa closed her eyes. When she opened them again, Harrison was peeping through the door.

She gave him the thumbs up.

Chapter 36

Harrison took Tessa out for a walk that evening, while Cally helped Peggy with the dishes.

'All good?' she asked.

He nodded. 'I think I shocked her. She may have been the only one except you and me who didn't see it coming.'

Tessa linked her fingers through his as they walked. The moonlight made the mallee trees glow silver and she smiled. 'I think everything is just about sorted. I've solved the family secret. I'm not drinking and feel the best I have in ages, and I've found you! All I have to do is get five minutes alone with Dad, tell him everything and my job will be done!' She bowed.

'Found me? You've always known me.'

Tessa shoved him on the shoulder. 'You know what I mean. Now Marni just needs to get pregnant and everything will be perfect.'

'Life isn't meant to be perfect,' Harrison said seriously. 'And I've got some news for you.' He stopped walking and turned to face her.

Tessa felt a shiver of fear rush through her as she stared up at him. 'What?' she breathed as her heart began to beat faster. 'What's wrong now?'

'Those photos you showed me on Facebook, Tessa. I've been thinking.'

'Oh no. No.' Tears sprung to her eyes. 'I was honest,' she whimpered, her voice breaking.

'Yeah, you were. And I have to admit they were fairly confronting and I hated what I saw.'

Tessa pulled away from him and wrapped her arms around herself as she waited for the hammer to fall on all her hopes.

'I couldn't believe there wasn't a way to find out who posted them. There had to be and I had a feeling someone was trying to deliberately discredit you. Well, maybe I was hoping. I found it hard to believe anyone could be so malicious without a reason.' He stopped and took a breath.

The silence, to Tessa, was deafening. There wasn't even a mopoke or an owl calling. It was as if the bush was waiting to hear what Harrison had to say.

'I've got a cousin who is a computer tech in Perth. I rang him and asked him how we could find out. He tried a few different techie tricks and didn't come up with anything. But then he saw something in the photo we hadn't seen. So he blew it up larger. I'm sorry I showed them to someone else, but

I thought it was really important to get to the bottom of this.'

Harrison felt in his back pocket and drew out a piece of paper. 'He emailed it to me and I printed it off last night. I think I know who did this, but you'll have to ask her why.'

Harrison handed over the piece of paper.

Tessa stared at it. She couldn't see herself in the photo and she was thankful. But she could see a window. And, reflected in the window, was the person taking the photo.

'Oh my God.' Tessa was struck dumb. 'Oh fuck, oh fuck, oh fuck!' She turned in circles of fear and confusion. 'Jaz took the photos? Why would she do that?' She stared wildly at Harrison, who stood a little way away from her.

'So it is Jaz? I wasn't sure, but I thought it might have been. If she was the one who took the photos, it would be fair to assume she posted them as well, wouldn't you think?'

'But why? Why?'

Harrison reached out and touched her cheek. 'I can't answer that, Tessa. But maybe you can. What went on between you two? Could it have something to do with Kendra's accident? Jaz was there, wasn't she?'

Tessa nodded.

'So what did happen that day?'

'We'd been drinking,' Tessa said, her arms crossed as she stared out into the paddock. We had a competition, who could get to the top of the windmill and back again. Kendra got scared the further she went up, so she didn't make it to the top. She froze.'

Tessa turned back angrily. 'Every goddamn time Jaz got the opportunity, she teased Kendra about not being able to make it to the top. Not just teased her, but really paid the hell out of her.'

She looked at Harrison with tears in her eyes. 'And then we played truth or dare, and Jaz dared Kendra to climb up the windmill again. Kendra wouldn't do it. But that night, when Jaz and I were asleep, she climbed up in the dark. The problem was, we'd been drinking all day. She wouldn't have had all her wits. I think she fell. Maybe she jumped because she was frightened. But I'd rather think she fell.'

Tessa looked at Harrison in horror. 'Then the dingoes came.' She shivered. 'It was awful. Awful!'

Harrison took her in his arms and held her. 'So why would Jaz do this to you?' he said finally.

Tessa looked up at him. 'I don't know! I don't know!' She buried her face in his chest and cried.

It was midnight on Danjar Plains when Tessa rang Jaz. Tessa could hear the hum of the office in the background when her friend answered the phone. She imagined Jaz sitting at Tessa's old computer, *her* files and *her* friends. She still could not begin to imagine why her oldest girlfriend could be so vindictive, but the shock had worn off and now there was a fury bubbling inside her.

'Marketing Matters. Jaz speaking,' the voice said.

Tessa half-smiled. Jaz hadn't recognised the phone number and now she had the upper hand.

'I know you did it,' Tessa began. 'What I don't understand is why.'

There was a silence, then Jaz said: 'I'm very sorry, but you must have the wrong number. This is Marketing Matters. To whom were you wishing to speak?'

'Oh I'm speaking to the right person. I just want to know why, Jaz?'

'Tessa? Is that you?'

'Yes.'

'What are you talking about? How are you? I haven't heard from you for ages!' Jaz gushed.

'No, and I'm sure you're pleased about it. The photos, Jaz. That's the only reason for the call. Tell me why you did it. And did you set me up with John Smith? Did you have a little plan?'

Harrison walked out of the bedroom, sleepy-eyed, and gave Tessa a questioning look. Tessa held her fingers to her lips but tilted the handpiece of the phone to him so he could hear, too.

'How did you work it out? Why are you accusing me? I'm your friend!' To Tessa that confusion of truth and lies was all the confirmation she needed.

'Jaz, come on. I won't ask you again.'

'There is no way you could've found out who posted those photos. Tessa, I'm really hurt you could even entertain the idea it was me.'

'Hold on a minute. Tell me this: whose job are you in now?'

'Yours,' she said, sounding defiant.

'Exactly. Did you set me up so you could get my job?'

There was a pause and then Jaz lowered her voice. 'You've lead a charmed life, haven't you? Even with everything that happened to Kendra, you got away with it. You deserved what you got. Yeah we both lied, but it was you who covered for me. Should I be grateful? Yeah, but I wasn't. I owed you. I wanted you out of here, out of my life. Every time I saw you, I hated myself more. If I didn't see you, I wouldn't have to remember. To feel what I feel. So yeah, I posted those photos. Happy?'

'You're the one who egged Kendra on, teasing her that she couldn't climb the windmill,' Tessa shot back.

'It was *you* who did that, or have you forgotten?' Jaz hissed.

Tessa reared back, shocked. She hadn't forgotten. It had been Jaz who had done all of that. But had she said something? She didn't think she had.

'Jaz, that was you. You said all those things.'

'Yeah, and it was your idea to hide it.'

'I didn't hide it. I just never dobbed on you for egging her on. Bloody hell, I had enough guilt because of it all without this. But I'm not letting you heap it on me again. For what it's worth, I'm glad you did it! My life now is much better than I could have ever imagined and it's because of you. So instead of ringing to have it out with you, I'm actually ringing to say thanks.' And with that, Tessa hung up, breathing hard.

Harrison took the phone, nodding. 'Well done. That was great. At least now we know.'

She shook her head. 'I don't get how her mind works. I just don't get her!'

Harrison grabbed her by the shoulders. 'Don't go there. We're not going back. It's fixed. Leave it and don't ever think about it again. Hear me?'

'Yeah, but . . .'

'No, don't. Come to bed. You need a release.' He smiled and raised his eyebrows at her. 'You can put all your anger into passion. With me, and enjoy it.'

She reached out to him and he pulled her close.

The next morning Tessa slipped out of bed before Harrison. She set off along the road to the homestead, only to run into Paul, who was heading out to do a water run.

'You're up and about early,' Paul said, slowing the ute to a stop.

'Couldn't sleep. Dad, I've got to talk to you.'

'No problem. I've got a Thermos of tea. We'll have a cup.'

Tessa poured out the story of Grace and Ali, holding nothing back. She watched Paul wince when she talked about the rape, and he rubbed his hands over his face when she spoke of the twins and Grace's death.

'That's a hell of a story,' he said, momentarily stunned, when she'd finished.

'Isn't it,' Tessa said flatly. She felt emotionally exhausted, like she had been run over by a truck. The weight of her family's history and the strain of tracking it down had become quite a burden in the last few days. Let alone the discovery and phone call to Jaz.

'But you know, Tessie, Elsie is right. It doesn't change anything. We are who we are. I'm still Paul Mathison, husband of Peggy, father of you and Ryan, and owner of Danjar Plains. It's nice to know, sure. But we already know who we are.'

Tessa smiled and threw her arms around her dad. 'I love you,' she muttered into his warm shoulders.

'And I love you, Tessie. Don't worry yourself anymore. It's all fine.'

'I'm so glad I came home. I nearly didn't.'

'We're glad you did, too. And I bet Harrison is as well.' He grinned as Tessa shot him a horrified look.

'Dad!'

He laughed.

'The other thing I wanted to tell you was that Brendan came over a couple of days ago. I'm sure he only made a beeline for me because everyone thought I'd be cleaning out her house. There must have been something in there that implicated him and his dad in something illegal.'

'Okay, it's my turn to tell you a story,' said Paul.

Tessa smiled, hoping nothing more shocking could be revealed.

'I know Ryan told you about the missing stock?' said Paul.

Tessa nodded.

'Well, he took it upon himself to find out who was doing it. I suspect he was pushed a bit by Spider. She hated anyone who profited by anything other than hard work.' He sighed and scratched his chin. 'I also found out later he was taking Spider with him on the nightly patrols. Not just taking her – she insisted on camping out there. By herself.' Paul shook his head.

Tessa gasped. 'By herself?'

'If I'd known I would have had something to say, I can tell you, but she'd sworn Ryan to secrecy.'

'What would have happened if she'd found out something? She could have been killed. My Lord! Ryan needs his head read for agreeing to it,' she burst out.

'She did come across someone. Brendan. Up on the top side of the place.'

'Brendan? And you didn't tell me?'

'I would have if I'd known,' Paul replied. 'That camera you found had photos on it. It was dawn when Brendan came along to drop the fences. From what Ryan has told me, she got the photos and then confronted him. I think we have to be grateful it was Brendan, not Ray, she came across. Ray wouldn't have thought twice about hurting her, especially after Joe, 'cos like you, I suspected there's more to Joe's death.' He twisted around for the Thermos. 'Top up?'

Tessa held out her cup. 'When did you find all this out?'

'Only in the last few days. Ryan had to find someone that would develop the old film, then when he saw the photos, he sent them to the Kalgoorlie Police.

'The other thing she managed to get photos of was Joe's crop.'

'What?' The cup stopped halfway to her mouth.

'Joe,' Tessa breathed. 'He was in with the McKenzies' then? I had wondered.'

'It certainly looks that way.'

They were silent for a moment and a magpie landed on the bullbar. 'She was so brave. How could a little old lady take on younger men and win?'

'You know Violet. Once she got a bee in her bonnet, especially if something was happening she didn't approve of, she'd move hell or high water to fix it. She knew Joe was growing marijuana and supplying it to Brendan and Ray to take to Perth to sell. Of course, *they* don't know she has destroyed all the evidence that links back to Joe. They can sweat on that. Spider would have never let anyone discredit Joe, even if he was trying to do the right thing in the wrong way. Looking after his sister, I mean.'

Tessa shook her head.

Paul shrugged. 'Doesn't matter now, anyway. Last I heard, the police had a search warrant and were heading out to the station to pay them a little visit.'

Tessa tried to digest what Paul had just said.

'Ryan's phone call floored me, I can tell you. All this cloak-and-dagger stuff going on behind my back. Doesn't make me very aware of my surrounds, does it?' He looked at her sheepishly.

Tessa shrugged. 'The end result is there, I guess. But . . .' She blinked a couple of times, trying to clear her head. 'Well, I'll be buggered.'

Paul's smiled widened as he put his arm around her shoulder and led her back to the ute. 'Now you're sounding like a real Nullarbor girl.'

Epilogue

Six months later

Dear Tessa,

I'm sorry things didn't work out for you over here in London.

I have since found out that Jasmine sabotaged your position, and although that doesn't annul your mistakes, I want you to know she no longer works for Marketing Matters and we have found proof she accessed your work, making some of the mistakes look like yours.

I hope you will stay in touch and I look forward to receiving a photo of the plaque I sent for Violet, in situ.

With best wishes,
Darcy Anderson

Tessa put the letter back in her pocket and let her head fall back against Harrison's chest. They stood and admired the memorial Darcy had sent. The sunlight reflected on the silver plaque and above, soft, white clouds sailed lazily by.

'Well, I reckon that just about does it,' said Ryan standing back with the drill in his hand and surveying his handiwork. Marni reached out and touched it, her fingers tracing Violet's name.

Paul stood with his arm around Peggy while Dozer snored under the tree, in the sun.

'I think she'd like that,' Tessa murmured. 'Right next to William and by the silver mallee trees she loved so much.'

'This is one woman who won't ever be forgotten. Imagine the tales we'll be able to tell our kids about her,' Ryan said, reaching over to pat Marni's protruding stomach.

Marni placed her hand over his and they shared a smile. 'They'd never believe us,' she said.

'You're dead right,' Tessa laughed. 'Come on, let's go home. I want to plant these in Spider's garden.' She held up two small tree seedlings she'd carefully dug up from under the big mallee and wrapped in newspaper. 'One for Kendra and one for Violet. It was Harrison's suggestion.'

'What a lovely idea,' Peggy said as they walked towards the utes.

'I think it will help,' he answered.

'So you heading to Mundranda tonight?'

'Yeah, but I'll be back in a couple of days with the trailer. I'm looking forward to seeing a bit more of Tessa.'

Tessa came up and nudged his shoulder. 'And I'm looking forward to moving in!'

'Shame Violet's house will be empty for a while, but once we've got it done up it will be perfect for holiday makers who want a taste of the Nullarbor and the history of a real station,' Paul said.

'There's that something else I'm looking forward to – getting the lamb and the tourist marketing going.'

Tessa stopped in her tracks. 'I have an announcement.' She motioned for them all to stop and come around her.

'I'm the luckiest girl in the world,' she said. 'Thank you for sticking with me, even when I was horrible. I know this is where I'm supposed to be.' She turned to Harrison and put her arms around his neck. 'And I know Harrison's the only one for me.'

The sun shifted behind a cloud and as a chorus of laughter went up, Tessa looked up and could have sworn the cloud looked silver with the sun rays behind it.

Silver clouds, silver linings, she thought and tightened her arms around Harrison. Then she turned her attention back to her dad, who was speaking. 'In your heart you've always been a Nullarbor girl,' Paul said. 'You never lost it and we knew you'd come back one day.'

With that they began to walk once more, apart from Tessa, who stayed a moment longer to look back at the grave. The magpie was there, watching with his beady eyes.

'And thank you, Spider. I'll love you always,' she whispered softly, then ran to catch up with the rest of her family.

Acknowledgements

Thank you to:

Angela Slatter, you are the reason this book is finished and I can't thank you enough, especially for that all-nighter we pulled from different sides of the country. Thank goodness for modern technology!

Amanda Day and Wendy Duncan, for answering numerous questions and for the photographs.

Kathy Mexted, for your time, ideas and support.

Jen Ford and Robyn Lane for your research. I couldn't have done the Afghan parts without your help. *The Washer Woman's Dream* by Hilarie Lindsay was also invaluable. Cal, I'm so glad you picked it up in the second-hand bookshop!

To every single member of my family, I love you. Thank you for being the centre of my universe and for loving me in return.

Carolyn, I don't think there is anything more I can say about how grateful I am to you. I've said it to you already.

The incredible Allen and Unwin team: Louise – thank you for enabling me to live this dream of writing. Siobhán, your friendship (and, of course, editorial skill) is a highlight of my journey. Amy, I'm looking forward to working more with you.

Jude McGee, for your careful crafting, gentle suggestions and time.

Gaby Naher, for your constant support, wisdom and encouragement, which keeps me on the straight and narrow!

To my writer friends, who know what it's like to go on this journey of ups and downs, highs and lows. I'm so glad I've got to know you all and appreciate your support.

To Robyn, Mrs Mackay, Margareta, Belle: you're worth more than words can say. And to all the Condy gang – you guys rock!

Finally, to you the reader. Samuel Butler once said, 'Books are like imprisoned souls until someone takes them down from the shelf and reads them.' Thank you for spending time reading *Silver Clouds*. I hope you enjoy it enough to see Tessa and the rest of the cast as friends. The story isn't mine anymore – it's now yours.

Psalm 46 verse 10